Her flat was a shrine to her late husband, and as soon as I stepped over the threshold I knew she would agree to help. Pictures of him littered every available surface and half the walls, too. The less-than-lily-white bookie had been elevated to saintlike status by his grieving widow. Any space in the spotless flat not dedicated to his memory was full of soft toys, dolls in frilly dresses, pictures of children. It spoke of a lonely woman living an empty life.

"Your kids?" I asked her.

"No," she said, a cloud passing across her eyes. "We weren't blessed. I hadn't given up hope, though, and nor had Jeff. We were still young enough." That was stretching it a bit but I let it pass. "Now it will never be," she said with a heavy sigh.

Anxious to get off the subject, I spun her a yarn about Cleo's dad taking the fall for the people who'd been using her beloved.

"I always knew Mike didn't do it," she said, taking everything I said as gospel. "I tried to tell that woman inspector, but she wouldn't listen."

"Well, obviously it's too late to bring Jeff back, but perhaps we can do something to clear Mike's name and find the real killer."

Her eyes came alight, and I felt bad about raising her hopes.

"He wouldn't have left me, Mr. Hunter," she said for the tenth time as we sipped stewed tea out of bone-china mugs. "I never believed that. We were blissfully happy together, but his work..." She stared at the opposite wall, overcome with emotion. I carried on forcing the tea down, waiting for her to regain control. "I hated him being a bookie," she eventually said. "Someone was always out to get him. If their horse didn't win they blamed it on him."

In that case someone must have bet a small fortune the day he died. But perhaps it would be better to keep that thought to myself.

# W. SOLIMAN

## RISKY
# BUSINESS

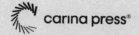

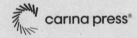

carina press®

ISBN-13: 978-0-373-00238-2

Risky Business

www.CarinaPress.com

**Printed in U.S.A.**

Recycling programs
for this product may
not exist in your area.

Dear Reader,

I was raised on the Isle of Wight, on the south coast of England, which just happens to be the headquarters of British yachting, famed for its regular visits from our royal family, and starting point for the world-famous Fastnet race.

I got plenty of chances to observe the glamorous yachting life at close quarters. I still can't believe the participants appeared to enjoy having regular drenchings in freezing salt water, took leaning precariously over the edge of boats tilted dangerously close to angry waves in their stride and didn't hop ashore praying for a quick and painless death. I decided at an early age that dry land had its advantages.

Many years later, helping my husband through a midlife crisis, I reluctantly agreed to take to the ocean waves, provided we were propelled by engines and not wind power. There were only so many sacrifices I was prepared to make. So started many years of a hate/hate relationship with the sea, during which I learned more about boats than I'd ever needed to know. The things I do for *lurve!* Still, never waste an experience, that's my mantra as a writer, and I spent many hours staring at great expanses of open ocean asking myself *what if?*

And so my Hunter Files series was born. The boat my hero, ex-policeman Charlie Hunter, lives on just happens to bear a striking resemblance to the one we owned. Many of the destinations he visits are also familiar to us. Does it show? Unlike Charlie, we didn't uncover Machiavellian plots, see bodies being dumped over the side, or anything remotely suspicious. In truth, I spent most of my time trying not to be sick!

Charlie gets a second chance at some of his old, unsolved cases, dragged back into a life he thought he'd left behind by a pretty girl with powers of persuasion that made it impossible to turn her down. In spite of my lukewarm enthusiasm for all things maritime, there's a certain camaraderie among the boating fraternity that holds an enduring appeal. I hope I've managed to express it in this series, and that you enjoy reading about Charlie's cold cases. Do let me know what you think. I'd love to hear from you.

Enjoy!

Wendy

www.wendysoliman.com

## Dedication

For my mother.
I only wish you were still able to enjoy reading as
much as you once did. I know you'd be proud of me.

# RISKY
# BUSINESS

# Chapter One

WE SHARED A piano stool, this scrawny black kid and me. Together we produced the strong swinging pulse of an old Art Tatum number, my fingers stiff and clumsy as they sought out the right keys. I showed the kid—Gavin his name was—how to imitate a ride cymbal by striking a beat with his right hand just after he'd produced a weaker one with his left.

The kid was a natural at this but was getting a hard time from his mates because he didn't conform to their version of normal. So here I was, doing what I'd sworn I'd never do again and tinkling the ivories. I was only making an exception for the kid's sake. If the exploitation of his talent was the only thing preventing him from falling into a life of petty crime, it was a no-brainer. I'd just have to work out my neurosis about music some other way.

When the session ended, I pointed my beloved Harley towards home. Preoccupied, it took me a while to realize that the same dark blue Vauxhall had shadowed me for more than five minutes. What was that all about? I swerved the Harley into the outside lane and opened up the throttle. The car followed, losing me on the straight but catching up again when I slowed the heavy bike in a snarl-up.

It confirmed my suspicions. I was being tailed. It was

Sunday afternoon, the road into Brighton was quiet, and the car following stood out like a fox in a henhouse in my wing mirrors. Its driver must have known from my frequent changes of lane that he'd been spotted, but it didn't seem to bother him.

Which bothered me.

I'd upset enough old lags during my time as a copper to have made a few enemies. If they were prepared to come after me in broad daylight, they must either be right cocky bastards, very determined to get me, or just plain stupid.

Whatever, it didn't look good.

In the end, instead of riding directly home, I decided to head into the centre of Brighton and lose the car in traffic. The narrow streets in my hometown weren't designed for modern-day traffic and were gridlocked practically 24/7. That was when a motorbike came into its own.

My plan worked like a dream. Or so I thought until I pulled into the multistorey at Brighton Marina and saw the Vauxhall illegally parked on a double-yellow in front of the supermarket, its driver watching the entrance to the car park. Why follow me if he knew I lived on my trawler in the marina?

I gave no indication that I'd seen the car, rode up the ramp and pulled the bike into a slot on the lower level. If the driver wanted to talk to me he'd have no choice but to follow me into the car park. If he left his vehicle where he was, it would be towed away in no time flat. As usual, there were no free spaces for cars lower down. The driver would have to try his luck on the upper levels and I'd get a good look at him before he saw me.

I concealed myself behind a pillar as the car passed my position. Moments later the sound of footsteps running down the concrete stairs heralded the arrival of my pursuer. Only one set of footsteps. That made me feel better, and I abandoned my half-formed plans to call reinforcements in the shape of my old colleagues. I was glad I hadn't when it dawned on me that the footsteps were light, the tapping sound almost certainly made by a woman's heels. My mates would laugh themselves silly if I'd called them to protect me from a woman.

Even so, I was still cautious and didn't immediately reveal myself. The woman stopped beside my bike and looked round, as though sensing I was still there. She was tall and slim, with short black hair that sat up in spikes. Her large brown eyes darted round the car park, as though she couldn't quite figure out how I'd disappeared so quickly. She looked familiar, probably because she was dressed in the uniform of a croupier. I often played poker in the marina casino and I figured she must be a dealer there. But that didn't explain why she'd gone to such lengths to follow me. Time to get some answers. I stepped out immediately behind her and placed a hand on her shoulder.

"Looking for someone?"

She started violently and clutched her chest. "Oh God, I didn't see you there! You almost gave me a heart attack."

"That's what you get for following people."

"Ah, you saw me then." That appeared to please her. "I thought you must have done."

"You wouldn't make employee of the month in the espionage business."

She shrugged. "I saw the bike parked opposite the house where I have a flat, and I thought I caught a glimpse of you talking to a kid about it. I've wanted to have a private word with you for a while now so I followed you. It seemed like a good way to get your attention."

I was almost tempted to smile at her lack of guile. "You certainly did that," I said, contemplating her for a moment, trying to place her. "Sorry, you seem to know me but I haven't a clue who—"

"No, I don't suppose you would. I'm Cleo Kendall. You've probably seen me in the casino." She stuck out her hand and I instinctively shook it.

"Hello, Cleo Kendall. Nice to meet you. Now, what is it you think I can do for you that made you resort to such drastic measures?"

"Well…" She hesitated, suddenly unsure of herself. "It's a bit complicated."

I rolled my eyes. "When isn't it?"

"I've got half an hour before I need to sign in," she said, checking her watch. "Can we go somewhere for a quick drink and I'll explain?"

I was too intrigued to even consider refusing. We headed for the local Wetherspoon's pub and I ordered myself a pint. She would accept only mineral water.

"If I report for work with alcohol on my breath, it's grounds for immediate dismissal."

"I suppose you do have to keep your wits about you."

"Yes, but don't let it stop you."

"It won't." I took a healthy swig of beer, just so she wasn't left in any doubt.

"We prefer the punters to feel relaxed."

I chuckled. "I'll just bet you do." I waved a hand. "No pun intended."

She obviously wanted something from me badly because she didn't roll her eyes at a feeble joke she must have heard dozens of times before.

"Anyway, Mr. Hunter—"

"It's Charlie." Every time someone called me Mr. Hunter I assumed they were talking to my dad. And my dad was very much on my mind right now. "Now, you were going to tell me what you want." I used a brusque tone to encourage her to get to the point.

"I've been trying to catch you in the casino but you haven't been in much lately." She made it sound like an accusation. "At least not when I've been on shift."

"Sorry, if I'd known I'd have made a point of checking your schedule."

She waved my sarcasm aside. "Besides, we're not supposed to fraternise with the customers. I knew you lived here on your boat. I've seen you around. And absolutely everyone knows the Harley is yours. It's a legend round these parts."

I grunted, inwardly conceding that she had a point. All the decorative artwork featuring the devil women that immortalised my early midlife crisis did make it stand out a bit.

"I didn't have any way of getting to you." She grinned. "So when I saw your bike I decided to follow you back, hoping for a quick word when you got here. You know my dad."

"Your dad?"

"Yes, your lot were responsible for banging him up."

I drained my glass and stood up. "I can't talk to you

about that," I said, feeling a moment's regret. She was surprisingly easy company.

"No, it's all right." She tugged at my arm. There was a desperate look in her eye that persuaded me to resume my seat. "I'm not here to have a go at you. I know you weren't directly involved. But something's happened and I need to—"

"I'm not on the force anymore, Cleo. And even if I was, I couldn't discuss your dad's case with you. Take it up with his brief if you have issues."

"That useless layabout." She blew air through her lips and simultaneously attracted the attention of the barmaid, ordering me a refill. "Do you actually remember my dad, Charlie?"

"Kendall." I sorted through my memory. "How long ago?"

"Ten years."

"Are we talking Mike Kendall?" I had a nasty feeling about this.

"That would be him. You did him for the murder of that bookie, Jeff Spelling."

"Not me. It wasn't my case."

"You knew about it though. You were around at the time."

"It was difficult not to know about it. It was splashed all over the papers for weeks."

"Yeah," she said, grimacing. "And so were we."

"Where is he now?"

She frowned. "Who, Spelling?"

"No, idiot, your dad."

"Oh, he's in Belmarsh, doing life." She flapped a well-manicured hand. "If he keeps his nose clean he could be out on probation soon. Overcrowding, you see."

I did see. It happened all the time. British justice at its finest. "Okay, so it wasn't my case and you don't appear to bear a grudge." I fixed her with a penetrating gaze. "So what is it that you do want from me?"

"He didn't do it."

I almost spilled my replenished pint. "I beg your pardon."

"I said he didn't kill that bookie."

"But I thought you accepted his guilt."

"I never said that. I said I accepted him being inside. There's a big difference." She shrugged. "My dad's a career criminal. He's been in and out of trouble with the law for as long as I can remember. But violence isn't his style. He's actually a very gentle person and a more unlikely murderer it's difficult to imagine."

"You'd be surprised what even the mildest-mannered bloke is capable of when provoked."

"I expect you're right but not in my dad's case. He didn't plead guilty this time, if you recall. He's always put his hand up to his other crimes because he knew it would get him a lighter sentence. But with this, even with all the evidence you had against him, he wouldn't roll over." She paused to sip at her water. "And that's my problem. I want him out of there but when his parole hearing comes up, unless he confesses and expresses remorse, they'll probably keep him locked up."

I didn't say anything. Instead I dredged up memories of the case in question. As soon as I called it to mind, my own misgivings surfaced.

"You didn't think he did it either, did you, Charlie?"

Was she a mind reader? "Okay, let's see what I remember about it, which isn't much. Like I said, I wasn't on the case."

"Do you want me to tell you?"

"No, let me work through it first. Your dad was at Spelling's betting shop the night he was killed. His prints were all over the room behind it, which he used as a private office, and on the baseball bat that was used to stave Spelling's head in."

"So were other, unidentified prints. Besides, he doesn't deny being there."

"He couldn't. He was caught on CCTV leaving the shop at about the time of the murder."

"I know it looks bad, Charlie, but it was a setup."

"I remember that Spelling had something to do with a betting scam."

"Yes, and my dad was a very small cog in that sophisticated wheel. More of a gofer really. But he was a friend of Jeff Spelling's, which gave him a good reason to be in and out of his place all the time. Anyway, he got wind that Spelling had fallen for a barmaid and was about to scarper with the takings from fixed dog races at Catford. Dad went round that night to try and talk some sense into him. You just don't cross the sort of people behind that scam and expect to get away with it."

"Who were they then?"

She shot me a look. "I'd have more sense than to tell you, even if I knew."

"So, if Spelling was alive and well when your father left him, how come the real murderer didn't show up later on CCTV?"

"Well, that's partly what got him convicted," she

said, biting her lower lip in evident frustration. "The defence couldn't produce an alternative culprit. Not that they tried too hard. Anyway, you don't need me to tell you how easy it is to dodge a camera if you know it's there."

"True, but even so—"

"Dad says Spelling was fine when he left and I believe him. I always know when he's telling porkies. His prints were on that bat because he moved it from a chair when he sat down."

I must have looked sceptical because she leaned towards me, her expression passionately intent.

"Jeff Spelling was my dad's friend, and Dad had nothing to gain from his death. Anyway, it would have been a really risky business, opposing Spelling's powerful connections by bumping him off, and Dad's not that stupid."

I looked at her without saying anything. She was Kendall's daughter. Of course she'd think that.

"Besides," she added passionately, "like I said before, whatever else he is, he's no killer. Whoever did it was in a real frenzy, and that absolutely isn't my dad. He didn't even raise a hand to us girls when we were small, no matter how much we played up."

Cleo crossed her arms as though defying me to argue with her. I didn't because she wasn't telling me anything that hadn't occurred to me at the time. That was one of the reasons why I recalled it so well. The other was Detective Inspector Jillian Slater, who led the investigation. Slater was a graduate fast-tracked into a position she didn't have the experience to handle and so she threw her weight about to counter her inefficiencies. She'd insisted upon going for a prosecution, not seeming to care that they might have the wrong man. A successful murder conviction to her name so soon after being promoted would work wonders for her career. It put everyone's backs up and made her universally unpopular with the troops. She hadn't seemed to give a toss.

"Why are you bringing this up now, Cleo?" I leaned back in my chair and crossed one foot over the opposite knee. "And why with me?"

"Because Dad said you were always straight with him." She met my gaze and held it. "He also told me that he suspected you thought he'd been set up."

"I don't know where he got that idea." I lifted my shoulders and took a swallow of beer. "And even if it's true, there's nothing I can do about it now. If you want to get the case reopened, you'll have to do it through his brief."

"Hang on, I haven't answered the second part of your question yet. Why I'm bringing this up now."

I said nothing. I wouldn't be rid of her until she'd said all she'd come to say.

"Mum was suffering from degenerative heart disease at the time of the trial."

"I'm sorry. I didn't know that. The strain of the trial can't have done much for her health."

"No, and nor did surviving on NHS care." She shuddered at some private memory. "But when Dad was convicted, she was moved to a swanky private clinic. I never knew who picked up the tab but I assumed—"

"You assumed your father had taken the fall for

Spelling's murder on the understanding that your mother would be looked after."

"Well, what would you think?"

"The same as you, I suppose. Did you ask your father about it?"

"Yes, but he clammed up tighter than a drum on the subject." She shrugged. "Said he had no idea but I knew he was lying."

Boredom was setting in. There was nothing I could do to help Cleo. Not that she'd got round to telling me what help she wanted yet but I could guess.

"Mum died a few months ago," she said, as though sensing my impatience.

Ah, I see. "I'm sorry. I lost my mother when I was still a teenager, so I know that can be hard."

"What happened?"

"She was a concert pianist." I shrugged. "I might have had a career in music too but—"

"But you had a change of heart after she died." Her smile was full of sympathy. "Can't say as I blame you."

"It was a long time ago now."

"It was a merciful release really, for my mum, I mean," she said, clearly sensing that I didn't want to say anything else about my mother's untimely demise. "But the thing is, her final bills were never settled and it's taken every penny of my savings to clear them."

"You don't have anyone else to help you out?"

She snorted. "A sister married to a stockbroker and living the high life. The amount involved wouldn't have made a dent in her dress allowance, but she hasn't wanted to know about any of us since she married so well. She knew about the bills but didn't offer to pay them and I wouldn't take it from the stuck-up cow anyway." She pulled a face. "Her own mother and she didn't even see her for the last two years of her life."

"So let me guess. Your mother's gone and the people you think your father did a deal with reneged on their promise to look after her. You don't see why your father should continue to rot in jail for a crime he didn't commit and you want me to help you get him out."

"Oh, Charlie." Her dazzling smile told me I'd worded that all wrong. "I knew I could rely on your help."

"Well, actually you can't because, like I already said, there's nothing I can do. Just get your dad to admit that he did it and then they'll let him out." I looked away, concentrating instead on my beer.

"That's what he ought to do but he flat-out refuses."

"Then I don't see how I can help."

"He's not well, and I don't want him to serve out his days in that rat hole when he doesn't deserve to be there. Besides, I want to know for my own peace of mind what went on. Who picked up Mum's bills, and why was I forced to use up my savings when they had a change of heart?"

"In your position I'd feel much the same. I can appreciate how frustrating this is for you, but even if I was still in the force there's nothing I'd be able to do. As it is, well…" My words trailed off. She was a smart girl. She could fill in the blanks without me labouring the point.

"You're right, of course," she said, sighing and collecting her bag. "Still, it was worth a try." She stood up. "Thanks for listening, Charlie."

I'd been in this situation before. An attractive woman wanted my help with an old case and when I didn't volunteer it, she deployed her feminine wiles to get me on her side. I'd been expecting Cleo to do the same thing but it obviously hadn't crossed her mind. Now that I thought about it, she hadn't even attempted to flirt with me. Perhaps that dented my male ego. Whatever, it was her straightforward approach that piqued my interest. That and the fact that I'd always suspected her father had been set up. I admired his stubborn determination not to make life easier for himself and confess to something he hadn't done, but Cleo had just lost one parent. She deserved to have the other one restored to her if he really was innocent.

"Even if you want to help your dad," I said, motioning her back to her seat, "it'll be next to impossible unless he's prepared to tell you who was behind the betting scam."

"And I don't suppose he will. He still thinks I need protecting from all that," she said glumly. "But he'd probably tell you."

"That won't happen. If I go to Belmarsh, whoever he's scared of will know about it before the visit's over. You know what the prison grapevine's like."

"Leakier than that restaurant," she suggested, nodding towards the dilapidated floating Chinese directly outside the window.

"Exactly. Look, I won't pretend I can do anything to sort this out…"

"But?" she prompted when I paused.

I sighed. "But, if you go and see your dad, tell him you've spoken to me. There are a few things I need to know if he wants my help. We'll see what he has to say and take it from there."

Her face lit up, elevating her from averagely pretty to knockout status. "Thanks, Charlie, I'll go next week. I usually only visit once a month but I don't want to wait another three weeks. You might come to your senses and change your mind if I leave it that long," she added, grinning. "What do you want me to ask him?"

I gave her a list of questions off the top of my head. She made no notes but I got the impression she was unlikely to forget anything. Unless my ability to read people had lost its edge, there was intelligence and fierce determination beneath that prickly exterior.

"Oh, and don't worry about being paid for your services. I'll get some money from somewhere. My sister will cough up if it means her father will no longer be labelled a murderer."

"We'll worry about that if I decide there's anything I can do for you."

"Fair enough."

I gave her my mobile number and we parted at the doors to the pub. I returned to the *No Comment,* my floating home and pride and joy. I'd inherited the fifty-foot trawler from my uncle and taken up residence on board when I quit my job with the police.

I received a rapturous welcome from Gil, my larger-than-life, soft-centred mongrel, who shared my bachelor abode.

"Okay, mate," I told him. "I know it's past time for your afternoon run."

I picked up his leash and let him out of the salon door. He leapt straight onto the pontoon, wagging like crazy as he turned in tight circles, somehow managing not to fall off the narrow slipway. He lifted his leg against the closest shore power box and I could almost hear him sighing with relief as he took an elongated pee.

We strolled along our favourite part of the shingle beach to the north of the marina but I didn't spend a lot of time dwelling upon my bizarre conversation with Cleo. Unless her father was prepared to rat out his partners in crime, nothing would come of it. Instead I concentrated on the week ahead. It was half-term and I was taking my son Harry to visit his grandfather in Yorkshire. It was a confrontation that was long overdue and I wasn't looking forward to it one little bit.

# Chapter Two

HARRY SQUIRMED ABOUT in his seat, asking me every half hour if we were there yet. Well, at least one of us seemed happy to be making this trip. I answered his barrage of questions in the way adults do when talking to kids, being selectively honest yet still able to think about other things.

We broke the journey in Sleaford and reached the bed-and-breakfast that Dad and his second wife Brenda run late the following afternoon. On the outskirts of Scarborough, high up in the Yorkshire moors, the rugged location was isolated in the winter. Undeterred, they'd settled into the local community and made a success of a business that was popular with hikers in the summer months. Immersing themselves in village life had earned them the grudging respect of the locals who were notoriously slow to place their trust in newcomers.

At least that was what I'd been led to believe from my spasmodic telephone conversations with my father. So I had trouble hiding my reaction when I pulled up outside the farmhouse. To say it was dilapidated didn't come close. The sign advertising its existence swung drunkenly from one hinge, which squeaked in the strong northerly wind. In fact the whole place looked as though it was on the verge of returning to nature. The thick stone walls were covered with green mould on the outside, and the window frames clearly hadn't seen a coat of paint for years. There were broken gutters, slates missing from the roof, and even a couple of smashed windows that had simply been boarded over and obviously forgotten about.

"Bloody hell!" I muttered.

Harry, unhampered by the shock that rendered me temporarily motionless, leapt from the car, Gil at his heels. Both of them had energy to burn after hours of being cooped up in the car. Harry ran towards his grandfather, waving and smiling good-naturedly, almost tripping over his own feet in his clumsy haste.

"Granddad, we're here!"

"So I see, son."

I was interested to see how my father would greet his only grandchild. He hadn't seen him for over three years but I wasn't surprised when he didn't even touch him. With a half smile he made some inane comment about him having grown since they'd last met and left it at that. His lukewarm response to Harry's sunny greeting annoyed me. I took my time getting out of the car and walked slowly towards my father, tamping down my irritation. I didn't want our first words to be spoken in anger.

His expression was unreadable as I extended my hand, and he hesitated for a fraction too long before shaking it. As he did so I took my turn to examine him. I felt a surge of affection and with it guilt for some of the thoughts about him that had run through my head on the journey up here. More guilt for not having seen him for so long.

My father was well into his seventies now and not

ageing well. His hair, once as thick and curly as Harry's and mine, was now straggly and thinning on top. His face was deeply etched with lines, his eyes faded and tired-looking. But it was the difference in his physique that troubled me the most. He must have lost at least four stone since we'd last met and he hadn't exactly been overweight then. His clothes hung off his frame as though they were using it as a hanger, and when his trousers flapped against his legs I could see how spindly they actually were. His shoulders seemed to have developed a permanent stoop and he moved as though every bone in his body protested at the pressure being placed on it. We used to be the same height but I now towered over him.

I wondered if he was ill and hadn't told me or whether his condition was simply attributable to the passage of time. If he was unwell, it would account for the downturn in the property but it wasn't something I could ask him about straightaway.

"Dad, how are you?" His hand was skin and bone in mine and I was careful to shake it gently.

"Fine, Charlie, and yourself?"

"Never better."

"Good journey?"

I shrugged. "Well, motorways, you know."

We seemed to have run out of things to say to one another already. This wasn't a good start. There was no sign of Brenda so I filled the awkward silence that threatened by hauling our bags out of the boot, and headed towards the house with them. Dad didn't offer to help. The inside of the farmhouse was in a similar condition to the rest of the place, the large kitchen cold and untidy with a thin film of grease clinging to every surface. Dirty plates were piled high in the sink. There was no way this place could still be a going concern. The Health and Safety bods would have apoplexy if they clapped eyes on it and close it down immediately.

"Not open for the season yet?" I asked him.

"We haven't been open for several years now."

I allowed my surprise to show. "You never said."

"Didn't think you'd be interested."

Well, that told me. I was standing at the kitchen window watching Harry and Gil charging to the bottom of the large and unkempt garden. Harry was throwing stones into the gushing stream and Gil was splashing about in it, flapping his tail and enthusiastically trying to retrieve them.

"What made you pack it in?" I asked.

He shrugged. "Not enough trade to make it worth all the hassle of keeping it up to the required standards."

I could relate to that, bureaucracy being what it is nowadays, and nodded sympathetically. "Well, I guess you've both earned your retirement."

"We've not closed through choice, if that's what you're thinking. We still need to earn a crust."

"But…" I closed my big mouth at the last minute. I was about to remind him that the life insurance had paid out over a quarter of a million quid when Mum was killed. It also paid off the mortgage on the detached house they'd owned, which he'd sold at the top of the market. I couldn't help wondering where all that dosh had gone. It sure as hell hadn't been invested in this place, but now wasn't the time to get on to the thorny subject of money.

"So, what do you do now?" I forced an upbeat note into my voice as I put the kettle on. Dad obviously wasn't going to offer me anything to drink so I helped myself.

"Not a lot." He slumped into a chair beside the open range, remembering to remove newspapers, a pair of spectacles held together with masking tape, and the remains of what appeared to be a curled-up cheese sandwich just before his buttocks hit the cushions. "Brenda plays in a local quintet, which brings in a bit of extra. That's where she is now, at rehearsals. Apart from that we rely on our pensions and just about make ends meet."

I thought of the property and cash I'd recently inherited from Jarvis, who'd been my mother's manager, and felt guilty for not offering to share it with Dad. But it wasn't too late. I'd been wondering what to do with it. The house would be sold eventually because I liked living on the boat and had no intention of being drawn back into a conventional lifestyle. A friend of mine, Kara Webb, was currently living in the house with her nephew and niece, but she was making noises about buying her own place.

I dunked a tea bag in a mug, added milk and sugar, gave it a quick stir and handed the resulting brew to my father. He grunted something unintelligible, which I took to be thanks. For myself a hefty spoonful of instant coffee with hot water poured over it was all it took.

With no further displacement activities to delay the moment, I sat in the chair opposite Dad's and searched about for something to say. "Harry's been excited about coming up. He's been going on about it for weeks."

"Oh yes?" He quirked a bushy brow. "I thought kids only wanted to go to Disney World nowadays."

"He does that with his mother."

"How is Emily?"

"She's well and happy with her new husband."

"You shouldn't have let her go, Charlie. She was good for you."

"Yeah, well…"

I let the conversation die. I hadn't been here ten minutes and already we were on to contentious issues, so I was glad when the door opened and Brenda came in. I'd never liked my stepmother much and knew the feeling was mutual. She was about ten years younger than Dad and had once been good-looking. She appeared to have gained the four stone Dad had lost and was bundled up in a weird assortment of clothing. A bright red jumper beneath a baggy shocking-pink cardigan and a shapeless long skirt in faded shades of mauve.

I stood to give her the obligatory peck on the cheek and we spent a few minutes exchanging trite pleasantries. To her credit she made more of an effort to pretend pleasure at seeing me than Dad had done. She was good with Harry too, asking him about school, what he was doing for the rest of the holidays and about Chelsea's chances of winning the Premiership. Thanks to her we got through the evening without coming to blows.

Even so, tension simmered just beneath the surface, and I knew it wouldn't be long before the cracks started to appear. Dad turned in not long after Harry. Not up to spending time alone with Brenda, I feigned fatigue and followed his example.

The following morning Harry, Gil and I set off for

a long ramble over the moors. It was early April and a bitter north wind bit into any parts of our flesh we'd been foolish enough to leave exposed. Neither Dad nor Brenda suggested coming with us, the latter offering to provide us with a packed lunch instead, implying she'd quite like us to stay away all day. I was happy to go along with that and enjoyed a day of fresh air and exercise with my son. But it was a day that could have taken place in Brighton. We hadn't come all this way to deliberately avoid spending time with the people we'd come to see. And that was precisely what I was doing, mainly because I still hadn't decided how to broach the real reason for my visit.

My opportunity arose that evening. Brenda provided us with a supper that Harry and I wolfed down, hungry after our day in the fresh air. Brenda ate as much as I did but Dad merely pushed his food round his plate. Much to Gil's delight, most of it finished up in his bowl. As soon as the food was cleared away I put Harry to bed. His eyes were drooping and he was tucked up, sound asleep by eight o'clock. Brenda had a performance that evening and was gone by the time I came back down from seeing to Harry.

I poured myself a large whisky. Something told me I was going to need it. Then I took the seat opposite my father and searched for the right words to express what was on my mind.

"Have you seen a doctor?" I asked.

He didn't pretend not to understand me and merely shrugged. "What's the point?"

"Well, you've lost a lot of weight, you have no appetite and no energy. There's obviously something wrong with you. You ought to get yourself checked out. They can do a lot nowadays."

"By prodding and poking and being intrusive? No thanks, I'll take my chances."

"It might be something that's easy to treat."

He lifted his bony shoulders and said nothing. That particular subject was obviously already exhausted so I broached the one that lay unspoken between us instead.

"You know about Jarvis?" I asked.

"Yes, you phoned to tell me. There's nothing wrong with my memory."

It was too much to expect any expressions of regret at Jarvis's passing but I was unprepared for the degree of bitterness lancing through his words. "He left everything to me, you know. His house, his savings, everything."

"Well, that's what I would have expected."

"He left me some of Marianne's papers too." Marianne was Jarvis's wife. She'd been confined to a wheelchair for much of her life due to a freak reaction to an over-the-counter pain medication. My father's bland expression underwent the narrowest of adjustments at the mention of her name. I had his full attention now. "Including her bank statements."

"Really." He stared at the flames licking round a log that gave off a pungent aroma as it crackled its way to disintegration. "Why are you telling me all this?" he asked a little too casually.

"Well, if you need money…" His bitter expression caused my words to stall.

"Thanks, but we're fine."

"I can see that." I glanced around the neglected kitchen and let my scepticism show.

"If you don't like the way we live, there's nothing to keep you here."

"It's not that. I just don't like to think of you going without when I can help."

"Keep your money, we're doing fine. Besides, Jarvis wouldn't have wanted you to share it with me."

I sighed. Why did it always have to be this way with us? We could never be together for any length of time without falling out. I should have known this time would be no different. Dad allowed his disappointment in me to be apparent and for some reason that made me feel guilty. I'm one of the most resolute people I know, not given to taking crap from anyone. Except when I get with Dad and one other person in my life. Beneath my father's indifferent gaze I seemed to regress to childhood, eager to earn a few words of approval from an exacting parent.

Annoyed with myself for being such a wimp, I took a large gulp of my drink and went for the jugular. "Why did Marianne lend you two hundred grand just before Mum died?"

My question took him completely by surprise, just as it was supposed to, and for the first time his reaction was entirely genuine. "None of your business," he said after a prolonged pause.

"So that's all you're going to say about it, is it?" I was starting to get annoyed. "Don't you think I deserve more of an explanation than that?"

"No, I don't. It has nothing to do with you. It was a personal matter and I have no intention of discussing it." He eyed me with cynical detachment. "If that was your reason for coming up here then you've had a wasted journey."

"Was it something to do with Mum?"

He looked at me for a long time before he spoke. "So, you think Marianne and I conspired to bump her off, do you?" His eyes narrowed with contempt. "Is that your latest theory? The conclusion you've drawn after years of stumbling about trying to find answers where none exist?"

"No, that's not what I meant—"

"Well, I can see why you might think so," he said contemplatively, talking over my interruption, "given your low opinion of me."

"It isn't what I think." But my voice didn't sound particularly convincing even to my own ears. Hardly surprising. I always lost objectivity when I talked about Mum's murder. She was assassinated by an unknown assailant right in front of me over twenty years before. That was when I stopped playing the piano and joined the police force, looking for answers. I had yet to find any. "It's just that reading those diaries was a real wake-up call. It brought it all flooding back like it was yesterday, and threw up a load more questions, too."

He drew a deep breath. "If you've been able to forget about it for more than five minutes at a time, then all I can say is that you're a fortunate man."

My father spoke with quiet dignity, the utter devastation in his faded eyes convincing me he'd not been involved in the murder. I breathed a sigh of relief and ought to have left it at that. But I couldn't. I was causing him further pain by raking over the coals but now that

I'd got him talking about it, expressing his true feelings without attempting to spare mine, I had to delve deeper.

"Jarvis told me that his affair with Mum was discreet but Marianne's diaries paint a very different picture. If she's to be believed, then he took pleasure in flaunting it in front of her. Do you think that's true?"

"Marianne had a lot of reasons to feel bitter about life." He shrugged. "But much as I disliked Jarvis, I don't think he would have been deliberately cruel to her."

I got up and threw another log on the fire, watching as a shower of sparks flew in all directions before fizzling out. "I haven't been able to stop wondering why Jarvis gave me those papers," I said. "The only conclusion I've been able to reach is that he thought Marianne was involved in some way. After all, you have to admit that Mum's killing came at a very convenient time and meant Jarvis didn't finish up leaving her."

My father suddenly looked very tired and every one of his seventy-four years. "This obsession you have with your mother's death isn't healthy. It's caused you to waste a rare and special talent that could have changed your life. It's cost your marriage to a woman who was good for you. It's prevented you from committing yourself emotionally to anyone else and turned you into a part-time father to a boy you obviously adore." He leaned forward in his chair and fixed me with a penetrating gaze, showing more interest in me than he'd done since the event that changed our lives and drove a wedge between us all those years ago. "You've thrown it all away, and for what?"

"You weren't there when it happened," I said, sounding peevish and, frankly, very lame.

"And you weren't the only one to love your mother. I idolised the ground she walked on and even if she had left me for that bastard, I would still have carried on loving her. You'll find out for yourself, if you're ever lucky enough to discover such an abiding love, that it's simply not possible to turn it on and off at will."

I was too stunned to speak. The animation in those rheumy eyes, the passion underlying my father's words, told me he was speaking from the heart. Never in all the years since Mum's death had he opened up to me in this way and I felt we'd finally bridged a huge divide.

"Understand this," he said emphatically. "Whatever that money was for, it certainly wasn't used to have your mother bumped off. If you believe for a single moment that I'd be capable of even considering such a thing, then I'm truly sorry for the person you've become."

"I believe you."

And I was relieved beyond words that I did, ashamed of the doubts which had briefly plagued my mind.

"Good." He leaned back in his chair. "And if you also believe that I loved your mother as much as I say I did, then you'll understand why I don't want to see a doctor. If my time's finally up then I'm more than ready for what comes next." He struggled to stand up and headed for the stairs. "I've been ready for more than twenty years."

"Yes, but even so—"

"Help yourself to another drink, Charlie. Good night."

And he was gone, leaving me to ponder upon our extraordinary conversation in the large untidy room, which suddenly seemed very quiet.

"Had a row, have you?" Brenda's voice startled me. I hadn't heard her come in and she was the last person I wanted to see right now. We'd coexisted for over twenty-four hours without falling out but that happy state of affairs couldn't last much longer, especially since Dad wasn't around to play referee. She slumped into the chair my father had just vacated, a glass of what looked like gin and tonic in her hand. "I'm surprised you lasted as long as you did." She sighed. "Why did you bother coming up here? You only upset him."

"That's not my intention."

"Perhaps not but it's still the way it is. Every time he looks at you, he remembers just what a talented pianist you were and that you threw it all away to embark upon a wild goose chase. It drives him demented so he tries not to think about it but I don't think he'll ever forgive you."

"It's my life." I sounded as petulant as Harry did when I ticked him off about something and he knew he was in the wrong.

Brenda chuckled. "Well, all I can say is that I hope your obsession has made it a happy one."

"I'm not obsessed, exactly."

She made a derisive sound in the back of her throat, something between a burp and a grunt, but didn't dignify my statement with a response. None was necessary since we both knew she was right.

"I just want answers," I said mildly. "Surely that's understandable. My mother's brains were blown all over me but everyone seems to think I should calmly accept that shit happens and move on."

"You're not the only one hurting. Your father still misses her every single day."

I elevated my brows. Brenda took pleasure in goading me whenever we met and I couldn't remember her ever speaking to me as though she cared about my feelings.

"Oh, he might not actually say so but I see it in his eyes. He gets this faraway expression, doesn't hear me when I speak to him, doesn't seem to remember what he was doing two seconds before. That's when I know exactly what he's thinking about."

"And it doesn't bother you?"

"Of course it bothers me! What a bloody stupid question."

I almost smiled. It was a relief to discover that the acerbic Brenda was still alive and kicking.

"But I have the sense to know there's sod all I can do to change things, and so I make the best of it and get on with my life. I don't waste time with pointless regrets and nor should you. I'm second best to your saintly mother and always have been. Still, I knew that's how it'd be when I married Robert so there's no point complaining."

"So why did you? Marry him, I mean."

"I should have thought that would be obvious even to a cold bastard like you." She shifted her bulk until she found a more comfortable position. "I loved him from the moment we met and, what's more, I still do."

"I understand that but you didn't know my mother, not really. You don't know how remarkable she was so you can't judge him or me for missing her. You came along afterwards."

She shook her head slowly, a spiteful half smile playing about her lips. I knew then that she was about to reveal something I probably wouldn't want to hear.

"For an intelligent man, you're sometimes exceedingly dense." She took a deep breath and a long sip of her drink, making me wait for what seemed like an eternity before she spoke again. "My affair with your father started two years before your mother died."

"What!" I leapt out of my chair, spilling whisky over my jeans without really registering the fact. "You're joking. Dad was devoted to Mum."

"Yes, but she was playing happy families with Jarvis. Robert waited, suffering in silence, hoping she'd get fed up and come back home. When she didn't, he decided to give her a taste of her own medicine. I was up for it, as the kids say nowadays, made sure he knew it, and that's how it started."

I sloshed some more whisky into my glass and slowly sat down again. "I had no idea," I said, feeling stupid for not having considered the possibility.

"I know. Robert was adamant that you shouldn't get wind of it. He felt you ought to benefit from having two parents permanently in your life, at least until you left school. He's got old-fashioned ideas about that sort of thing. That's why he feels so strongly that you ought to have made a go of things with Emily, if only for Harry's sake."

"Did Mum know? About you and Dad, I mean."

"I think so but she never actually said anything." Brenda lit a cigarette and blew smoke at the ceiling. "Robert's attempts to make her jealous backfired and if anything I think she was glad that he'd found someone else. It would have made it easier for her to leave when the time came."

I shook my head. How had I not known these things? It seemed so obvious now. Snatches of conversations I'd overheard that abruptly stopped when my presence was noticed. Angry telephone conversations, missed appointments. But most of all, the tension that was always there between my parents. It could all now be explained.

"What did you and Robert argue about just now?" Brenda's voice brought me back to the present. "About Jarvis. He left everything to me and I offered Dad money."

Brenda chuckled. "That wouldn't have gone down too well. He'd starve before he took a penny from that man's estate."

"Yes." I grimaced. "So much for my good intentions."

"Well, I don't share his principles so if you feel like spreading some of your inheritance in my direction, I'll make sure your dad benefits without knowing where it came from." She shuddered. "God alone knows, we could do with a bit of extra to make our lives more comfortable."

I had to admire her nerve. She's never had a good word to say for me, but that clearly wouldn't stop her tapping me for a loan. No, make that a handout. "I'll pick up the heating bill, if you like."

"Thanks." She dipped her head. "That will help. But to get back to Robert, your offering him money wouldn't be enough to make him lose his rag and storm off to bed. I assume that's what he did because he usually waits up for me. Come on, what else did you fall out about? I know there's more."

I didn't see any reason not to tell her. "I found out Marianne lent him a load of dosh just before Mum died and asked him what he wanted it for."

She slapped one palm against her fat thigh and roared with laughter. It was the last reaction I'd expected. "And you assumed he used it to hire an assassin?"

I couldn't meet her eye. "The thought did briefly cross my mind."

"Oh, Charlie!" Brenda shook her head, causing her multiple chins to wobble. "You really know how to rub him up the wrong way."

I spread my hands. "I didn't want to believe it."

"Oh well, that makes it all right then."

"Look, Jarvis obviously wanted me to know about the money so you can't blame me for being curious."

"And he wouldn't tell you?"

"No."

She leaned back in her chair and dealt me a look. "You should have asked me."

"You!"

"Yes." Her noxious smile caused deep grooves to appear on either side of her mouth. "Your father borrowed the money because I asked him to."

"You?" Shock was causing me to sound more moronic by the minute.

"I was fed up with playing second fiddle, no pun intended." Her halfhearted attempt at a self-deprecating joke didn't altogether conceal her glee at making this latest revelation. "To your mother and to you. I wanted Robert and me to make a life together but knew it would never happen, not all the time Julia was still dithering about what to do. And so I gave him an ultimatum. Get me that money or it was over between us."

"I see." I didn't, not really, but I couldn't seem to string a coherent question together. "But what did you want it for?"

"I didn't. It was for Paul."

"Paul." My gut contracted at the mention of the only person other than my father who could intimidate me. "Ah yes, that would explain it," I said almost to myself. "Now it's starting to make sense."

Paul Flint was her son from her first marriage and was five years older than me. We'd never got on and that wasn't because he'd always been demonstratively gay. That sort of thing didn't bother me. It was more that he was such a flash bastard, always on the lookout for an easy option. Never fussy about what he did to earn a crust provided it didn't involve too much hard work. His parents split when he was a toddler and he moved in on my father, ingratiating himself with his mother's lover before Mum was cold in her grave. I resented that, feeling as though he was intruding on our grief and taking my place in my father's affections. It annoyed me that Dad couldn't see through his insincere blandishments.

Brenda and my father married a year after my mother's murder. Paul, flamboyant in a yellow suit complete with matching hat and black shirt, was so overbearing that I left the small reception before it even got underway and didn't go home again for over a week.

"What did Paul want the money for?" I asked Brenda.

A whole new range of possibilities that this time I

had no difficulty believing flooded my brain as I waited for her answer. She watched me closely and didn't speak for what seemed like an eternity. When she finally did, her words were no help whatsoever.

"Well, Charlie," she said, lumbering to her feet and flashing a final spiteful grin in my direction. "If you want to know that, then the person you need to ask is Paul."

# Chapter Three

WE LASTED ONE more day in Yorkshire. I think even Harry sensed the tension, and we were all relieved when I cut our visit short two days earlier than planned. The weather had fooled us into believing that spring had arrived early but got its revenge by chucking it down until we got back to Brighton. All the treats I had planned for Harry on the return journey were rained off but I made it up to him by taking him to Chelsea's home fixture on Saturday. We scored the winning goal in injury time and Harry was now convinced the trophy was all but ours.

Emily, dressed to the nines, came to pick Harry up. The boat seemed very quiet without his constant chatter and it would take me a while to get used to him not being around. I poured myself a beer, put on a Fletcher Henderson CD and finally settled down to have a good, uninterrupted think about all I'd learned in Yorkshire.

I closed my eyes and absorbed the music as though through osmosis. Gil turned in several tight circles, contorted his body into an impossible angle and flopped down beside me. He rested his huge head on my feet, let out a mournful sigh and promptly dozed off. If he stayed there for long I'll lose all feeling in my toes, but I figured he was missing Harry too so I let him stay put.

Eyes still closed, I mentally catalogued the progress I'd made. Dad and Brenda started their affair two years before Mum was killed. Dad definitely wasn't involved in arranging her demise but did borrow two hundred thousand pounds from Marianne and gave it to Brenda's son for an undisclosed purpose. Brenda had wanted to formalise her relationship with Dad but knew that would never happen whilst Mum was still on the scene.

I took a large swallow of beer but it didn't make things any clearer. All I knew for sure was that the finger of suspicion had now swung in Brenda's direction. I couldn't somehow see her searching for unemployed hit men on the internet, but I didn't have much trouble picturing Paul going down that route. He knew how badly his mother wanted to have Dad all to herself and probably also knew about the money Dad stood to make if Mum departed this world. Looked at from that perspective, things were starting to fall into place. Paul was one of the most self-centred people I had the misfortune to know and I wouldn't put anything past him. I sighed, resigned to the fact that I wouldn't have any peace until I found out what he had to say for himself.

I shifted my position, thankfully dislodging Gil's head from my numb feet. He obviously thought it was time for his afternoon run and started jumping about, wide awake again. How did dogs do that? Switching from deep slumber to fully *compos mentis* in no seconds flat? I ignored Gil, my mind reverting to Paul. I didn't mind thinking the worst of him but was already having second thoughts about getting in touch with him. He enjoyed winding me up even more than his mother did and was a damned sight better at it too. If he was behind my mother's assassination he'd hardly admit it. Knowing Paul, he'd make snide innuendos and set me off on the trail of a whole flock of wild geese. His mother would have warned him to expect my call so he'd had plenty of time to think up juvenile ways to taunt me.

Maybe Dad and Brenda were right. It was time to let the past go and get on with my life. I'd think about it for a day or two before I made my move and let Paul wonder why I hadn't got straight on to him. If he was guilty perhaps the waiting would unsettle him. Paul disconcerted by me? The poetic justice lent me some satisfaction.

I gave in to Gil's nagging and took him for his run. I thought more coherently in the open air and since I had so much to think about I delighted him by walking almost twice as far as usual. My mobile rang just as we were returning to the boat. Cleo Kendall's name flashed up. I hadn't expected her to get back to me this quickly.

"Cleo, how are you?"

"Are you back in Brighton, Charlie?"

I almost smiled at her single-minded attitude. "Yes, I'm fine, thanks."

"Look, sorry, but I don't have time to make nice. I need to talk to you about a few things before I go to work."

I sighed. "Yes, I'm in Brighton. Come to the boat." I gave her the code to the gate and hung up, matching her for verbal economy by not saying goodbye.

I'd barely got back to the *No Comment* when she knocked on the hull. I opened the sliding salon door and did a double take. She stood on the pontoon wearing a very short skirt—several inches shorter than anything I'd seen on her before—which gave me a very good idea about the condition of her legs. There was nothing on display to take exception to. Quite the reverse. My eyes lingered for a moment or two, letting her know that her efforts were appreciated.

But I was instantly on my guard. Talk about déjà vu. Kara Webb had pulled exactly the same stunt when she wanted me to help her find her lost sister. Was I that predictable? I held out a hand and helped Cleo over the gunwales. A gentleman wouldn't have looked when her skirt crept even higher up her thighs. I looked with impunity, and the shapely nature of said thighs had me nodding my approval.

"You might wanna take those shoes off," I said. Her pumps had low, spiky heels that would play havoc with the teak.

She did as I asked and stepped barefoot into the salon, only to be almost knocked from her feet by Gil. I'd forgotten about him. Fortunately she appeared to like animals and knelt down to give his big head a thorough rub.

"This is lovely," she said, glancing round. "I've never been on a posh boat before."

"This is hardly posh. More like a labour of love."

"Well, your adoration shines through. I like it."

"Thanks. Drink?"

"Just tea, please. I have to work."

"Ah, right."

She was turning out to be a cheap date. I made tea for her and opened a beer for me. As soon as we were seated, she got straight down to business.

"I saw my dad a couple of days ago."

"And I take it from your glum expression that it didn't go well."

She grimaced. "That's a bit of an understatement. It's partly my fault. I handled it all wrong."

I leaned back and made myself more comfortable. "Tell me what happened."

"Well, I think he was a bit suspicious, what with me going to see him only a week after my last visit. I said it was to tie up Mum's business but he wasn't buying that. Anything to do with Mum's affairs could be handled by me alone and we both know it. Anyway, we chatted generally for a couple of minutes and I tried to work round to your questions subtly."

"Was that a good idea? I don't mean to insult you but you haven't actually grasped the concept of subtle, have you?"

She flashed me a brief grin. "You've clocked that about me already?"

"I'm a detective," I said, winking at her.

Her hair wasn't quite so spiky today. Flat against her head, it looked longer, feathering her face with soft jet-black fronds. They fell in silky wisps across her forehead, emphasising the size of her eyes and length of the thick, curling lashes that guarded them. I preferred this softer look.

"If I've got something to say I go right ahead and say it." She shrugged. "It rubs some people up the wrong way but we can't help the way we are. Anyway, at least people know where they stand with me. If they ask my opinion they tend to get an honest answer."

I allowed my amusement to show. "How to make friends and influence people."

"What can I say?" She flashed a mirthless grin. "What you get is what you see."

"So your dad sussed you out?"

"Yeah, I asked him about Mum's bills and who'd been paying them, just as you said I should."

What I'd actually said was that she should have asked as soon as her mother was moved to that fancy clinic. If her father hadn't told her at the time he was hardly likely to do so now.

"And he wouldn't say?"

"He just said a friend owed him a favour and it was none of my concern."

"Well—"

"It might not have been at the time but it certainly became my business when I had to use all my savings to settle her account. Now that," she said, leaning towards me, her remarkable eyes blistering with intensity, "was obviously news to him. He didn't have a clue that I'd been stuck with her expenses and wasn't too happy about it."

"So it upset him." I'd been counting on his injured feelings to loosen his tongue. "How did he deal with that?"

"When Dad's upset he gets defensive. When he was on the outside and up to no good, Mum and I always knew because he'd get all argumentative. And that's what happened this time. He said I should have asked my sister to settle up because she wouldn't have missed the money."

"He knows your sister's disowned you all so why would he say that?"

Cleo stared off into the distance. "I don't know. Just to ease his conscience, I suppose. All I can tell you is that he's dead scared of whoever financed Mum's stay in that clinic. And Dad doesn't scare easily."

"What makes you think he was scared?"

"I could see it in his eyes. I told him I'd been to see you and he hit the roof. Told me to forget it, to leave you out of it and basically to let him rot inside in peace."

"But you didn't let it go?"

"No, I guess I lost it a bit too. I mean, all this 'poor me' bit is starting to wear a bit thin. Life on the outside isn't exactly a bed of roses for the rest of us. Well," she conceded, "it is for my snobby sister but she doesn't count. I've had to worry about Mum all this time, live with the emotional turmoil of watching her die, arrange her funeral and, well…I told him that if he wouldn't accept help to prove his innocence then the least he could do was admit to killing Spelling and express remorse. That way he stands a chance of getting out and could be of some use to me." She pulled a face. "Not that he would be. Any use, I mean. But if a guilt trip is what it takes to get him to act responsibly for once, then I don't have a problem with that."

"But that suggestion didn't go down too well either?"

"Nope, he dismissed it out of hand." Gil was resting his head in her lap and she absently rubbed his ears. "Said I was better off forgetting all about him."

"Then I don't see what else we can do. I told you at the start that unless your dad was prepared to cooperate, we didn't have a hope in hell of proving he was innocent."

I expected counterarguments, tears, coercion. Hell, I was still suspicious about that shorter-than-short skirt, expecting her to flash those dynamic legs even more obviously in my direction. And the mood I was in, she wouldn't have had to work too hard at it. But instead of all that, she just levelled her eyes on me in a manner that made me feel mean-spirited for deserting her when she was at her most vulnerable.

"We could try and find out who he's afraid of," she said quietly, not an ounce of flirtation in her body language.

"We could, but have you considered what that might mean for your dad?"

"I don't understand."

"I think, for what it's worth, that your dad knows he's in above his head. Your unscheduled visit won't have gone unnoticed by the prison snouts, and news of it will already have reached whoever he's frightened of—"

"Yeah, there's that, but I still don't see why he should have to—"

"Strange as it might seem, he's trying to protect you in the only way he can."

She expelled a long, frustrated breath. "By staying inside and keeping his mouth shut."

"Precisely. You're the only thing left on the outside that matters to him and these people will know that."

"I can take care of myself."

I levelled my eyes on her but she didn't flinch. What would it take to make her understand she could be in danger?

"I'm not the helpless female you have me pegged for," she said. "I've had to cope with all sorts of shit as well as having a criminal for a father."

"I don't doubt it but if your dad's frightened then these have got to be pretty hard men. They wouldn't think twice about hurting a woman, or threatening to, if that's what it takes to keep your dad in line."

"So you *are* just an establishment figure, then. Dad was wrong about you, just like he's wrong about most things." She gathered up her bag and got abruptly to her feet. "Thanks for listening."

I should have been relieved to see her leave. I really didn't need this. But, I don't know, perhaps my manly pride had been bruised by her disinclination to flirt or look upon me as anything other than a means to an end. There again, even though it hadn't been my case, perhaps I felt guilty for not expressing stronger doubts about her dad's involvement in Spelling's murder at the time. Either way, I couldn't let her leave until I'd at least tried a bit harder to help her.

"There is one thing we could do, I suppose."

She was at the door but my voice stopped her and she turned back to look at me, unsmiling. "And what would that be?"

"Ask a few questions at the clinic your mum was in. Find out who settled her bills all that time."

Her eyes widened. "Could it really be that easy?"

Somehow I doubted it but I tried to sound more optimistic than I felt. "It can't hurt to ask but you'll need to come with me. I don't have the authority to go poking around since I'm no longer a copper and I'm no relation. But you'd have every right in the world."

"Okay. When can we go?"

"I'm off to France next week but whenever you're free before that."

"Great. I'm off duty for three days after tonight."

"Then there's no time like the present. Where is the clinic?"

"In Hove."

"All right. Pick me up in the morning at about eleven and we'll drive out there together."

I thought I'd adjusted to Cleo's disinclination to look upon me as anything other than…well, a partner in crime, and so I was taken completely unawares when she wrapped her arms round my neck and kissed me hard on the lips. Her kiss was as firm and decisive as everything else she did, her tongue warm and moist as it invaded my mouth. My arms instinctively folded round her waist whilst my best friend stood to attention and took a keen interest in the proceedings. But before I could take control of matters she broke away, ending the kiss as abruptly as she'd started it.

"What was that for?" I asked.

"It was my way of thanking you," she said, stepping into the cockpit and retrieving her shoes. "Right now it's the only form of payment I can offer you." I quirked a brow but said nothing. "And," she added, grinning, "I got the impression that it was appreciated."

I WAS WAITING for Cleo the next day on the landside of the marina, not surprised when her Vauxhall arrived dead-on eleven. She was wearing jeans and a sweatshirt, acknowledged me with a brevity that bordered on rude and seemed all business. I might still be remembering that surprisingly passionate kiss but she'd obviously forgotten all about it. So much for my legendary charm.

"How are we going to play this?" she asked.

"Presumably they have an accounts office. I suggest

you say you need a copy of your mother's final bill because your sister wants to reimburse you for half of it and you've lost the original."

Cleo rolled her eyes but made no comment about such an unlikely development.

"Whilst we're in there, we'll try and get the clerk talking, see if she'll reveal the information we need." I shrugged. "No reason why she shouldn't."

And that proved to be the case. The elderly woman in the accounts office was sympathetic towards Cleo and happy to tell what she wanted to know. Up until a few months before her death, her mother's bills had been settled by an offshore company called Holder Enterprises with an address in Jersey.

"What does that mean then?" Cleo asked as we drove back to the marina.

"It's what I expected. It's easy enough to buy dummy corporations off the shelf and use them for all sorts of purposes. Mostly to remain anonymous or launder ill-gotten gains."

"So we need to find out who the directors are."

"Yes, that information will be available from Companies House but I doubt whether it'll get us very far."

"Oh, why not?"

"Think about it. If these people want to remain anonymous, their names won't appear anywhere. My guess is that the corporation will be fronted by their accountants. Or solicitors. Or someone with a fake identity."

We arrived back at the boat and received a rapturous welcome from Gil. I phoned my old mate Detective Sergeant Jimmy Taylor and caught him at home. He'd be able to access Companies House records from the nick and get me the information I needed. I could do it myself but I'd have to register and leave a trail for anyone paranoid enough to check. If Jimmy did it from the nick, it might raise a flag or two but no one would know why he was looking if I asked him to keep stum about it. Jimmy was about to go on duty and said he'd get back to me later that day.

Cleo and I passed the time by taking Gil for a run and stopping for a bite of lunch at one of the restaurants attached to the marina.

I felt Cleo's eyes assessing me and wondered what she was thinking. I was a good judge of character—you had to be in my previous line of work—but this girl had me puzzled. It was almost as though she'd become accustomed to expecting the worst from life and so was seldom disappointed. Given that she had a career criminal for a father and my ex-colleagues regularly knocking on the door was probably something she'd learned to take in her stride, I couldn't say as I blamed her. But she'd done what she could to rise above it all and make a decent life for herself, only to have her savings whipped away from her and no way of knowing why that should have happened. In her position I'd have kept people at arm's length too.

And that was what she'd been doing with me. With everyone. She'd built a shell round her emotions and seldom let them out for air, afraid of being disappointed. She wasn't dishonest herself but trusting the police still had to go against the grain. She'd obviously expected me to turn her down flat, and when I didn't her kiss was a rare, spontaneous reaction. One which she obviously regretted. I really must be losing my touch.

Now that we were in a social setting, with no pressing engagements, I waited for the inevitable questions. The ones people always asked. Why had I left the police so young? Why had I joined in the first place? Why was I divorced? But she said nothing and the silence between us was in danger of becoming embarrassing. But I was good at silences and waited it out, determined that she'd be the first one to talk.

"How was Yorkshire?" she eventually asked.

I toyed with my pasta, not surprised that she's chosen such a safe subject. "Cold," I said succinctly.

"Well, what else can you expect at this time of the year?"

"How long have you worked at the casino?" I asked on impulse.

"Two years."

Two years. That was all she said. Nothing about whether she liked it, if she planned to make a career out of it or was just marking time. *Nada.* I'd never met a woman so disinclined to talk about herself.

"Was your father hanging out with anyone in particular at the time of Spelling's murder?"

Surprise registered on her features at the abrupt change of subject but it got her complete attention. "I'm not sure. Why?"

I said nothing, thinking the question ought to be self-explanatory, and it didn't take her long to catch on.

"He was tight with Reg Turner," she said eventually, "but no other names stand out."

I nodded. In my former life Turner had been well-known to me as a small-time criminal and regular face on the dog-racing scene. I couldn't imagine him having anything to do with murder but there could well be a link here. Reg was involved with the dogs, and so had Cleo's father been, and Spelling was a bookie. Before I could push Cleo for more information, my phone rang. It was Jimmy with the information I needed.

"An accountant is the company secretary," he said, reeling off a name and address which I dutifully made a note of. "And a solicitor's down as director."

"Figures," I said. "Who is he?"

Jimmy told me but my pen stalled when he gave me his address. I knew Jason Miller by reputation. He represented some of the wealthier cons in the area. What I hadn't known was that he lived and worked from a flat in the same block as my stepbrother Paul Flint. The very person I was putting off visiting.

I felt the adrenaline kick in along with my suspicions. Coincidences like this just didn't happen in real life. There had to be something more in it. Hell if I knew what, but I fully intended to find out. It seemed that I was destined to be involved in this thing with Cleo whether I liked it or not. And not just to get a man who might or might not be innocent released from prison.

# Chapter Four

CLEO'S IMMEDIATE SUGGESTION was that she pay Miller a visit.

"Not a good idea," I told her.

"Why not?"

"Because he'll know who you are and won't tell you a thing. Solicitors are a cautious breed at the best of times. They have to be. Client confidentiality and all that." I leaned back and stretched my arms above my head. "If their clients are, as in this case, adamant about remaining anonymous then you'll be showing your hand for no good reason and that could rebound on your dad."

She glowered at me, as though it was my fault. "I suppose so but it's frustrating to have got this far and not do anything about it."

"Who said we weren't going to do anything?" I drained my beer, wondering if I'd live to regret my next words. "There's nothing stopping me popping in to see Miller."

She visibly brightened. "I suppose not. But on what pretext?"

"Well, it's fairly common knowledge that I was disillusioned with the police force, which is why I left before my time. I might suggest that I have some business to transact that's on the dodgy side of legal."

She looked sceptical, with good reason. It wasn't

much of a plan. "The moment you mention my father's name he's bound to smell a rat."

"Credit me with a little intelligence," I said, pulling a wounded face. "Your father's name won't pass my lips. I'll tell him I've been contacted by Spelling's wife. She's come across some papers to do with Spelling's activities immediately before his murder and wasn't sure what to do with them."

"Papers that are incriminating to certain people," she suggested, looking a bit more enthusiastic about my brilliant master plan.

"Precisely."

"But why would she come to you and why would you pass that information to Miller?"

"She came to me for the same reason you did. I'm the caring face of modern policing," I said. Her expression clearly conveyed her thoughts about that piece of self-aggrandisement. "And I've gone to Miller because the papers name one of his clients."

She frowned. "But won't he ask who that client is?"

"Yes, I'm sure he will, which is why I'll have to do a spot of digging before I make the appointment. We know your dad was hanging out with Reg Turner. If I can get my old colleagues to find out who Turner was working for at the time—"

"Will they know?" She seemed surprised by the suggestion.

"They'll have a pretty good idea. I'll ask Jimmy to see what he can unearth and then take a punt on it. The worst it can be is a massive waste of time."

"But won't it put Spelling's wife in danger?"

"Well, obviously, I'll have to run it past her first, if I

can find her. But it's true what I said earlier. She never could understand why her husband was hit."

"She attended Dad's trial every day looking very tragic."

"Hardly surprising given that her husband *was* murdered and the man accused of bumping him off had been a regular guest in her home. It would be enough to upset anyone."

"I was so stunned by Dad being charged that I didn't give her situation much thought." She dropped her head. "I ought to have done. She was always nice to us girls."

"She probably wouldn't have appreciated anything you had to say back then."

"Probably not but I still should have tried." She briefly covered one of my hands with her own. "But thanks for trying to make me feel better."

"All part of the service, ma'am."

"Going back to Miller," she said reflectively. "Even if you hit on his right client's name, he won't admit to knowing anything about it. So short of tapping his phone to see who he contacts after you leave, I don't see how your dangling carrots under his nose will help."

"Even if we could tap his phone it wouldn't get us anywhere."

She looked surprise. "Why not?"

"Because he might phone the person to say I've been sniffing around but he won't talk business over the phone. Someone with stuff to hide would never risk it."

She plucked at her lower lip, looking deflated. "It always works in the movies."

"This is the real world and Miller's type doesn't get to survive without being super-cautious."

"So they'd meet in person."

"That's my guess. Hopefully, if I'm convincing enough, they'll do it soon after I meet with Miller, and we'll be able to—"

"But won't that mean watching him all the time?"

"I've got people who'll do that for me."

"Charlie, are you sure?" She leaned across the table, her intense expression wary but full of gratitude. It brought that bloody kiss to mind and I wondered if she would express her gratitude in a similar fashion again. "It all seems a bit tenuous."

"Catching crooks isn't an exact science."

"I guess you know what you're doing."

I was glad one of us thought so. She finished her drink and signalled for the bill, but when it arrived I wouldn't let her pay. She'd already told me she was broke. Perhaps that was why she didn't put up much of a fight when I reached for my wallet.

"Thanks," she said, smiling. "What can I do whilst you're playing cat and mouse with Miller?"

"Keep well away from me." I glanced at a man I'd seen lingering for ages over one drink a few tables away from us. A man who was pretending to read the paper but kept glancing at us over the top of it. I had a nasty feeling about him.

"Oh, why?"

"Because we're unlikely bedfellows, unfortunately. If I stir up this hornet's nest, it won't do for us to be seen together for a while."

"I suppose." She seemed disappointed but not, presumably, because her thoughts were veering in the same direction as mine.

"I'll call you as soon as I have any news."

"Thanks." She kissed me on the cheek as though it was a chore to be got out of the way as quickly as possible. After ruffling Gil's ears she strode off towards the car park without a backward glance.

The man at the nearby table left as well, following Cleo but keeping a good distance behind her.

Jimmy drew a blank on Reg Turner's amigos from ten years back. In view of that I couldn't decide whether to go through with my plan or admit defeat. In the end I figured it wasn't my call to make. Spelling's wife would have the final say. There would be a degree of risk for her, and she needed to be made aware of that. I recalled a bemused woman with a whole load of questions that none of us could fully answer at the time. I was the only one who tried, even though I wasn't directly involved in the case, and was relying on that to work in my favour now. I found her address in the local phone book. She remembered who I was and agreed to see me at once.

Her flat was a shrine to her late husband, and as soon as I stepped over the threshold I knew she would agree to help. Pictures of him littered every available surface and half the walls too. The less-than-lily-white bookie had been elevated to saintlike status by his grieving widow. Any space in the spotless flat not dedicated to his memory was full of soft toys, dolls in frilly dresses, pictures of children. It spoke of a lonely woman living an empty life.

"Your kids?" I asked her.

"No," she said, a cloud passing across her eyes. "We weren't blessed. I hadn't given up hope though and nor had Jeff. We were still young enough." That was stretching it a bit but I let it pass. "Now it will never be," she said with a heavy sigh.

Anxious to get off the subject, I spun her a yarn about Cleo's dad taking the fall for the people who'd been using her beloved.

"I always knew Mike didn't do it," she said, taking everything I said as gospel. "I tried to tell that woman inspector but she wouldn't listen."

"Well, obviously it's too late to bring Jeff back but perhaps we can do something to clear Mike's name and find the real killer."

Her eyes came alight and I felt bad about raising her hopes.

"He wouldn't have left me, Mr. Hunter," she said for the tenth time as we sipped stewed tea out of bone china mugs. "I never believed that. We were blissfully happy together but his work…" She stared at the opposite wall, overcome with emotion. I carried on forcing the tea down, waiting for her to regain control. "I hated him being a bookie," she eventually said. "Someone was always out to get him. If their horse didn't win they blamed it on him."

In that case someone must have bet a small fortune the day he died. But perhaps it would be better to keep that thought to myself. "This might come to nothing. You must be prepared for disappointment," I told her.

"Well, it doesn't seem right for Mike Kendall to be in prison. He and Jeff were the best of mates. He would never hurt him."

"Even so."

"Do what you have to do, Mr. Hunter. Don't worry about me. I might go and stay with my sister for a while. Just until this all dies down."

"That might be best.

"Just one more question and I'll leave you in peace. Do you know who Reg Turner hung out with back then?"

She shook her head. "No, not really. Jeff kept his business world separate from our private life. Sorry. Is it important?"

"No, don't worry about it. I just thought you might know."

She wrinkled her brow. "Well, if I think of any names, I'll let you know."

"Thanks."

I gave her a card with my number on it and left her flat, ready to rattle Miller's cage with her blessing. I'd always enjoyed stirring it with smug bastards like Miller. Even though I didn't have much, I reckoned I could still wind him up enough to send him running to his client. I rang his number and made an appointment to see him the following day. Then I rang someone else who owed me a favour and got him to stand sentry outside Miller's building with my zoom-lens camera. I gave Bill instructions to stay well hidden and get pictures of everyone who went in and out for the rest of the day. I promised to relieve Bill myself when darkness fell. It felt a bit like old times.

Miller's flat was opulent. If Paul could afford to live in the same building, it probably explained where Marianne's money had gone. Miller answered the door himself, dressed in an immaculate three-piece suit that obviously hadn't come from a High Street chain store. He eyed my uniform of jeans and biker's jacket with distaste, just as he was supposed to.

"Inspector Hunter," he said, opening the door wide enough to let me in.

"It's just Mr. Hunter now." I followed him along a panelled hallway and caught a glimpse of a large lounge to the left that was obviously his private domain. He led me into a room at the back of the apartment with a full-length bow window overlooking the street. A log fire was burning in the grate, and a large mahogany desk dominated the room, flanked by rows of leather law tomes that looked as though they'd never been opened.

Miller ignored the cosy arrangement of sofas facing one another in front of the fire, which were clearly reserved for his wealthier clients. He seated himself behind his desk, indicating the visitor's chair on the opposite side. I took my time sitting, keeping him waiting for a few seconds out of sheer devilment.

"Ah yes," he said, steepling his fingers and regarding me with something akin to amusement. "I did hear something about you taking early retirement, now you mention it."

"I was surprised when you asked me to call here," I said. "I thought you were a partner with a firm in town."

"I am but in this day and age it's possible to work from just about anywhere. I enjoy the comforts of my own home and only go to the office for board meetings."

"I see. But don't you need a secretary or some sort of backup staff?" I looked round but couldn't see another desk in the adjoining rooms.

"The joys of the internet age. Everything's done electronically and I can enjoy my privacy here. A lot of my clients prefer it that way."

*I'll just bet they do.*

"I must confess that your request for an appointment surprised me. What can I possibly do for a renowned ex-policeman?"

*You could offer him refreshments, like you would any other client.* But I clearly didn't rate that common courtesy.

"I received a visit the other day from the last person I expected to see again," I said.

"Someone known to me presumably or you wouldn't be here."

"Hmm, I expect so." I crossed one foot over my opposite thigh and leaned one elbow on the arm of my chair, striving for relaxed body language. "She was married to someone who met an untimely end. Does the name Anne Spelling mean anything to you?"

Miller's expression froze momentarily but he recovered quickly. "Spelling," he said, frowning. "Not sure I recognise the name."

"You don't remember the case? It was about ten years back but you couldn't pick up a paper at the time without reading something sensational about it. Her husband was the bookie who got murdered."

"Ah yes, I think I do recall something now." He tutted. "A most torrid affair." I almost smiled. The guy had had his brains bashed in, and Miller described it as "torrid." He made it sound as though he was talking about the weather. "But I don't see what it has to do with me?"

"Not you exactly but a couple of your clients. She's not managed to put what happened behind her. From what I know about him, Spelling was no great loss but naturally his wife doesn't share that view."

"Hardly surprising if she loved him, Mr. Hunter."

"Yes, but ten years." I spread my hands in a what-can-you-do-about-obsessive-women kind of gesture. "She latched on to me and plagued the life out of me for months afterwards, even though I didn't work the case. Anyway, she's convinced that the guy jailed for her husband's murder was acting on someone else's orders, and she's been tenaciously trying to ferret out the truth ever since."

"Good heavens." Miller beetled his brows. "It never fails to surprise me, the manner in which grief manifests itself."

"It now appears that Mrs. Spelling knew a great deal more about her husband's activities than we, the police that is, realised at the time. She came to me the other day and produced some pretty damning evidence against the people she suspects had it in for her husband."

"I see. And she hasn't taken this alleged evidence to the police because…"

"Because she's out for revenge and financial compensation." I enjoyed watching Miller trying to pretend an indifference he clearly didn't feel. "Why else?"

He frowned, feigning concern. "Then she's probably playing a dangerous game."

"That's what I told her but you know how women can be." I shrugged, wondering if he actually did. This place certainly lacked a woman's touch. "She says the papers she showed me were just an example and that the rest are lodged in a safe place with instructions that they be released to the authorities if she meets with an accident."

"Goodness, how very cautious of her."

"Well, what can I say?" I flashed a grin, man-to-man, intended to lament our inability to understand what made women tick. "We live in a dangerous world."

"Forgive me, Mr. Hunter, but I still don't see what this has to do with me or any of my clients."

"You don't?" It was my turn to feign surprise. "Oh well then, she must have got it wrong. You clearly don't represent these people so I won't take up any more of your time."

"Who are the people she's accusing, just as a matter of interest?"

"That's something I'd rather not reveal. Not if they're nothing to do with you. The fewer people who know about this, the safer it will be for Mrs. Spelling." I stood up and he joined me, leading the way towards the door.

"Indeed. But I still don't see why she came to you." He frowned. "You may not be a policeman anymore but, forgive me, leopards don't change their spots."

"She's got this bee in her bonnet about me being the only person to listen to her at the time of the killing and, to be frank, I feel sorry for her so I didn't brush her off."

"Ah, I suppose that would explain it then."

"And she knows that I left the force under something of a cloud."

I could see that he was itching to ask me more but I'd done enough and had no intention of being caught out with unnecessary embellishments. Anne Spelling was safely in Leicester spending a couple of weeks with her sister, but if anyone wanted to get to her badly enough it wouldn't be that hard to find her.

"What will you do now?" Miller asked in an indifferent tone.

I shrugged. "What can I do? Anne wanted me to contact these individuals direct but I'm not that stupid. I compromised by saying I'd have a word with you but that's as far as I go."

"So you think she'll give up on this wild goose chase?"

We'd reached the front door and as I waited for him to open it I glanced again into that sumptuous lounge. There was a photograph on a sideboard in a silver frame. I only caught a brief glimpse of its subject but was fairly sure I recognised the person whose image took pride of place in this man's home. My head was reeling with the implications it threw up but I had the presence of mind to look away quickly, not wanting to let on that I'd noticed.

"Sorry," I said. "I missed what you said."

"I merely asked whether you thought Mrs. Spelling would give up."

"I'll try and persuade her to see sense but I'm not holding my breath." I shook my head and his hand simultaneously as I stepped into the corridor. "Thanks for your time."

"Always a pleasure, Mr. Hunter."

He remained standing in the open doorway. I could feel his eyes boring into my back as I made my way to the stairs. I figured that if Miller was going to contact his clients then he'd do it the moment I left. He'd then either go and meet them or they'd come to him.

BUT IT DIDN'T work out that way. At six o'clock my mate Bill called me to say that Miller had left the building.

Bill tailed him to an upmarket restaurant but couldn't risk following him inside. I joined him there. Bill had a nice collection of pictures of all the people who'd come and gone after I left but there was no one that I recognised. Not even my stepbrother.

Together we watched Miller and another man enjoying a cosy dinner for two. Something about their body language made me wonder. Miller didn't strike me as being gay but, I don't know…there was nothing suspicious about this meal, other than it being easy to imagine the two men finishing up in bed together. If I'd rattled Miller with my questions it certainly wasn't evident in his current demeanour. We were wasting our time here.

"Thanks, Bill," I said, handing him a few notes. "It was worth a try anyway."

"Fancy building like that ought to have a doorman we could bribe," Bill complained.

"They make do with CCTV instead."

"Fucking cheapskates."

"Shame we can't get hold of the feed into that camera."

"I might know someone who could help there."

"No, but thanks anyway." There were limits, and right now I wasn't so desperate to help Cleo that I'd actually break the law.

"Do you want me to hang round the guy's building for a bit longer then, just in case any familiar faces appear?"

"No point. It was always going to be a long shot. If the people I wanted to see were worried, they'd have appeared by now. Let's leave it."

"You're the boss."

I phoned Cleo with the glad tidings. As always, she took the lack of progress in her stride and thanked me for all I'd tried to do. I didn't tell her that it was far from over. If there really was a conspiracy to do away with Spelling then the people behind it couldn't risk any evidence turning up that might point the finger at them. Anne Spelling was out of harm's way for the moment, and so I was the obvious target. I'd waved papers under Miller's nose and his clients would want to know what they contained. All I had to do now was wait for a visit.

But no one called and I started to wonder if I'd got it wrong. I tried to carry on as usual but the waiting was starting to get to me. To take my mind off things I returned to Miller's building two days later, not to see him but to make that long overdue call on my stepbrother. Sod's law, he wasn't home. I'd psyched myself up for the confrontation and left feeling deflated, as though Paul had somehow managed to get one over on me yet again.

I parked the bike and walked back towards the boat. Cleo was waiting for me at the gate to the pontoon. My initial reaction was one of pleasure, even though it was dangerous for us to be seen together. Still, no one had stopped by yet so I was probably being paranoid. My need for congenial company overcame my caution and I waved a greeting.

"Hi, what brings you here?"

"Just wanted to say a personal thank-you for trying to help."

She was wearing jeans, a sweatshirt and minimal makeup. This girl wasn't trying to make an impression or coerce me into chasing more wild geese. So what did she want?

"Well," I said as I keyed in the code for the gate and ushered her through it ahead of me, "if you're prepared to risk my cooking then you're welcome to join Gil and me."

"Oh, I'm the type that likes to go out on a limb."

"Can I have that in writing?"

Grilled steaks, baked potatoes and frozen vegetables. Even I can't cock up a simple meal like that. We washed it down with a bottle of decent red, talking about anything and everything except her father's situation.

"Come on," I said as we settled down with our brandies. "Now's the time to tell me what you're really here for."

She flinched as though I'd hit her. "You think I have an ulterior motive?"

"Don't you?"

"Actually, no. You're right about my father. If he doesn't want to help himself then there's sod all I can do about it." She tucked a foot beneath her thigh, leaned an arm along the back of the seating unit and stared out of the portlight at the pontoon pilings. Not the most attractive view when the tide's out but she didn't appear to be taking it in so I guess it didn't matter. "Perhaps he's become institutionalised and is better off where he is."

"Perhaps."

I wondered if that was what she really believed. She'd obviously learned to keep her thoughts to herself and it was impossible for me to read anything from her expression. She closed her eyes for a second or two, revealing in that simple gesture her unwillingness to show weakness by crying. It made me wonder just how close to the edge she actually was. The desire to comfort her was compelling. Without thinking it through I reached for her and pulled her into my arms.

She responded to my kiss with an urgency that matched my own and I knew that if I didn't bring this thing to a halt right now then we'd finish up in bed. So what? I wanted her and the feeling was obviously mutual. Why did I feel the need to fight it?

"Cleo, I don't think we should—"

"Shush!" She brushed a finger across my lips, sweeping my feeble objections aside just as easily. "I need you. Nothing else matters. Nothing needs to be said."

But before we could get down to specifics, a knock on the hull made us both start.

"What the fuck?"

The timing was lousy, bringing all my concerns to the fore. Someone *had* been watching us, waiting until I was with Cleo before coming to call. Whoever it was presumably intended to use her as leverage to get what they wanted out of me. But when I stepped into the cockpit, it wasn't some murky underworld figure waiting on the pontoon but my nemesis, Detective Chief Inspector Jillian Slater, as she now was. Jimmy Taylor was right behind her, looking as though he'd much rather be somewhere else.

"Not interrupting anything, are we?" Slater asked with a malicious glance in Cleo's direction.

"Evening, Jimmy," I said, ignoring Slater. "Kind of late for a social call, isn't it?"

"Hi, Charlie, we're…er, just—"

"This is official," Slater said, cutting across Jimmy's attempts to explain.

Her air of smug satisfaction suggested she knew something I didn't and intended to use that information to cause me maximum embarrassment. Slater enjoyed her petty attempts at revenge but as I'd always been able to run rings round her I wasn't unduly worried.

"Must be important if it can't wait until a more civilised hour." I thrust my hands into my pockets and leaned casually against the door frame. "But then I'm always at your service, Chief Inspector, you know that. Need my help catching local villains, do you?"

My reference to Slater's questionable abilities as a thief-taker was greeted with a predictable scowl. "It might surprise you to learn that we're managing very well in your absence," she said, making to step onto the deck.

I levered myself away from the door, glowering. "What's occurring?"

"I just need a word."

"And you'd walk into someone's house without being invited?"

"We're old colleagues. I didn't think I needed an invitation."

"All right," I said reluctantly, curiosity overcoming my distaste. "Come aboard if you must but remove your shoes first."

"You have got to be joking!" She looked at me askance but I didn't dignify her comment with a response, focusing my eyes on her heeled court shoes instead. With an elongated sigh she finally bent to remove them.

"You're all right in those, mate." I nodded towards Jimmy's trainers, just to rub salt into the wound. Jimmy caught on straightaway and flashed a grin.

"Sorry," Jimmy whispered as he stepped aboard first and left Slater to struggle over the gunwales unaided. I had no idea what he was apologizing about and he had no time to explain.

"We need to talk. Now." Slater pushed past Cleo as though she didn't exist and stepped into the salon. "And alone if you don't mind."

"Well, Charlie," Cleo said, reaching for her coat. "It was about time I was off anyway. We'll finish our chat later."

"No." I put a restraining hand on her arm. "There's no need to go."

"Don't push your luck, Hunter, or we'll take this down the station."

"It's Mr. Hunter to you, Detective Chief Inspector. And if you have a valid reason to take me in then by all means be my guest." I stared at her, and when she dropped her eyes first I knew I'd been right to call her bluff. Even she would think twice before pulling a respected ex-copper in for questioning about an as yet unspecified matter. "Now, as you're obviously on duty I won't put temptation in your path by offering you a drink."

I resumed my seat, pulling Cleo down beside me and making a big thing out of swirling the brandy round my glass. Irritated that Slater was already getting under my skin like only she knew how, I took a long sip. Hell would freeze over before Jillian Slater told me who could and couldn't remain on board my own boat. Gil appeared to be of the same mind and offered the occasional growl in Slater's direction as he settled warily at my feet.

Slater looked round the boat with obvious interest. I watched her impassively, waiting for her to get to the reason for her visit. She was short for a copper. Probably only just made the minimum height requirement, but was attractive and made the most of herself. She had short brown hair, pale blue eyes and a decent figure. Although most people wouldn't believe it from their dealings with her, she also had a wicked sense of humour when she allowed herself to relax—which wasn't often.

"Who's your friend?" she asked, giving Cleo an officious once-over.

"Cleo, this is Detective Chief Inspector Slater and Sergeant Taylor, both ex-colleagues of mine."

I left it at that. Cleo's full name was no business of Slater's. I didn't invite her to sit down but she took the other end of the seating unit to Cleo and me anyway. Jimmy stood behind her, still looking glum, which bothered me. Jimmy was one of the most irreverent, upbeat people I knew and a bloody good copper to boot. Something unpleasant, other than having to spend half the night traipsing round Brighton in Slater's company— which would be enough to upset anyone—must have happened to make him look so apprehensive. I was slightly mollified when his eyes lingered upon Cleo and, reverting to type, he winked at her.

"Right then," I said briskly. "What's so important that it's brought Brighton's finest calling at such an unsocial hour?"

"Sorry to interrupt your cosy little evening," she

said, looking anything but sorry, "but I need to talk to you about a local solicitor named Jason Miller."

Cleo stiffened beside me. I covered her hand with mine to prevent her from speaking. "What about him?" I asked.

"You know him?"

"I asked first."

She pursed her lips. "He's been murdered, Mr. Hunter, that's what about him."

# Chapter Five

"MURDERED?" I EXCHANGED a look with Cleo. "When?"

"Time of death is yet to be established but it was sometime within the last twelve hours."

"And you came knocking at my door because…" I knew what was coming but felt the question needed to be asked.

"Because your name was in his appointment book for two days ago." Slater's eyes glistened with malicious intent. "And because you were seen on CCTV leaving his building today."

Fuck it, I should have let Bill's mate doctor that bloody camera. I forced my limbs into a more relaxed pose and felt Cleo shift imperceptibly closer until our thighs were touching. Possibly she'd picked up on Slater's latent interest in me and was staking some sort of prior claim. Either way, having her leg pressed against mine wasn't something I intended to complain too strenuously about.

"Care to tell me what you were doing there?"

"Nope."

"Come on, Charlie, you know you can't keep quiet when murder's involved."

"How did he die?"

She hesitated before replying. "He was stabbed."

"So the killer would have been covered in blood."

She pursed her lips. "Not necessarily."

"Yeah, necessarily. And if you have me on CCTV leaving the building, you'll know I was as fresh and clean as a daisy."

"You were wearing a biker's jacket. You might have taken it off before doing the deed."

"You're really anxious to pin this on me, aren't you, Jill?" I knew she hated her name being shortened. "But as usual you haven't considered all the angles." I shot a glance at Jimmy, who was heroically attempting to smother a grin. "Why am I not surprised?"

"This doesn't look good for you. Just tell me why you were there and we can leave you and your friend to carry on doing whatever you were doing."

"*If* I was there to see Miller then it would be privileged."

She rolled her eyes. "How often have I heard that one?" She laughed but no one else appeared to get the joke.

"I wasn't there to see Miller," I said, standing to indicate that they'd overstayed their welcome. "And that's all I'm prepared to say."

"Tell us who you were there to see, and he or she can give you an alibi."

"Do I need one?"

She resorted to a smile that would frighten small children. "What do you think?"

I sipped at my drink and took my time responding. "Since you ask, I think you're sounding a bit desperate."

"And you're in a pile of deep shit unless you cooperate."

I actually smiled at that one, taking a tighter grip on

Cleo's hand as I did so and making sure Slater noticed. Hardly the best way to get myself out of this mess, flaunting Cleo beneath the nose of a woman who'd tried every trick in the book to get up close and personal with me when we'd worked together. But I was tired of being jerked about and really didn't give a toss about Slater's injured pride.

"I won't be able to sleep," I said, hoping I sounded unconcerned as I showed them off the boat and Slater clambered rather inelegantly onto the dock.

"Sorry, mate," Jimmy said, hanging back as Slater busied herself putting her shoes back on.

"Not your fault," I said. "In her position I'd have pulled myself in for questioning."

"She probably will."

He wasn't telling me something I didn't already know. Slater wanted to get me so badly that she'd do everything by the book, running my possible involvement past the brass before making her next move. She'd already convinced herself that I knew more than I did and would want to make sure there were no cracks I could slip through. I figured I had until the morning.

"What the hell's going on?" Cleo asked the moment our visitors left.

"Good question," I said, refilling our glasses.

"What a mess." She expelled a long breath. "Sorry, Charlie."

"What for?"

"I got you into this."

"You didn't get Miller killed. And Slater knows I don't have it in me to commit murder. She just wants it to be that way. That's why she'll try and find a way to make the facts point to me."

"She's already doing a pretty good job of it." Cleo frowned. "She's the woman who dealt with my dad's case, isn't she? She looks different now but I thought I recognised her."

"She hasn't improved with age."

"Why is she trying to fit you up?"

"We don't like each other." I slipped an arm round Cleo's shoulders and pulled her closer. "Now, where were we?"

"Charlie! This is more important."

I grinned at her. Actually grinned. "Nothing's more important than sex."

"You silver-tongued devil, you."

"You have no idea."

"I'm getting there. But you won't be. Not until you tell me why that woman was so antagonistic towards you."

I huffed a bit, annoyed with Slater for spoiling the moment. "You must know that I'd tell you any old story right now just to get your cooperation." I placed her hand over my erection, just in case she still didn't get the message.

She shot me an irritated glance and reclaimed her hand. "Try and think with your other head for a while and tell me what the hell's going on."

"Okay, okay." I knew when I was beaten. "Jillian Slater is a graduate who was fast-tracked into a position she was ill-equipped to handle. She's brilliant at manipulating the brass but a bloody awful copper. She was a detective inspector, the same rank as me, when she came to Brighton. I tried to help her out but she misinterpreted my friendly overtures."

"Oh dear!" She covered her mouth with her hand, presumably to try and stifle the giggle that escaped anyway. "You repulsed her advances. No wonder she's so pissed with you."

"I don't mix business with pleasure. Ever. Besides, I was still married at the time."

"But she forced you out of the force?" Cleo rolled her eyes at her clumsy choice of words.

"She was one of the reasons I got out, certainly, but not the only one."

"Because she was promoted above you?"

I took a moment to consider the question. "If you're implying that I resented having a woman boss, you're dead right. But only because it was her and she was promoted for all the wrong reasons." I stretched my arms above my head, trying to decide whether I ought to say more. In the end I chose to get it over with so we could turn our attention to more pressing matters. "My marriage broke up, I inherited this boat, Slater was compensating for her own inadequacies by throwing her weight around and making life difficult for me. Who needs it?"

"You obviously didn't." She kissed me gently and quickly pulled away again before I could take advantage of the situation. "But why were you at Miller's place again?"

"Has it occurred to you that other people besides Miller live in that block?"

"Well obviously they do." She furled her brow, her index finger absently plucking at her lower lip as she thought about it. "But you have to admit that it's a bit of a coincidence, you being there to see Miller one day and someone else another. Even I can see why Slater would be having a hard time with that."

"That's because she doesn't know my stepbrother lives there and I went to see him."

Her concerned expression evaporated. "So he can vouch for you?"

"No, because he wasn't in."

"Oh."

"Yes, oh indeed." I pulled her to her feet. "Come on, we're taking Gil for a run."

"Tell me more about the horrible Inspector Slater," she said as we strolled along together. "I didn't have much to do with her when Dad went down. I flew beneath her radar because I was never a suspect."

"She's the face of a modern force that's not afraid to promote women and people from ethnic minorities into positions of authority at a young age," I said succinctly.

"But she can't hack it?"

"Nope. She's intelligent but that's not necessarily helpful when it comes to outwitting your modern-day criminal. All the talk you hear about a copper's nose is right on the button." I lifted one shoulder. "You need street smarts. An inbuilt sixth sense that will tell you who's feeding you a line—which would be ninety-five percent of the people you talk to, in case you're wondering—and when to cut them some slack. Slater does everything by the book, which is why I know she'll cross the t's and dot all the i's before she comes back for me."

Cleo gasped. "You think she'll be back?"

"Oh yeah, but not until she's sure she's covered her own arse."

"Then why aren't you more concerned?" Cleo was frowning again, like I wasn't taking this seriously enough for her liking. "You ought to talk to your lawyer."

"What, and really give her a reason to suspect me?"

"Everyone has a right to legal representation."

"Hopefully it won't come to that," I said, wishing I felt as confident as I sounded.

"It can't have been easy for Slater, not if everyone knows why she's in the position she's in. How long has she been in Brighton?"

"She was promoted to inspector by the Met and moved down here just before your dad's case came up."

"You think they wanted rid of her in London?"

I flexed one brow. "The possibility did occur to me."

"Is that why she was so keen to prosecute Dad then? To make her mark."

"I always thought so."

Cleo's expression reflected her disgust. "Will she survive in the force?"

"Her sort always do." I snorted. "She's a useless thief-taker but bloody good at sucking up to the right people. The paperwork always shows her in a good light. She makes sure of that."

"But the antagonism? The sparks flying between the two of you. What's that all about?"

"Like I said, she hit on me and made something of a fool of herself in the process. The lads in the squad room got wind of it and she became a laughingstock for a while."

"That can't have been pleasant for her."

"In our line of work you have to be able to take it

as well as dish it out. Sometimes the banter is the only thing that gets you through. Anyway, I guess you can say that Inspector Slater doesn't take rejection well."

"She's very attractive."

I tried for an innocent expression. "Is she?"

"Like you've never noticed."

"Nothing gets in the way of her ambition, that's something I have noticed. But I've just learned tonight that she never forgets a slight either."

"Is that why you asked me to stay?"

"I didn't see why she should force you out."

"Oh, Charlie, that's so sweet!"

"Yeah well, I was already thinking about quitting the day job, and having her around made the decision that much easier. She's younger than me but she'll be promoted again and inflicted upon some other unsuspecting division before too long, especially if she can pin this murder on me."

"But she can't, can she?"

I wished I shared Cleo's optimism. "There won't be any evidence but, jaded old cynic that I am, I guarantee that won't stop her from trying."

She offered me a lilting smile. "I could describe you as many things, Charlie, but cynical…" She shook her head. "I don't see it."

"Perhaps that's because you don't know me too well."

"We can easily put that situation to rights."

"Ah, at last! The lady gets the message."

She bashed me playfully on the arm as we went back to the boat and did precisely that.

Cleo was an aggressive lover who knew what she liked and wasn't afraid to go after it. None of the reti-

cence she displayed in her daily life was evidenced between the sheets. She shed her inhibitions along with
her clothes, vociferously making demands that didn't
have me complaining.

We were in the shower together the following morning when Slater came for me, earlier than I'd anticipated.
She could hardly keep the glee out of her expression
when she requested that I accompany her to the station.

"Walk Gil, if you don't mind," I said to Cleo calmly,
"and hang on here until I get back. I shouldn't be long."

"Don't count on it," Slater said, walking into the
cabin where Cleo and I were having this conversation
and casting a scathing eye over the dishevelled bed.

"Do I need to call you a lawyer?" Cleo asked.

"No need for that." I led the way back to the salon
and out onto the pontoon. Slater had ostentatiously
posted two uniforms there, presumably in the hope of
embarrassing me. "Oh, and Cleo," I called over my
shoulder. "If anyone tries to search this boat, don't let
them on board."

"Got it."

And I knew she had. With her father's background
she'd be well aware of the grounds necessary to issue
a warrant. But I wouldn't put it past Slater to try and
get her people on board, implying that I'd given permission. It was just the sort of stunt she'd pull because
no magistrate would issue a warrant on the flimsy evidence she possessed. Slater glowered at me, which told
me I'd guessed right but said nothing as we walked
away from the boat.

I travelled in the backseat of the car driven by Jimmy.
Slater occupied the passenger seat and no one spoke for

the duration of the journey to the nick. Slater took great delight in walking me through the squad room. Since it was almost the end of a shift it was especially full. A coincidence? Somehow I didn't think so. Old colleagues recognised me and raised hands in greeting, only to drop them with uncertainty when it became apparent that I wasn't making a social call. Their friendliness turned to disbelief as I traversed the room, and I could imagine the sorts of rumours that would be doing the rounds before I'd even made it to the interview room. All part of Slater's petty revenge.

"Do you want a brief?" Slater asked, sitting herself next to Jimmy opposite me.

I leaned back, deliberately casual, and made myself as comfortable as I could on the uncomfortable metal chair. "Why, am I under arrest?"

"Not yet."

"Then I don't."

"Okay, you know the drill." She switched on a tape recorder, went through the usual rigmarole of introducing all the people present and got straight down to business. "You are Charles William Hunter and live on a boat called *No Comment* in Brighton Marina." I confirmed that I was. "What can you tell me about your recent visit to a solicitor called Jason Miller?"

"You just said all there is to say about that."

"What do you mean?"

"No comment."

Jimmy stifled a chuckle, which earned him a reproving look from his boss.

"That's hardly helpful."

"Why do you need my help?" I settled as comfortably as I could in the uncomfortable chair, hoping to convey the impression of being totally unconcerned about her allegations. "You obviously think you know it all already. Bring out the handcuffs, why don't you?"

"I'd like to hear your version."

"I'm sure you would but I'm equally sure that anything I said to a solicitor is privileged."

"Not if it impinges upon his death."

"It doesn't."

"Allow me to be the judge of that."

I actually laughed aloud at that one. "Oh, I'm sure you'd love that."

"Come on, Charlie." She leaned towards me, predictably allowing her impatience to show. One of her many shortcomings was a lack of finesse when interviewing suspects. "Why did you visit Miller on the day he died?"

I half smiled at her, almost enjoying myself, tapped the side of my nose and asked Jimmy for a coffee.

"Later," she said when Jimmy nodded and stood up. "You were about to tell me why you went to see Miller."

"Was I?"

I made my voice come out all croaky, grasping my throat in a dramatic parody of a man dying of thirst. Jimmy snickered but when Slater glowered at him he realigned his features into a passive expression and slid a little further down in his chair. He knew as well as I did that this whole thing was a crock of shit. We both waited in silence for Slater's next move. With a protracted sigh she suspended the interview, turned off the tape and nodded towards the door.

"Get me one too," she said to Jimmy as he left to fetch my coffee.

"Yes, ma'am."

I wondered if she could hear the sarcasm in his tone but figured that even if she could, Jimmy was too far down the food chain for her to care what he thought of her.

"Okay," she said as soon as the door closed behind him, "we're alone now and off the record so you might as well tell me what's what."

"I'm not sure about that." I stroked my chin as I tried to decide how much help to give her.

"Humour me."

"All right. I went to see Miller a couple of days ago. You know that because my name's in his appointment book, right?"

"Yes, and you saw him on the day he died too."

I let out a long breath and tried to remain patient, never my strong point when dealing with idiots. "Did I?"

"Nice try, Charlie, but I've got you squarely in the frame for this one. If you had an innocent reason for being there, why not help us out and save yourself a lot of grief."

"Really, Slate." I waggled my brows at her, using the station's nickname for her to her face. "Let's see if I've got this right. I'm an experienced ex-detective who's decided to swap sides and kill someone I barely know and have had few dealings with. But I'm daft enough not to notice the CCTV camera that's in plain view." I paused, waiting to see if she'd realise how impossible that sounded. It quickly became apparent that she was so anxious to pin this on me that the tiny logical part of her brain was closed for business today.

"It's how it looks from where I'm sitting, given the overwhelming evidence."

"Okay, let's look at your so-called evidence." I shifted my position and pinioned her with a direct look. "I was in that building for less than five minutes on the day in question. Not only was it not long enough to stab someone to death but it didn't give me nearly enough time to get the blood off my clothing."

"It could have been enough time and you might have overlooked the camera. People have done dafter things."

"What room was he killed in?"

"His bedroom."

"And I've never set foot in there."

"Well, I hardly thought you'd leave prints. Even you would think to wear gloves."

"But you thought I'd forget the camera." I rolled my eyes. "Really, I'm flattered that I still figure so prominently in your thought process, but I've left the force now so you don't have to feel threatened by me."

Colour spread across her cheeks. "You really think you're something, don't you?"

I winked at her. "Just telling it like it is."

Jimmy returned with the coffee and the tape was turned back on. She carried on for half an hour, trying to get me to say something incriminating.

"You know how it looks, Charlie, your refusing to say why you went to see Miller again."

"Not guilty, guv," I said, causing Jimmy's lips to quirk.

I felt like smiling myself at how easy it was to wind her up. But smiling at the best of times didn't do a lot for me and at that particular moment it was hardly appropriate.

Slater was right about one thing. This didn't look good for me. That meant I'd have to find out who really did kill Miller, because Slater would never get there on her own.

Bored now, I finally told her what I'd been holding back.

"Has it occurred to you that I might not have been visiting Miller on the day he was killed?" I could see from her expression that the thought hadn't crossed her mind. "Look up the names of the rest of the residents before trying to pin this thing on me." I drained the last of my coffee from its plastic cup and grimaced. I'd forgotten just how vile it tasted. "Now, I'm done here, and if you're not arresting me I'll be off."

"Sit down, Mr. Hunter," Slater said authoritatively.

I remained standing. "Or what?"

"You're not under arrest now but you soon might be if you don't cooperate."

"You've had all the cooperation you're gonna get out of me." I moved towards the door. "But don't take it badly. You know where to find me if you ever get enough to bring me in. Thanks for the coffee, if that's what it actually was. I know the way out."

She sighed. "Go with him, Taylor, and make sure he leaves the premises."

"Christ, Charlie," Jimmy said as soon as we were alone. "Sorry about that. She's a real bitch, but then you don't need me to tell you that. She couldn't believe her luck when she saw you on that CCTV footage. It was like all her Christmases had come together. But then

she's had it in for you ever since you pissed her off."
Jimmy pulled a doomed face. "Talk about bearing a
grudge. You should have given her one when you had
the chance. It would have done us all a favour."

I shuddered. "Think I'd prefer to take my chances,
if it's all the same to you."

Jimmy grinned. "It's your funeral, mate."

I sauntered through the squad room beside Jimmy
as though I didn't have a care in the world, and waved
to some of my old mates. They waved back, regarding
me in a friendly way now that it was clear I was no longer under suspicion about anything.

Once we were outside, Jimmy's entire demeanour
changed. He concentrated his gaze on the pavement
as he formulated his next words. I could already guess
what was coming.

"Look," he said, "I didn't tell her about what you
asked me to do."

"I know you didn't and I appreciate it."

"I might have to though if she carries on with this
vendetta against you."

"Do what you have to do, mate. Don't drop yourself
in it because of me."

"I know you didn't murder anyone, Charlie, and she
probably knows it too. If I thought for a moment that
you had anything to do with it then we wouldn't be having this conversation."

"Jimmy, you don't have to—"

"The super only allowed her to bring you in for questioning because he wants to play this by the book and
not have it look as though he was going easy on one of
our own. But if she knew of your interest in the offshore

company Miller fronted then it would give her what she needs to hold you on suspicion and to search your gaff."

He wasn't telling me anything I didn't already know. "She won't find anything because there's nothing to find."

"No, but she'd enjoy embarrassing you."

I conceded the point with an irritated nod. "Yeah, but all she's got right now is circumstantial."

"You think that'll stop her." He kicked moodily at a loose drinks can. "But I owe you big time, mate, and I'll keep stum for as long as I can."

He was right about that. He did owe me. When I'd been in the job, he'd stupidly jeopardised his marriage by having a meaningless fling. His wife found out about it, took the kids and ran off to her mother's. Jimmy, full of remorse, hit the bottle and fell apart. I covered for him and helped him to get his act together. His marriage was now solid again, his career back on track and I wasn't about to let him risk it again because of me.

"Look, Jimmy, I can't tell you what's going on. Even if I could, it's better that you don't know. I'll clear it up myself but it would help if I knew what other names were in Miller's appointment book immediately after I called on him."

He was silent for a moment. "I could probably find that out," he said a bit reluctantly.

"Don't take any risks." What I'd really like to see was the contents of Miller's file on Holder Enterprises but I knew the likelihood of that happening was just about zero. I asked the question anyway. "What about his files?" Jimmy shot me a disbelieving look. "Just asking," I said mildly.

"There weren't any that I saw."

I thought about that. "I didn't see any evidence of paper records whilst I was with him either but I figured they might be in another room."

"Well, if they were, they aren't now. One of his partners called the murder in. Apparently Miller didn't turn up for a vital board meeting and wasn't answering his home phone or his mobile. That was so unusual that alarm bells rang and someone went round to see if he was all right."

"How did they get in?"

"Spare key at the office. His firm own that flat and Miller rented it from them. By the time we got there, Miller's laptop was gone and a desk drawer had been unlocked and emptied. His partners are claiming client confidentiality and won't let us near his computer without a warrant."

"Yeah, I'll bet."

"They're trying to act like concerned citizens and have said that if there's anything on it to help our investigation they'll pass it on."

I expelled a long breath. "More concerned with the image of the firm than with seeing justice done."

"That's how it came across to me."

I started walking slowly along the pavement. It wouldn't do for anyone in the nick to see us in conversation for too long. "There's something going on here and I'm not sure yet what it is. I'll do some digging if only to exonerate myself. Presumably you're looking at Miller's phone records."

"Of course."

"Well, if any interesting names crop up—"

"I'll let you know."

"Thanks, mate."

"What were you doing at that building on the day Miller died?" Jimmy asked. "Just as a matter of interest, like."

I flashed a brief smile. "Paying a social call on my stepbrother."

The wrinkles on Jimmy's brow immediately flattened themselves out. "Then why didn't you tell her that and get her off your back?"

I quirked a brow. "Where's the fun in that?"

Jimmy guffawed. "But it puts you in the clear. You have an alibi."

"No, unfortunately I don't. If I did I'd have told her. Eventually. But Paul wasn't in. That's why I was in and out of the building so quickly."

"Fuck it!"

"Yeah."

"Anyway, I'd better get back to work but I'll give you a bell with the names in Miller's appointment book when I can."

"And if anything interesting comes up on his phone records?"

"I'll let you know that too."

"Thanks, Jimmy, I owe you one."

# Chapter Six

I RETURNED TO a rapturous welcome from Gil and a more guarded one from Cleo.

"What happened?" she asked. "You've been gone for ages and I was getting worried."

I reached for a beer and then changed my mind, going for whisky instead. Cleo seemed angry but I figured that was just her way of dealing with stressful situations. She wasn't the emotional, weepy type and for that I was grateful.

"Oh, just my ex-colleague trying to peg me as a murderer." I shrugged, trying to make light of it.

"Don't be so flippant, Charlie."

"Sorry, it's been a long morning." I slumped onto the seating unit and took a healthy swig of my drink. Cleo paced a couple more circuits of the limited floor space before she joined me. "It looks as though I'm going to have to get to the bottom of this whole business myself," I said wearily. "Slater won't let it go until I can prove I'm not involved."

"But you *can* prove it. You were in and out of the building too quickly to have murdered anyone."

I harrumphed. "That won't stop her from needling away at me."

"She can't do that, can she?"

I shot her a look that said *don't be so naïve.* "You

ought to know the score by now. How many years did you live under the same roof as your old man?"

"Yeah but he *was* a career villain. He expected your lot to come calling whenever anything with his moniker on it went down locally and didn't hold it against you." She flashed me a sapient smile. "Bet you never thought you'd be on the receiving end of police harassment."

"You wouldn't get very good odds on a bet like that." I twisted my lips into a parody of a smile that quickly faded as I thought the matter through. "Slater will keep at me just because she can. And one thing's for sure, she'll be so obsessed with pinning the whole thing on me that she won't look too hard anywhere else and then—"

"And then the murderer's trail will go stone-cold."

"Yeap." I exhaled slowly. "That's about the size of it."

"All right then. What can I do to help?"

"I'll let you know if I think of anything."

"That won't work. I got you into this so I'm staying around for the duration."

"All right then, it's your turn to cook." I ducked the blow that she aimed at me, pleased to see her finally crack a genuine smile.

"I had something a little more practical in mind."

"There's nothing more practical than food."

She rolled her eyes but got up and rummaged about in the galley without further protest. "I certainly don't believe that."

"I'm emotionally drained after my ordeal at the hands of the brutal police," I said, milking the situation for all I was worth. "Besides, I can't think properly on an empty stomach."

"Okay, you've made your point. But, just so that you know, I'm no Delia Smith so don't expect any sort of gourmet experience."

She rustled up a pasta dish with salad and crusty bread. I wolfed it down, causing Cleo to make some cryptic remark about my *ordeal* not having affected my appetite.

"So, Charlie," she said when we'd cleared up and were back on the seating unit, my arm draped round her shoulders, jazz playing softly in the background. "What's our next…say, what's that music?"

"It's Oscar Peterson."

"It's cool." She tilted her head and regarded me quizzically. "You listen to a lot of jazz. Isn't that what was playing in your cabin last night when we—"

"The rhythm helps me to maintain my…er, rhythm."

She laughed at my lame attempt at humour.

"I was rather hoping you'd appreciate my harmonic diversity."

"I'm sure I did. Whatever that is." She smiled at me. "But there's more to it than that, isn't there. Jazz is a big part of who you are."

I narrowed my eyes at her. "What makes you say that?"

"I don't know really." She threw her head back and rotated it slowly, as though forcing herself to relax. "It's just that at times of high emotion, or stress, you automatically turn to music. And it's always some sort of jazz. I think I could get to predict your moods through your choice of music, is what I'm trying to say."

I didn't want to get into a discussion about jazz,

aware of where it would lead, and brought the conversation back to more pressing matters. I told her Jimmy had promised to get me more information about Miller's recent appointments and phone calls.

"How will that help?"

Good question. "Who knows? Can't say until I know who he's been dealing with. That's how detecting goes. You niggle away at every little angle until something interesting pops up. It usually does, eventually."

"If you say so." She stretched and settled herself into a more comfortable position, her tucked up knees resting on my thigh. "So, what do we do in the meantime?"

"What, right now?"

She giggled. "I have a pretty good idea what's on your mind right now."

"Hey, I'm still traumatised."

"You could get counselling."

"I prefer my method of coping."

I kissed her because it seemed like the right thing to do. Because it was what I wanted to do. She leaned towards me and returned that kiss with fervour. Five minutes later, clothes indiscriminately discarded along the way, we were in bed having brutal sex. I was starting to understand her. She enjoyed harsh physical contact, no talk and little emotional investment. She wrapped those long legs of hers round my neck and lifted her hips, taking everything on offer with a hunger that was infectious.

In all other aspects of her life she appeared to be self-contained and completely in control. But between the sheets she was insatiable, which was a definite turn-on.

I liked to think it was my skill as a lover that wrought such a change in her but suspected she was one of those women who simply enjoyed sex and wasn't ashamed for her partner of choice to know it.

We fell asleep afterwards, me feeling strangely unsatisfied despite having had completely satisfying sex. Then Gil's reproachful whining reminded me that he hadn't had his run. I sat up and reached for my clothes. As I stepped into my jeans my phone rang. It was Jimmy, with interesting information to impart.

"Thanks, mate," I said. "I appreciate it… Sure I will. As soon as I know anything I'll be in touch."

"What was that all about?" Cleo asked.

"Something odd. Jimmy tells me that Reg Turner had an appointment with Miller the very day before me."

"Reg?" She elevated her brows. "That mate of my dad's. How can he afford the services of a top-end brief like Miller?"

"That's what I'd like to know," I said, buckling my belt. "I told you something interesting would pop up."

"Are you going to take Gil for his run?" Cleo asked. "I'll come with you."

I manfully resisted reaching for her pert breasts by not dwelling on the way they bounced when she sat up. "Better not. I need to track Turner down and it's probably best if I do that alone."

"Do you know where to find him?"

"Unless he's changed his habits since I quit the force, which I rather doubt."

"Oh, all right then." She frowned. "What else did Jimmy say?"

"He mentioned another name that was in the appointment book, but I'm not sure if it means anything."

"Who was it?"

"Andrea Garnet."

Her head shot up. "Garnet?"

"Yes. Her husband has fingers in all sorts of pies. He owns racehorses, has a string of nightclubs here on the south coast and a posh health spa in Hove."

"I know it by reputation. It recently had a huge makeover."

"He used to hang out with all sorts of dubious characters but we were never able to pin anything on him. Nowadays he's respectable, on the surface anyway, and has friends in high places. If he'd been the one contacting Miller, it wouldn't have surprised me but I'd like to know what business his wife had with him."

"Andrea Garnet." Cleo leaned up on one elbow and supported her head on her hand. "She comes to the casino sometimes. She plays poker for high stakes and doesn't seem to care if she loses."

"With the sort of money her husband brings in, she wouldn't have to."

"I've never met him. She always has a guy there with her but I don't think he's her husband."

"Well then, that might be a useful way to get chatting to her. You can give me a call the next time she comes to the club."

"She'll eat you alive, Charlie. She loves men in general and something tells me you'd be right down her street."

I offered her a mock bow. "I aim to please."

She threw a pillow at my retreating back.

Gil and I caught a bus to the less salubrious part of town. By the time we reached our destination it was gone nine o'clock. Exactly right. I pushed open the doors to the old-fashioned saloon bar of the equally old-fashioned Dog and Duck and was almost asphyxiated by the cigarette smoke that drifted out to greet me. The bar itself was as shabby as the rest of the place, the ceiling a dull nicotine colour, the wallpaper faded and peeling away in places. I preferred not to dwell upon the origins of the substances that stuck to the soles of my shoes, impeding my progress as I traversed the uneven floorboards. The lighting was dim, its effectiveness further reduced by the cloud of smoke hovering just below ceiling height like a vengeful celestial body. I wasn't surprised to discover that the smoking ban had passed this establishment by.

Two men sat in front of an ineffective single-bar electric fire and looked up briefly as Gil and I entered. Two women, obviously working girls taking a break, sat at one end of the bar. They were drinking what looked like gin and tonic, adding to the polluted atmosphere by puffing away on unfiltered cigarettes. They visibly brightened when I walked in but turned away in disgust when I shook my head.

Reg was just where I expected to find him, holding up one end of the bar, the remains of a pint of bitter in front of him. I slipped onto the stool next to him and attracted the attention of the brassy-looking barmaid. Gil gave Reg's trousers a thorough sniffing and, finding nothing too objectionable adhering to them, flopped onto the greasy floor between us with a heavy sigh.

"Evening, Reg," I said cheerfully. "Refill?"

"Don't mind if I do, Mr. Hunter. Just so long as it won't cost me nothing."

"There's no such thing as a free lunch, Reg, or a free pint, come to that." I ordered a pint for myself and another of whatever Reg was having.

"I heard you'd got out," Reg said morosely. "So what do you want with me? Can't somehow imagine that you hit upon this fine establishment by accident."

"Nope, it was you I came to see."

Reg sniffed, took his time rolling a paper-thin cigarette, tapped it several times on the bar and fired it up with a plastic lighter. "Oh yeah, what about then?" he asked warily.

This was where it got tricky. If he was still involved with the people behind Spelling's murder then they'd get to hear of my interest before I even made it back to the boat. Even so, I had to take that chance.

"Your name cropped up in conversation the other day," I said, taking a long pull on my pint. I wasn't surprised to discover that it was excellent. Shabby décor meant nothing to the clientele of such establishments, but a poorly tapped barrel would likely cause a riot.

"Yeah, what about?" Reg's attitude changed from guarded to hostile. "Don't you lot ever let a body alone and mind your own bloody business?"

"Ah now, Reg, where're your manners? It was a woman who spoke to me about you. Said you were tight with her dad."

He scowled at me. "Why do I get the feeling that there's more to this than a social call?"

"What, there's somewhere else you need to be?" I

feigned surprise. "What were you and Mike Kendall up to before he went down for Spelling's murder?"

Reg slopped beer over his hand and dissolved into a bout of coughing.

"Ought to give up those cancer sticks, Reg." I nodded towards his half-smoked fag. "They'll kill you in the end."

"Gotta die of something."

"True enough but that won't be a pleasant way to go." I paused for a sup of beer. "Come on then, tell me about Kendall."

"And I'd do that because—"

"Because I'm asking you nicely," I said, steel in my voice. "Because you know me well enough not to want to make an enemy of me. Oh, and because I'll make it worth your while."

The offer of financial gain secured his attention but he wasn't about to give anything up easily. "It was a long time ago," he said.

"And you've got the memory of an elephant."

He ground his cigarette out on the floor and sighed. "Look, it was a scam, all right?"

"What sort of scam?"

"Dog fixing. I was just a gofer and never knew who was behind it all." That had to be a lie but I let it pass. "Mike Kendall was higher up the food chain but still a small cog."

I nodded. "Go on."

"It was money for old rope, weren't it. Thousands of letters were sent out to known gamblers telling them that the person sending it had a score to settle with a particular bookie and was going to break him by betting big time on a specific race." Reg paused to scratch vigorously at his scalp. I moved out of range to avoid the ensuing shower of flakes. "Dead simple it was, but then the best dodges usually are."

"Don't tell me. The recipient of the letter had to ring the number quoted and was given the name of the winning dog for free."

"Got it in one, Mr. H." Reg sniffed his contempt. "Course, three dogs were picked, with three different numbers to ring and one of them was almost sure to win the race. Well, put it this way, one of them always *did* win the race but don't ask me how that could possibly have been arranged, dog racing being the upstanding, whiter-than-white sport what it's always been. Anyway, out of the thousands of chancers who rang the numbers, a lot of 'em hit on the winner. Greed almost guaranteed that they'd phone again and this time pay for another tip."

I nodded, having heard of such schemes before. "Simple and undetectable."

"Yeah, pretty much, until that wanker Spelling went and got himself offed and spoiled it all."

"He was the bookie who coordinated it?"

"Yeah, he supplied the names of the punters who were targeted but as far as I know, once he was killed and Mike went down for it, the scam was wound up." He shrugged. "My services became surplus to requirements anyway and I never heard of it starting up again at another track."

"Who's Peter Garnet then and what was his part in it all?" I asked, hoping to catch him off guard with the abrupt change of subject.

"Dunno." But he was lying. I could see it in his

ferret-like eyes when he focused them everywhere except on my face.

"Don't lie to me, Reg. Not when you were doing so well."

"Look, I don't know the man and what's more I don't want to." But Reg was terrified. I could tell by his defensive body language and shuttered expression. "I've heard stories though and he ain't the sort you'd want to cross."

"So it's coincidence that you happen to share the same brief as someone in Garnet's league."

This time his eyes did focus on me. "What do you mean?"

"You went to see Jason Miller, who charges three figures for a ten-minute consultation, a day or two before he was murdered. What am I supposed to think about that?"

Alarm flashed through his eyes. "Here, that was nothing to do with me. Don't try sticking me with that one."

"So why did you go to see Miller?"

Reg ground his teeth, clearly trying to decide how much to tell me. "It was personal."

"Is that what you told my ex-colleagues when they came calling?"

He shrugged. "Haven't had that pleasure yet."

I wasn't surprised to hear it. Looking at the people who'd been at Miller's office on the day of his death would have been my priority too. But unlike Inspector Slater, I'd have also flipped back a few days to see if anyone of interest had been getting his attention before then. Turner's name would have stuck out like a fox in a henhouse, and he'd have been one of the first people I spoke to. Jill obviously thought she had her man in yours truly and wasn't bothering to look further afield.

I kept at Reg but he refused to say anything more. Whoever sent him to see Miller obviously frightened him a lot more than I did so I decided to call it a day. It would only be a matter of time before he remembered that I no longer had a right to be asking him questions.

"What can you tell me about Garnet, then?" I asked him instead.

"Like I said, he's a hard sod. All smarm and good nature on the surface but he'd knife you as soon as look at you if you cross him."

"Has he then?"

"Has he what?"

"Knifed anyone."

"Fucked if I know. It's just an expression. Word is that he's gone all respectable nowadays."

"But you don't buy that?"

He shrugged. "People don't change."

"All right. What else can you tell me about him?"

"I did hear something interesting on the grapevine the other day, as a matter of fact."

"And that would be?"

Reg said nothing more until I put my hand in my pocket and produced a tenner. I held it just out of his reach. "You have to earn it," I reminded him.

"Rumour is that he's on the verge of bankruptcy and is cooking something up to get himself out of the mire."

It was the first thing Reg had told me that truly surprised me. "I'd heard that he was rolling in it."

Reg took a long swallow of beer and passed his glass across the bar for a refill. "Yeah well, what with the recession, that fancy health club of his wasn't doing so well. So he decided on an expensive refit to attract more punters."

"I'd have thought his nightclubs would keep the coffers full."

"What can I say? Even the kids are feeling the pinch right now. Guess they don't go clubbing quite as often as they used to. Or could be Garnet's got competition in that field too, just like with his health club."

"Somebody deliberately targeting his market, you mean?"

"Dunno, do I. Haven't heard anything. It was just a suggestion."

I thought about it. If Garnet had been behind the payments to Cleo's mother's clinic, his financial problems could explain why they'd stopped so abruptly. Could Reg have been in Miller's office, acting as go-between for Garnet? It seemed tenuous, especially since Garnet's wife had also been there, and presumably he'd be much more likely to trust her if he needed someone to act for him. None of it made sense. Yet. But my sixth sense told me I was on to something. Besides, I had bugger all else.

"Here, why are you asking about Kendall anyway?"

"He's up for parole."

Reg looked surprised. "Is he? I hadn't heard."

"But he won't get it unless we can prove someone else killed Spelling."

"Yeah, but why would you care? You were around

when he was banged up and I don't remember hearing that you had any doubts."

"Mistakes are sometimes made."

"Leave it alone, Mr. H. You don't know what you're getting yourself into. You always treated me fairly, not like some of your lot, and I wouldn't like to see you lose your kneecaps."

"Thanks. Warning duly noted."

We drank for a moment or two in contemplative silence.

"What I can't understand, Reg," I said eventually, "is why Mike Kendall would have killed his mate."

Reg chuckled. "There's no honour amongst thieves. You of all people ought to know that."

"Do you think he killed him then?"

He sniffed. "Doesn't matter what I think, does it?"

"See what you can find out about Peter Garnet for me, Reg. There'll be a decent drink in it for any information you come up with."

He looked at me for a long time. "A woman." He nodded vigorously. "It's got to be a woman."

"What has?"

"Whoever persuaded you to start asking dangerous questions. Kendall's daughter, I shouldn't wonder. Can't say as I blame you. She's a bit of all right but is she worth all the aggro?"

"So will you do it?" I asked him. "Get information on Garnet for me, I mean?"

He mulled the question over and took his time replying. "If that's the only way to get you off my back. Not that it'll do you much good, mind. I only see him occasionally at the dog track and he don't talk to the likes of me. But I'll keep my ear to the ground. Where can I reach you?"

I gave him the tenner and my number, whistled to Gil and I left the pub.

# Chapter Seven

GIL AND I had to wait a while for a bus to transport us back to civilisation. It didn't particularly bother me. I had some thinking to do and was barely conscious of the passage of time. What or who was Reg so frightened of that he'd be prepared to turn down good money rather than ferret out the information I wanted? And he *was* frightened, which bothered me because it took a lot to frighten an old lag like Reg.

All right, so he'd said he'd help if he could but in all the years I'd known him, and used him as a snout, I couldn't ever recall him backing away from a financial negotiation. Reg loved money and didn't care too much what he had to do to earn it. Villain or snout, it was all the same to him. In his case it was true what he'd said to me in the pub. There was definitely no honour amongst thieves. But moral colatitudes aside, whatever information Reg had fed me over the years had always been good value. To the best of my knowledge, none of his partners in crime had ever discovered who'd grassed them up. If they had, he'd no longer be able to walk unaided. That was one advantage in being so far down the chain of command. Reg had a way of ingratiating himself and keeping a low profile. Suspicion never seemed to fall his way.

Perhaps I was imagining something that didn't exist,

and Reg was simply being cautious about helping me out because I no longer had the might of the police force behind me. But somehow I didn't think so. Reg had landed himself in something out of his league. I didn't need his visit to Miller's office to tell me that. So what the bloody hell was going on?

Another bloke was waiting at the bus stop too, doing his best to avoid eye contact but that was nothing unusual in a city like Brighton. What did surprise me was Gil, usually the most compliant of dogs, taking an immediate dislike to him. A soft growl rumbled in his throat and his tail was rigid with tension. I tried to apologise to the guy but he seemed determined to act as though I didn't exist. I thought nothing more of it until the bus finally trundled into sight. I stood back to let the other passengers board ahead of Gil and me but the chap who'd caught my attention didn't do so.

Only then did I cotton on to the fact that something wasn't quite right about him. He couldn't be waiting for another bus. The vehicle belching out toxic fumes as passengers took their time getting on and off and whose driver took forever trying to decide whether or not Gil could come aboard was the only one serving this route. Perhaps he was meeting someone off the bus. It was odd but I was too preoccupied to think much more about it.

Only when the bus pulled away and I happened to glance back and see a car screech to a halt did the penny drop. The guy got into the passenger seat and the car fell into the bus lane, seemingly content to follow behind the slow-moving vehicle in spite of there being plenty of room to overtake.

The feeling of unease I'd experienced over Reg's behaviour intensified. Was the guy following me or was I getting paranoid in my middle age? I tried to remember what he looked like, wishing now that I'd spared him a bit more attention. I could recall that he was tall and well built, as if he worked out or something. Mid-to late-thirties. A ball cap had prevented me from seeing his hair colour. A denim jacket and jeans. A description that would fit half the male population in Brighton. I briefly wondered if Slater had set him to watch me but dismissed that possibility. He hadn't been in the pub whilst I was talking to Reg. I'd have spotted him even if he'd been in the other bar because it was visible through a large archway. Old habits die hard, and wherever I am, I always keep half an eye out for trouble.

Anyway, if he was watching me he was a joke. Unless he wanted me to know he was there, of course, in which case he'd done a pretty efficient job. I wondered about that as the bus slowly made its way into the more prosperous part of town. I hadn't been followed to that pub, I'd bet a lot of money on that, so how did anyone know where I was?

Reg? Could he have tipped someone the wink? He'd gone to the bathroom midway through our little chat. I doubted whether he'd embraced the cell-phone age but there was a pay phone on the wall in the corridor leading to the gents.

By the time Gil and I got off the bus and set out to walk the rest of the way back to the boat, I was a fair way to believing that the guy *had* been watching me and had wanted me to know it. The car he was in had stayed behind the bus all the way into Brighton. I'd only lost sight of it when it got stuck at a red light.

We turned down the road to the marina, passing the casino where Cleo would be back on duty tomorrow, when I heard footsteps behind me. I had a feeling I'd know who it was as soon as I looked over my shoulder, which was presumably the point. And so I refrained from looking. I hated being predictable. The guy was walking at the same pace as me but I knew by now that he didn't wish to harm me. Merely intimidate. Fortunately I didn't scare easily.

I deliberately took the long route back to the boat, passing several glass-fronted restaurants in the process and using them as mirrors. Sure enough, my denim-clad friend was a hundred feet behind me. Just for the hell of it, I carried on through the marina, towards the rocky beach where I often take Gil for a run. He was delighted to find himself there at this time of night. We had it to ourselves and he tore off to the water's edge, keen to chase anything foolish enough to be loitering within his range.

That would include men he'd taken a dislike to. Men who were afraid of dogs. It was always possible to tell. Gil knew as well of course. He abandoned the pile of seaweed he'd been nosing through in the hope of finding something sufficiently rotted to appeal to his doggy palate, lifted his head and sniffed the air. His entire body stiffened. Then he let out a volley of barks and tore off in the direction of my shadow, growling and snarling like he meant business. Perhaps he did. I'd never seen him like this before so I couldn't have said. I wasn't surprised when I finally turned my head and found myself alone. With a grimace of satisfaction, I whistled to Gil and we headed back to the boat. My pursuer obviously knew where I lived so my detour had done nothing other than make me feel I'd come out on top of this particular skirmish.

"God, Charlie, you've been gone forever." Cleo greeted me in the salon wearing nothing but a thin robe and a worried frown. "What kept you?"

I gave her a brief rundown of all that Reg had told me but didn't mention anything about being followed. I was concerned about it and would give a lot to know who'd been after me, and why. I could take care of myself but what would happen if Cleo became their next target? She'd have no idea how to shake her pursuer off and if they wanted to know what I knew—which was bugger all—they could easily nab her. That meant keeping a close eye on her and being careful about how much I told her.

"The dog scam is just the sort of thing my dad would have got involved with," she said, thinking through all I'd just told her as she poured me a drink. "And Spelling too—but I find it hard to believe that he chucked in something that lucrative just to run off with a woman."

"Ah, so cynical." I winked at her. "You underestimate the power of *lurve*."

She snorted. "More like lust."

"Now that I *can* identify with."

"Tell me something I don't know." She flopped down next to me. "So, what do we do now?"

I shrugged, deliberately vague. "Not much we can do unless Reg comes through with anything useful."

"You don't sound too hopeful."

"That's because I don't think he knows anything that will help us."

She frowned. "I don't buy that."

Somehow I hadn't thought that she would. "He used to be a reliable source but nowadays he's more scared of whoever he works for than he is of me." I spoke with casual finality. "Probably best not to get your hopes up."

"He knows you can't make his life awkward now that you're no longer a policeman."

"Exactly."

"I'd still give a lot to know why he went to see Miller and how he could afford to."

"Me too."

"Has he got a wife? A family? Perhaps it's something to do with them."

"Good question." I rubbed my chin, trying to think if I'd ever seen him with anyone, or heard him talk about someone special. "I recall going to his drum once or twice. A grungy bedsit, it was." I shook my head. "No, I think he's a loner. No woman would have put up with a pigsty like that."

"You'd be surprised."

"After twenty years on the force I think it's safe to say I've seen it all."

"Well, perhaps he was making his will, swearing an affidavit, something like that."

"Hardly. Unless he has ill-gotten gains we know nothing about, then Miller's fee would be in excess of the value of his estate. And an affidavit…" I shook my head again. "The only swearing Reg knows anything about is restricted to four letters."

"It just doesn't make any sense."

"No, it doesn't."

"Still," Cleo said, brightening, "I'm back at work

tomorrow and perhaps Andrea Garnet will come in."
She grinned. "I'll call you if she does and you can bam-
boozle her with your lethal charm. Who knows what
she might reveal?"

I sighed dramatically. "The things I do for the forces
of law and order."

"And to extricate yourself from a murder rap."

"Ah yes, that too."

I kept Cleo with me the following day on various
pretexts, going with her when she returned to her flat
to change into work clothes. I didn't see anyone watching me or the boat but then it wouldn't be so easy for
people to get close, given that the pontoons are locked.
It wasn't that difficult to slip through the gate on some
pretext or other but anyone loitering on a pontoon without a good reason would stand out like a spare part.
That wasn't to say we weren't being watched from one
of the many bars overlooking the boats, but at least no
one was trying to get close enough to invade my living
space. If that happened I wouldn't be a happy camper.

Cleo wasn't too pleased about me tagging along, and
when we reached her flat I could see why. It was a glorified bedsit with kitchenette and minuscule shower
room. She'd made the best of it, giving it the feminine
touch, and it was scrupulously clean and tidy. But it
clearly wasn't what she was used to and the fact that
she'd been reduced to this, just because she'd had to settle her mother's bills, made me angry. She was grouchy,
embarrassed by her circumstances, and I couldn't think
of anything to say to put her at ease. I had the good
sense not to make any observations about her living
arrangements but could now understand her determi-

nation to get some answers. I would do everything I could to provide her with them.

"Charlie, your determination to dog my footsteps has nothing to do with the relentless attraction you feel towards me, has it?" Cleo emerged from her bathroom, clad in her work uniform. "Come on, what gives?"

"I'm not with you." I tried to look innocent but she wasn't buying it.

"If I didn't know better I'd think that you're trying to protect me." She narrowed her eyes. "Something else happened, didn't it? Something you're not telling me."

"What, I can't be gentlemanly without arousing suspicion?"

"I'm a big girl. It's not that I don't appreciate your concern but I can take care of myself."

"Maybe I just enjoy your company."

"And maybe I enjoy my job too much to risk being late and getting the sack," she said, glancing at the clock. "Come on, Mr. Gallant, I'll drive you home." She smiled sweetly over her shoulder, more like the girl I'd got to know over the past few days. "It just so happens that it's on my way. But," she added, wagging a finger at me, "don't think this lets you off the hook. I fully intend to find out what it is you're *not* telling me."

She rushed to her car, failing to see the guy stationed across the road. He was leaning against a lamppost, his face concealed behind a newspaper that he obviously wasn't reading. I knew immediately that he was in the job. So Slater had set someone to follow me as well. At this rate I was going to start looking like the Pied Piper. Whilst the idea amused me, having my old colleagues looking upon me with suspicion didn't.

Slater was sensible enough to have used a young guy, one who usually wore a uniform and wasn't personally acquainted with me. Even so, word of her actions was bound to spread through the squad room and I wasn't happy about that. I was willing to bet that my old boss, D.S. Dormer, didn't know what she'd done. And that might be my saving grace. Dormer liked Slater but I wasn't so sure that he respected her abilities as a copper. I'd had my ups and downs with him over the years. He liked to do things by the book and didn't always approve of my methods, so we'd never been friends exactly. But he had acknowledged my talents and knew I was one hundred percent straight. If he found out what Slater had done, there'd be hell to pay. And if push came to shove, I wouldn't hesitate to drop her in it.

Cleo went to work, promising to be in touch the next day to see if I'd made any progress. Sooner if Andrea Garnet put in an appearance at the casino.

I spent the evening tinkering on the boat, doing all the usual routine maintenance checks. I was due to take it to Le Havre for the weekend. A mate who'd retired from the job a couple of years back had opened a small hotel there and had invited some of the lads for the weekend. The boat was overdue for a run and I was looking forward to making the trip. Perhaps a few days away from Cleo's problems would put things into perspective.

I hadn't forgotten about my stepbrother Paul and all that money he'd borrowed but I knew better than to go anywhere near his flat right now. Slater would know about my visit before I crossed the threshold and would be down on me like a bull elephant. It had waited twenty-odd years so a few more weeks couldn't hurt. But it kept niggling away at me like a physical ache. Paul borrowing a huge sum of money. Paul living in the building where a vicious murder had been committed. What did he know about either, or both, events?

Cleo didn't phone me that night. It would have been too much to expect Andrea Garnet to appear to order. She did ring the next morning but when I told her I had nothing to report she said she had errands to run and wouldn't be stopping by. I sensed that she was deliberately distancing herself from me and was relieved that she hadn't read too much into our finishing up in bed. I thought about inviting her along for the trip to Le Havre. It would have been a good way to keep her in my sights, but in the end I decided against it. It would be better to leave things the way they were.

I spent the day making a few calls, trying as casually as possible to garner information about Reg Turner's background. All I knew at the end of several hours working the phone was that Reg had never been married and no one was aware of his having any relatives that he kept in touch with. He still lived in the same rundown bedsit at the back end of beyond and hadn't won the lottery or received an unexpected windfall.

I leaned back in my chair and thought about that. What was it Sherlock Holmes used to say? Eliminate the impossible and everything else is fair game. Well, those weren't his exact words but the premise still rang true. If Reg hadn't gone to see Miller on his own business then he must have been there on someone else's. Possibly Garnet's, which would account for his evasiveness when I mentioned his name.

I took Gil for his afternoon run, tempted to wave to the guy who'd been following me since my meeting with Reg. I didn't bother and instead pretended not to see him. If Slater had anyone on me today he was better at keeping a low profile than her previous minion. I wasn't sure whether to be relieved or insulted by her sudden lack of interest in me.

They couldn't have anyone else in the frame yet or Jimmy would have let me know. Perhaps she thought I'd be so rattled by the grilling she'd given me that I'd do something stupid the moment I was out of her sight. A lot of criminals acted that way. Given her lack of imagination, it didn't surprise me she actually thought I would fall into that category. I definitely deserved to feel insulted.

I fed myself and settled down at my desk with a beer, intent upon surfing the Net to see what else I could learn about Peter Garnet. I hadn't got far when my phone rang and Cleo told me Andrea Garnet had just come into the casino. I glanced at my watch, surprised to see that it was already ten o'clock.

"She's on her own," Cleo told me. "I'll see which table she goes to and try to inveigle my way in as dealer."

"See you in a bit," I said, already shedding my rumpled clothes and heading for the shower. I could hardly play poker wearing a Harley T-shirt and with hands stained by engine oil.

Half an hour later I strolled into the casino. An unusually large crowd was loitering around the table Cleo was dealing at, watching the action. I didn't recognise my shadow or any potential ex-colleagues amongst them and wondered what the attraction was. I soon found out.

A woman whom I assumed was Andrea Garnet, co-cooned in a waft of expensive perfume, was flamboyant enough to make people stop and stare. Tousled brown hair, too much makeup and a blue dress that clung to a decent figure drew the eye. She drank constantly from what looked like a glass of scotch and chatted the whole time she played.

I joined the crowd of watchers and could see at once that what Cleo had said about Andrea was true. She was a reckless player but then she needed to be because she was hopeless at hiding what was in her hand.

All poker players had "tells." Giveaway signs that indicated how good a hand they had. Unlike on television, not many amateur players bothered to wear shades inside a windowless casino but a lot wore ball caps, thinking the brims would conceal their expressions. They didn't. The guy at the far end, for example, blinked repeatedly when he had a decent hand. His betting technique was good but that simple habit told me after just a few hands not to go up against him when he started exercising his lashes. The guy next to him tapped his foot all the time, until he got dealt something useful, when he tried so hard to behave casually that his entire body tensed up. Andrea Garnet kept up a constant flow of chatter, aware that every male eye at the table was drawn to her ample cleavage. But when her hand was respectable the chatter turned from a flow to a torrent.

I bought some chips and took one of the two remaining seats at the table, two down from her. I could feel her eyes assessing me as she reached out a hand to shake mine and introduced herself.

"Hi, I'm Andrea."

"Charlie. Pleased to meet you."

"Oh, no, the pleasure's mine."

I caught sight of Cleo in the periphery of my vision, struggling not to roll her eyes as she dealt the cards. Andrea was the small blind and threw the appropriate chips into the pot. The big blind did the same. Andrea won that hand, mainly because I deliberately folded a decent one, but lost the next two. She committed a cardinal sin by turning over her cards when she folded, before the hand was over. If any of the men at the table had done that they'd have been lynched, and rightly so. But Andrea was clearly a law unto herself. She clicked her fingers at a passing waitress, drained her glass and asked for another scotch. Her pile of chips was rapidly diminishing and I was waiting to see what she'd do when they ran out.

I could tell by her increased chatter that she'd been dealt a decent hand. Everyone else folded and it was my turn. Being on the button, I was in the best position but since just she and I were left in, that advantage didn't help me much. I had to play this hand, even though I had only a queen and ten, offsuit. I raised.

"Well, Charlie," she said. "It's just you and me then."

"Seems that way," I said. "Good luck."

"Oh, I never rely on luck, darling."

"Really." I quirked a brow. "You'll have to let me in on your secret sometime."

"Just as soon as I've relieved you of some of those lovely chips." She reached across the table and stroked my forearm.

I offered her the glimmer of a smile and covered her hand with mine. "You're certainly welcome to try."

Cleo cleared her throat, offered me a brief scowl and dealt the flop. A nine and two tens. I'd tripled my tens and now had a shot at a full house. A sharp intake of breath on Andrea's part told me that she'd hit the card she wanted. She'd probably got three of a kind. Since I had two tens in my hand and one was in the flop, the odds were against her having the remaining one. Perhaps she now had three nines. My assumption proved correct when she went all in and, with a flourish, turned her cards over. I matched her bet and turned mine over too.

"Oh, bad luck." She bit her lower lip, whether to appear vampish or to prevent herself from smiling I was unable to tell.

"May the best player win," I said calmly.

"Oh, she will, darling, she will."

The turn card was a four. No help to either of us. I needed a queen to get a full house, otherwise the hand was Andrea's. She eventually stopped talking as Cleo took her time dealing the river.

The queen of hearts.

Andrea's smile faltered fractionally and then, with a reckless little laugh, she pushed the pot in my direction.

"Are you as lucky in love?" she asked.

"Usually." I scooped up my winnings and winked at her, wondering what she'd do next.

She called to one of the pit bosses, asking for additional credit on her account. He disappeared and another, more senior, manager appeared and whispered something in her ear.

"What do you mean?" she demanded crossly.

It was obvious that her credit was no longer good. I

exchanged a brief glance with Cleo. This lent credence to Reg's suggestion that her husband was skint. But if he *did* have problems of that nature it was obviously news to Andrea and she looked furious. As she turned back to the table, I pushed half of my chips towards her.

"Please," I said. "I'm sure it's just a glitch. You can pay me back when it's sorted out."

She looked surprised by my largesse and I thought at first that she might refuse. But slowly her face lost its angry flush and returned to a more natural colour, her disinclination to borrow superseded by the pressing desire to gamble.

"Thank you. I don't know where they find the brainless idiots they employ here." She shot a hostile glance at the manager who'd refused her credit. "When my husband hears about this, there'll be hell to pay." Her features relaxed into a flirtatious smile as she turned back to me. "And you won't be out-of-pocket for long, Charlie. I intend to win and pay you back immediately."

In spite of her optimism, I knew I could kiss those chips goodbye. I'd already written them off in my head. I thought of Cleo's squalid living conditions and reminded myself that I was making the sacrifice in a good cause.

"Obviously." I deliberately let my eyes linger on her cleavage. Cleo, for whose sake I was manfully pretending to be impressed by Andrea's rather too obvious charms, glowered as she dealt the next hand. Women! "Why else would we be here?"

"Exactly."

I wasn't surprised when half an hour later Andrea had lost the lot. I cashed in, threw a generous tip Cleo's way, for which I received a curt thank-you, and joined Andrea at the bar.

"I'm so sorry about that." She clicked her fingers at the barman. "You must let me know where I can find you so that I can send you a cheque."

"Not necessary." I slid onto the stool next to hers. "Like I said, I'm sure it's just a misunderstanding. You can repay me the next time you come in."

We ordered our drinks but she made no attempt to move away from me when they were served.

"You're a regular here then?"

"Yes," I said. "I like to play."

"Well, I haven't seen you before. I would have noticed you," she said, fluttering her lashes. "I dislike the idea of being in debt to a stranger."

I scribbled my number on the back of a drip mat and handed it to her. "There, does that make you feel better?"

"No, darling, not nearly but I suppose it'll have to do." She took a sip of her drink and observed me over the rim of the glass. "For now."

"Can't help wondering why that husband of yours lets you come here on your own." I nodded towards a wedding ring that was almost buried by an enormous diamond solitaire. "He's obviously not the jealous type."

"Oh, he only ever thinks about work, the poor darling."

"Really? What does he do?"

"He runs nightclubs, amongst other things." She flapped the hand not holding her drink, as though talking about anything other than herself bored her rigid. It probably did. "I come here to get away from all that."

"From that or from him?"

She shot me a look and I wondered if I'd overplayed

my hand. She could do one of three things. Get up and walk away, throw her drink in my face or answer my question. I waited out the ensuing silence, curious to see which way she'd jump.

"A bit of both, I suppose," she said, not meeting my gaze. Her mood had turned introspective and for the first time I sensed that I was catching glimpses of the real woman beneath all that flamboyance. "Peter collects possessions and I suppose that includes me."

"But you're here alone so he can't be that possessive."

"Am I?" She nodded towards a guy I'd seen loitering all evening, apparently watching our table but never playing. I'd thought he might be yet another person tailing me but now knew that it was Andrea he had in his sights. He looked vaguely familiar. I was pretty sure I'd had dealings with him in my previous life but couldn't put a name to the face. "One of my husband's flunkies," she explained. "Peter never likes me to go out at night alone."

"And during the day?" I dropped my voice to a suggestive whisper.

"Well now," she said, draining her glass and signalling for a refill. "That's another matter." She slipped the mat with my phone number on it into her bag and smiled at me. "Besides, I always pay my debts. Let me know when you'll be back in again and I'll see you straight."

"No hurry. Besides, I live on my boat in the marina here. I'm off to France for a few days so it'll have to be when I get back."

"That must be an interesting lifestyle."

"It has its moments." I leaned an elbow on the bar and rested my chin in my cupped hand, looking directly at her. "I've been trying to think where I know you from. Did I see you the other day, coming out of a solicitor's office in town?"

She wrinkled her brow. "When?"

"I can't remember the date but I do remember coming out of my brief's place in Montpelier Road last week and passing someone who looked a lot like you." I treated her to one of my rare smiles. "I never forget a beautiful face."

"Oh, you charmer you!" Her new drink arrived and she took a healthy swig, enjoying the flattery. "Yes, it might have been me. I was there last week."

"You know Miller's dead, don't you?"

"Yes, isn't it shocking? The police came to see me. Some officious woman inspector who seemed to want to pin the crime on me." She shuddered. "Can you imagine a little thing like me stabbing a great hulk like Miller? Anyway, why would I?"

"If it's any consolation the same woman came to see me and actually took me down the nick for questioning."

She looked surprised. "You? Why would you kill Miller?"

"That's what the inspector was hoping I'd tell her." I shrugged. "Like it's any of her business why I was seeking legal advice."

"I told her exactly the same thing when she asked me what I'd been to see Miller about. Anyway, even if I'd wanted to tell her, I could hardly say I'd gone to consult him about divorcing Peter."

My eyebrows shot skywards. "Things that bad, are they?"

"A woman likes to be loved, not possessed."

Her glance strayed towards the man watching her and it struck me that I wasn't targeting Andrea Garnet. It was the other way round. Absorbing the blow, I wondered what game she was playing, and on whose orders. Miller wasn't a divorce specialist but he *was* her husband's brief. If Andrea really did want a divorce then Miller was the last solicitor on earth she'd consult. Besides, Garnet would have known that the police visited his wife at home. Even if he hadn't been there at the time, something like that would soon get back to him. If Andrea didn't tell him the truth, one of his contacts sure as hell would. I was definitely being played but went along with the charade, hoping to discover why.

Andrea turned towards the man who was guarding her and beckoned him over. "This is Tommy," she said. "You can talk freely in front of him."

The man shot a questioning glance at Andrea but didn't speak.

"Your husband doesn't sound like the type to let you go."

She pulled a face. "Even if he was I'd never get a fair settlement. You've seen for yourself how mean he can be. Besides, half his assets are hidden and even I don't know where they are."

The man she called Tommy was regarding me with suspicion. He and Andrea seemed very friendly, which got me wondering. He probably thought Andrea was being too open with a stranger and I was with him on that one. I definitely knew him but his last name just wouldn't come. It irked me but was hardly something I could ask. One thing was for certain, though. If I recognised Tommy whatever, he as sure as hell knew who I was. This was definitely a setup.

"It's a shame Miller finished up with a knife in his guts instead of Peter," she said, draining her glass and standing up. "That would have solved all my problems."

"Nice meeting you," I said, shaking her hand and then kissing her on each cheek.

"You too, Charlie. And I really will repay that money soon. I promise you."

As I watched them leave the room, I wondered how she knew Miller had been stabbed in the stomach. That detail hadn't been made public and I only knew myself because Jimmy was keeping me informed.

# Chapter Eight

"Why would she tell you all that then?"

Cleo had called at the boat the following morning, wanting a full account of my conversation with Andrea. I'd given her the abridged version.

"Tell me what?"

"Don't play dumb, Charlie, it doesn't suit you. Why did a complete stranger tell you she wanted to divorce her husband? It's hardly the sort of thing that would crop up in conversation."

"You'd be surprised what people told me when I was in the job."

"Only because you got the thumbscrews out."

"Good point."

"So," she said, her sweet tone belying her determined stance. "Are you going to tell me why you think she opened up to you like that?"

I shrugged. "Perhaps she just liked my face."

"I noticed."

"Ah now, don't go getting upset. I only flirted with her because you said I had to."

"And you didn't enjoy it one bit."

"How well you know me."

"Be serious, Charlie."

"I am."

She pulled a face. "I don't like this. It's a little bit too convenient that Andrea came into the casino the day after I went back on duty."

"Well, you said yourself that she was a regular."

"Not that regular. And anyway, that still doesn't explain why she bared her soul to you?"

"You told me to use my charm."

"You're not that charming."

"You know how to wound," I said with a dramatic sigh, waving the kettle in her direction.

"Don't change the subject."

"I'll take that as a *yes* then."

Cleo was worse than Gil with his Frisbee when she got her teeth into something. She absolutely refused to let go. I was ahead of her though. The same questions she was plaguing me with had already occurred to me. The only conclusion I'd been able to reach was that the guy in denim who'd been following me was employed by Garnet. That being the case they'd know about the questions I'd been asking and my association with Cleo. So we had to be getting close.

But close to what?

"I phoned Jimmy when I got back last night and asked him to have a look on the quiet at the papers for the Spelling case," I told her.

"Oh, why?"

That worked like a charm. I had her full attention now and she'd forgotten all about Andrea Garnet.

"Just to see if there's something obvious we're overlooking. I'd like to know if there were any other names in the frame, besides your dad's."

"So would I. When will he get back to you?"

"When he can." I handed her a mug of coffee. "Don't worry, he won't hang about."

"But how will that help us?" She had a penchant for good questions today.

"Dunno, but the more I think about this, the more it comes back to betting. Sport was the key to everything back then and it looks like it still is today."

"What, Miller's murder, you mean?"

"Yes. And my gut tells me that Garnet's up to his neck in the whole mess."

Cleo seemed subdued and didn't speak for several minutes. "This is getting dangerous."

"There's an element of risk in what we're doing but I don't envisage finishing up like Miller."

I regretted the words as soon as they'd left my mouth. She was starting to realise what she'd got herself—got us—into, and if I voiced similar doubts she'd probably give up her sleuthing. But it didn't occur to me. I guess I needed answers. And there was still the trifling matter of Slater trying to pin Miller's murder on me.

"Want to give it up?" I asked belatedly.

"God no, I'm still game but I didn't mean to get you into this."

I squeezed her hand. "I know that."

My phone rang. I glanced at the screen and saw the call was coming from France. It was my mate, the one I was due to see at the weekend, cancelling because his wife had been taken ill.

"Problem?" Cleo asked as I hung up.

"My trip to France has been called off."

"I'm sorry. You were looking forward to it."

"Well, it can't be helped. There'll be another time."

SHE'D BEEN GONE less than half an hour when Jimmy did call, giving me the names of two suspects in the Kendall case.

"They were both grilled at the time," he said. "But you probably wouldn't have been aware, not being on the case. They were both known associates of Spelling's but they had airtight alibis."

"Do these faces have names, Jimmy?"

"Yeah, and you'll recognise at least one of them. Frank Glover."

"Now him I have no trouble seeing as a murderer," I said, calling up a mental picture of the muscle-bound, heavily tattooed thug in question. "We obviously couldn't get anything to stick."

"No, and the other one's called Mallet. Tommy Mallet."

"Tommy?" Of course, Andrea's friend.

"Yeah, does it mean something?"

"No, not much." Jimmy didn't need to know how my mind was working any more than Cleo did. "Who do they work for now?" I asked, already knowing the answer.

"Peter Garnet."

"Did Garnet alibi them both?"

"Yes. So did Garnet's wife."

What a surprise. "Why were they suspects?"

"They'd both been seen with Spelling on the night he died but they weren't on the CCTV tape."

We talked round in circles for a while. Speculating. It was a bit like the old days. I had a feeling Jimmy was enjoying it too. Unless Slater had changed her ways since I got out, she didn't have much time for the opinions of her junior officers.

"Have you looked at Garnet and Mallet for Miller's killing?" I asked.

"No, any reason why we should?"

"Nothing specific but it might be worth trying to find out where they were on the day in question."

"If she'll let me," Jimmy said morosely. "I'll have to run it past her first and she'll want to know why I suspect them. Garnet's well connected nowadays and I won't get away with asking questions of his employees without a good reason."

"Okay, leave it with me. If I can come up with a reason for you to look at them I'll get back to you."

I was still trying to figure out why I suspected Garnet's lackeys of bumping off his brief when my phone rang again. They say when one door closes another opens, and this was a prime example. A call from my stepbrother's employer brought with it an invitation.

Hal Faraday owned a powerboat team and was married to Gloria, a violinist who'd been a particular friend of my mother's. She'd left the orchestra a few years before Mum's death to marry him. A multimillionaire, Hal had ignored the hordes of women trailing in his wake and pursued Gloria relentlessly until she succumbed to his coercive charm. Hal came up from nothing and was now CEO of Spectre Sports and Leisure plc, a company he'd started from scratch back in the eighties by investing in one small leisure complex.

Perhaps because of his humble origins, he was no pushover and was wise to just about every dodge in the book. That was why I was astonished that Paul, my stepbrother, had remained in his employ for over a year. Paul might be loosely connected to Gloria through his mother and my father, but Hal wouldn't cut him any slack because of that. If he'd tried his usual crap with Hal, he wouldn't have lasted five minutes in his organisation. If he was still clinging on, he must really want that job for some reason. Paul instinctively knew how far he could push people and when to back off.

"Hal, how the hell are you? I was just thinking about you."

"Good thoughts, I hope."

"Are there any other kind?"

"You have no idea."

I could hear the smile in his voice and didn't need him to tell me that he was in good health. He had to be over sixty now but was blessed with an inexhaustible supply of energy that left me standing when he got a bee in his bonnet about something he decided needed doing immediately.

"To what do I owe the pleasure?" I asked him.

"I'm under orders to invite you down for a few days. Gloria has a party planned for Wednesday night and you're on the guest list."

I thought about it, but only for a moment. Hal and Gloria had a massive house on the Beaulieu River complete with its own mooring. I could take the *No Comment* and make up for the aborted trip to France by spending a few days with my old friends. And perhaps I'd bump into Paul there. Kill two birds with one stone. If I was in the same room with him I wouldn't be able to find a reason to put off tackling him.

"Okay, you're on. What's the occasion? For the bash, I mean."

Hal groaned. "When you get to my age the last thing you want is to celebrate the passing of yet another year. Unfortunately Gloria doesn't see it that way."

I chuckled, suspecting that his protestations were entirely feigned. There was nothing Hal enjoyed more than a good party and he certainly knew how to throw one in style. "So you're in need of a little masculine support?"

"Something like that." Hal's throaty laugh echoed down the line. "Bring the boat and a date. I'm sure you can persuade some unsuspecting lady to keep you company."

"I'll see what I can do."

He paused. "Oh and, Charlie, Paul will be here. Hope that won't cause any problems."

Quite the reverse. "Not at all."

"Great, we'll expect you late tomorrow afternoon. That way we can catch up before the hordes descend upon us on Wednesday. High tide's at 6:00 p.m."

I told him I'd be there and cut the connection. Then, without stopping to think about the consequences, I rang Cleo and invited her to join me. She sounded intrigued and a little reluctant.

"Big houses on the Beaulieu River." She paused. "It sounds great but I'm not sure I can get off work at such short notice."

I knew it wasn't work commitments but rather her insecurities that made her hesitate. I wasn't having that. A lot of the people at the party would be wealthy. Many would not. Few, I suspected, would be as honest as Cleo, especially given the role model she'd had as a kid. Besides, I wanted her where I could keep an eye on her and Garnet's people couldn't. Eventually I talked her round.

"Bring your party shoes," I told her.

IT WAS ABOUT fifty nautical miles from Brighton to Beaulieu, so although my tub only cruised at about eight knots, it was a comfortable distance to cover in a day. Cleo and I remained protected from the elements as I steered from the enclosed wheelhouse. Because of that, the weather being a bit iffy, with quite a swell running, didn't particularly bother me. It would be necessary to time my arrival at the mouth of the river to coincide with high tide. It was either that or hang about until there was enough water beneath the hull to navigate to Hal's house without running aground.

Normally I'd have slowed down and trawled a fishing line through the area where the bass like to lurk, but it was too rough for that. Besides, Cleo looked distinctly green, and slowing down even more would make the motion of the boat worse.

"Don't look down," I told her. "Stare at the horizon and you'll feel better."

"How can people say that boating's glamorous?" She pouted. "I'll never forgive you for putting me through this, Charlie Hunter. I told you I wasn't a good sailor but you forced me to come."

"I'll make it up to you. Promise."

"Short of calming this bloody water down there's absolutely nothing you can do." She managed a humourless grin. "Unless you know of a speedy and painless way for me to end it all."

"Drink some more water." I handed her a plastic bottle. "It helps."

She clamped a hand over her mouth. "If I put anything inside me it'll come straight up again."

I was about to tell her the reverse was true when I felt a vibration rattle through the entire boat.

"What the fuck?" I checked the echo sounder, wondering if we'd hit an uncharted sandbank, but there was still plenty of water beneath the hull.

"What's happening?" Cleo asked.

"Not sure." I was even more concerned when a second shudder swayed the boat violently sideways. I slowed the engine to just above idle. In such a big sea stopping altogether would be worse than keeping a little power on.

"Stay put, we're quite safe." I tried to sound calm and convincing. "I just need to take a look in the engine room."

"What do you need me to do?" she asked, whey-faced but gamely offering to pull her weight.

"Just keep a lookout and shout if you see any other vessels anywhere near us." I didn't add that we might need their help. "There's nothing showing on the radar so I doubt you'll see anything."

"Nothing else stupid enough to be out in this sea," she grumbled.

"I won't be a moment."

The conditions made it difficult to stand upright, and I was only able to open the hatch to the engine room after several attempts. I donned earphones, descended the ladder into my spotless shrine and groaned. Several inches of seawater had flooded the bilge and was rising fast towards the metal floor, and I didn't have a clue where it was coming from. There was a Force Six wind whipping up the sea, and we were still miles from the Beaulieu River with no other ships currently anywhere near us.

I waded farther into the enclosed space, crouched double since there was insufficient headroom for me to stand upright, trying to think where the water could be coming from. It didn't take me long to figure it out.

The stern glands kept all but a controlled drop of sea-water out of the boat. If loosened, there would be some vibration but it wouldn't be immediately noticeable at the helm if there was a big sea running, as there was right now. Had that not been the case, and had I not been concerned about Cleo's seasickness, I'd probably have noticed the problem before it got this bad. Water had gradually flooded into the engine room, almost over-whelming the bilge pumps. That would have set off an alarm but fortunately the vibration had alerted me to the problem before it got to that stage. Even so, I couldn't figure out how it had happened. I'm obsessively care-ful about things like this and check them regularly. I'd done so just before leaving for this trip.

Or had I?

I'd certainly intended to but I'd been preoccupied with Cleo, who'd again been grilling me about Andrea Garnet. I'd taken several calls simultaneously whilst doing the engine room checks and I suppose it could have been overlooked. I examined the bolt, which had worked loose enough on the port side to let all this water in. Cursing the oversight, I attempted to screw it back in but it fell apart in my hand.

I was left holding one half of a bolt that had sheared completely through. This was deliberate sabotage. Who? Why? Feeling ready to commit murder, I grabbed some rags and tried to tie them in thick, tight bundles round the two parts of the shaft. It was an almost impossible feat. Crouched double, I was constantly knocked sides, cursing as I battled the elements and the confined space. Progress was abruptly halted when a particularly large wave crashed against the starboard beam, pitching me off my feet. I fell awkwardly, bashing my head against the protruding dial on a pump. The insecure rags fell away from the shaft, treating me to a shower of dirty water straight in the face.

"Fuck it!"

I saw stars as I knelt in the grimy water, blinking my way back into focus, and felt blood trickling down the side of my face. I ignored it and renewed my efforts, striving to remain calm and focused.

At the third attempt I managed a rough repair. It was slipshod but would only need to hold for the next hour.

Exhausted from fighting the conditions, the water in the engine room and the engine itself, I all but staggered back to the wheelhouse.

"What's happened?" Cleo asked, looking paler than ever.

"A loose pipe, that's all."

No point in us both worrying. I pushed the throttle forward and increased our speed. At least the wind appeared to have shifted direction and was now behind us, pushing us along and giving us a slightly smoother ride.

"You're bleeding," she said.

"It's nothing. I just knocked my head on a pipe."

"I'll clean it for you."

"It can wait."

"No, it can't."

In spite of her seasickness she insisted on getting the first aid kit out and patching me up. I let her do it, figuring it would take her mind off her queasiness. And stop her asking questions about what was wrong with the boat.

"There you go," she said, slapping a plaster over the cut. "You'll live."

"You have a wonderful bedside manner, Ms. Kendall."

"Which is more than you deserve, given what you've put me through."

I actually chuckled at that one, earning myself a light punch on the arm. Then I unfastened my sodden jeans and stepped out of them.

"Get me a clean pair from the cabin, would you?" I asked, throwing the dirty ones at her.

Whilst she was gone I returned my attention to our situation, wondering how best to deal with it. We were too early to get down the river safely but I couldn't afford to wait. I had no idea how long my repair would hold. The alternative was to put out a distress call, but by the time help arrived, we could be at Hal's. What to do?

We'd reached the mouth of the river so it was decision time. If I stuck to the centre of the channel, I had a chance of making it. If something was coming the other way it would be another story, but there was no point in thinking about that unless it happened. I radioed the marina and told them I had problems.

"*No Comment,* we'll warn any other vessels using the river," the marina office said, "but a lot of people don't bother to switch their radio on. Nor are they required to."

As if I didn't already know that. Still, if I got into an argument with another boat at least I'd covered my back.

I slowed right down again, my eyes swivelling between the river and the echo sounder, hoping to hell that we'd touch sand and not rocks if we did hit the bottom. Cleo looked much better now that we weren't being thrown about but had the sense to keep quiet and let me concentrate on keeping us afloat.

Sod's law, we'd almost made it when a sailboat came the other way, its helmsman gesticulating wildly and letting forth with a string of foul language when I didn't give way, as I should have done. I tried him on the radio but he didn't respond. Sailors resented motorboaters at the best of times, and when we behaved in the manner I was, it did little to restore relations. Well, they weren't exactly perfect themselves if they didn't turn their bloody radios on. Fortunately the yacht was able to lurk in a deep mooring until I'd passed him. I had no doubt my behaviour would be reported to the harbourmaster and was glad I'd forewarned the marina of my problems.

We reached Hal's house and he was standing on his dock, long salt-and-pepper hair blowing around his face like an untidy halo as he raised an arm in greeting. I acknowledged him as I fired up the wing engine, engaged the bow and stern thrusters and eased the *No Comment* sideways until I made soft contact with the floating pontoon. Satisfied the boat wouldn't drift far from the dock, I disengaged the thrusters to prevent running the batteries down, left the wing station and threw the ropes to Hal.

Now that we were safe, the gravity of my situation struck home. If I'd gone to France as planned, this incident wouldn't have happened close to the mouth of a friendly river but in the middle of one of the busiest shipping lanes in the world. Somebody wanted me dead, or at the very least badly frightened. And given my recent activities, it didn't take a rocket scientist to figure out who that someone had to be.

Hal caught the lines, looped them round the bollards on the pontoon and threw them back to me so I could make them fast on the deck cleats. Once the boat was secure, I cut the engines, closed down all my navigational equipment and uncoiled the shore power cable. I'd turned off the radar before negotiating the river. I could navigate by sight and couldn't understand why people kept the old microwaves churning away unnecessarily.

Once Hal had attached the power cable to the box on the dock, I plugged in my end and checked the gauge on the switch panel to make sure the supply was coming through. I nipped down to the engine room, relieved to see that my unsophisticated repair had held and that the water level hadn't risen. Now that there was no water flowing over the propeller, the bilge pumps would be able to do their job. Even so, I needed to get someone to repair that stern gland pronto.

"Ready?" I asked Cleo, emerging from the engine room.

"As I ever will be."

"You look a little better." I pinched her cheek.

"You have some colour back now. Sorry you had to go through that."

"Not as sorry as you will be when I get you alone," she growled.

"Don't make promises you have no intention of keeping, wench!"

"Oh, I shall keep it. And, just so we're clear, it's not a promise. It's a threat."

I winked at her. "That's good to know."

She glanced ashore and gasped. Well, Hal's house was the size of a country hotel and tended to have that effect on people. I squeezed her hand, helped her step ashore and then did so myself, Gil bounding ahead of me as I took Hal's outstretched hand. He clasped my shoulder in the way that men do when they're pleased to see someone but don't want to appear effeminate.

"This is Cleo," I said to Hal. "Cleo, meet our host, Hal Faraday."

Hal offered Cleo an appreciative smile and took her hand in both of his. "Welcome, my dear."

"Thanks," she said, looking slightly less apprehensive.

Gil, not wishing to be excluded, leapt up at Hal, who admired the scruffy hound and tickled his ears. Having satisfied himself that he was welcome, he tore up the steps to the garden, lifted his leg against a plant pot and peed for an eternity.

"Oh, by the way, I hope you don't mind this mutt coming along." I nodded towards Gil.

"Not at all. We like dogs. What's his name?"

"Guilty but it causes less confusion when I shorten it to Gil."

Hal chuckled. "So I would imagine." He glanced with amusement in Gil's direction, apparently unconcerned by the use of his garden as a toilet. "Good trip, Charlie?"

"A bit lumpy in places but this boat is made for those sorts of seas."

Cleo made a disgruntled sound at the back of her throat but remained silent.

"Probably takes them better than my tub."

My lips twitched. His *tub* was a hundred-and-twenty-foot superyacht. "Actually, I did have a spot of bother with a stern gland coming loose. Does Mike still run that marine engineering shop in Bucklers Hard?"

"Yes, you can ring him from the house. I'm sure he'll be able to pop over." Hal grabbed one of the overnight bags I'd hauled onto the dock and smiled at Cleo. "Come on, Gloria's anxious to see you both."

We walked across the pristine lawn together, Gil bounding ahead of us, anxious to explore this new environment. Gloria was standing on the terrace, waving and smiling as we approached her. Dressed casually in wide leg trousers and a soft sweater that was probably cashmere, she was the epitome of country chic. No one would think she was in her fifties. I could still see why Hal had pursued her so relentlessly once he got over the death of his first wife. There was just something about her, some innate elegance and air of self-containment, that set her apart.

"Charlie!" She had no compunction about hugging me and proceeded to do precisely that. "It's been too long. How are you?"

"I'm fine, thanks. And I don't need to ask how you are. You look as lovely as ever."

"Oh, you old charmer you." She turned towards Cleo with a smile. "But who's this?"

I introduced Cleo. Gloria's welcome was as warm as her husband's and I felt Cleo's hand relax in mine. Gloria linked her arm through Cleo's and led us into the house. "How's Harry?" she asked over her shoulder. "You should have brought him along."

"I've just had him for a week but he's back with Emily now."

"That's a shame."

I followed them into the spacious living room that afforded an uninterrupted view over the river. Hal handed out drinks. He didn't bother to ask us what we wanted, assuming that vintage champagne covered all the bases. It was wasted on me so I quickly drained my glass and asked which room they'd put us in.

"I'm not fit for company right now." I nodded towards my hands, which still bore traces of oil. "A disagreement with my engine on the trip down," I explained. "Let me have a quick shower, if that's okay, and then we can talk. But first I'd better walk that mutt before he completely destroys your garden." We all looked towards Gil, who was barking frantically at the base of a tree, presumably thinking that would entice the squirrels down from their lofty vantage point.

"Okay," Gloria said. "You do that whilst Cleo and I get better acquainted. But don't be long. I want to know everything that's happened to you since we last met."

"She means it." Hal rolled his eyes. "Don't say that you haven't been warned."

I left them to enjoy their drinks and rounded Gil up. We walked to Buckler's Hard and I called at Mike's marine engineering business. He understood my problem and promised to have it fixed first thing in the morning.

When I rejoined Hal and Gloria I felt cleaner and more respectable. Cleo was on her second glass of champagne and appeared more relaxed. I sat down beside her and took her hand.

"Ready for a proper drink now, Charlie?" Hal asked.

"Yeah, whisky would be good."

"Coming up."

We chatted about inconsequential matters for a while but I could see that my scintillating small talk wasn't exactly holding their attention.

"How's it going with the team?" I asked. His powerboat racing team was Hal's abiding passion. He'd pulled back a bit on his commitments in order to follow the team around Europe. Canny businessman that he is, he set the team up with his own funds but then had his company act as its sponsor, taking advantage of the tax breaks that afforded him and providing himself with a glamorous stage upon which to entertain his corporate clients. "When does the season start?"

"Next month. The first Grand Prix is in Malta." Hal exchanged a look with Gloria. "If we make it, that is."

"Any reason why you shouldn't? I thought you did okay last season, for a new team with money to burn, that is."

Hal managed a weak smile that didn't come close to troubling his eyes. "It was a steep learning curve. We ought to do better this season."

"Do I sense a *but* in there somewhere?"

"Well, we've had a few problems with our preparations."

"In what respect?"

"Oh, just trivial things at first," Hal said, "and we hardly gave them a thought. Dirty fuel made the engines misbehave, but we put that down to bad luck." He shrugged. "It happens. Then spares didn't arrive when they should have because someone forgot to pay for them, that sort of stuff. Lots of little niggles. I figured at first that the team was being lazy so I gave them a rollicking, warned them to get their act together and thought no more about it."

"Until the drivers missed their annual medicals and the team almost got disqualified as a consequence," Gloria said.

"How the hell did that happen?"

"They weren't informed of the date, apparently."

"Who, your crew or the team manager?"

"Oh, Josh Harling knew. He's team manager and swears he sent emails to Simon, Dave and Paul confirming the date. And I know he did because he showed me them in his sent file. Trouble is, Simon and Dave didn't confirm they'd received them and Josh forgot to chase them up. Paul was the only one who turned up at the appointed time."

"Paul?" I already had a nasty feeling about this. "He drives for you?" I elevated a brow, trying to keep my tone casual. "I didn't know that."

"He's our reserve. Every team has to have at least three licenced pilots to comply with the rules."

"So how come Paul received his email and the other two didn't?"

"I've no idea frankly but they say they didn't and I believe them. They know how important the medicals are and wouldn't risk disqualification by missing them." Hal frowned. "But I don't understand how they went astray. One disappearing into cyberspace I can accept, but two…"

I didn't say anything for a moment but was put in mind of Kara Webb's sister, whose husband had turned his nefarious talents to cybercrime. After that particular skirmish I knew only too well that anyone who knows what they're doing can infiltrate someone else's computer system with ease. I immediately suspected Paul. Deflecting emails from a given server ought to be child's play but that might not have been necessary. Not if he knew the other two pilots' passwords. People were incredibly lax about that sort of thing, often keying them in when others were watching. Paul would have been able to access their email, delete the incoming messages before they had a chance to read them, and no one would be any the wiser. And it was just the sort of thing he wouldn't have any scruples about doing.

Paul had always been a snoop. Just after Mum died, I'd found him in my room on a couple of occasions. He said he was looking for something to read but I knew that was bullshit. What he was actually doing was going through my stuff, looking for chinks in my armour so he could use them against me to ingratiate himself with Dad. Knowledge had always represented power to Paul and I doubted whether that situation had changed.

"Does seem like a little more than coincidence," was all I trusted myself to say.

"Yes, I agree." Hal's expression was sombre. "And

things have gone from bad to worse. We had a practise session arranged off Cowes with another team last weekend but Simon and Dave both went down with stomach bugs at the eleventh hour and we had to back out. Paul wasn't affected but they recently changed the rules and it's not possible to race with only one pilot on board."

"Did Paul know about the rule change?"

"He didn't even suggest racing alone, so I guess he must have. Anyway, it didn't go down well with the other team when they'd made a special effort to be there. Besides, it made us look unprofessional." Hal grimaced. "We've rearranged it for Torquay in a couple of weeks' time. I just hope to hell that we make it this time. We won't get another chance and we need the practise."

"Who do you think would want to do this to you and why?" I asked. Anything involving Paul interested me. "One of your competitors, perhaps, jealous of your fast rise up the ranks?"

"No, Charlie, I don't think so." Hal stood with his back to us, staring at the river but probably not seeing it. "The sport is fiercely competitive and growing in stature all the time, but we respect one another's outfits and would never deliberately seek to sabotage them."

"A dissatisfied team member then?"

"No, nothing as simple as that." Hal shook his head emphatically. "I haven't been able to come up with anyone who'd have a reason to go to such extremes."

"Has anyone joining the team coincided with the onset of these problems?"

"No, we haven't taken on anyone new for a couple of years."

"Okay." So much for my fledgling theory about a mole in the camp. "Has anyone left under a cloud then?"

"No again." Hal dredged up a half smile. "I've gone through all the most likely scenarios myself and drawn a complete blank." His eyes were flat and hard. "I have no idea who would want to do this to me, or why, but when I find out…"

His words trailed off but then he didn't really need to say any more. I was in no doubt that when the identity of the guilty party became known, retribution would be swift and brutal.

"How long has Paul Flint worked for you?" I asked.

"More than three years now."

"I didn't realise it had been that long. How do you keep him in line?"

Hal turned to look at me again and this time his fierce expression was replaced with a sympathetic smile. "I know you don't have a high opinion of your stepbrother, Charlie, but he's passionate about the sport and is a very good Logistics Manager."

"Logistics Manager? I thought you said he was your reserve pilot."

"He is but that doesn't mean he can't do something else as well." Hal shrugged. "He has to if he wants to stay with me. I can't afford to carry passengers. He's responsible for moving the whole circus from one venue to the next."

"And moving with it, presumably." Which would explain why he hadn't been at home when I'd tried to reach him there.

"Yes, he likes the locations and the glamour as-sociated with the sport, there's no denying that, but all he really wants is to drive the boat. He's totally single-minded about that, and it's what keeps him on the straight and narrow. He knows that if he pisses me off then he'll be out in the cold. Pilot's jobs are competitively sought after and I doubt if any other team would take him on."

"I think you said earlier that they have to be licenced?"

"Oh yes, the governing body have a strict policy about that. Each pilot has to have competed in a specific number of races before he can apply for a licence to compete in the Grand Prix."

"And Paul has?"

"Yes, some years ago he put money of his own into a fledgling team on the proviso that he could drive for it."

I nodded thoughtfully. A lot of things were starting to make sense to me now. Not only the question of where Marianne's money had gone but very possibly where the bulk of my father's dosh had finished up too.

"It proved to be a disaster. Paul totalled the boat, his team ran out of money and that was when he came to me."

"Has he learned from the experience? Will he ever make it?"

Hal shook his head. "He's too impulsive and tries too hard, which almost always ends in tears. It's an intangible skill having the ability to drive a boat at over 120 miles an hour. You either have an intuitive sixth sense to excel at it or you don't. Having nerves of steel isn't enough. I've been straight with him and told him that he doesn't have what it takes but he's determined to prove me wrong." Hal shrugged. "And if things carry on the way they're going, I might lose my driver and throttle-man to another team anyway and he'll get his chance. Experienced pilots with decent track records are few and far between and therefore highly sought-after. They won't stay with me if I can't enhance their reputations."

"Then surely that's your explanation. Paul's trying to get the team a bad reputation so that he'll get to be the new glamour boy."

"You're letting your dislike of your stepbrother cloud your judgment, Charlie," Hal said. "To be fair, the thought did cross my mind too, but it can't have been him. Even if he did somehow manage to divert those emails there's no way he could have done the fuel thing. He was fifty miles away at the time. And he has nothing to do with ordering spares so that can't have been him either."

I wasn't convinced but let it pass. "How did he come to work for you in the first place?"

"He totalled that boat at about the time when I was setting up my team. Your father rang me and asked me to give him a trial as a driver."

*Of course he did.* "I see. And did you? Give him a trial, I mean."

"Sure, but like I said, it was obvious that he'd never make it. I offered him the reserve seat and the opportunity to be our logistics man instead, and he's proving to be quite good at the latter."

"Have you thought about tightening security?" I asked, attempting to push the thorny question of Paul aside until I'd had time to think it through.

"How?" Hal scratched his head. "The things that

have happened have all been in different areas of the operation and could almost be construed as coincidence."

"But you don't think they are?"

"No, I have a bad feeling about this."

"Hal is really worried that someone's going to wreck the show," Gloria said, covering one of my hands with hers. "Everyone seems to know that things aren't going right for us, even though we've tried to keep it from them, and there's lots of tension and dissatisfied rumblings in the ranks. It doesn't exactly make for team unity. We need them to be focused and pulling in the same direction, not looking at one another with suspicion and sniping behind each other's backs, which is what's starting to happen."

"I'm not surprised. Bad news always has a way of leaking out."

"We really had a chance to make it this year," Hal said. "We could certainly have won several races. But now I'm not so sure."

"What are we thinking of," Gloria said, smiling at Cleo, who'd been following the conversation with interest but hadn't contributed to it. "Poor Cleo must be bored rigid."

"Not at all."

"Well, no more shop and that's an order," Gloria said, wagging a finger at Hal and me.

"It doesn't matter on my account," Cleo said. "I can see that Hal values Charlie's opinion."

"Perhaps, but he's not being fair, putting him on the spot like this. Charlie's supposed to have retired from sleuthing."

Cleo flashed me a guilty smile. "He likes to keep his hand in."

Gloria chuckled. "Come along, Cleo. You and I are going to make ourselves beautiful and then we'll have dinner."

Nothing more was said about the team's problems that night. But when Hal casually mentioned over dinner that they'd all be at the party tomorrow, I knew he wanted me to question them and see if I could come up with an explanation for his troubles. And because there was a chance that Paul was involved, I knew I'd do precisely that.

# Chapter Nine

"DO YOUR SLEUTHING powers get called into play wherever you go?" Cleo asked as we slipped into bed that night.

"Yeah, it happens all the time."

She laughed. "How do the police cope without your help?"

"I've often wondered that myself." I tried for a modest expression. "It's a bit like going to a party and admitting you're a doctor, I suppose. Everyone just kind of assumes you won't mind them running their symptoms past you."

"Which is what Hal did tonight?"

"Yeah, but in his case I don't mind at all."

I pulled her into my arms and kissed her, attempting to distract her. I didn't want to get into that right now. Besides, it would be a pity to waste the opulent comfort of the bed in Hal's principal guestroom with unnecessary talk.

"But do you really think your stepbrother would resort to sabotage?" Cleo asked, returning to the subject of Hal's team as soon as I gave her the opportunity to speak again.

"Nothing would surprise me about Paul. But—"

"But what?" She leaned up on one elbow and looked at me intently, as though my answer really mattered to her.

"It pains me to say so but I think on this occasion he might be a convenient scapegoat."

That surprised me. I hadn't realised my thoughts were veering in that direction. I don't have a particularly high opinion of mankind in general. Hardly surprising after twenty years of the shit I've had to deal with. Being cynically minded, I think the worst of everyone, especially Paul. But I also try to be fair. Paul is many things but he's not stupid. If he wanted to bite the hand that feeds him he'd have found a way to do it without the finger of suspicion pointing his way.

"He's being set up?"

"Possibly, but hell if I know who by."

"And I suppose you're going to try and find out."

"I'll see what I make of things at the party. Talk to a few people, for Hal's sake. But that's it." It would suit me to clear Paul and have him indebted to me for a change. "But it won't distract me from your father's case. Honest, ma'am."

"See that it doesn't," she said, wagging a finger beneath my nose.

I sucked that finger into my mouth, flipped her onto her back and held her there. By then we'd both lost the desire for conversation, and a different sort of need took precedence. It was quite a while before I let her get some sleep. And a lot longer still before I drifted off myself. I stared at the patterns dancing across the ceiling, wondering what the hell was wrong with me. Sex with Cleo was dynamite but I'm ashamed to say that I spent much of the time whilst engaged in the act, imagining I was with Kara, my friend and previously intimate acquaintance who lived in my house with her nephew and niece. I was stunned by the path my sub-conscious had taken me down. Up until that point I hadn't realized how much I missed Kara's company.

The following morning Gloria assured me that the preparations for the party wouldn't be disruptive. But when a massive marquee was dragged onto the lawn by a posse of burly men, I figured she was being overoptimistic. I'd either be roped in to help or would just be in the way. I left Cleo and Gloria, heads together, getting on like they'd been friends for years as they discussed stuff I didn't even pretend to understand. Gil and I headed for the relative safety of the boat and waited for Mike to turn up and repair the stern gland.

"This looks like a clean break." Mike held up one end of the bolt in question. "You were lucky that it didn't give when you were farther out."

I didn't reply. It clearly hadn't occurred to Mike that someone had sabotaged my boat and I didn't want to get into that with him. But I'd been thinking about little else since the incident occurred. How had it been done? Brighton Marina isn't exactly Fort Knox but it does have some security so a stranger hanging around the *No Comment* would stand out like a gentile in a synagogue. Said stranger would also have had to pick a time when Gil and I weren't on board *and* have enough knowledge about boats to know which bolt to loosen without me spotting it when I did my engine room checks.

Peter Garnet was the obvious candidate but he never did his own dirty work. That was where the guy following me earned his crust. Presumably he reported when I wasn't aboard and your local boat saboteur was in business. Except he'd not done a thorough enough job. Garnet knew I was going to France because I'd helpfully informed his wife of my plans, so presumably the bolt was supposed to give way when I was mid-Channel.

In such a busy shipping lane as the English Channel, help would have been close at hand and the saboteur would know I'd be rescued. It was against maritime law not to go to the aid of a vessel in distress if she put out a Mayday. But the bolt held almost all the way to Beaulieu, twice the distance, and if anyone was still keeping tabs on me they'd know I'd arrived without putting out a call for help.

It was probably intended as a warning. *Keep out of my business if you know what's good for you.* I must have struck a nerve, stumbled across something significant.

There was just one problem with that theory. I was buggered if I knew what it was.

I was still mulling it over after Mike left when another possibility hit me like a tidal wave. Perhaps the person behind this knew I wasn't going to France. I felt the bile rising in my throat. My beloved stepbrother would have been aware that I was on Hal's guest list. Gloria would have told Brenda, who in turn would warn her son. Paul knew I wanted to ask him about that money Marianne loaned him. Was he so desperate to avoid that confrontation that he'd try and stop me getting here? Being involved with Hal's team, he'd certainly have the necessary knowledge to do the dirty. And he lived in Brighton.

Peter Garnet or Paul Flint? I needed to find out which.

Cleo joined me just after I'd given Gil his afternoon walk. We'd be sleeping on board tonight because Gloria needed all the space in the house for other guests who were staying over. After I showered, I changed into the only smart trousers I possessed and a fancy shirt Kara had coerced me into buying for some do she'd taken me to. Then I sat in the salon with a drink, waiting for Cleo.

The wait proved to be worth it. She was wearing a dress that finished just above her knee. In a shade of mid-blue that suited her colouring, it was sculpted to her body and showcased her remarkable legs. Not an ounce of cleavage was on show but it looked much classier because of that. Some sort of black pencil outlined her eyes, the lids of which were all sparkly, and her full lips were painted a deep burgundy colour. I let my eyes rove slowly over her body and whistled.

"Why thank you, sir." She gave me a twirl.

"Just remember that you're all mine tonight," I said, slipping an arm round her waist and giving it a squeeze. "I don't want you getting any fancy ideas about those glamorous speedboat pilots."

She pouted. "Only for tonight, Charlie?"

"Well, if you're a very good girl, I suppose we could stretch it to two."

"You drive a hard bargain," she said, teasing her lower lip between her teeth as she pretended to think about it. I figured she'd end up with burgundy-coloured teeth but her lipstick stayed right where it was supposed to be. *How do women do that?*

"That's me," I agreed, tweaking her nose. "Hard as nails."

"And I thought I was about to embark upon a glamorous life, mixing with millionaires and all."

"You'd get seasick."

"Thanks for the reminder," she said, grimacing.

"Come on then, let's get this thing over with."

"Aren't you looking forward to it?" she asked as I took her hand to help her to step ashore.

"Parties aren't really my thing."

Nor was confronting my stepbrother but I refrained from saying so. As soon as Cleo's feet touched the pontoon, she donned a pair of shoes that had to have four-inch heels. They did wonders for her already spectacular legs but they'd probably cripple her within an hour.

"Won't you lose all feeling in your feet?"

"The torture we women put ourselves through just to make an impression." She sighed. "You have no idea."

I chuckled. "Well, on behalf of mankind in general, I want you to know that your efforts haven't gone unappreciated."

She linked her arm through mine and we strolled across to the house with ten minutes to spare before the guests were due. I barely recognised the place. A team of caterers was bustling about with platters of food, a bar had been set up in the marquee and, worryingly, a live band with monstrous-sized speakers was also making itself at home. A series of tables was set with shimmering white cloths and sparkling crystal glasses. Fresh flowers were absolutely everywhere, filling the place with a delicate perfume.

Gloria had overseen all the arrangements and must have felt knackered before the event even got underway. Even so, she still managed to look fresh and sensational in a floaty red chiffon number. I told her so.

"Ah, thank you, Charlie, and you don't look so bad

yourself." Her eyes flickered towards Cleo. "But neither of us can hold a candle to Cleo."

"Thanks," Cleo said, looking embarrassed.

"Hope it isn't black tie," I said, glancing at Hal, who was in full monkey-suit attire, "because this is about as formal as I get nowadays."

"No, you're fine." She walked the length of the marquee with us, chattering about nothing in particular, casting a critical eye over everything we passed. Every so often she stopped to make an adjustment or issue a quietly spoken instruction to one of the caterers.

"That's the glamour boys, just arriving." From which I assumed Gloria meant the pilots. "I'm surprised they're on their own but perhaps Josh is providing the entertainment," she added, almost to herself. "The one on the left, the taller, dark-haired one who thinks he's good-looking is Simon French, the driver of the boat. He fancies himself as quite a ladies' man, Cleo, so watch yourself."

"Thanks for the warning."

"And the shorter, stockier guy next to him is Dave Mason, his throttleman."

"Are they friends as well as colleagues?" I asked.

"Yes, they grew up together on the Isle of Wight and have never wanted to do anything other than play the powerboat game."

"Only those with nerves of steel and oversized testicles need apply."

Gloria smiled. "Quite."

"French looks like a natural leader," I remarked.

"Oh, he is, very much so."

I wondered if Mason resented playing second fiddle

and had resorted to underhand tactics to take over the driver's seat. But I didn't see how he could be behind the things that had happened so far since all the sabotage had affected him as much as French. Still, it was best to keep an open mind and not dwell upon Paul being the only pilot not inconvenienced so far. I was determined that my antipathy towards him would not cloud my judgement.

"Gloria!" French enveloped her in a fierce bear hug, lifted her clean off her feet. She extracted herself from his grasp, smiled at Mason with genuine warmth and then introduced us to both men.

"Charlie's parents are old friends of mine," she explained as Cleo and I shook both men's hands.

"That your trawler on the mooring, is it?" Mason asked.

"Sorry if it lowers the tone."

"It's an unusual craft. What engine do you have in it?"

I fell into conversation with Mason about my floating home. He asked a lot of intelligent questions and I found myself being drawn away from Cleo, leaving French free to make a move on her. I resisted the urge to intervene. Cleo was a big girl, well able to deal with the likes of French. Or so I hoped. I watched him from the corner of my eye as he oozed artificial charm. Mason and French were chalk and cheese, which possibly explained why they connected as a team.

"What does a throttleman do exactly?" I asked Mason. "I have a feeling there's quite a bit more to it than just keeping an eye on the rev counter."

Mason cocked a brow. "Just a bit. Have you ever ridden in a powerboat when it's crashing through seas that are supposed to be calm but never are at speeds of over a hundred miles an hour?"

My back twinged at the mere prospect. "Can't say I've had the pleasure."

"You're strapped into a flimsy fibreglass cockpit. It's like being in a straitjacket, or a ruddy coffin. I've never been able to decide which." He flashed a good-natured grin. "You're surrounded by other lunatics in boats as flimsy as your own and wonder what the fuck you think you're doing. I tell you, Charlie, it makes your teeth rattle when you hit the waves wrong, and that's on a calm day. You don't want to know what happens when there's a swell running."

"Sounds like a masochist's game."

He took a sip of his drink and grimaced. "If you mean it helps to be a head case, then yeah, you've got it dead right."

"Then why do it?'"

Mason's grimace turned into a puerile grin and he suddenly looked years younger. "What, apart from the glamorous locations, the accolades and the gorgeous girls anxious for a part of me?"

I wasn't buying it. "There must be more to it than that."

"I do it for the rush," he said. "There's nothing like it. I've tried sex, drugs, booze, you name it, but nothing comes close to crossing that line, knowing you've driven a near-perfect race."

I nodded. A bit like my stubborn determination to live on my boat, I supposed, even in the depths of winter when it was freezing, damp and uncomfortable. I'd given up trying to explain to my ex-wife what made me do it. She'd never understand because she didn't want to.

"You were explaining what you do on the boat, apart from sitting back and admiring the view."

"Cheeky bastard." Mason waved to someone across the room. "Simon has to keep his hands firmly on the wheel and watch for rival boats, often just yards off our stern. There are strict rules about overtaking that can make a big difference to the points the team scores. If you miss a buoy you can't retake it so you go through all that torture just to be penalised for something you could have avoided if you'd taken a little more care. It's fucking infuriating."

"I can imagine."

"Simon uses his eyes and the GPS system in the boat. My job is to keep blipping the engines on and off to avoid over-revving them. I also have to keep control of the trim tabs, make sure the engine temperatures and oil pressures stay within the right parameters, and provide a second pair of eyes. The hard-to-spot corner buoys are real bastards."

I nodded. "So wouldn't it make sense to have a navigator on board to take care of that sort of thing? I thought Hal mentioned that it's permissible to have a three-man crew."

Mason shook his head. "We tried it a couple of times with Paul on board but it didn't work out. Simon and I are used to one another and perform better as a two-man team."

From which I surmised that he and French weren't exactly Paul's greatest fans either. I'd lost sight of Cleo but she appeared out of nowhere at that precise moment and grasped my arm.

"I think Gloria's trying to attract our attention," she said.

"Okay, duty calls. Catch you later," I said to Mason, allowing Cleo to lead me away.

We drifted across to Gloria, who greeted us with a smile.

"Oh, Charlie, Cleo, I'd like you to meet Josh Harling, the team's manager."

Harling was stockily built, wearing a cream linen suit over a shirt that was unbuttoned halfway down his chest. His hair was thinning and I figured he must be in his forties. He was sporting artfully cultivated designer stubble and had a woman clinging to each arm. He was not more than five-nine and his leggy companions both towered over him, although he seemed smug rather than embarrassed by that. Maybe these girls were the entertainment Gloria had predicted he'd supply for the pilots. Part of his job description, perhaps.

Harling chatted about the team and its prospects for the coming season. He might present a ludicrous figure with his pathetic attempts to appear trendy but he seemed to know his business backwards. Given that he was employed by Hal, that shouldn't have surprised me. But he could sure as hell make an exciting sport sound tediously dull and had the pedantic nature of a methodical man born to organise. He must have beaten himself up about the fiasco with the pilots' medicals.

"Seem to have lost my companions," he mumbled at one point. He obviously hadn't noticed when French and a couple of other guys lured them away.

An exceptionally statuesque waitress with chocolate-coloured skin walked by, carrying a tray full of drinks.

Harling wasn't the only man in the room who stared at her with his tongue hanging out, myself included.

"Angie!" Harling raised a hand to attract her attention. "I didn't know you'd be here tonight."

"Good evening, Mr. Harling," she said politely. Her eyes ran briefly over me, lingering for a moment as though she was trying to place me.

"Who was that?" I asked Harling as we watched her walk away.

"Her name's Angie Bradley," he said. "She's the stewardess on Hal's boat but she gets drafted in to do other jobs if the boat's not being used."

"Really," I said casually. "I don't recall seeing her on his boat before."

Harling smirked. "And you'd hardly forget, right?"

"She'd stand out in a crowd," I agreed.

"Right, and she's comparatively new. Been with Hal less than a year."

That got me wondering. She was so attractive, moved so instinctively well, that she was obvious model material. From the few words I'd heard her speak she appeared to be educated and could probably have landed a far better job than the one she'd settled for. And there was something niggling at the back of my brain. Something I ought to remember about her but couldn't.

"You've got that pensive look I'm starting to recognise," Cleo said as we strolled away from Harling. "What are you thinking?"

"That Mason doesn't enjoy playing second fiddle to French in all aspects of his life."

"Oh, but he seems so nice. Surely you don't suspect him of being the saboteur?"

"If all guilty people looked the part then my old job would have been a lot easier."

"Hmm, I suppose." She helped herself to a glass of champagne from the tray of a passing waitress. "But still—"

"It's just an observation, that's all. And Harling's another candidate. He has a severe case of small-man syndrome and a point to prove."

"Hence his tall lady friends."

"They weren't here for his benefit. How would you feel if you were expected to act as a glorified pimp?"

"Point taken."

"And then there's the lovely Angie."

"So you think she's lovely?"

"Turn of phrase, love. Didn't really notice."

She offered me a kindly smile. "No, of course you didn't."

"Seriously though, she's too well qualified for the work she does."

"What's better than working on a superyacht and seeing the world?"

"Lots of things. It sounds glamorous but in reality it's nothing more than domestic service wrapped up in pretty packaging." I shot her a look. "And then there's the seasickness to consider."

"You enjoy bringing that up, don't you? Stop being such a dork and tell me why Angie interests you. Apart from the obvious reasons, of course."

"Well, that boat goes to all the races, and Angie wouldn't be monitored like the others. She'd probably have opportunities to do all sorts of things she shouldn't, and no one would think about suspecting her.

I asked Hal if anyone new had joined the outfit since the sabotage started and he didn't mention Angie."

"You've got a suspicious mind, Mr. Hunter."

"No, gorgeous, I've got a copper's mind."

"So you've already figured out three possible culprits."

Four actually. I hadn't mentioned the obvious suspect, aka Paul Flint, nor did I intend to. Time was getting on and Paul had yet to put in an appearance. That shouldn't really have surprised me. Paul liked to make an entrance, and I idly wondered just how long he'd leave it before he deemed the time right to honour us with his presence.

We joined a queue at the buffet and filled our plates with all sorts of delicacies, few of which I could have named. I'm more of a steak and chips man myself. Our table had been filched by a crowd of musicians, some of whom I recognised from the old days. I returned their waves and promised to catch them later. Cleo and I wandered outside with our plates and settled on the balustrade on the edge of the terrace. I went in search of alcoholic refreshment and returned with two brimming glasses.

We'd only just finished eating when ominously loud static squawks emanated from the giant speakers inside the marquee. Some long-haired kid seized the moment to murder a Clapton guitar riff. His efforts earned him a round of muted and undeserved applause. I'd bet a lot of dosh that it wasn't being led by my mum's old colleagues. The tables were now pushed back to form the perimeter of a dance floor, and that was my cue to distance myself. Loud rock music, especially when it's badly executed, simply isn't my thing.

"I think I know where we can go to escape that racket." Cleo nodded towards the marquee where figures were energetically gyrating on the makeshift dance floor.

"Lead me to it," I said with feeling.

The inside of the house was deserted and thankfully a rock-music-free zone. Only as Cleo led me up the stairs did I realise, too late, what she had planned. On the first floor was a huge room devoted to Gloria's music and—surprise, surprise—it was now almost full to capacity with some of the musicians I'd seen in the marquee.

I shot Cleo a look, wondering who'd put her up to this, but she'd already been swallowed up by the crowd, leaving me to fend for myself. I was greeted warmly and felt myself being inexorably swept back in time. Instruments were being tuned and the abbreviated conversation that would sound like a foreign language to anyone else was…well, music to my ears. Everyone wanted to know what I'd been doing with myself. I diverted their questions and told them not to let me interrupt their improvised session.

"You're not interrupting," someone said. "In fact you're just the person we need. We're short of a pianist."

"Sorry." I turned my hands palms-outwards and shook my head. "I don't play classical piano."

"Oh, that's all right, Charlie," said a female violist who looked familiar but whose name escaped me. "This is no time for the classics. In fact, a little jazz would be in order, if only to block out that racket from the marquee."

In spite of my anger at being manipulated, I didn't say that I no longer played. Instead I found myself being propelled towards the Steinway grand piano and didn't protest. God knows why not.

"What's it to be, Charlie?"

I ran my fingers over the keys. In spite of my misgivings I felt as though I was being welcomed back into an exclusive club. The beautifully tuned instrument made my clumsy attempt at a major seventh sound almost melodic. Until panic seized me and I abruptly stopped tinkering. What the fuck did I think I was doing? I was about to leg it but glanced up and could see there was no way they'd let me back down now. Sighing, I figured the only way to escape was to jam with them and get it over with.

"How about this one?"

Someone tapped out the basic rhythm of Scott Joplin's "Maple Leaf Rag," which was when the panic turned into outright fear. My brow felt damp. My fingers shook. "Maple Leaf Rag" was a masterpiece in syncopation. I'd just about nailed it, after hours of sweat and toil, when my mother was killed. Some of these people knew that but none of them remarked upon my hesitation. Instead, a double bass picked up on the sixteen-note rhythm, a cello joined in and then so did a snare drum.

Inexplicably my fingers had stopped shaking and were now itching instead. Before I could stop myself, I launched into the number. Fast, like Joplin played it, just to show them that I really was a lost cause. It required good left-hand control to play it right and I very much doubted that I was still in possession of that particular skill. Still, an assault on their collective eardrums was the least they deserved for railroading me into this.

The generic ragtime beat rang inside my head and it took a moment for me to realise that everyone else had stopped playing. Instead they were all looking at me, smiling encouragement. Perhaps it wasn't quite as bad as I'd feared. Caught up in it now, I closed my eyes and gave it my best shot. As I did so I found myself wondering where I'd be with my music today if I'd stuck with it. But I'd learned the hard way never to let my thoughts dwell upon *what-ifs,* and distracted myself by running with a few ostinato patterns, nodding to encourage the rest of the ensemble to rejoin me.

I hadn't noticed Cleo and Gloria materialise. They were standing immediately behind me, watching my fingers pick out the notes. I glanced up and scowled at them.

"You'll pay for this later," I warned them.

Cleo's lilting smile was almost my undoing and I hit a wrong note.

"Stop looking so smug. It won't be pretty."

"Don't blame me," she said. "I was only obeying instructions."

I sighed. She wasn't the first pretty girl who'd enticed me back to a piano recently. Talk about being led by the balls. Did being unemployed imply that I'd somehow get involved again when I'd always been adamantly opposed to the idea?

"When all else fails it's the messenger who should

face the music. Er, pun intended," I told her, bringing the number to an end with a flourish of my right hand.

The rest of them actually stood to applaud. Coming from professionals that was praise indeed, and I'll admit I was pleased by their reaction. I caught Gloria's eye. She looked genuinely moved and mouthed a thank-you to me. I inclined my head, realising now that she hadn't once asked me if I still played. Anyone in the music world who knew me back in the day always asked that question. Presumably she already knew the answer and had recruited Cleo to help her change my mind. Well, I was glad to have pleased her, if only for Mum's sake, but not to the extent that I was prepared to play anything else.

They let me go without protesting too much. Cleo and I drifted from the room and found Paul leaning nonchalantly against the doorjamb. He was dressed as flamboyantly as ever in a pale blue suit with a black shirt and tie and a fedora tipped over his left eye.

"Well, well, little brother," he said, taking his time to straighten himself up and giving me a slow, ironic round of applause. "I guess you still have what it takes."

# Chapter Ten

CLEO GLANCED AT Paul as I made the introductions. Perhaps sensing the animosity already building between us, she kissed my cheek and said she'd see me later. Left alone, neither of us offered to shake hands. I couldn't think of a single time when we ever had, which said a lot about our relationship.

"How are the old folks?" he asked as we drifted off in search of a quiet corner. "I hear you honoured them with a royal visit."

"Starting to look their age."

"Aren't we all, dear."

Paul paused to examine his reflection in the hall mirror. About the same height as me, he could never pass a mirror by without checking on his appearance. Today, though, the mirror didn't detain him for long. He was also less than his usual sarcastic self, leading me to suppose that he was worried about something. If he was responsible for sabotaging my beloved boat then he had good reason to be. But if he was behind my mother's murder…I suppressed that thought. If it crept past my guard I'd lose all objectivity, and I needed to be at my sharpest in my dealings with Paul.

How to start our conversation? Small talk was the last thing he'd expect so that was the route I took, hoping to catch him off guard.

"Enjoying working for Hal?" I asked.

He shrugged. "It has its compensations."

"Like travelling the world at someone else's expense."

"Someone has to do it."

"True." I looked round for a waiter, in need of something to do with my hands. Needless to say, there wasn't one in sight.

"So, brother-dear," he said. "What brings you here?"

Like he didn't know. "Any reason why I shouldn't come?"

"None at all except that whenever Hal's invited you before, he's mentioned that you either couldn't make it or had to cancel at the last minute."

"That was when I was in the job. I've retired now."

"Hmm, so I hear. And nowadays you take your house with you wherever you go, a bit like a mollusc."

I refused to let him rile me. "I enjoy my comforts."

"Goes well, does she?"

We'd wandered outside and perched ourselves on the terrace in much the same place that Cleo and I had eaten our supper. Paul nodded towards my boat moored at the end of the garden as he posed the question. As far as I was concerned that was all the proof I needed of his guilt. He was burning to know what damage his sabotage had done.

"Like a dream. The trip down was as smooth as silk."

"Go on, then," he said a little too casually, brushing imaginary specks from his trousers with the back of his hand. "Ask me whatever it is you want to know."

I took my time responding, trying to read his body language without making it obvious. It didn't tell me much. "I guess you've already been primed," I said laconically.

Paul scratched his chin and pretended to think about it. "Well, unless you've undergone a character transplant since giving up sleuthing for a living, I assume you're still looking for answers about your mother's untimely demise."

Up until then I'd felt in control of the situation. That in itself was something of a rarity in my dealings with Paul. But his taunting tone, his deliberate provocation, now made me want to hit him.

I clenched my fists, aware of the indolent smile playing about his lips as I strove to remain calm. "Actually I'm not." He snorted. "But I'd still be interested to learn why you persuaded your mother to borrow money from Marianne on your behalf."

"Even though you no longer care who killed your mother?"

I flinched. "Exactly."

He wagged a finger at me. The nail was covered with clear varnish. "Wouldn't you like to know?"

"If there's an innocent explanation it can't hurt to indulge my curiosity."

"Now isn't that just like a policeman, always assuming the worst about everyone?"

It was my turn to pretend indifference. "Perhaps that's because you've never given me any reason to think well of you."

"My, my." He placed a hand mincingly on a jutting hip. "Aren't we the grouchy one today." But his ostentatious display of contempt lacked bite.

"It seems to me," I said, staring at some of the revellers now spilling out onto the lawn, "that neither of us is enjoying this encounter. So why prolong it? Just tell me what I need to know and I'm out of here."

"Ah, now that is a tempting offer, but you're wrong, little brother. Marianne didn't lend the money to mother. She lent it to Dad."

He'd deliberately referred to my father in that possessive way to irritate me. Usually it worked but this time I felt implacably calm, immune to his childish attempts to rile me.

"And he lent it to you. No," I amended, "make that he *gave* it to you." I lifted my shoulders. "You have to admit it's enough to make anyone curious."

He quirked a brow. "If not resentful?"

"Not at all. I just want to know why a kid of…what were you, twenty-one at the time?" He neither confirmed nor denied the accuracy of my maths but his amused expression showed signs of strain. "What I want to know is why a twenty-one-year-old would require such a large sum of money. I'd also quite like to know why Marianne was so keen to give it away."

"Yes, dear, I expect you would, but it's none of your bloody business."

"Well, that's up to you, of course." I fell silent, staring off towards my boat with an attitude of detached indifference. Since I'd never displayed indifference when speaking about my mother it was safe to assume that his interest was piqued.

He confirmed that suspicion by speaking first. "What strange little habits you've developed, darling. Going all dark and moody on me. It really is rather fetching. Such a shame you're not gay."

"Have the police been to see you yet?"

The change of subject clearly surprised him and he responded for once without putting on an act. "What do you mean?"

"The man murdered in your building. They'll want to speak to all the neighbours, just in case they saw anything."

His taunting attitude fell away and just for a moment I thought I detected genuine grief in his expression. He gathered himself quickly but still looked as though I'd thrown a bucket of cold water over him. "Well, I wasn't there so I couldn't have." He paused. "But I gather you were."

If that was supposed to unnerve me he didn't know me very well. "Can you prove you weren't there?"

"That's what CCTV's for."

"Not if you park in the garage beneath the building. There are no cameras down there."

He looked rattled now. "If you say so, dear."

"But the dead solicitor, you knew him socially?"

"Did I?" He quirked a brow, trying to look bored, but it wasn't working. I had his complete, undivided attention and we both knew it.

"Rather well," I said, enjoying myself.

"Bullshit!"

I'd rattled him. I felt a childish need to run circuits of the garden, punching the air and letting out delirious whoops.

"Even so, you'd prefer not to be questioned too closely about your friendship," I said mildly.

"You're way off the mark, little brother."

"Am I?" I paused. "I wonder if my ex-colleagues would agree?"

He produced an exaggerated sigh. "Okay, what do you want?"

"What I've always wanted. I'm not interested in any scams you had going with the dead solicitor."

He let out a long breath. "Why do you always think the worst of me?"

"Because you've never given me any reason to think otherwise." I met his gaze and held it. "I need to know what happened to that money. If I believe what you tell me, then there's nothing more to be said about the other business."

"If you really think I spent that money on having your bitch of a mother done away with, then you've lost what few brain cells you used to possess." He was speaking straight into my face, his lips twisted with malicious spite. "I'm many things, Charlie, but a coward I am not. If I'd done the world a favour by ridding it of your mother, don't you think I'd have done myself one at the same time and made sure you went with her?"

"Contact me by the end of the week," I said, letting his words wash over me. "I'll keep the police off your back until then. But when we speak again I'll need some answers about that money. Understood?"

With that I turned on my heel and disappeared into the night.

The party was in full swing, loud and raucous. In no mood to socialise, I headed for the boat. Cleo would be fine and she'd know where to find me. I was still some way off when I noticed a barefoot figure silhouetted on the aft deck, swinging her legs casually over the gunwales. I liked Cleo but right now I could do with being alone so I could figure out what precisely I'd just learned from Paul.

"Hi," I said. "I thought you'd want to dance the night away."

"Not without you."

"I'm not very good company right now."

"Was it as bad as all that, talking to Paul?" she asked, resting a hand lightly on my arm.

"He enjoys winding me up and I always seem to let him."

"I find it hard to imagine anyone getting the better of you for long."

"I'm bushed," I said, turning to unlock the salon and trying not to look at her. It wasn't easy because I liked looking at her. Gil came bounding out and made a beeline for Cleo. She ruffled his ears and made cooing noises. Gil lapped it up and then rolled on his back for more.

"I'm too old for all this hell-raising so I'm gonna turn in."

"Surely you've got enough energy for a nightcap."

"No, really I—"

"Charlie, don't make me beg."

I knew when I was beaten so I headed for the drinks cabinet and poured us both hefty measures of brandy.

She stood to take her glass from me. "I didn't know you could play the piano like that. Why didn't you tell me?"

I shrugged. "I don't play much anymore."

"Well, I don't know anything about jazz but it sounded pretty good to me. Everyone was talking about it."

"That was a nasty trick you played on me."

"Sorry!" She clamped a hand over her mouth to stifle a giggle. "It was Gloria's idea. She said if you knew what she was planning, you wouldn't have gone anywhere near that room." My expression must have told her Gloria was right. "Well," she said smugly, "there you are then. You enjoyed it so don't bother denying it. It showed on your face."

I acknowledged that with a reluctant nod. "I didn't realise I was such a pushover."

"Subconsciously you must have wanted to do it."

"Don't go all philosophical on me." I drained my glass and placed it on the galley counter. "Well, that's it then. Time to hit the sack."

Before I realised what she had in mind, she scooted across the seating unit until no space separated us, plonked herself on my lap and kissed me. It was a searing, tongue-down-the-throat sort of kiss, and my heroic attempts at resistance last for all of five seconds. Quite why I was trying to resist wasn't altogether clear to me. It was just that Paul had shown his vulnerable underbelly, I needed to think, and I still felt confused about Kara, and…oh, what the hell.

We were naked and in one another's arms in seconds.

HAL JOINED US for breakfast on the boat the following morning.

"It's a three-ring circus up at the house," he said with a martyred sigh. "Musicians pretend they don't like parties but they're certainly not averse to the drinking bit."

"It went on a while then?" I said, chuckling.

"After four, I think. Can't say for sure. Hope it didn't disturb you."

"Didn't hear a thing."

"That's good. Anyway, I left them to it when it started to get silly."

"Very wise."

"Coffee?" Cleo asked, waving the pot in our direction. We both nodded.

"So," Hal said, leaning back in his chair. "Any blindingly obvious suspects for the sabotage, Charlie?"

"I spoke to quite a few people but no one stands out." I paused. "But then we could be coming at this the wrong way."

"What do you mean?"

"Well, we're assuming it's someone directly connected to the team, trying to queer your pitch. But you're a businessman."

Hal lifted his shoulders. "Yes, and no successful businessman gets to the top of his tree without treading on toes and squelching egos."

"And presumably if the powerboat team folded, then you'd be disadvantaged financially."

"Yes, I would." He rubbed his chin, deep in thought. "Very much so. To say nothing of my own ego. I hadn't considered that possibility."

"It's no secret that the team's your abiding passion, so if someone was out for revenge it would be a prime target. And since none of the sabotage has been technical, anyone with a bit of gumption could have organised it."

"It's possible, I suppose. I'll give it some thought, and if I come up with any candidates I'll let you know." He paused, frowning. "But if it was a business rival they'd still need someone on the inside, wouldn't they?"

"Possibly. Where were all the team before last night, by the way?"

"Why do you ask?"

"No reason. Just curiosity."

"Were they closeted together, scheming to bring about my downfall, is what you're asking?"

"Humour me."

"Josh Harling's the only one who's employed full time. The rest are paid to work for me during the season, when I need them."

"Which isn't yet?"

"No, another month before we join forces."

"So, what does Josh do for support staff?"

"He uses people from my organisation for PR and stuff like that."

That would explain the two women he'd brought with him. Someone mentioned that they worked for Hal's organisation. "Everyone arrived from different points for the party?"

"Pretty much, yes."

So Paul could have been in Brighton and could have sabotaged my boat.

"When do you plan to leave, Charlie?"

"In about an hour, with the tide."

"Oh, but Gloria was hoping—"

"Cleo has to work tonight and I've got some other stuff on."

"Of course, I should have thought. But don't leave it so long next time. And come up to the house to say goodbye before you go, or my name will be mud."

We made our fond farewells and put to sea as planned. My engine room checks were extra diligent but everything appeared to be in order. The boat behaved beautifully, and the weather was calmer as well, so Cleo was saved a repeat bout of seasickness.

As soon as we were tied up in Brighton, Cleo dashed home to change for work. I hit the phones and asked Jimmy Taylor if he could meet me for a pint later. I also asked him to check a few names out before he did so. Then I got on to the internet and did some background research on Peter Garnet.

Jimmy and I settled at a quiet table in the back of his local, two foaming pints of beer in front of us. Jimmy didn't look comfortable and I got the impression he'd suggested the location because no one else from the job was likely to see us there.

"Cheers," I said, raising my glass in salute. "And thanks for making the time."

"My pleasure." He paused, grinning over his beer. "I think."

"I'm still public enemy number one then."

"Oh, Slater's busting her balls trying to pin the murder on you. Well," he amended, grinning again, "she would be if she actually had any, but you get the picture."

"Sure." I tried not to show how unsettling I found her determination to nail me.

"No one else suspects you for a moment, not even the boss."

"That's reassuring."

"Yeah, and I think Slater realises she's over-played her hand. You know what she's like about self-image and keeping in with the people that matter. The guvnor's told her to back off you and since she hasn't got anything definite linking you to the crime, she's pretending to look elsewhere."

"But still having me followed."

Jimmy's eyebrows shot up. "Is she?"

"I'm pretty sure she was."

"Well if she is, it's not official."

"Much good may it do her." I took a long draft of beer. "Did you bring those crime scene pictures I asked for?"

"Yeah." He reached into a document case and produced an envelope. They didn't show the body but then those weren't the pictures I wanted to see. I was more interested in that lounge I'd caught a brief glimpse of. My ex-colleagues had done a thorough job of photographing it from every angle. That was how I knew the silver-framed photograph I'd seen was missing. The frame that I was sure held a head and shoulders shot of my stepbrother.

Paul's reaction to my accusations at Hal's party had all but confirmed it. It accounted for his despondency and so much more. Miller didn't look gay but he probably hadn't come out and didn't want people to know. Men in his profession often didn't. The picture's disappearance gave me a pretty good idea who'd offed Miller but I tried not to let it show in my expression. It was a delicate situation for all sorts of reasons, and I needed more proof before I started throwing accusations about.

"Thanks," I said, handing the pictures back to Jimmy.

"Find what you were looking for?"

"No." Or rather *yes*. "About those names I asked you to check out, Jimmy. Any news yet?"

"Nothing on Tommy Mallet. He hasn't got a record but he does have a few brain cells and is known to be Peter Garnet's fixer. Anything he wants done."

"And Garnet's clean too, I take it."

Jimmy nodded. "As a whistle."

"Any other interesting names connected to Garnet then?" I asked, already knowing the answer.

"Yeah, he has some muscle by the name of Frank Glover. He and Mallet are a bit of a double act but, like I said, Mallet's the brains and—"

"—and Glover supplies the brawn."

"Yeah." Jimmy produced a mug shot from his inside jacket pocket. "Know him?"

I took the picture and studied it. I was fairly certain it was the guy with the ball cap and denim jacket who'd followed me. I leaned back and thought about it for a moment. Why were they worried about me? What didn't they want me to find out?

"Yeah, I think our paths crossed once or twice back in the day."

"He's got a record for petty stuff but has been clean for some time." Jimmy looked at me, his eyes troubled. "What's this all about anyway?"

"Well, obviously Garnet's wife had been to see Miller not long before he died," I said, striving for a casual tone. "I wondered if there might be a connection."

"Nothing to do with Mike Kendall then?"

"What?"

Jimmy's perpetually cheerful expression gave way to a scowl. "Don't take me for an idiot, Charlie, and don't keep me in the dark here either. I ain't a fucking mushroom. And," he added belligerently, "I'm sticking my neck out for you."

"Look, mate, I'm not trying to—"

"I recognised Cleo Kendall the first time I saw her

with you and couldn't help asking myself why you were hanging out with the daughter of a known con."

"Well, if you've seen Cleo," I said, spreading my hands, "the answer's pretty obvious."

But Jimmy wasn't buying it. "I know you better than that. She's come to you with some hard-luck story about her dad, you've been poking your nose in and now you're in the shit." He shook his head. "Besides, my dear Watson, you asked me to look into the original Kendall case."

"Yeah, okay, there is something, but it's probably better that you don't know."

"It's a bit late to keep me out of it."

"I will tell you when I can but if you don't want to help me, I'll—"

"No, it's okay. I know you're sound, and if we can get one over on Slater it'll be worth it."

"Thanks." I lifted my shoulders. "And there just might be a collar in this for you at the end of the day."

"Fair enough."

We'd finished our drinks and I insisted on paying for the second round even though I'd already got the first. It was the least I could do when Jimmy was putting his career on the line for me.

"What about that other name I ran past you yesterday?" I asked him, returning to the table with our refills.

"Angela Bradley?"

I nodded. "I thought there was something sensational from a couple of years ago. I don't know exactly what but it's niggling away."

"If there was, it's not on record. She's clean."

So much for my incubating theory. "Oh well, thanks anyway."

"But I got curious so I did a bit more digging, just using the name Bradley." His eyes lit up and I knew he had something.

"And?" I prompted.

"Do you remember the Katrina Simpson case?"

I slapped my thigh. "Of course! She was the girl who got jailed for defrauding her stockbroker employer out of a shedload of money."

"She was indeed."

"Okay, so what has Angie to do with Katrina Simpson then?"

"She's a long-standing friend. They were at school together. Angie testified on Katrina's behalf. Insisted she knew she was having an affair with her boss, who talked her into opening the accounts for all that stolen dosh, and that Katrina knew nothing about it. Trouble was, she had no actual proof and the crown prosecutor tore her story to shreds on cross."

I felt a surge of excitement. I was on to something. I remembered Hal talking about the Simpson girl at the time. He was involved somehow and conflicted about it. "You might want to delve a little deeper," I said.

"Why's that?" Jimmy paused to take a sup of his ale. "Good drop of bitter this," he remarked, placing his glass almost reverently in the centre of his drip mat.

"Well, I can't be absolutely sure, but I have a feeling that Miller worked in the city at the time and that his name was connected to the case."

Jimmy sat bolt upright. "So you think someone from

Miller's past with an axe to grind might have come out of the woodwork seeking revenge."

"It's worth looking at but, like I say, keep it low profile. If it pans out you don't want Slater stealing all the glory."

Jimmy perked up considerably, and I felt I'd repaid him in part, even if there proved to be nothing in it.

I headed back to the boat, needing to talk to Hal. I managed to get hold of him and didn't waste time with small talk. "What can you tell me about Katrina Simpson?" I asked.

If the question surprised him it wasn't apparent in his voice and he answered me without pausing to think. "She was a junior trader with the firm of stockbrokers I use and was jailed for stealing. Over three million quid went missing from their client accounts."

I let out a low whistle. I'd forgotten that so much dosh was involved. "Yes, but you were involved somehow." I waved a hand, even though he couldn't see it. "Not with the theft, obviously. Remind me where you fitted in."

"I know Katrina's boss and his wife quite well. Gloria and I socialise with them." This time Hal did hesitate but I waited him out. "Katrina claimed to be having an affair with Max and that he'd embezzled the money so that they could disappear into the sunset and play happy families. All she did was open the accounts on his instructions, or so she claimed. But there was no evidence that Max was involved, and she didn't have any proof of an affair."

"So if there was an affair, your mate had been careful to cover his tracks."

"Actually, Katrina's defence team asked me to testify that I knew about the affair."

"Why?"

Another hesitation. "Some months before the fraud came to light, I'd arranged for Max to call at my office to discuss a big investment I wanted to make. I got held up, so my secretary put him and Katrina, whom he brought with him, in the small conference room off my office.

"When I arrived, the door was ajar and I overheard Katrina and Max having a muted yet heated conversation. Max's back was towards me, so he didn't know I was there. Katrina was so intent upon the conversation that she didn't see me for a while, either." He sighed. "I should have made them aware of my presence, but something held me back. Max was holding her hand, stroking the back of it and assuring her that she didn't need to do anything other than open the accounts." Another pause. "That's when Katrina looked up and saw me."

"What conclusion did you draw from that?"

"I didn't know what to think. Max laughed it off. Said she had cold feet about a big account he'd given her to handle and he was trying to reassure her. I didn't think anything more of it, until the theft case hit the headlines."

"Do you think there was an affair?"

"I didn't at the time. They were friendly, Katrina and Max, but that was never in dispute. She was a knockout, and you can't blame him for mentoring her, but I never saw or even suspected that there was anything between them, other than that kiss on the wrist. I've often wondered about that in the light of subsequent revelations."

"Her brief asked you to say what you saw?"

"Yes, but how could I? I felt bad about it. Katrina comes from a good family and wasn't the sort to do something like that without a compelling reason. But I couldn't kill off Max's career, to say nothing of his marriage, on such flimsy evidence."

"I guess not."

"Why did you want to know about her? Has it got something to do with my problems?"

"No, I don't think so." I was unwilling to let him in on my suspicions until I knew more. "It's just something that someone said to me. I'll tell you more when I know."

"Fair enough."

"One more thing, Hal, and then I'll let you go. Angie Bradley," I said. "How did you come to employ her?"

"You suspect her?" he asked, tension in his tone.

"Not necessarily. For now I just need to know what brought her to your attention."

"I needed a hostess for the boat. I advertised in a trade journal and my PA whittled the applicants down to a short list, one of whom was Angie. I interviewed them all but she was head and shoulders the best candidate."

If Hal had read about her testimony at Katrina's trial, he obviously hadn't made the connection.

"Has she done that sort of work before?"

"No." He hesitated. "But her CV was impressive, I could tell she was intelligent and I figured she'd pick it up quickly enough. And she has. I haven't had a single complaint against her."

"Where did she work before?"

"She was a masseuse, I think."

Adrenaline shot through my veins. "Can you remember where she worked?"

"Just a moment," Hal said. I heard the clatter of computer keys. Presumably he had all his employees' records digitalised. "Yes, a health club in Hove. Her boss gave her a glowing reference."

"Don't tell me, let me guess. A guy by the name of Peter Garnet."

"How the hell did you know that?"

## Chapter Eleven

I GOT OFF the phone to Hal, promising to answer his questions as soon as I could. In the meantime he agreed not to do anything to alert Angie that she was under suspicion. She couldn't be in this alone and we needed to find out who her accomplice was. Every which way I turned, it came back to Peter Garnet. How did he manage to have fingers in such a disparate range of pies? And, more to the point, why? Spelling and Miller I kind of got. But what possible link did Angie Bradley have with Garnet?

My research revealed that at the time of Spelling's murder Garnet had a few racehorses, a run-down health club off the beaten track in Hove, and was allegedly involved with a couple of betting scams. The police were regular callers, and he must have known it would only be a matter of time before we got him for something. Perhaps that was why, after Spelling's murder, he changed tack and became legit. He bought his first nightclub about then and set about climbing up the local business ladder. Now he had three thriving nightclubs. He'd also revamped his health club, made it very exclusive and charged a fortune for membership. He enjoyed a position of respect within the local community, was a well-known figure in sporting circles, and still had racehorses in training. Jimmy hadn't heard about him being involved in anything shady.

I was still thinking about Garnet the next day when I got a call from Reg Turner. I hadn't expected to hear from him again so soon, if at all. He sounded agitated and asked if we could meet. I agreed immediately. I rode the Harley to a street close to his local and found the greasy spoon he'd directed me to.

He lived close by and obviously had his routine down pat. A stroll to the café for a late breakfast, a detour to the betting shop and then straight on to the boozer. No deviations apart from an occasional visit to the dog track, and yet he still managed to know absolutely everything that was going on in the manor.

I joined him but didn't risk the food, settling for a strong black coffee.

"What's up, Reg?" I asked. "You look a bit shaken."

"I had a visit from your lot, didn't I."

"I did warn you that they'd come knocking sooner or later. It wouldn't normally bother you."

"Some god-awful, pushy woman inspector came throwing her weight around." He pulled an aggrieved face. "What happened to a bit of good old-fashioned professional respect, Mr. H, that's what I wanna know?"

"Times are changing, Reg."

"Yeah," he agreed morosely, wiping up dollops of egg yoke with his bread. "And not for the better. Knew where we stood, we did, back in your day."

"I've only been gone for a bit more than a year, Reg," I said, amused.

"Whatever."

"You didn't ask me here to talk about Inspector Slater's myriad shortcomings."

"Kept on and on at me, she did, demanding to know why I'd gone to see Miller. How could I afford his fees?" He glowered at the opposite wall as though he bore it a grudge. "Like it was any of her business, the nosy cow."

"She was only doing her job."

"Well, someone ought to show her how to do it right. She can't speak to people like that and expect them to tell her what she wants to know."

I chuckled. "You wouldn't have told her anyway."

"That ain't the point. We could have a nice little thing going. A polite exchange of information, beneficial to both parties, like what I had with you. But not if there's no respect there."

"Okay, Reg, you've had a good bitch. Now tell me why I'm here."

"It's about why I went to see Miller." Fear replaced the sullenness in his expression. "I've had a long think about it, and now that he's gone I reckon I need some insurance."

I frowned. "You're not making any sense."

"That's because it don't come natural to break confidences but I don't reckon I've got any choice now. If I finish up like Miller, then the truth'll die with me."

I'd never seen Reg so shaken before. "Just tell me. You know I won't blab."

"It's about Jeff Spelling. He wasn't going to leave his missus for a barmaid. He wasn't going to leave her at all, that's just what Mike told Cleo when he was nicked and she demanded to know what he'd been up to."

"Why? What was really going on?"

Reg rubbed his bristly chin. "He needed money, and fast. When Mike got wind of it and asked him what he was doing, he told him the truth."

"What did he need it for?"

"His daughter." Reg flashed a mirthless grin, presumably because my expression reflected my surprise. "Yeah, I knew that would shake you. Jeff was dead faithful to his missus. He wasn't the type to put it about. But he had a thing going before he married her, with—"

"Don't tell me. A barmaid."

"Right, anyway she had his kid, but Jeff didn't even know at the time that she was up the duff. He only found out after he'd married Anne." He paused, lost in reflection. "Now Anne was dead set on having a family," he said round a mouthful of toast. I recalled all the stuffed toys and pictures of her sister's kids dotted round her house and could easily believe it. "It never happened but Anne dragged Jeff off for all the tests under the sun. There was him wanking into a plastic cup to make sure all his little soldiers were alive and kicking when he knew full well that he wasn't firing blanks. Couldn't tell Anne that though. Not without giving the game away."

"Would she have minded knowing that he had a kid with someone else before he met her?"

"Dunno." He shrugged. "Jeff must have thought so. Anyway, the kid's mum asked him not to say. She'd managed to bring the kid up pretty well on her own and didn't want anyone else sticking their oar in."

"So why did she contact Jeff?" I signalled the waitress for a refill. She sashayed over and spent an unnecessarily long time bending over, giving me a good view of her cleavage as she poured.

Reg chuckled. "Reckon you're in there," he said.

"Must be my lucky day."

"Anyway, you asked why she contacted Jeff after eight years." He paused, staring off into the distance. "Apparently the kid was ill. Leukaemia."

"Ahh."

"Yeah, well, the NHS. You know how it is, even with kids. The treatment she needed was expensive and she wouldn't necessarily get it straightaway. It was possible for her to get the best of everything abroad but it cost money."

"And Jeff gave it to her."

"Every penny and more besides. He didn't hesitate."

"Did he actually have the money?"

"That's a bit of a grey area, isn't it. I don't suppose he did but then he was a bent bookie so it didn't really make much odds."

I wondered if the pun was deliberate. "Unless he skimmed off the top of money that was coming in from Garnet's scam."

Reg nodded. "Glad to see you haven't lost the edge, Mr. H."

"Is that what he was doing?"

"Dunno, do I, but it wouldn't surprise me."

"And you think Garnet had him done in?"

"Possibly." He shot me a glum look. "More than likely. No one crosses Peter Garnet. Not if they've got any sense."

"Seems a bit extreme."

"I've thought about it a lot and I suspect it wasn't meant to go that far. Garnet probably sent that goon Glover round to have a quiet word and things got out of hand. Glover ain't too bright but he does like his work and gets a bit overenthusiastic sometimes."

"Thanks for sharing, Reg." I didn't bother to ask him why he hadn't come to me with his theory at the time instead of letting an innocent man go to jail. He'd obviously been thinking about his own skin. "But it still doesn't tell me what you were doing at Miller's."

"I was getting to that." He paused to take a noisy slurp of tea. "Jeff was right taken with being a dad, even if he couldn't boast about it. The kid had the treatment and Jeff decided he wanted to do something more for her."

"Hang on. I thought Garnet caught him skimming and did him in?"

"Yeah, but only when he realised dosh had gone missing. That didn't happen until some months after the kid had her treatment. That's when Kendall tackled him. He must have heard word that Garnet, or whoever, was out to get him and went to warn him. Obviously, Kendall knew why Jeff had, er, borrowed the funds and probably tried to persuade him to save his own skin by telling the truth and offering to pay it back. Even hard men like Garnet tend to lighten up a bit when a sick kid's involved." Reg paused for breath. "It might not have been Garnet, of course. Jeff was involved with some pretty heavy hitters."

"A bent bookie's always in demand," I said with a wry smile.

"Jeff was determined to do something right with his life so he set some money aside for the kid."

"Set up a trust fund," I said, anticipating where he was going with this.

"Yeah, some dosh for the kid when she turned eighteen or if she had a relapse and needed more medical treatment. He went to Miller and had it all drawn up legal like and invested somewhere. If the kid's mother needed money she could go to Jeff or Miller and ask for it."

"And in the event that something happened to Jeff, you took his place as trustee?"

"Yeap."

"Why you then, Reg?"

But I thought I knew the answer to my own question. Spelling had to be careful not to upset his wife and keep his promise to the child's mother not to let on that the kid was his. Reg might look like a down-and-outer but he wasn't daft, had an old lag's code of honour and, crucially, no relatives to ask awkward questions.

"Just doing a mate a favour. Anyway, I went to see Miller at his invitation because the kid turned eighteen recently and the money had to be signed over to her."

"I see." I sipped my coffee as I thought it through. "You don't think Miller was murdered because he set up that trust with money stolen from his main client?"

"I doubt it after all this time." He added three spoons of sugar into his refilled mug of tea and stirred it vigorously, slopping some onto the plastic tablecloth. "Besides, I don't think he knows anything about it. Only Miller, Jeff Spelling, me and the kid's mother knew, and I don't imagine any one of us blabbed. But it shook me a bit when Miller turned up dead, and I needed someone I could trust to know about it." He shrugged. "Just in case, like."

"You'll be quite safe, Reg," I said, wondering if it

was bad luck to give assurances when…well, when I wasn't sure about anything to do with this whole business.

"If you say so, Mr. H."

"I'll need the name of the kid's mother. And the kid too."

"Why? You said this wouldn't go no further."

When he still hesitated, I pressed him. "You came to me with this, Reg, because you trust me."

"I suppose." He paused. "The mum's name is Sheila Randall. She lives in Hove." He rattled off the address from memory. "Her kid's a student at the university here in Brighton. Her name's Carolyn."

"Right." I made a note of all that, paid for his breakfast and gave him a few quid for his trouble. "Keep your ear to the ground, Reg," I said, putting my biking jacket back on. "Let me know if you hear anything interesting about Garnet or about Miller's murder. And you know where to find me if Slater keeps hassling you."

"Will do, Mr. H."

I left him drinking his oversweetened tea, looking as though he bore the weight of the entire world on his shoulders.

As I rode back to the boat I mulled it all over. Where did this leave Cleo's dad? This alternative information might cast doubt over his guilt but that wasn't much help if we couldn't put someone else in the frame. And we couldn't. I might suspect who was behind it all but that was very different from being able to prove it. Besides, I wanted the organ-grinder, not the monkey.

I decided against contacting Cleo with this latest information. Instead I spent the evening with just Gil and

Scott Joplin on the stereo for company. It was mild and
I sat out in the cockpit, staring at the sky as I thought it
all through, planning my next move. My options were
limited. I had information concerning Jeff Spelling's
activities that no one else knew about but which got me
precisely nowhere. Jillian Slater was still baying for my
blood and I also had the identity of the boat's saboteur
to uncover, Andrea Garnet financially in my debt, Paul
at a disadvantage, Mike Kendall's situation to sort…
oh, and Hal's problems that I'd promised to look into.

Retirement was turning out to be bloody hard work.

THE FOLLOWING MORNING I still had no clear idea what
to do next. My phone rang at just after ten, making the
decision for me. It was a subdued-sounding Paul asking
for a meeting. I agreed and at midday, Gil, Paul and I
were sitting at a quiet table outside one of the bars attached to the marina. Paul and I drank designer lager
straight from the bottle. Gil stuck with water.

By his standards Paul was conservatively dressed.
In his jeans and tank top, he would have passed unnoticed in a crowd. The designer shades covering his eyes
were the only indication of his flamboyant personality.
Although I had a pretty good idea what had brought
about the transformation, I had no intention of pulling
my little surprise just yet. He'd called this meeting so
I left it to him to break the silence.

"So, little brother," he said, a trace of the old, taunting Paul in his voice. "Here we are."

"Yeap." I leaned back, regarding him with a level
expression. "To what do I owe the pleasure?"

"Well, I thought you'd like to know that your colleagues came to see me yesterday." He paused, presumably expecting me to say something.

I didn't oblige, wondering why he needed to meet just to tell me that. Knowing Paul, he'd said something to drop me in it and wanted the satisfaction of seeing my reaction.

"A charming lady inspector," he said.

Slater being described as charming. Well, there was a first time for everything. "I didn't think she'd be your type," I said.

"I can appreciate beauty in all its forms. Doesn't mean I want to own it."

I didn't reply. There wasn't really anything to say.

"I told her I'd been away at the time of the crime, could prove it and knew nothing about it."

"You lied, in other words."

He reacted with a sharp intake of breath. "Well, you would think that, wouldn't you?"

"You didn't think your romantic attachment to the late Mr. Miller was relevant?" I stared straight ahead as I spoke but was aware of his sharp gaze resting on my profile. I expected him to carry on denying it but instead he merely shook his head, almost smiling.

"Nothing gets past you, does it?"

"Not a lot, no."

"How did you know? Jason hadn't come out. No one knew."

"You asked to see me," I said, answering his question indirectly. "When did you last actively seek my company, unless it was to cause trouble or to seek my help?"

He chuckled. "Good point."

"You want to know what the police know without

breaking faith with Miller by revealing his secret, even in death."

"It was important to him that no one knew," he said with a quiet dignity I found hard to associate with him. "And yeah, I figured you'd know where the police are going with this."

I quirked a brow. "Even though I'm a suspect?"

"Unfortunately even I'm having a hard time imagining you as a murderer."

I wasn't too sure if I liked this new, chummy Paul and wasn't about to be taken in by him. "Then you definitely want something."

He threw up his hands but whether to indicate that I'd guessed right or as a sign of surrender I was unable to tell. "How did you know about us?" he asked.

"Your framed picture. I saw it in Miller's lounge. Don't think I was supposed to but I'm nosy by nature. It was careless of him to leave the door open."

"The fool!" He shook his head, speaking the words with obvious affection. "I told him to hide it when you asked to see him. In fact I told him not to see you at all but he was curious to know what you wanted."

*I'll just bet he was.* "You saw him before he was killed?"

"No, we spoke on the phone."

I believed him. At least about that. "But you found the body and didn't report it. That in itself is a crime. The police lost precious time tracking down the killer because they didn't know anyone had been killed until much later."

"How the—"

"The crime scene pictures," I said slowly, as though

speaking to a backward child. "I've seen them and your silver-framed shrine is missing."

"Damn, you're good." He fell silent.

I left him to his cogitations, signalling a waitress for another round. Me buying Paul a drink. Who would have thought it? I watched him struggle to contain his emotions, feeling almost sorry for him. He'd removed his glasses to reveal eyes that were dull and lifeless. The dark circles beneath them suggested he hadn't been getting a lot of sleep. He'd clearly had strong feelings for Miller and was having a hard time coming to terms with his murder. I resisted the urge to tell him that he now knew how it felt. It also made me wonder if I was right to suspect him of having committed the crime.

"Yes," he said, his voice low and completely devoid of any artifice. "I must have got back not long after the murderer had done his stuff. It was a hell of a shock. All that blood. The smell." He shuddered, his face deathly pale. "Don't think I'll ever get the image out of my head. How did you do it, Charlie? Dealing with shit like that for so many years."

I shrugged. "You get immune after a time and tell yourself it's just a job."

"I threw up in the john until my throat was raw. Felt a bit better after that, got over the initial shock and knew the first thing I had to do was clear out anything that linked the two of us. There was that picture, a few cards, not much else. We were careful."

And chalk and cheese. A stuffy, middle-aged solicitor unsure of his sexuality and an overtly gay peacock proud of who he was. Opposites attract, I guess.

"But you still didn't call the police?"

"How would I explain having a key?" He shook his head. "Better to leave it. I cleared off again and didn't come back for several days. I couldn't bear to see…" His voice broke. "I couldn't bear to see his body being removed like a lump of meat."

"How did you get into the building? Through the garage presumably."

"Yeah, I parked up and took the stairs."

"Crap security then."

"The garage is only accessible with a zapper thing and residents are presumed to be upstanding citizens, entitled to some privacy."

I snorted. "Like I said, crap security."

"I probably deserved that."

I thought about all the grief he'd given me over the years. All the cruel things he'd said about my mother, even as recently as at Hal's party. "There's no probably about it."

His eyes were flat and hard when he looked at me again, a spark of defiance lurking in their otherwise lifeless depths. I could sense how badly he wanted to get up and walk away. How much it was costing him to come to me, cap in hand.

"You're enjoying this, aren't you?" he said.

I didn't reply. But he was wrong. He was hurting badly and I wouldn't wish that sort of pain on anyone. Not even Paul.

"I need you to find out who did this, Charlie, and why."

"You don't want much then. The police don't have a clue but you think I can crack it."

"I know you don't like me." His expression was as

close to being contrite as I'd ever seen it. "I suppose I've given you plenty of reasons not to over the years, but I was hoping that you'd be able to put your own feelings aside and—"

"Why me?"

"You've drawn a blank regarding your mother's murder but I still respect your instincts as a detective. If anyone can find out, it's you."

I was almost touched by the vote of confidence but knew Paul too well to be taken in by it. "You know nothing about my abilities."

He blew air through his lips. "In the early days, when I still had regular contact with the aged parents, it's all I ever heard from your dad. Drove Mum and me up the wall, it did."

"What?" If he'd told me I'd won the lottery I couldn't have been more surprised. "That can't be right. He hated what I did."

"He hated you giving up music but he was proud of your climb up the ranks in the police. Kept cuttings about anything mentioning you. Probably still does."

I shook my head. "Even so, why would I help you, Paul? You've never done anything except ridicule me."

"And why the fuck do you think that was?"

I was almost relieved by the reemergence of the old Paul. "Beats the hell out of me."

"You had it all. Looks, talent, a full set of parents, people who put you before themselves." He puffed out his chest, his expression glistening with resentment. "Even an old man who was proud enough to keep a scrapbook charting your career." He glowered at a woman unfortunate enough to bash her hip against our table. She opened her mouth, presumably to apologise, took one look at Paul's face and left without saying a word. He watched her go, then turned to face me. "I was jealous, pure and simple. There, feel free to gloat any time you please."

I said nothing.

"It all came so easily to you. Especially the music."

"Yeah and the more I practised the easier it came." I sighed. "Jealousy is for kids, Paul. You didn't need to keep up that vendetta."

"Perhaps not." His elbows were planted on his splayed thighs. He dropped his head into his hands and stared at the floor. "But it was either that or face up to what a prat I'd been. It's different now. I need to know what happened to Jason and why. And if that means baring my soul to you, then I'm even prepared to go down that route."

"What's in it for me?"

"Marianne's money. You wanted to know what I did with it. If I tell you, will you help me?"

I tried to remain casual but felt my entire body tense. "If I think you're telling the truth."

"Oh, you'll know I am."

"All right then, I agree to consider helping. That's the best I can do."

"Okay, I guess I have no choice then."

"Not much, no." Why wasn't I enjoying this more?

"Like I said, I was driven by my jealousy of you. It fired me with determination to make decent money. Give the old folks someone else to be proud of."

I didn't bother to mention what I thought of his doing so with someone else's dosh.

"I used some of it to buy my apartment. They were far cheaper back then."

"And the rest?"

"A racehorse syndicate."

I sat bolt upright and stared at him. "You have got to be joking!"

"Well, I always did enjoy the thrill of the chase. Besides, it was a great opportunity."

"But it obviously didn't pay off because you're now working for Hal."

"When I say opportunity, it got me noticed by the right people. People who could open all sorts of doors that would otherwise have remained firmly closed."

"Okay, so who are these paragons of virtue?" I had a horrible feeling I knew what he was going to say.

"A guy called Peter Garnet." His mouth curved. "I think you've heard of him."

I'd been stupid enough to think that Paul was opening up to me because he cared about Miller. The moment he mentioned Garnet's name, doubts surfaced. It was one coincidence too many and I felt sure I was being set up. But there again, was it so very unlikely? All along the way this had been about gambling in one form or another. And in this part of the world, you couldn't do much of that without crossing paths with Garnet. Anyway, I decided to play along, just to see where Paul was going with this.

"Okay," I said, ignoring his jibe. "If it was so successful, where are the proceeds?"

"I used them to start my own powerboat team," he said, looking a bit sheepish. "But it didn't quite work out the way I'd planned. That's why I'm with Hal. I still love the sport, the buzz I get from it, and want to stay involved."

Against all the odds, I believed him. He really hadn't used that money to have my mother killed. I didn't know if I was more relieved or discouraged to be back to square one.

"But you still run errands for Garnet, don't you?" I asked, looking him squarely in the eye.

"What makes you say that?"

"I'm a detective. It's my job to know these things."

"I still have a couple of horses in syndicate with him. When I was short of dosh and couldn't pay my share of the training fees, he helped me out."

"And he's owned you ever since?"

"Of course not!"

"Then why did you tamper with the stern gland on my boat?" I hadn't been sure that it was Paul, but the moment I threw the suggestion into the ring his expression gave him away.

"Garnet knows you've been sniffing round his business and doesn't like it. He wanted you warned off."

"So he had someone follow me?"

"I don't know about that." He lifted his shoulders a little too nonchalantly. "Probably."

Thanks, Reg, I thought without rancour. He obviously had tipped Garnet off that first time we met in the pub. Not that I blamed him. He'd survived for as long as he had by playing both ends off against the middle. If anyone saw us talking and Reg didn't cover his back by telling Garnet himself, he'd get a visit from Glover. Knowing Reg, he wouldn't have told him much. But enough to have someone follow me from the pub. And when that didn't work, to have my boat tampered with. It had to be one hell of a secret he was trying to protect.

"I'd say definitely," I said mildly.

"Well, Garnet never tells anyone anything they don't need to know. He got wind of the fact that you were going to France, and wanted your boat to break down mid-Channel. Just as a warning to stay out of his business."

"And he asked you to do it." I shot him a withering glare. "You did as he asked and then come to *me* asking for a favour."

"Have you ever met Garnet?"

"Nope, can't say I've had the pleasure."

"Well, if you had then you'd know better than to ask why I did as I was told. No one crosses him and gets away with it."

That gelled with what everyone else had told me about him. "That's still no reason. If I had been going to France it could have been serious. Do you have any idea how busy the channel is?"

"That's why I didn't tell Garnet you'd had a change of plan." He looked at me intently. "It's also why I didn't sever the bolt so it would snap when you were still miles from land."

I snorted. "Do you expect me to thank you?"

He ignored my sarcasm. "And it's why I made sure it would be obvious someone had tampered with it. I realised once you knew, you'd start asking who." He paused. "And that it wouldn't take you long to suspect me."

"What did Garnet expect to gain from doing that to my boat?"

"He didn't confide in me. But I guess he wanted you to know he was on to you. Garnet doesn't like people looking into his affairs." He paused to take a swig of his beer. "He's not too keen on them flirting with his wife either."

"They're happily married then."

"Oh yes. Cut from the same cloth, are those two."

"So Andrea isn't considering divorce?"

Paul spluttered with laughter. "Hardly."

"What about Tommy Mallet?"

"What about him?"

"He and Andrea seem quite tight."

"He's her minder, that's all. Peter doesn't gamble. He knows it's a mug's game but Andrea enjoys the odd flutter." He shrugged. "Peter doesn't like her going to the casino alone."

"I got the impression there was more between them than that."

"Tommy bats for my team," he said, smirking.

"Ah, I see."

"Andrea's a drama queen. She so enjoys winding people up. I don't know how you came to meet her in the casino, but if you thought you'd made it look accidental, I suspect it was you who was being played."

I nodded. I thought so too.

"Jason was going to join Hal's team," he said, shocking me out of my introspection.

"In what capacity?"

"The team needs a full-time lawyer and I asked Hal if he'd consider Jason. It would have meant he'd have to travel with the team and we'd have been together."

"But he'd also have had to give up his partnership and stop working for Garnet."

"Yeah, that was the stumbling block."

"How did Garnet take it?"

"He didn't know. Jason kept putting off telling him."

Which didn't mean he didn't know. Garnet seemed to have ears everywhere.

"So why have you been sabotaging Hal's team then?"

He shot me a withering glare. "I know you don't have a very high opinion of me, but if I wanted to start a new life with Jason away from all this other shit, why bite the hand that feeds me?"

"Well now, let me see." I flexed my jaw as I pretended to think about it. "If Jason sells out his share of his partnership in that fancy law firm and sells his apartment, I reckon he might be in the market for a powerboat team at bargain basement prices."

Paul laughed in my face. "You're way off base, little brother. You need to be of multi-millionaire status to even think about running one of those teams."

"Like Hal?"

"Like Hal and all the rich bozos from Asia who so love their gambling."

That surprised me. "Is there heavy betting on powerboat racing?"

"There's heavy betting on anything that goes by the name of sport. Especially if Asians are involved."

I conceded the point with a nod. I believed Paul wasn't responsible and switched to another tack. "Is Garnet hard up?"

Paul hesitated a long time before responding. "It's possible."

"Come on, Paul. I need more than that."

"You're still a policeman at heart. I'm not saying anything about his activities that'll get back to him and drop me in it."

"But you want my help."

"There's only so far I'm prepared to go to get it." He looked genuinely afraid. "Garnet's all sophistication and charm on the surface, but beneath it all he's just as much a thug as the goons that work for him."

I didn't point out that Paul was, at least indirectly, one of his employees. He'd already told me a lot, including confirming that Garnet was short of cash. Time to see what else he let slip. "What's Garnet's connection to Katrina Simpson?"

He blinked. "I've no idea. Is there one?"

His reaction was too swift and spontaneous to be a lie.

"But Jason knew her, didn't he."

"He was going to represent her at her trial. He was looking forward to it."

"So why didn't he?"

"He was spotted by one of his partners coming out of a gay bar. Real stuffed shirts about it, they were."

"So they eased him out."

"Yes, they knew that trial would get a lot of press and they wouldn't take Jason's word that he had no skeletons in his cupboard. They gave him a generous severance package and he set up on his own."

"So Katrina Simpson would have felt let down by him?"

"No, they only met once before the case was passed to another firm."

"I see." So much for that theory. "Any other clients from his past who might have held a grudge?"

"He talked about a couple of guys who didn't think he'd given their cases his best shot."

"Can you remember names?"

"Not really. He didn't mention any details, because he wasn't supposed to talk about that stuff."

"Okay, fair enough." I'd get Jimmy to check back on the cases he'd worked whilst in London to see what names popped up. If I'd been running the case, I'd have done that as a matter of course, but Slater might not have thought of it.

"So he gave up criminal work. Too much hassle, he reckoned. He'd spent a couple of days a week working from his firm's Brighton office for a number of years and had a lot of contacts here." Garnet amongst them, presumably. "As he lived here, it made sense to set up shop on his home turf."

I harrumphed. "He worked for Garnet and you say he gave up criminal work."

"Not quite the same thing."

I didn't bother to say what I thought of that. "Why did Andrea go and see Miller a few days before he died?" I asked instead.

He produced a leather-bound notebook from his pocket and brandished it in front of my nose. "If you agree to help me, you'll be able to find out for yourself."

"What's that?"

"Jason didn't really trust computers, and with all the sensitive work he did for Garnet, I guess no one could blame him. He got into the habit of keeping private notes about all his appointments."

"His appointments?" I said sharply.

"Yeap. It's all in here. Brief notes about everyone who came to see him for the past six months, including you. That's how I know you were asking about Jeff Spelling."

I disciplined myself not to reach for the book.

"You have to promise not to let the police see this," Paul said. I nodded. "It makes for interesting reading and implies that Garnet had a very good reason to kill Miller." He stood, handing the book to me. "Call me as soon as you know something." He waved as he started to walk away. "And make it soon."

# Chapter Twelve

I SOMEHOW MANAGED not to fall on a notebook that had to be pure dynamite and refrained from even taking a quick peek. Instead I shoved it into my jacket pocket and zipped it securely in place. If I was still being watched, I didn't want anyone to know that our meeting had been anything more sinister than stepbrothers shooting the breeze. I picked up someone's discarded newspaper and pretended to read it for the next ten minutes, keeping an eye out for anyone watching me. No one stood out, and since the people who'd been tailing me up until that point were pretty inept, it was safe to assume that I was no longer flavour of the month. I wasn't sure whether I ought to feel relieved or read something more sinister into it.

I finished my beer and settled the bill. Gil uncurled himself from beneath the table, had a good stretch and shook himself. He then looked up at me and wagged his tail, as if asking what we were hanging about for.

"Come on then, mate," I said, leaning down to scratch his big head. "Let's see what surprises your Uncle Paul has landed us with this time."

We headed towards the boat but hadn't even reached the gate to the pontoons when I changed my mind and turned towards the bus stop instead. It hadn't taken long for my insecurities regarding Paul to resurface. I told myself not to be such a trusting idiot and to think before I went charging it feetfirst.

"Help me out here, Gil," I said. "How likely is it that Paul would do an about-face after all these years of open warfare and actually put his trust in me?"

Gil wagged.

"Fat lot of use you are. *Not very* is the answer you were looking for," I added with a cynical curl of my lip.

Even though Paul was genuinely cut up about Miller's murder, I still found it easy to believe I was being set up. When I goaded him, he must have wanted to tell me to go fuck myself *so* badly. Asking me for a favour would be akin to poking himself in the eye with a blunt stick. But he still did it. It could have all been an act, though. Paul could be very persuasive when it suited his purpose, and if he really did still harbour jealousies about me, then he'd been handed the opportunity for revenge on a silver platter. Besides, if he was acting on Garnet's orders, he'd already made it clear that he wouldn't have the nerve to say no.

The only thing preventing Slater from arresting me was lack of proof that I was in Miller's actual apartment on the day he was murdered. An anonymous tip-off to the police and Slater would be back at the boat with a search warrant before I had time to blink. She'd be looking for this book, and the moment she found it I'd be in handcuffs. I couldn't really blame her. In her position I'd probably arrest me myself.

Gil and I caught the bus to Saltdean and headed for the bungalow I inherited from Jarvis. Kara, who'd been on my mind lately, currently lived there with her nephew and niece. She'd been making noises about buying her own place with the money her sister had left in trust for the kids. I'd encouraged her to do so. Not because I wanted her to move out but because it would be a good investment for the children's futures and would give them a much-needed sense of permanency in their lives. Kara and I had grown apart since she gained custody of the children. That was hardly surprising. She'd had a lot of adjustments to make.

Six months ago she came to me, asking me to help locate her long lost sister. We managed to find her, only in time for Kara to witness her murder. She'd now taken on two young children and was learning how to be a mother and hold down a career at the same time. The responsibility hung heavily on her shoulders, and she didn't always have time to fit me into her busy schedule.

She'd become very friendly with Anton, a guy who'd worked for her sister's husband. The kids loved him, just as he had loved their mother from afar, and I sometimes wondered if he and Kara were finding comfort in one another. If so, I didn't mind. Well, actually I did, but there was sod all I could do about it. Besides, I wanted Kara to have the happiness she deserved.

Kara was home and seemed gratifyingly pleased to see me. She greeted me with a prolonged kiss that I was more than happy to return.

"Hello, stranger," she said when I finally broke it.

Then it was Gil's turn. Their love for one another was mutual and it was a while before Gil stopped turning in circles, wagging, making soppy squeaking noises and jumping all over her.

"How are you?" I asked her. "How are the kids? Sorry I didn't call ahead. Hope I'm not interrupting."

"I'm fine, the kids are thriving and you couldn't have called at a better time." She indicated the kitchen table, strewn with paper. "I'm trying to organise an annual re-union for some of our lonely hearts." Kara was the co-owner of an online dating site. "I've hit a few glitches and would welcome an excuse to take a break, even with you." She shot me a cheeky grin. "But especially Gil. It's supposed to be a weekend of activities to suit all ages, and I'm having trouble finding the right venue at the right cost."

"What sort of activities did you have in mind?" I asked, waggling my brows at her.

"Same old Charlie," she said, laughing. "Still only one thing on your mind."

"Not my fault."

I let my eyes drift over her body and grinned. There was just something about Kara. There always had been. She was wearing jeans and a sleeveless top. Nothing special. It was the way she wore them that got to me. Her glorious red hair was pulled up on top of her head and there wasn't a scrap of makeup on her face but she still looked sensational.

She rolled her eyes as she filled the kettle. "What brings you out here? Not that you need a reason."

"I needed somewhere quiet to read something. And to store it."

"Then it's just as well that you came whilst school's still in. You'll get a bit of peace for the next few hours."

"That's what I was hoping for."

"Hungry?"

"Mmm."

I looked at her again and didn't say anything else. I

didn't need to. The next thing, she was in my arms and I was kissing her with an urgency that always surfaced when I was anywhere near her. One of the reasons I'd distanced myself from Kara was that I was as close to falling for her as I'd ever been with any woman since... well, what seemed like forever. And it frightened me. I thought she felt the same way and neither of us knew how far we wanted to take this thing. Not in the long term anyway. But right now we both only had one destination in mind.

And it couldn't wait, not even until I'd read that bloody book.

"Come on," I said, leading her by the hand towards the bedroom.

We tore one another's clothes off and fell onto the bed. That was how it had always been with us. With Cleo I felt affection and a mutual need for release. With Kara it was a very great deal more. She's intelligent, beautiful, funny, great in the sack. And she doesn't get seasick.

Soon, too soon, the only thought in my head was the cataclysmic climax building deep within me. We got there together and collapsed in a sweaty heap in one another's arms afterwards. I felt satiated to the tips of my toes. Boneless. Totally content. Completely incapable of movement.

I also felt a fiercely possessive, overwhelming tenderness towards Kara. The moment I admitted to that, I also understood then what had been lacking in sex with Cleo. She was great-looking, uninhibited and unselfish in bed.

But she wasn't Kara. It was as simple as that.

"Wow," Kara said, grinning at me. "I think we both needed that."

"Yeah, but it wasn't what I had in mind when I came here. Honest. I wouldn't have you think I only want you for your body."

"Even if it's true?"

"It's not," I said lightly. "You know better than that."

"Then why have you been avoiding me?"

*Ouch.* "I haven't. I went to Yorkshire with Harry and then—"

"How was your father?"

I grimaced. "It didn't go well. No, scratch that. I didn't handle it well."

She knew about the money and my suspicions. I briefly told her what I'd learned.

"Poor Charlie," she said kissing the end of my nose, her eyes brimming with sympathy. She knew how I felt about Paul as well. Come to that, there wasn't much Kara didn't know about me.

"Yeah, poor Charlie," I said, pulling an injured face.

She dug me in the ribs. "Don't push it! Now, what is it you came here to read?"

I reached for my discarded jacket and extracted the notebook. She immediately started throwing questions at me and it wasn't long before I'd told her everything about Cleo's problems.

"The poor girl," she said. "Fancy having to live with the fact that your father's in prison for murder. Especially if he didn't do it. Will you be able to help her?"

"I'll certainly try."

"Is she pretty?"

I should have expected that one, even from Kara. "She'd stand out in a crowd," I said carefully.

"Have you slept with her?"

"Have you with Anton?" I shot back at her.

"Okay, I get it. We don't have an exclusive arrangement." She swallowed several times and blinked rapidly. She obviously didn't like the thought of me in bed with anyone else. She needn't have worried about it changing how I felt about her, but I had no intention of trying to explain that to her. "Just so you know, I haven't slept with Anton. He doesn't come round as much as he did. I think at first I just reminded him of Jas. And the kids were used to him. It helped them to make the transition. But he's got a job up in London now."

"You didn't need to tell me that."

"I know how insecure you macho types really are underneath all that posturing." She grinned at me, apparently in control of herself again. Then she sat up in bed, cross-legged, completely comfortable with her nakedness. Her hair fell in a tangled mess over her shoulders, partially covering her breasts. I moved it aside.

"It's blocking my view," I explained.

"You've had your fun," she said, shaking her head so her hair fell back again. "Now tell me about this book. I'm intrigued."

I briefly gave her a rundown of all I'd learned from Paul, including details of Miller's murder.

"Oh no!" Her hand flew to her mouth. "You're a murder suspect?"

"Not a viable one and Slater knows it. But still, this little treasure trove might clear up a few mysteries and point me in the direction of the real killer."

"Come on then, let's have a shufty."

She scooted over and sat next to me, propping pillows behind our backs until we were more comfortable. I turned to the first page, which was dated several months previously.

"He uses a kind of shorthand," I said, discouraged.

"By the looks of things, it's just the initials of his clients."

"K.P. to sign papers for A.A." I harrumphed. "Makes him sound like a bloody social worker."

"Why don't we look at the pages that refer to the time period in question and then work backwards if we need to?"

"I would have thought of that," I protested, "if you weren't sitting there deliberately distracting me." I flicked a finger across her nipple to emphasise my point.

"Charlie! We only just—"

"Yeah," I said, rustling up an innocent expression. "And your point is?"

"You're insatiable, and we're not doing it again until we've done what you came here to do."

"You're a hard woman, Kara Webb."

With a put-upon sigh I returned my attention to the book, finding the page that related to Reg's visit to Miller. There were a couple of other notes for that day that meant nothing to me. Next to the initials R.T. was the entry *Signed papers to liquidate trust for C.R.*

"C.R.," I said. "The girl's name is Carolyn Randall so that bears out what Reg told me."

"Hey, you don't suppose the girl's mother murdered the bookie, do you?"

I quirked a brow. "Why would she? She didn't want

Spelling to have anything to do with her daughter until she got ill. But when she did approach him, Spelling did everything he could, and more."

"Yes, but we only have Reg's word for it that she didn't want him involved. She was a barmaid, remember. It can't have been easy bringing up a kid alone on what she made pulling pints."

"You have a point," I said. "If necessary I'll look into her background. But that's not a priority right now."

"I thought you wanted to get *your* Cleo's dad out of jail."

I shot her a look. "Not by exposing skeletons that have nothing to do with it. I'm ninety-five percent sure who murdered Spelling. Or at least, who ordered that killing."

"Your friend Andrea Garnet's husband, presumably."

"The idea had crossed my mind."

"And so, when he couldn't discourage you from poking about in his affairs, he set his wife after you. He must have heard how easily a beautiful woman can distract you." She shook her head, trying for a disapproving expression that didn't quite work. "What am I going to do with you?"

"Well," I said, "if you're looking for suggestions…" She rolled her eyes. "Anyway, who said anything about Andrea being beautiful?"

"Lucky guess."

"You're wrong, as it happens."

"Humph."

"Let's see why she went to see Miller." I turned to the appropriate page. "Hmm, 'A.G. signed papers to transfer G.H. to her name.'"

"G.H.?" Kara wrinkled her brow. "I wonder what that is."

"Probably one of Garnet's companies. If they're in her name and he gets his collar felt, the funds can't be confiscated. He's being cautious." I thought about it. "It explains why she went to see him on her own though."

"But she told you she was there seeking divorce advice?"

"Yeah." I feigned surprise. "A woman telling porkies. Who would have thought it?"

"It's hard to believe, isn't it?" She played absently with her lower lip as she thought about it. "But why did she feel the need to lie?"

"Because her husband sent her to the casino deliberately to see if I let anything slip. It means, of course, that they know about my connection to Cleo."

"Wouldn't that be obvious, if he knows you and Cleo are tight? You said you thought she was being followed as well as you."

"Yeah, but he obviously doesn't know if I really do have information from Anne Spelling and has no way of getting to her because she's left town."

"That's a good thing." She paused. "But would he really expect you to say anything indiscreet to his wife?" She frowned. "It smacks of desperation, if you ask me."

"We're playing cat and mouse with each other. He thinks I want something from him but doesn't want to show his hand too openly until he finds out what it is."

"Poor Charlie, being played at his own game."

I sighed. "Kara, I swear to God, if you keep looking at me like that you're gonna finish up on your back again."

She batted her lashes at me. "Promises, promises."

"Just concentrate, woman." I turned to the page that covered my visit. "'C.H. kept his appointment. P. said not to see him but if it concerns P.G. then it's best to know what he wants. Says he has info. regarding J.S. murder. Should I tell P.G.? P. says no but my first duty is still to client until I sever that connection.'" I threw the book aside. "Well, if Garnet didn't know about me before, he did by then."

"If Miller got round to telling him."

"Good point. They might have spoken on the phone but I doubt it. Not about something so sensitive."

"And Miller was killed two days later, before he had a chance to see his client face-to-face, presumably." Kara wrinkled her brow. "Do you think there's a connection? No, that wouldn't work. There couldn't be if he didn't tell Garnet what you told him?"

"I honestly don't know." I stared at the opposite wall, thinking it through. "But Paul says there was a reason in here that explains Miller's killing."

"We haven't read the entire book yet."

"No, and obviously I will but I still think that reason coincides with my visit. Miller was reluctant to tell Garnet that he wanted out. Perhaps he knew how the killing went down, actually did speak to Garnet and implied that I knew more than I did."

"Which would get you killed and not him."

"It would put us both in the frame if Garnet wasn't aware that Miller knew about the murder and assumed I told him. That would be clever, but dangerous. He was demonstrating his loyalty to Garnet and also using the opportunity to speak about getting out. I know all this stuff, I've always known it but have never said any-thing…blah, blah."

"Hang on, how would he have found out?"

I shrugged. "Same way as I did. He had occasion to see Reg quite a bit after Spelling was topped. They must have talked about it. And Miller wasn't stupid. He would have put things together. But when Garnet found out he knew, he didn't trust him to keep quiet if he no longer worked for him."

"But that would be privileged information, surely?"

"A word here or there in the right ear would be enough to get my former colleagues salivating. They'd been after Garnet for years and hadn't been able to get anywhere near him. And that was before he went all respectable. As things stand, they have no chance." I settled my shoulders more comfortably against the pil-lows. "Garnet knows that and would quite like for that state of affairs to continue. He can't afford to have skel-etons falling out of cupboards."

Kara grabbed the book from me and turned to the final page. "Look. 'Lunch with P.G.' Now we're get-ting somewhere."

"What else does it say?" I asked, peering over her shoulder.

"'Told him about visit from C.H.'"

"No wonder my ears were burning."

"'Didn't take it well. Cross-questioned me at length. Scared about what he might do. Told him I was plan-ning to resign from the firm. Didn't take that well ei-ther. I rather bungled it. He told me I knew too much about his empire and was too valuable for him to let me go.'" She slammed the book closed. "Well, that seems clear-cut enough."

"A little too clear-cut, perhaps."

"You don't like things being too straightforward, do you?"

"It's not that. It's just that I can't see Garnet offing someone so valuable to him, just on the basis of my fishing expedition to see Miller, which is all that it was."

"You said yourself that he's survived by being cautious."

"Even so." I fell silent, thinking it through. "Whoever did it must have been known to Miller. He didn't open his door to anyone unless he was expecting them. Or knew who they were. I had an appointment but he wouldn't let me over the threshold until I proved who I was."

"He looked after the affairs of some of Brighton's foremost criminals so I'd say he had good reason to be cautious."

"Talking of skeletons in closets—"

"Which we weren't."

"I wonder how long Paul and Miller had been an item, and if Paul was Miller's first male lover. I mean, he was reluctant to come out of said closet, which might suggest that he was only just getting to grips with his sexuality. That sort of thing doesn't matter too much to most people nowadays, especially here in Brighton, but his partners in the law firm might have taken a different view. It still happens."

"I think I see where you're going with this," she said speculatively. "If he liked to keep his private life private and didn't indulge in short-term relationships, then there could be an old lover whom he dumped in favour of Paul with a grudge to bear."

"Yeah, but most dumpees don't resort to murder." I sighed. "Pity that. I thought I was on to something there for a moment."

"But how would he have got in? Everyone on the CCTV has been identified and cleared."

"Except yours truly," I said grimacing.

"You will be."

"I wish I had your faith." I slipped an arm round her shoulders and gave them an affectionate squeeze. "But as to how he got in, that would have been simple. Just wait until someone opened the garage door and slip in behind them."

She frowned. "Wouldn't he be spotted by the driver who opened the door?"

"Unlikely. The driver would be concentrating on getting his car into his space and wouldn't have any reason to check his rearview mirror. Besides, those garage doors stay open for some time after the car's gone in. He could wait until the car was out of sight and then walk in like he had every reason in the world to be there. One thing I learned on the job, if people look like they belong rather than behaving furtively, no one looks at them twice."

"And there's a door from the garage to the upper floors, presumably."

"Yeah, and the lift goes down to the garage as well." I paused. "If I'm right and the killer got in that way, I doubt whether he used the lift and risked it stopping at the ground floor. Someone else might have got on. But if he took the stairs, the chances are he'd have got in undetected." I flashed a wry smile. "No one walks nowadays if they can avoid it."

"Yes, that makes sense. Have you suggested the possibility of the killer getting in that way to Slater?"

"What, and do all her work for her?" I pushed my hands away from my torso, palms out, as though warding off the devil. "Not on your life."

Kara laughed. "I'm beginning to understand why she doesn't like you."

"I can live with that, just as long as you don't stop liking me."

"That's not gonna happen. Believe me, I've tried to but it doesn't seem to work." She blushed, as if she'd said more than she intended to. "I'll make us some coffee, shall I?"

Without waiting for a response, she slipped out of bed, pulled on a T-shirt and headed for the kitchen. I heard cupboards opening and the sound of coffee beans being ground. I flipped through the rest of the book whilst she was gone and paused at a page near the front dated a month before the murder. The entry related to someone Miller had bumped into on the street. *D.H. is out. Accosted me today, making threats. Thought he had more time to serve. Rather unnerved me.*

Could this be what Paul meant about an obvious suspect? Was I letting my obsession with Garnet obscure my vision?

Either way, I had a more immediate problem to wrestle with. This book was evidence so I ought to pass it to Slater, even if I did so anonymously. That wasn't going to happen of course but there was nothing to stop me giving Jimmy a few pointers. I wasn't ready to let him abandon his check into Katrina Simpson on Paul's say-so, but he might as well look at this D.H. character. Apart from Garnet, it was the only real lead the book gave. Miller having dinner with Garnet so soon before the solicitor met his end was obviously relevant, but any competent detective could find out about it if they took the time to delve into Miller's final days. Besides, Garnet would merely say that they'd discussed his legal affairs over dinner and anything they talked about was privileged. To interview him would serve no purpose other than to put him on his guard.

My conscience salved, I picked up my phone and dialled Jimmy.

"Jimmy," I said when he answered. "You didn't get this from me but someone with the initials D.H. got out of nick recently. Miller unsuccessfully defended him and he held a grudge."

Jimmy, to his credit, asked no questions but merely groaned at the prospect of having to track someone through the prison records on initials alone.

"And you'd know this because…"

"A friend of a friend," I said, tapping the side of my nose even though he couldn't see the gesture.

"Yeah, right. Well, thanks, mate," he said. "I'll see what I can find."

Kara returned a while later with a tray laden with coffee and bacon sandwiches.

"Thanks, sweetheart." I grabbed a sandwich and wolfed it down.

"You've got grease dripping from your chin," she said, proceeding to lick it off.

I sucked in a breath, determined not to let her distract me. "Shameless hussy."

"That's why you love me."

"Have I ever denied it?"

"Nope." She grinned. "But you've never admitted it either."

"I can't help wondering if and how this all fits in with Hal's problems," I said speculatively, deliberately changing the subject.

"Hal? Your friend in Beaulieu?"

I told her about my visit there.

"You took Cleo with you?"

I nodded, realising too late that I should have kept my big mouth shut.

"So you have slept with her." She wasn't going to let this go.

"Kara," I said, placing my hands on her shoulders. "Don't do this."

"It's all right, Charlie. I understand." But the hurt in her eyes was telling a different story.

"You know how it is with me," I said, keeping my tone light. "I like my alternative lifestyle and have a phobia towards commitment. But," I added, meeting her gaze and holding it. "You're the only one who matters. You know that, don't you?"

"I said it's not important," she snapped, dropping her eyes from mine.

Which meant that it was. Our relationship mattered to her a great deal more than I'd realised. She'd seemed so concerned about her nephew and niece when she first took responsibility for them that I hardly figured in her plans. Now that things had settled into a routine, she was obviously rethinking her position. Or rather, thinking more about herself. And I was glad about that.

*Well, I think I am.*

"I could be sitting with Cleo now, discussing all this stuff. The idea of going to her didn't even cross my mind." I treated her to one of my rare, full-on smiles. "You're a great person to brainstorm with." It was true, we'd done enough of it when we were looking for her missing sister, and she always managed to see things from a different angle. "Besides, you make a great bacon sandwich."

She threw a pillow at me, and the moment passed without her castrating me. Or making demands I wasn't sure I was up to fulfilling.

"I also make insightful suggestions. Like, if this guy kept notes about all his meetings, where are the rest of the notebooks?"

"Good question. Jimmy didn't mention that the police had found them."

"Perhaps his partners took them when they removed his computer and files." She paused. "It was them who took those things and not the killer, I assume."

"Yeah, but Jimmy says they can't get near them. They're yelling about client confidentiality and saying there's nothing on them that would help their investigation."

"So how come Paul has this latest book but none of the others?" Her eyes flashed with suspicion. "Or does he?"

"I shall make a point of asking him." I drained my coffee mug and placed it on the bedside table. "The question now is how do I use what I've found out to point Slater towards Garnet without letting her know where the information came from?"

"Hmm, it's a toughie." She wrinkled her nose. "You also need to think if you've learned anything to help your lady friend's father."

"No, I don't. I'm no further forward in that respect."

"Everything comes back to this Garnet, doesn't it?"

"More than you know." I updated her on Hal's problems. We'd been distracted into a discussion on our personal relationship before I could do so earlier. "Garnet doesn't have an involvement there but Paul does, so it's much the same thing."

"You still don't trust him?"

"Not as far as I could throw him." I told her I suspected Angie Bradley of being one of the saboteurs.

"And she worked for Garnet?"

"Yes, and has a connection to Katrina Simpson."

"This is all getting a bit weird. And confusing. Who's Katrina Simpson and what has she got to do with Garnet?"

"I can tell you who she is, but what she's got to do with Garnet, I don't have a clue. Even so, I'm willing to bet that there is a connection."

"Want me to do some digging?"

"I thought you'd never ask."

"Okay." She grabbed a pad and scribbled down Angie's name. And Katrina Simpson's too. "So you think Angie could have done some of the sabotage, doctoring emails, diverting spares to the wrong place, stuff like that."

"Mmm, but she'd need someone hands-on to do some of the other stuff, like the wrong fuel additives. Still, she's an attractive girl. If she spun one of the grease monkeys a line, I dare say she'd get him eating out of her hand without too much trouble."

"I rest my case."

"Come again?"

"Oh, I intend to," she said with a potent smile. "You owe me. But what I meant was that you never seem to get involved with ugly women."

I spread my hands. "I'm responsible for that?"

Kara grabbed her pad and turned to a clean page. "Let's take these things one at a time." She wrote Peter Garnet's name in the centre of the page and drew a circle round it. "Spelling's murder," she said, writing his name with a line connected to Garnet. "We know he almost certainly ordered that because Spelling was stealing from him." Miller's name came next. "He didn't want to let him go because he was afraid of what he knew about his organisation." Another line linked directly to Garnet. "And now Hal's problems, almost certainly perpetrated by someone who used to work for Garnet." She was doodling now as she said absently, "He's like a big predatory spider, sitting in the middle of his web and drawing everything in that passes within his reach."

"A good description."

"We really need to find out what his connection to Katrina Simpson is. It must be something pretty powerful if he's going to so much trouble to wreak revenge."

"If it is just revenge."

"What do you mean?"

"Well, Paul said something that's only just clicked

with me. I didn't know that powerboat racing attracted such high rollers and so many hefty wagers."

"No, nor did I."

"Well, apparently the Asians are big players and you know how they like to gamble."

"Yes, half our football clubs have been taken over by them."

"Garnet's probably got a deal going with someone to nobble Hal's team. It also provides him with a timely opportunity to get revenge for Katrina Simpson, who obviously matters to him. What I can't decide is whether he wants to buy Hal's team on the cheap when it's had the stuffing knocked out of it."

"But you said Paul told you it took a multimillionaire to afford one."

I made a scoffing sound at the back of my throat. "Paul said it so it has to be true."

"Point taken." She jotted another note. "I'll research that too."

"Do you have time?"

"For you, I'll make time. Besides, it occurs to me that going to watch a local race might be a good thing for my singles."

"All those powerful engines will get your men revving their own engines."

She treated me to a droll look. "Very amusing."

"I aim to please."

"What are you going to do now?"

"What, right now?" I reached for her and pulled her T-shirt over her head. "You said something about a repeat performance."

Her beatific smile was almost my undoing. "So I

did," she said, throwing the discarded shirt onto the floor and falling into my arms.

"I REPEAT MY earlier question," she said afterwards. "What are you going to do about all this mess now?"

"I don't know. Talk to Paul again, I suppose. Read this book more thoroughly."

"Why do you want to leave it here?"

"Just in case I'm being set up," I said grimly.

"You really don't trust Paul, do you?"

"He's never given me any reason to."

She looked at her watch and groaned. "I have to go and get the kids soon." She paused, half in and half out of the bed. "How's Harry, by the way?"

"He's fine. He's with me this coming weekend." I suddenly had a bright idea. "Say, why don't we all go to Cowes for the weekend? It'll be like old times." We'd stopped there on our way to Weymouth in search of her sister. "And you can update me on the results of your research."

"You don't have to butter me up, Charlie. I said I'd do the research."

"Kara, I asked you and the kids to come because I want you to."

She looked at me for a while, as though searching my face to see if I really meant it, and then nodded. "Okay, that would be great. The kids will love it."

"Come to the marina as early as you can Saturday morning and we'll get straight off. I think they have a special event on at Robin Hill for the kids. I saw something about it somewhere."

"You're on!"

She went to collect the children but I stayed on for a while, going through that notebook. I didn't learn much else and carefully hid it away in plain sight amongst a load of other books.

Riding the bus back to the marina with Gil, I knew one thing for certain. I never wanted to cause the hurt I'd seen in Kara's eyes ever again. She meant too much to me and I felt like a prize prick for upsetting her. Cleo wouldn't be sharing my bed again. Nor would any other woman. What that said for my hard-fought indepen-dence I didn't have a clue, and I had no intention of dwelling upon it.

It was simply the way it was.

# Chapter Thirteen

I'D MISSED TWO calls from Cleo during my afternoon with Kara. I hadn't seen her since our return from Hal's. She'd been working and I'd been chasing my tail.

She rang again just after I got back to the boat, sounding in a bit of a state.

"I couldn't get hold of you," she said when I asked her what was wrong. "I was worried. I thought something might have happened to you."

"Sorry, I was with someone and couldn't answer my phone."

Typically, she didn't ask me who and got straight to the point. "Have you found anything more out?"

"Are you working tonight?"

"Yes."

"Come a bit early and I'll meet you in the pub. We'll talk then."

"Okay. Eight o'clock?"

"Fine."

She was already there when I reached Wetherspoon's pub, a glass of mineral water in front of her, a fresh pint waiting for me.

"Thanks." I gave her a peck on the cheek. "Sorry to keep you waiting."

"You didn't. I was early."

I'd stopped at the marina office on my way over and

picked up my post. I threw it on the table and devoted my attention to the beer.

"Cheers," I said, raising my glass to her.

"Come on then, Charlie, give," she said, not bothering to acknowledge the gesture. "Don't keep me in suspense. I can tell from your expression that you have news."

"Okay, there is something but I'm not sure what we can do with it."

Her face lit up as I told her about my meeting with Reg.

"It explains so much," she said, mulling it over. "You think Peter Garnet was behind the murder?"

"I'm sure of it. I just don't have a clue how to go about proving it."

"My dad's known Jeff's secret all this time but never confided in me." She shook her head. "How could he do that? He must have known I would have kept quiet."

"Perhaps, but it wouldn't have stopped Jeff getting killed or your father's name being in the frame for it."

"I suppose." She fell into a temporary silence, fiddling abstractedly with the drip mat in front of her. "There must be a way to use this information to get Garnet to confess," she said morosely.

"Unfortunately not. Reg would never repeat what he told me to the police."

"But the woman." She leaned towards me, eyes sparkling with determination. "The mother of the child. Couldn't we ask her to say where the money for her daughter's medical bills came from? There must be a paper trail to back it up."

"There probably is and I dare say she wouldn't mind

saying now that the child's grown, but it won't get us any closer to Garnet."

"Damn!" She thumped the table so hard that our glasses jumped. Several people glanced at us and quickly looked away again. They probably assumed we were having a domestic and didn't want to get involved. "There must be something we can do. It's the first solid lead we've had. Perhaps we can have another go at proving Garnet paid Mum's bills."

"Even if we managed to unravel all the false trails behind that company, and they led us to Garnet, it would still be circumstantial. Garnet would come up with a plausible reason for paying your mother's bills. He'd probably say he felt sorry for her and wanted to help."

"And come out of it smelling of roses." Cleo's lips twisted into a mirthless smile.

"Right. I can just see the headlines now. Local Businessman Comes to the Aid of Sick Woman." I made a scoffing sound at the back of my throat. "People like him who can afford top-end briefs always manage to put a positive spin on their actions."

"It's so unfair, Charlie. So bloody frustrating."

I briefly covered her hand with mine, conscious of the tears shimmering in her eyes. "Try not to worry. We're not giving up yet. I'll think of something."

We drank for a few minutes in speculative silence. I didn't mention my meeting with Paul. It didn't directly impinge on her problems but the connection to Garnet would probably engender all sorts of wild suggestions.

"Andrea Garnet," she said, brightening considerably. "She took a liking to you in the casino. If you worked on that, perhaps…"

"Perhaps what?"

She visibly slumped. "No, of course, if she implicates her husband she'll finish up on a slab too, just like Spelling."

Now she was starting to think straight. "Short of wheedling my way into Garnet's organisation, or turning someone on the inside," I added, thinking of Paul, "we're all out of options."

"So Dad will just have to stay where he is and I'll have to get on with my life."

"It looks that way at the moment." I briefly held her gaze. "Sorry."

"Don't be. It's not your fault. You did all you could."

"Something will turn up. It always does."

We lapsed into another lengthy silence. I flipped through my mail to avoid facing the disappointment in her eyes. A mobile phone bill, junk mail, something from Harry's school. And a thick cream envelope, hand-addressed and hand-delivered. My curiosity piqued, I opened it then and there. Cleo gasped when she saw me extract a printed invitation to Mr. Hunter and guest to attend a cocktail party that Friday evening at Peter Garnet's health club in Hove. A note written on the back, presumably by the man himself, said he understood his wife owed me money. He would be pleased to reimburse me on Friday and looked forward to meeting me then.

"Well, well," I said, thinking of Kara's analogy. "So the spider comes to the fly."

"What does it mean?" Cleo asked.

"It means that Garnet has something he wants to say to me in person." And I had a feeling I wasn't going to want to hear it.

"To us, Charlie, to us. It says to bring a guest. I'll get the evening off."

"No, you won't."

She glowered at me. "Why not?"

"Because he knows of my interest in your father's case. It might be dangerous. Besides," I added, keeping my expression resolute, "knowing how you feel about him, I wouldn't put it past you to do something stupid."

"Thanks very much!"

"You're emotionally involved. I've seen it happen more times than enough."

"Yes, but I know how to play my cards close to my chest. I bloody well ought to, given what I do for a living."

I chuckled. "Point taken. Even so, I'm afraid I can't invite you along." I paused, wondering how to let her down gently. "I've already arranged to spend the weekend with someone."

"Oh, I see." Her face briefly fell but she quickly rallied. "That's different. You should have said."

"I'll be in touch after the event to let you know what I find out."

"Fair enough." She glanced at her watch. "I have to run. Can't afford to be late for work."

I walked her to the casino, returned to the boat and did a bit of sleuthing on the internet. Then I called Kara.

"Charlie," she said. "Missing me already?"

"Hey gorgeous, wanna go to a party with me on Friday?"

"What's it all in aid of?"

I told her about the invite.

"It sounds a bit dodgy," she said dubiously.

"When did that ever stop you?"

She giggled. "True, but are you sure he's not setting you up for something?"

I wasn't sure about anything. "I've checked it out. There was a bit in the local rag about it. He's done a revamp of the club and this is the official reopening. There'll be heaps of people there. Besides, if Garnet wanted to do anything sinister, he knows where I live and could arrange for me to be abducted easily enough."

"Well, that's all right then, I suppose." But she still didn't sound too sure.

"Hey, have I ever led you into trouble? If memory serves, it's always been the other way round."

"Guess I can't argue with that." She paused. "What do you think he wants to talk to you about?"

"No idea. We'll have to wait until Friday to find out."

"I'll get Mum to babysit. She never says she can't."

"Don that sexy dress you wowed me with once before and pick me up at seven," I said.

"Shouldn't you be taking Cleo with you?" she asked tentatively.

"She's working."

"Oh, so you asked her first?"

I sighed. "I met her this evening to talk about her father, that's all. She saw me open that invite and said she wanted to come. I said no. End of story." I took a deep breath and softened my tone. "Even if she wasn't so keen to see Garnet taken down that she's likely to do something stupid, I still wouldn't have asked her along."

"Okay."

"Good, I'll see you on Friday then."

Whilst I cooked my supper I wondered about the

speed with which things were now happing. Rattling people's cages often had that effect, but I was only used to doing it with the might of the police force to back me up. Even so, seeing Garnet in company couldn't do any harm and I was way too curious to know what he wanted to even think about backing out.

The following morning I rang the number on the card and told the posh-sounding woman who answered that I'd be attending. She told me Mr. Garnet was looking forward to meeting me. I wondered how she knew.

After that I thought about giving the boat a thorough wash but then remembered I was supposed to be listening to Gavin play jazz. I climbed on the Harley, thinking as I rode the busy streets about all the things that had happened since I'd last made this journey. Gavin was slightly less suspicious of me this time and we enjoyed making music together. I even got a reluctant smile out of him on a couple of occasions. Progress came in many guises.

"Right, that's it for today," I said, after about an hour. "Do you want a ride back on the bike, Gavin? I'll drop you well short of the estate."

I was gratified when he agreed and threw him the spare helmet I keep in my top box. In my rearview mirror I saw him smile spontaneously when the engine roared into life. I felt good about making him…well, feel good about the things in life that kids are supposed to enjoy. When I dropped him off he actually asked me if I'd be there next week.

Friday morning came round. Jillian Slater hadn't come calling again so presumably Paul's intention wasn't to set me up. On the negative side, I'd been calling him three times a day since our meeting and hadn't been able to get hold of him. I asked Hal but he wasn't due on duty again for another couple of weeks. Where the hell was he? Whatever, I assumed he'd be at Garnet's tonight.

Kara surprised me by appearing two hours early, clutching an overnight bag.

"Hey." She climbed onto the aft deck and Gil and I competed with one another to hug her first.

I won. Just. "What brings you here so early?"

"When I told Mum about our plans for the weekend she said it was stupid for me to drive back tonight, only to return again in the morning. She'll stay with the kids tonight and drop them here tomorrow." She grinned at me. "So we'll have one whole night all to ourselves."

"Hmm." I pretended to think about it. "What are we gonna do with it?"

"Oh, I'm sure something will come up," she said with an angelic smile.

She wandered into the salon and glanced around. It didn't take a rocket scientist to figure out she was looking for evidence of Cleo's presence.

"She isn't here," I said quietly from the doorway.

She turned to face me, guilt in her expression. "I'm sorry, Charlie, I'm being a dork."

"No, you're not." I took her hand and pulled her onto the seating unit. "In fact we probably ought to talk about it."

"There's nothing to talk about." She snatched her hand away. "I know how you feel about these things."

"About being independent? About having no commitments other than Harry?" I asked. Kara nodded, not quite meeting my gaze. "Perhaps I've changed."

She did look at me now. "What do you mean?"

"I've been thinking about it since our last…er, meeting."

"Me too." She ran a hand along my thigh.

"Don't do that." I trapped her hand with mine anyway. "I need to be serious for a moment or two, say what's in my head and then you can have your wicked way with me."

"Sounds like a plan," she said with such a glorious smile that I almost shelved the serious talk and got straight down to business.

"Look, the thing is, I don't want to change the way I live. I really don't want to go back to the semidetached, the saloon car, the golf club…"

"You don't play golf."

"You know what I mean."

"Yes, I do. I sometimes feel a bit trapped by the kids. Oh, don't get me wrong, I love them to death. It's just that I hadn't planned to become mother to my sister's children out of the blue like that. Especially when I saw her murdered with my own eyes."

"I know. Life can be a real bitch sometimes." But I hadn't known, not really. I thought she was completely content with the turn her life had taken. I should have asked her instead of just assuming. "What I was going to suggest," I said, "if it's all right with you, is that we keep things the way they are—"

"Oh, I see." She dropped her eyes but not so quickly that I didn't see disappointment written all over her face.

"No, you don't. I was going to say, let's keep things the way they are, with one big change."

"That I stop nagging you about your other conquests." She grimaced. "Okay, point taken."

"Actually—" I paused, wondering how to phrase this. Wondering how she'd react. "Look, the thing is, how would you feel about becoming my only conquest?"

She snapped her head round, her expression so startled that I was tempted to laugh. It was obviously the last thing she'd expected me to say. "You mean that?" she asked warily, tears suspiciously close.

"You think I'd say it if I didn't? I'd have asked you before now," I said, realising that I meant it, "but I thought you were tied up with Anton."

"You should have asked."

"I guess I was afraid of rejection."

"Oh, Charlie!" Her laughter echoed round the salon. "Humility doesn't suit you."

"Okay, do I get my reward now?"

Relieved as I was that she hadn't turned me down, or told me to get real, as far as I was concerned that was all there was to be said about the arrangement. I moved the hand I still had trapped on my thigh closer to my groin. Things were stirring in that region and it was starting to become urgent. But I should have known it wouldn't be that easy to get laid.

"You're not doing this because you feel obligated in any way, are you?"

"No, sweetheart, and just so we're clear, I'm not making you any promises beyond an exclusive relationship. It just feels kind of right, so if you're up for that, let's see how it goes."

"Fine by me."

Even so, I could sense her formulating further questions and knew she'd want to analyse my suggestion to death. I didn't. Without giving her the opportunity to speak, I swept her into my arms, negotiated us both rather inelegantly down the winding steps to my cabin and dumped her on the bed.

"Now, would you kindly shut up and give me my reward."

"Gladly," she said with a specious smile that convinced me I'd done the right thing.

Only afterwards did I get round to asking her how she was doing with the research she'd volunteered to undertake.

"Not much to tell, I'm afraid."

"You failed me." I tutted. "How much of himself must a guy give to get good help nowadays?"

She punched my arm. "Do you want to know what I did manage to find out?"

"Sure I do," I said, idly tracing patterns on her breasts with my forefinger. "Shoot."

She reeled off a load of background leading to Katrina Simpson's downfall. Nothing I didn't already know.

"And I can't trace any connection between her and Peter Garnet. There's nothing on public record that I could find anyway."

I was disappointed but not surprised. "Never mind. Thanks for looking."

She couldn't shed any additional light on Angie

Bradley's involvement either, but she did come up with the goods on the powerboat teams.

"They are all owned by mega-rich guys, Charlie, mostly Asian. Unless Garnet's got hidden funds I can't see how he could hope to take one over. Not even a failing one."

"Perhaps Hal's has become such a drain on his resources that he's decided to cut his losses and write it off as a tax deduction."

"Could he do that?"

I shrugged. "I've no idea but anything's possible when you're that rich."

"I read quite a lot of stuff online about his team and they were a force to be reckoned with at the end of last season."

"But there won't be much team camaraderie this year if things keep going wrong."

"I would imagine not. There have been a few articles in the trade press hinting at problems within the team."

"And those sorts of rumours would be enough to start a whispering campaign." I levered myself from the bed. "Thanks, sweetheart, you've helped a lot."

"My pleasure." Still sprawled naked amongst the twisted sheets, she smiled up at me in that provocative manner of hers that severely tested my resolve to take Gil for his run.

I left her to make her preparations for the party to come. I knew she wouldn't take long but it would still be a damned sight longer than I needed. Gil and I ambled along the beach, giving her time. I waited for panic to set in about the commitment I'd made to Kara but it didn't happen. By the time I got back to the boat she was looking sensational in the clinging emerald-green dress I'd seen her in before, her hair freshly washed and curling around her shoulders in orderly disorder. I whistled, my decision to keep her all to myself suddenly vindicated.

"Going somewhere nice?" I asked her.

"I'm going with someone nice," she countered, giving me a hug.

"Anyone I know?"

"Stop being silly and get in that shower. We'll be late."

"Isn't that supposed to be fashionable?"

"I'LL DRIVE," I said as we made our way along the pontoon a short time later, Kara swinging a pair of killer heels by their straps. If she wore them to walk down the floating dock they'd get stuck between the planking. "Don't want you to ruin your fancy footwear."

She threw me the keys and blew a kiss. "My hero."

"You better believe it!"

"Oh, I do. I absolutely do."

"That's more like it," I said, slipping an arm round her waist. "A bit of respect at last."

"Ah, but it worked. You've offered to drive so I can drink as much as I like."

I whacked her backside as I opened the car door for her. We arrived at the club at seven-thirty, by which time the car park was almost full. I slotted Kara's VW into one of the few remaining spaces and took my time checking the place out. It was on the corner of a country road in a decent area just outside Hove. As well as the car park at the front there also seemed to be an extensive wooded area fenced off, part of the property.

"Probably couldn't get permission to cut the trees down and build on that bit," I speculated.

"Yes." Kara followed the direction of my gaze. "I looked the club up online. They call it their meditation wilderness. It covers several acres apparently."

"And makes the place more like a country club."

We headed for the door and I handed my invite to a monkey-suited lackey. He checked my name against a list and we were granted admission to an impressive atrium. Mature tropical plants dominated but the immediate eye-catcher was a plunge pool with attractive women wearing miniscule bikinis draped on swings above it. Steam rose from an unoccupied hot tub. I wondered if that situation would change before the close of play. My first impression of the rather straitlaced crowd made me doubt it.

One wall was completely taken up by a caterer's table, and waiters circulated with trays of champagne. Soft music—the sort of stuff I associated with lifts and absolutely hated—was being piped through hidden speakers. It reinforced my premonition that I wasn't going to like Mr. Garnet much. I already had reason to question his taste.

"It reminds me of the Sanctuary in Covent Garden," Kara said, grabbing two flutes of champagne from a passing waiter. "I reckon he's copied their formula."

"Is that what you do at these swanky places then?" I indicated one of the babes on a swing, pushing herself across the pool slowly enough to give the men beneath her a good view of her bikini-clad rear.

She chuckled. "You have no idea."

"Perhaps I ought to sign up."

"They wouldn't have you, Charlie, not at the Sanctuary anyway. It's women only."

I sighed. "Such a waste." I felt her eyes on me and squeezed her arm. "Hey, I didn't agree to stop looking."

"True," she said, grinning, "but then neither did I."

I followed the direction of her gaze. Lounged against a pillar, a couple of fit-looking guys were lazily assessing her with their eyes. I didn't blame them. As far as I was concerned she was ten times classier than any other woman in the place. But then, perhaps I was biased.

"Will I be letting the side down if I ask for a beer?" I asked, turning my nose up at the slightly warm fizz.

"Probably, but as we've agreed you're the designated driver you might as well save yourself the embarrassment and abstain altogether."

I feigned horror. "I hope we're only referring to the booze."

"Even I wouldn't be that cruel."

"Self-deprivation not being in your nature."

She tilted her head and offered me a sultry smile. "Well, there is that."

I put my glass aside and we circulated a bit. Kara knew a few people and nodded to them. The only familiar face I saw belonged to Tommy Mallet. We made eye contact and left it at that. Then I saw Paul. He'd regained his flamboyant flare and was wearing a pale linen suit with a turquoise T-shirt beneath it. I felt myself tense up as I guided Kara in his direction.

"Let the theatricals begin," I said quietly.

"Hey, little brother," he said. "Welcome to the lion's den."

"Paul, this is Kara. Kara, Paul."

They shook hands. "Pleased to meet you," Kara said politely.

"Where have you been?" I asked him. "You were supposed to be contactable." He glanced at Kara and raised a questioning brow. "It's okay," I said.

"I needed time to get my head together." He paused. "I went to Yorkshire to spend a few days with the folks, if you really want to know."

It had to be the truth because he knew I could check. It also explained why he hadn't been answering his mobile. There was no signal in their particular part of the back of beyond.

"We can't be seen talking too animatedly," I said. "I assume Garnet knows we're not the best of friends."

"I might have given him that mistaken impression."

"Cut the crap, Paul," I said tersely.

"Relax, little brother. This is supposed to be a party."

"More like a bloody wake." I cast an eye over the sober crowd. Paul and I appeared to be the only two men in the place not wearing ties. Some were even in dinner jackets. None of them appeared to even notice—let alone enjoy—the eye candy in the plunge pool, which struck me as entirely unnatural.

Paul grinned. "You have a point there."

"What happened to Miller's other notebooks?" I asked abruptly.

He didn't insult my intelligence by asking me what I meant. "They weren't there. He has a storage facility somewhere and kept them in it once he started a new one."

"Why?" Kara asked.

"Because he was a cautious guy."

"Does Garnet know about this storage place?"

"I doubt it." He shrugged. "Even I don't know where it is."

Kara dumped her empty glass on a waiter's tray. Paul did the same and took fresh ones for Kara and himself. He looked at me but I shook my head.

"Did Miller have another male friend before you, or were you his first?"

"Why do you ask?"

"I should have thought that would be obvious."

"Well, yes, there was one other. They had a long-term relationship. It lasted several years."

"Do you know his name?"

"I know the man. Miles Fisher."

"Miles?" Amusement caused me to temporarily forget about keeping this brief. "Who the hell calls their kids Miles nowadays?"

"A small price to pay in return for a sodding great trust fund."

"Not much love lost between you, then?"

"Hardly, darling," Paul said derisively. "I met Miles here at this club. He was with Miller. They were trying to look as though they didn't know each other but my gaydar was on full alert and I picked up on their little secret at once."

"And moved in on Miller."

Paul shrugged. "These things happen."

"How did Fisher take it?"

"Badly at first, but Jason had dinner with him again one last time, not long before he died as a matter of fact. He told me they'd worked it out and he was okay with it."

That must have been the cosy tête-à-tête I'd witnessed. I wondered about it. A man scorned was probably just as vindictive as his female counterpart.

"Didn't that strike you as suspicious?"

Paul shrugged. "No, not really. I know the guy was upset but…well, get over it, baby. It never even crossed my mind that he'd resort to murder."

"Do you know where I can find a picture of this Miles character?"

"I have one of the three of us somewhere at home."

"Cosy," I said, elevating one brow.

"It's not what you're thinking. It was taken here at a do, before I moved on Jason."

"Can you get it to me?"

"I'll email it."

"Did Miles know you were Jason's new significant other?"

"No. We didn't see any point in hurting him by flaunting it."

"Okay, that makes sense. Now, one last question before you start making loud, derisive innuendos about me."

Paul struck a pose. "What insults could I fire at you now we're so chummy?"

"I can help you out there," Kara said sweetly.

Paul chuckled. "I'm starting to like this lady."

"Why has Garnet asked me to come here today?"

"No idea but he's heading this way so I guess you're about to find out."

I followed the direction of Paul's gaze and saw a tall, thin, unremarkable-looking man with a receding hairline working the room. He was wearing a three-piece suit, tie, the whole works. It certainly hadn't come off the peg. He oozed insincere charm as he paused to greet people. The women appeared to love him. I watched for Kara's reaction but she didn't seem to be particularly impressed, which was good for my male ego.

Garnet was detained by another group and I didn't notice his wife approaching us from another direction until I felt a hand tugging at my sleeve.

"Ah, there you are, Charlie. You came."

Andrea Garnet was wearing a skintight red dress that was too short for her age. Her face was overly made-up, and foundation was settling into the lines round her mouth, emphasising the cracks instead of conceal-ing them. She batted her lashes at me and reached up to give me a kiss. Kara watched her with open interest.

"Good evening," I said politely.

"Isn't it too boring for words, darling," she said, slip-ping an arm through mine.

"There are some interesting people here," I said dip-lomatically.

"Interesting, bah! They all latch on to Peter like leeches. They're just out for what they think he can do for them."

I could see her eyeing Kara, presumably trying to gauge the precise nature of our relationship, but she didn't ask for an introduction. Kara stood her ground, even though Andrea had rudely half turned her back on her and Paul, trying to cut them out of our conversation. I almost smiled. Kara's a redhead. A genuine redhead. I've yet to see her back down from a confrontation and woe betide Andrea if she lost her temper. Before the sit-uation reached that stage, Peter Garnet joined the group.

"Paul," he said, not shaking hands with my stepbrother. Presumably big men like him didn't shake with the hired help. "Won't you introduce me?"

"Sure," he drawled. "Meet my little brother, Charlie Hunter. And this is Kara."

"It's a pleasure," he said, shaking my hand and then kissing the back of Kara's. I got the impression that she wanted to wipe her hand clean on the side of her dress. I admired her restraint when she didn't actually do so. "Kara? I don't think I caught your other name."

"She didn't offer it."

"Ah, a lady of mystery." Garnet accepted my put-down without missing a beat.

I wasn't sure why I did it. He'd be able to find out who Kara was easily enough if he really wanted to know. I guess I wanted him to understand that, unlike most of the men here whom I'd seen kowtowing to him, I was no pushover.

"I like that," he said, smiling directly at Kara. "But you haven't got a drink, Charlie."

"I'm driving."

"Then I admire your restraint. So many people don't stop to think."

When none of us said anything in response to his rather inane comment, he spoke again.

"Have you eaten? The salmon is locally smoked, and the devilled kidneys are a particular favourite of mine."

"Perhaps later," I said, eyeing the queue at the buffet. "When the rush dies down."

"In that case…Paul, if you wouldn't mind entertaining Kara, Charlie and I have business to discuss. I can call you Charlie, can't I?"

"That's my name, Peter." I suspected that few of his

underlings addressed him informally so I made a point of doing so. I turned towards Kara. "Won't be long." I could see from her expression that she wasn't too happy about me being whisked away by Garnet. I wasn't keen on the idea myself but needs must. "You'll be perfectly safe with Paul."

"No arguments there," Paul said, taking her elbow and steering her away from us. "I'm sure we can find some common ground. For a start you can tell me where you got that gorgeous dress. Is it Versace?"

Andrea opened her mouth to speak, but before any words came out her husband stepped in.

"Go and keep Paul and Kara company for a while, dear. I have things to discuss with Charlie."

"Why must you always mix business with pleasure?" she asked, pouting.

"To keep you in baubles," he said tersely, indicating the diamonds sparkling on her fingers. "Now run along."

I couldn't help wondering about that. Paul had indicated that they were devoted to one another. That exchange indicated the precise opposite but I tried not to read too much into it. I already knew she was a consummate little actress who enjoyed playing games.

"This way, Charlie," Garnet said.

Our progress towards the back of the atrium was slow. People stopped Garnet for a quick word every step of the way, almost all of them women. He introduced me to quite a few of their men, all respectable bastions of the local business community. He seemed to take particular pleasure in making me known to the Assistant Chief Constable. He probably thought a lowly detective inspector wouldn't be personally acquainted with the boss. He was wrong. I knew Bennett quite well and thought he respected me, so I couldn't understand why he pretended we were strangers.

"We get quite a diverse crowd in here," Garnet said, finally opening the door to an office somewhere in the back of the building. I'd tried to keep track of my bearings but behind the glittering façade the place was a rabbit warren and I was now hopelessly lost. "Women want to keep themselves looking lovely, and they persuade their men to sign up with us as well. Where would we be without the ladies, eh, Charlie?" He moved to a sideboard, picked up a crystal decanter obviously containing whisky and waved it towards me. "A proper drink? One can't hurt you."

"Okay then. Since you insist."

"Good man. I get the feeling that you're not really into all this champagne nonsense."

I didn't feel the comment required a response so didn't bother to make one. Instead I glanced round his office whilst he poured the drinks and fussed about with ice. Like the rest of the place it was showy. High-end furniture, leather settees in front of a fireplace filled with an extravagant flower arrangement. A huge polished desk with absolutely nothing on its surface other than a computer monitor and a telephone. And pictures absolutely everywhere featuring Garnet with some dignitary or other or at sporting events.

"Let's make ourselves comfortable." Garnet handed me my glass and indicated the sofas in front of the fireplace.

"Thanks," I said, taking a decent sip of my drink.

"Cheers." He raised his glass to mine and also drank. "I do so hate these affairs but it has to be done occasionally."

"You draw a good crowd."

"Course I do." He chuckled. "It's free."

"There is that."

"And talking of money, let's get this out of the way." He handed me a fistful of cash, which I suspected was more than his wife owed me.

"Thanks." I put it straight in my pocket.

"Aren't you going to count it?"

"Do I need to?"

"Ah, a man who trusts."

If that was what he thought, then he really had lost the plot. I trusted him about as much as he trusted me, which was not at all.

"So rare nowadays." He paused to sip more of his drink, still sizing me up. "Thanks for helping my wife out but I'd prefer it if you didn't do it again." The warning was couched as a mild request.

"Not if you'd rather I didn't. It's none of my business but it looked as though there'd been some misunderstanding with her credit. I don't like to see any lady embarrassed when it's within my ability to help her."

"Chivalrous as well." His smile would have caused a shark to back off. "There was no misunderstanding, Charlie. My wife has, shall we say, a desire for cheap thrills. When it comes to gambling there's no such thing, of course. The house always wins and it gets very expensive. She won't heed my warning to stop playing when she's losing, and so I told the casino not to extend her more credit."

"You don't sound as though you share her love of cards."

"I've been involved with games of chance all my adult life," he said, leaving me to interpret that any way I wished. "That's why I know it's a mug's game unless you're the one in charge."

He was right, of course. Too many people got caught up in it, my old partner included, with dire consequences. "It's okay if you have self-discipline."

"Which is what I count on most punters not having." He chuckled as he nodded towards all the pictures of horseracing lining the walls.

"I see your point." I drained my glass, placed it on a side table and stood. "Well, thanks for the drink. I'd better go and rescue Kara from Paul before he completely poisons her mind against me."

"Just a minute more of your time, Charlie."

"Sure." I sat down again, aware that we were getting to the real reason for his inviting me here.

"I know a bit about you," he said.

I feigned surprise. "I can't imagine why you'd want to?"

"Oh, I think you can. Good men are hard to find nowadays and I'm always on the lookout for trustworthy employees."

This time my surprise was entirely genuine. "You're offering me a job?"

"On a freelance basis."

"What could I possibly do for you?"

"You have useful connections."

"The police?"

"Amongst others. The word on the street is that

you're respected and people know not to mess with you." He paused. "Or it was, until you came under suspicion of murdering my old friend Jason Miller." I disciplined myself not to react. "You wouldn't tell the worthy Inspector Slater what you were doing in the building that day and she's now dead set on pinning the crime on you." He shook his head. "Mud sticks, you know, Charlie."

"Only at low tide."

"Ah yes, you're a boating man."

"What is it exactly that you want of me, Peter?"

But we both knew the answer to that. Stop digging into his affairs and he'd see me okay in return for not very much. The alternative was to finish up like Spelling. He was also telling me that he had reliable sources within the police force. How else could he know the details of my interview with Slater? But I also bothered him. He obviously thought I had more on him than I did.

"What were you doing in that building on the day of the murder, as a matter of interest?"

"I wouldn't tell Slater but I'd tell you because…?"

He laughed. "An honest man who's not afraid to stick to his guns. I like you more and more, Charlie."

"Glad to hear it."

"Since Slater's harassment I don't suppose you feel so loyal towards the police?"

"Don't presume to tell me how I feel."

"I wouldn't think of it." But annoyance flashed through his eyes and I doubted if many people had the balls to contradict him. "Now, about that job offer."

"I'm not sure I'd be of much help to you."

"Like I said before, I'm diversifying." He hadn't actually but I let it pass. "All sorts of information interests me if it pertains to betting of any sort. Information is power, never forget that."

*Yes, and you enjoy your power. You enjoy controlling people and making them dance to your tune, you arrogant little prick.*

"And what particular information are you after?" I asked.

"You're a friend of Hal Faraday's, I believe."

"Yes," I said evenly. "What of it?"

"So you might be able to drop me the odd hint about what's happening with his team. The likelihood of them winning particular races, stuff like that."

I regarded him with distaste. "Paul can do that for you. It's right up his street."

"Don't try hogging the moral high ground, Charlie. You're hardly whiter than white yourself."

"Why does Hal interest you so much? There are other, more successful teams."

"Yes, but Hal's is the most vulnerable."

I resisted asking how he knew that. "Why would I rat out my friend?" I asked instead, a nasty taste in my mouth.

"I'm not asking you to do anything illegal."

Like hell he wasn't. I couldn't believe his front but knew he was offering me a face-saving way to back off my enquiries into his affairs. Again I stood up. "Tell you what, why don't I think about it and get back to you. Where can I reach you?"

He delved into his pocket and handed me a card. "That has all my contact numbers on it."

"Thanks."

I turned towards the door but a picture I'd only just noticed stopped me in my tracks. Garnet and a familiar face leading a horse into the winner's enclosure.

"Pretty girl," I remarked. "Who is she?"

"Oh," he said, a genuine smile breaking out across his face for the first time. "That's my goddaughter."

Well, I thought as I followed the noise until I found the party again. At least now I knew the link between Garnet and Katrina Simpson.

## Chapter Fourteen

I TOLD KARA about Garnet's proposal as I drove us home. Her jaw literally dropped.

"You're joking," she said when she finally found her voice. "Why would he offer you a job?"

"Whatever he's up to, it's big. He knows I'm interested in him and he doesn't want me on the opposing team. I suspect that even he would draw the line at doing away with an ex-copper, which might be his only alternative."

"You've got him rattled."

I indicated and moved out to overtake a bus. "Evidently. Wish I knew why."

"So, what will you do?"

"That's something else I'm not sure about."

"Well, you were right about Miller having a vengeful lover. I'm surprised Paul didn't mention it before."

"Paul would have dismissed him as an irrelevance as soon as he was off the scene. His ego doesn't allow for competition."

"So will you tell Slater? About this Miles character, I mean."

"Not yet. Maybe not at all."

"Charlie! I know you don't like her but she is supposed to be one of the good guys."

"That's debatable."

"You don't seriously think she's bent."

"No, just incompetent. Anyway, I'll wait until Paul sends me that picture and think about it a bit more first. Besides, if Garnet has a mole inside the force, then he'll know what I pass on before Slater even has time to act on it."

"That's true."

"If Garnet really is looking for Miller's killer himself," I said pensively, "then he'll probably get to Miles first and beat the shit out of him, even if he's got nothing to tell him."

"Why would he care so much about getting the killer?"

"Dunno. Perhaps he's worried that Miller was killed because of him."

"Someone after papers pertaining to his business, do you mean?"

"I'm not sure what I mean yet." I paused to mull it over. "Perhaps Garnet knew of his notebooks. If he did, he'll know the police don't have them and that will worry him. It would explain why he was so keen to know why I was in the building that day."

"Be careful, Charlie," she said, touching my arm. "He's dangerous."

"That's why I said I'd think about his job offer. I got the impression that he wouldn't take too kindly to being turned down."

"No, I don't suppose it happens to him very often. There's something about him. Something creepy. Well, he made me shudder but the women there were all over him."

"But not the men. Did you notice that?"

"Now that you come to mention it, they did seem a bit reserved."

I told her about Katrina Simpson being Garnet's god-daughter. "And he's obviously very fond of her."

"So he wants to punish Hal for not testifying on her behalf and get his claws into his business at the same time."

"Yeah, it looks that way. And I do think he has designs on taking the team over."

"He's not hard up then? Well, he can't be, seeing how much he's spent doing that club up."

"Oh, I don't think that was him. In fact I'm sure it wasn't. He got a syndicate of local businessmen to finance it. Half of them were there tonight, with their wives swanning about like they own the place, which they do in a way. I heard one or two snippets of conversation about it."

"How did he manage that?"

I snorted. "Probably better not to ask."

"If he wasn't hard up, why did he stop paying Mrs. Kendall's medical expenses?"

I'd been wondering that myself. "I'm not sure. My guess is that he wound up the company they were being paid from and simply forgot about transferring the payments to another account." I shrugged. "Who was there to remind him? Cleo didn't tell her dad that they'd stopped. She didn't want to upset him so she just coughed up the money out of her savings."

"Why would he close that account?"

"I don't know that either but I suspect he moves things around whenever anyone shows too much interest in a particular undertaking. My guess is that he

has a whole raft of offshore accounts hidden behind
shell corporations. Either that or he transfers his ill-
gotten gains to his wife's name."

"I didn't like Andrea Garnet at all."

I chuckled. "No kidding."

"Talk about mutton." She shot me a reproving look.
"Your standards are definitely slipping."

"Hey, she's a suspect." I looked at her askance.
"Whatever it takes."

She pulled a face. "Not that, surely?"

"No, definitely not that." I covered her hand with
mine and gave it a gentle squeeze. "I'm a one-woman
man nowadays."

"Of course, how could I have forgotten?"

"Very easily, apparently." I placed her hand on my
thigh. "A reminder will shortly be forthcoming. You
have been warned."

She let out a soft, throaty laugh. "Warning duly
noted."

"What did you make of Paul? What did you two
talk about?"

"Well, he has a lot of issues with you, but obviously you already know that. He was quite subdued
but camped it up every so often because he enjoys the
attention. But I got the impression his heart wasn't really in it." She turned towards me in the snug interior of
her car. "I think he really is upset about Miller."

"Yes, I think so too."

Back at the marina, Kara changed out of her silly
shoes and came with me when I took Gil for his con-
stitutional.

"Charlie," she said, slipping her hand into mine.

"You didn't tell me that you played the piano again when you were at Hal's."

"I was railroaded into it by Gloria and half a bloody symphony orchestra."

"Paul told me about it. He was very scathing but I could tell that even he was impressed."

"Is that supposed to make me feel all warm and fuzzy?"

"Don't get all defensive." She slipped our joined hands into my pocket. "Are you still helping Gavin develop his skill?"

I kicked at a loose drink can. "Yeah."

"Why not say you just don't want to talk about music, Charlie, instead of going all moody and monosyllabic on me?"

"I don't want to talk about music, Charlie," I said. Kara dug me in the ribs. "Anyway, it's all your fault. You were the first one to make me play again."

"And you're not enjoying it?"

"There're other things I'm going to do very soon that I'll enjoy a hell of a lot more." I turned back towards the marina. "Come on."

I HOPED THAT Emily would deliver Harry the following morning and leave again before Kara's mum arrived with Sergei and Saskia. No such luck. Mrs. Webb called at first light. By the time Emily arrived, two redheaded children were tumbling all over the aft deck, aided and abetted by Gil, and I knew I was in for a grilling. I gave Harry a swift hug and swung him aboard. He immediately joined in the rough-and-tumble.

"Who are those children?" Emily asked, narrowing her eyes suspiciously as soon as I joined her on the pontoon.

"Friends who'll be spending the weekend with us."

"Friends?" She made the word sound like a contagious disease. "You didn't say anything about friends coming along."

I sighed. "Any reason why I should?"

"Well, I don't know. It's just that it would be nice for me to know Harry's friends too. Then when he talks about them, I'll know who he's on about."

She was fishing. Desperately wanted to know about my relationship with the children's mother. Or in this case, their guardian. And, law of sod, Kara sauntered down the pontoon at that precise moment, hands full of supermarket bags. How did I get myself into these situations?

"Oh hi," Kara said awkwardly.

With no other choice available to me I introduced the two women.

"Nice to meet you," Kara said politely.

Emily muttered something unintelligible, enough for Kara to get the message.

"If you'll excuse me," she said, "I'll just get this stuff put away."

I picked up her shopping bags and hauled them onto the deck.

"Who is she?" Emily watched as Harry threw himself at Kara. She hugged him back and then disappeared into the boat.

"Em," I said, exercising extreme patience, "it's really none of your business. She's not an axe murderer and that's all you really need to know."

"She seems to know Harry quite well."

"She does."

"Well, he's never mentioned her. Or her children."

"Perhaps, even at his age, he knows he'd get the third degree if he did. And they aren't Kara's kids, by the way. She's their guardian."

"Oh, now I get it." Emily scowled at me as if I'd just confessed to some heinous crime. "She's the woman whose sister was married to that gangster. And you let our son mix with her? Charlie, have you lost your mind?"

"Get over it, Em. I'll drop Harry back on Sunday night." I stepped back onto the boat before I did or said something I might later regret.

"Oh dear." Kara came up behind me in the wheelhouse and wrapped her arms round my waist. "That was unfortunate."

"That was Em," I said shortly.

My phone rang and I inwardly groaned when I saw Cleo's name on the display. I'd promised to ring her when I got back from Garnet's but had forgotten all about it. Other things on my mind at the time, if memory served. I didn't really want to talk to her in front of Kara but couldn't bring myself to keep her in the dark any longer.

"Hey, Cleo," I said. "I was just about to ring you."

I lied, telling her that Garnet merely wanted to repay me and show off his overhauled club. Sometimes it was necessary to be cruel to be kind. I didn't want to give her false hope. I'm not sure if she believed my watered-down account of events but she didn't challenge it. I promised to let her know if anything new transpired.

Typically she didn't bother to say goodbye and simply rang off.

"The women in your life don't give you an easy time, do they?" Kara said sympathetically as I snapped my phone closed.

"You're the exception to the rule." I gave her a brief kiss. "Now, come on, let's get out of here. If we get to Cowes by lunchtime, the small people can get rid of their excess energy at Robin Hill."

The crossing was smooth and the kids loved it. Kara's two were used to sailing with their mother and Saskia kept asking where our sails were. The boys giggled and told her she was stupid, which almost caused a riot. We calmed them down and Harry started showing off a bit. He demonstrated the wonders of the fish finder and then I let him pretend that he was driving the boat. Gil took a break from three small pairs of hands dragging him all over the place by wandering onto the foredeck. He slumped down by the windlass, big face turned into the breeze as it blew through his thick coat.

"He looks like a fury figurehead," Kara said, blowing kisses to the stupid mutt.

I'd radioed ahead to the marina and they'd arranged a half-day's car hire for me. We had a sandwich lunch on board and then set off for Arreton Downs. Robin Hill is a great place for children. It has rides, woodland walks, all sorts of animals and a great falconry display that the boys found awe-inspiring. Saskia talked us into four pony rides. We had dinner early and they were all tucked up, fast asleep, by eight o'clock.

"Peace!" Kara flopped down next to me on the aft

deck, a glass of wine in her hand. "And I even got Harry to clean his teeth."

"Blimey, what did you bribe him with?"

"You don't want to know."

I grimaced. "Probably not."

"Thanks, Charlie, it was a great suggestion going out for the day. They enjoyed it."

"So did I."

"I could see that." She rolled her eyes. "The kids are supposed to persuade you to go on the rides, you know, not the other way round."

I flashed a puerile grin. "What can I say? Boys will be boys. Never have been able to resist those things."

We lapsed into a companionable silence as Kara curled her feet under her and settled into a comfortable position against my side. It felt good having her nestled there and I draped an arm round her shoulders and pulled her a little closer. The mellow sound of Fletcher Henderson drifted from the speakers, enhancing the mood.

But in spite of the comfortable domesticity of the day, I hadn't forgotten about my problems. I'd been hoping that a weekend away and the distractions provided by three boisterous kids might result in a flash of inspiration. My best ideas often occurred to me when I wasn't actually concentrating on the difficulty at hand.

And I had plenty of those to wrestle with. I needed to get Cleo's father out of jail, me out of Slater's line of fire, and Hal's team back on track. Nothing as taxing as world peace or a cure for cancer but it felt like it.

It seemed to me that I needed to play Garnet at his own game, and a way to do it was taking shape inside my head. Kara asked me what I intended to do next. I wasn't ready to share my thoughts with her yet but there was one thing she needed to know.

"I spoke with Hal whilst you were putting the kids to bed."

"Has anything else happened?"

"No, it's a quiet period for the team. The lull before the storm, he called it." I paused to take a swig of beer. "How do you fancy stopping for lunch in Portsmouth on the way back tomorrow?"

"Why?"

"Because Hal's yacht is at Gunwharf Quays."

"Ah, I get it. Angie will be on board."

"She sure will, and on Sundays no one's on board except Angie and a skeleton crew. It's a long shot but I reckon she won't risk communicating with her fellow saboteur by email or phone."

"Especially if she's getting him to help her by trading sexual favours."

"Very delicately put." I kissed the top of her head. "And, since you mention it, not a bad idea."

"Don't you *ever* think about anything else?"

"Not when I'm with you."

"Thank you." She laughed. "I think."

"It's all this fresh air. It makes a guy randy as hell."

"Everything makes you randy."

"True." I drained the last of my beer in one swallow. "Anyway, if we hang about, have lunch somewhere that lets us keep an eye on the comings and goings on Hal's yacht, pun intended, then we might get lucky as well."

"Sounds like a plan."

"Angie didn't know who I was when she saw me at

Hal's but she looked at me like I worried her. You can bet your life that Garnet's found a way to warn her about me—"

"But if he wants you to work for him, why would he?" She frowned. "He'd think you're both on his side."

"No, it isn't his intention to let me know what he's really up to. He just wants to keep me quiet. Besides, I reckon he likes playing people off against each other, never letting any of them into the full picture. That's how he keeps one step ahead."

"He's not a nice person, Charlie."

"That's an understatement." I paused. "You know, I was thinking a bit more whilst you were on bedtime duty, and I reckon we're coming at this the wrong way."

"How so?"

"Perhaps it's a lot more straightforward than we're making it."

"The best plans usually are." She snuggled a little closer. "Tell me what you're thinking."

"This all started with Spelling's murder, right? We know he was a bent bookie and that he was helping Garnet to run his dog-racing scam. When he found out Spelling was skimming off the top, he only meant to warn him but his goon got overenthusiastic."

"Which meant the scam was over, unless he found another bookie to help him run it."

"Exactly. But I don't think he managed it."

"No, he got into horseracing scams instead."

"Did he? We don't know that for sure. Reg said he thought he did but that his services were no longer required so he couldn't be sure. But if it had been going on, Reg *would* know for sure. Not much gets past him."

I pulled the tab on a new can of beer and lifted it to my lips, sucking up the froth before it could spill. "I don't think the dog scam was paying off as well as he'd hoped, and horseracing cons are even harder to work. The dog world is notoriously shady but the horseracing scene is far higher profiled. Not only do you have to get a jockey to pull the favourite, but you also have to get him to do it so it doesn't look obvious. The stewards are down on them like a ton of bricks if they even suspect they're not trying, they finish up having their licences suspended and have no means of making a living."

"Don't they sometimes do horrible things to the horses? Give them stuff in their feeds that makes them slower, giving them water just before they race, things like that?"

"Not so easy nowadays. They do random drug testing on the horses, just like they do on athletes."

"So, let me see if I've got this straight. You think Garnet *was* hard up when he packed the dog-racing scam in but he's now apparently loaded. Okay, so he got investors to pile into his health clubs but how did he do it?"

"I've got a feeling he's an old-fashioned blackmailer."

She sat bolt upright and stared at me. "You're joking!"

"Think about it. Why did that party seem more like a wake?"

"Well, the men didn't particularly want to be there, I suppose. But health clubs are more a woman's thing."

"True, but they all know each other, the booze was flowing freely. That usually loosens tongues and inhibitions. But you didn't get the usual cluster of men talking about manly stuff whilst the women huddled together and talked about…" I looked down at her. "What do you girls talk about at parties, just as a matter of interest?"

"Charlie," she said, with an enigmatic smile, "what we talk about at parties stays at parties."

"Hmm, probably just as well." I tweaked her nose. "Did you notice the young ladies on those swings?"

"They weren't easy to miss."

"No, they weren't, but I didn't see many men ogling them." I shook my head. "That's just not natural."

"I'll take your word for it."

"I know their wives were with them but, even so, they appeared to actively avoid looking at them."

"You think Garnet got these men into compromising positions with the girls somehow?"

"It's an interesting possibility. Honey traps are amongst the oldest and most reliable forms of blackmail known to man."

"And woman."

"Obviously." I rotated my neck, thinking aloud. "If Garnet got men alone with them and recorded it somehow, he could then ask them for investments in return for keeping stum."

"Would he really risk doing that?"

"I think it makes a lot more sense than racing scams that no one knows anything about."

"Perhaps, but how will you go about proving it?"

"Ah well, that's where my incisive powers of detection come into play."

"In other words, you know someone who knows someone."

"Better than that, I saw a guy there tonight who I

know. We just nodded across the room and didn't get a chance to speak. I helped his kid avoid a drugs possession charge so he might be willing to talk to me, off the record."

She twirled a strand of her hair round her forefinger. "But if you don't think Garnet's into betting anymore, why is he so interested in Hal's team that he'd try to destroy it?"

"For his goddaughter's sake. Like I said, the only time I saw a genuine smile on his face was when he looked at her picture. He probably believes she was having an affair and the guy persuaded her to lift the money so they could make a life together. Hal told me the guy's wife is loaded. She introduced all the money into their marriage and if he left her, she'd take him to the cleaners and alienate him from his kids. The guy's job probably wouldn't survive the fallout and having got used to the high life he wouldn't fancy slumming it."

"So he set it up but covered his own back."

"Exactly. If the affair did take place then he was clever. When the axe fell it looked as though Katrina Simpson had acted alone."

Kara wrinkled her nose. "What a charmer!"

"Hal agonised over it. He said he couldn't blame his mate if there was an affair because his wife's a real ballbreaker. But he had no firm evidence, just an overheard conversation that he could easily have misinterpreted. And you don't destroy marriages and careers because you suspect all is not well in paradise."

"Do you think Garnet asking you to tattle on Hal is just a smoke screen? He's testing your loyalty by putting you up against your mate."

"It looks that way."

She frowned. "But this thing about destroying Hal. I don't buy it, Charlie. He might love his goddaughter but it's a hell of a lot of effort just to gain revenge."

"Ah, but we're not talking about a normal person here. Garnet's a megalomaniac. Everything has to be on his terms. Cross anyone he loves and he takes it personally."

"Hmm." She covered her mouth with her hand and yawned. "Sea air always makes me sleepy."

"Not too sleepy to play, I hope," I said, pulling her to her feet.

"Never."

Her mouth, warm and mobile beneath mine as I bent to kiss her, assuaged all doubts on that front.

WE STRETCHED OUT our lunch the following day until the kids started to bicker, earning us censorious glances from other diners. The restaurant we'd chosen was part of the shopping complex just outside the marina gates. We could see the *Glorianna,* which was attracting a lot of attention from passersby, but weren't close enough to see if anyone was on board. Still, if and when someone left, he'd have to come through the marina gates, and I hoped to recognise whoever. It seemed a bit tenuous but stranger things have been known to happen. Besides, we had to eat somewhere.

As I paid the bill, distracted for a moment as I tried to stop Harry and Sergei squirting ketchup at each other, someone emerged from the *Glorianna.* I only caught a glimpse of him as he slunk through the gates. He was obviously trying to look inconspicuous with a hood pulled over his head when the day was warm. It made him stand out and aroused my suspicions.

"Is that him?" Kara asked.

"Not sure. It could be. His features aren't that clear but I think…"

As soon as he turned the corner into the shopping centre and pulled his hood down I recognised him. He'd been at Hal's party. A junior member of the maintenance team, perfectly placed to do Angie's dirty work. I snapped off a few shots of his profile on my mobile.

"That's him," I said. "Don't remember his name but Hal will know who he is."

"Aren't you going to email that picture straight to him?" Kara asked as she shepherded the kids through the restaurant door.

"Not immediately, no. Garnet probably suspects Hal's asked me to look into things, and if Angie and her mate get the push he'll know who orchestrated their downfall. I don't want him to think I'm actively working against him—at least not yet." I lifted Saskia aboard the *No Comment* and whistled to Gil, who was paying a little too much attention to a female beagle.

"What will you do next then?" Kara asked.

"I'm going to start by talking to that guy I recognised at the club."

# Chapter Fifteen

I DIDN'T HAVE Gerry Binder's number but it wasn't difficult to find in the local directory. He had a massive
double glazing business that was bucking the recession. A lot of home improvement businesses apparently
were. People weren't moving but upgrading their exist-
ing properties instead. Every lining has a silver cloud.

I got through to Gerry's PA, gave my name, said it
was personal and was told he'd get back to me. He rang
less than an hour later.

"Charlie, how the hell are you?" he asked.

"Good. And you?"

"I saw you at that god-awful shindig the other night,
but when I looked for you again you were gone." He
chuckled. "Not that I blame you if you were with that
redhead."

"How's it going, Gerry?"

"Well, you know, I'm scraping by." He paused and
I heard someone in the background asking him something. "Sorry about that," he said, coming back on the
line. "Now, what can I do for you?"

"I wondered if you could spare half an hour for a
beer sometime. There's something I need to ask you."

"The local nick in need of double glazing, is it?" he
asked hopefully.

"Hardly. Besides, some toe-rag would probably lift

it before it could even be installed. Anyway, I got out of that line of work a while back."

"Can't say as I blame you. All that abuse. Never could understand why anyone would want to be an officer of the law."

"I'm starting to come round to that point of view myself."

We arranged to meet at the marina later that day. He'd tried to get me to say what it was about but I didn't want to frighten him off by giving any clues. I had a feeling he might already suspect the truth, given the way we danced round the issue of the party by only giving it a passing mention.

I was waiting for him when he arrived that evening, ten minutes late.

"Sorry, Charlie," he said. "Bloody customers kept changing their minds about the frames they want. I ask you, how hard can it be? It's enough to drive you to drink. Talking of which, what're you having."

"It's my shout. I asked to meet."

"Forget it." He attracted the barmaid's attention and pointed to my half-empty glass. "Another of whatever that was and a pint of special for me, please."

We took our drinks to a quiet corner table. "How's Andy?" I asked.

"Doing great. He's at university now, in his final year and straight as a die, thanks to you."

"I didn't do anything."

"You put the fear of God into him. He realised the error of his ways and dropped the bad crowd he was mixing with." He paused. "At the time it seemed like

the end of the world but I can see now that it was probably the best thing that could have happened to him."

I waved aside his gratitude. "I have a young son of
my own. If he got into bad company, I'd like to think
that someone would take the time to set him straight."

"Yeah, well, any time I can do something for you,
you have but to ask."

"That's why we're here." I paused to take a sup of
beer. "Peter Garnet," I said, watching him closely.

"Ah." He slowly replaced his glass on the table and
met my gaze. "I thought it might be."

"What can you tell me about him?"

"Why do you want to know? I'll tell you what I can,
provided you really are no longer a policeman?"

"I really am no longer a policeman. Cross my heart."

He chuckled. "Just checking."

"Tell me how you got involved with Garnet."

"I rue the bloody day," he said with feeling. "The
man's bad news and you'd be well advised to steer well
clear. He looks like butter wouldn't melt but beneath
that smarmy exterior he's as hard as fucking nails." He
picked up his glass again but didn't drink. "You still
haven't told me why you're asking about him."

"I do a bit of freelance investigating for individuals
nowadays, and his name came up."

"The women love him." He spread his hands. "They
get primped and pampered at his fancy club, and he knows
just how to keep them on his side. But you won't find too
many men who have a good word to say for him."

"Yourself included, it seems."

He saluted me with his glass. "You obviously haven't
lost your touch."

"And yet you invested in his revamped club."

His glass hit the table so hard that beer sloshed over its rim. "How the fuck did you know that?"

"You just told me."

He realised his mistake and grimaced. "Well, it seemed like a good opportunity. I might not like the guy but business is business."

I leaned back in my chair and grinned at him. "Bullshit!"

"I beg your pardon."

"Look, Gerry, you said you owed me a favour so how about cutting the crap and being straight with me?"

"There's nothing sinister about it," he said defensively.

I allowed an uncomfortable silence to lengthen between us. If he was desperate to keep his indiscretion from his wife and invested in the business of a man he despised for that reason, he was obviously going to be cautious about opening up. Especially to me, what with my connections to the establishment.

"Let me hit you with a hypothetical situation then," I said, sitting forward and leaning my elbows on the table. "I go, in all innocence, for massage at a new club because my wife's nagged me into it. She says it's a great place, everyone who matters is joining, and they're offering a special deal to get more men to sign up. I'm stressed out. I work too hard. It'll do me the world of good. I go to shut her up, expecting a twenty-stone Swedish masseur to pummel the life out of me. Instead I get a gorgeous babe who's willing to rub a great deal more than my back." I glance up at him. "How am I doing so far?"

He didn't answer me but then he didn't need to. His expression said it all.

"Afterwards I feel great. A bit guilty but, hey, it was just a blow job. No one needs to know. But then I start getting pictures in the post, sent to the office, marked for my personal attention. Damaging pictures of my pecker in this nearly naked woman's mouth, making it look a damned sight worse than it actually was. Hell, the woman's not wearing much but what she is wearing differs from picture to picture, as though it's been going on for some time. I'm terrified that the next picture will finish up on my home doormat. Then there'll be hell to pay. My wife doesn't have a forgiving nature, and I can't afford a divorce. Heck, I don't want a divorce. So, when I'm invited to partake of a good business opportunity, I don't really have a lot of choice." I focused my eyes on his face, which he'd turned slightly away from me. "But that doesn't mean I'm happy about it. Well, who would be? No one likes a blackmailer."

I stopped talking and waited out the silence. Finally he broke it.

"Hypothetically speaking, I guess it could happen that way," he said. "If a couple's relationship was under strain because their only son had been experimenting with drugs. If the mother wanted to mollycoddle him and the father wanted to go down the tough-love route, it's easy enough to imagine him being a bit frustrated because the wife was no longer giving out."

"How much would he need to invest to buy the blackmailer's silence?"

"I should imagine something in the region of two hundred grand."

I let out a soft whistle. "That much?"

"If he had a going business then it might even be a shrewd investment," Gerry said, guilt making him sound even more defensive.

"How many people would our slimeball need to snare?"

"That I couldn't say. Not even hypothetically. Judging by the way that none of the men wanted to be there the other night and certainly didn't want to talk about their investment, I'd say as many as fifteen."

A cool three million then. "But the women love being able to say that they're investors in the club. That's clever."

"Garnet gives them a special category of membership. All sorts of perks not available to the general mob that they can boast about to their friends," Gerry said, giving up all pretence. "It makes me sick to the stomach to be in the same room as the prick." He paused, staring into the depths of his glass as though seeking inspiration there. "And another thing. He's given that club a superficial makeover, imported that jungle you saw in the atrium and made a flashy reception area, but I can't see that he's done much to the rest of it other than slap on a fresh coat of paint in the places that show."

"You don't think he used the money for the intended purpose then?"

Gerry shrugged. "Beats the hell out of me. If he doesn't want anyone to know what he's doing, then no one will find out. Not if they value their health. He'll produce invoices and stuff to satisfy his accountant but I doubt if they'll be kosher, and you can bet your life that no one will cross-question him. He's not the sort you accuse of being bent."

So, if he didn't want the money to refurbish his clubs, what was it for?

"There must have been some marks who told him to fuck off," I said. "Not everyone would care about being caught with their pants down. Some couples do have open marriages."

"Yeah, but he could still embarrass the bloke by letting the pictures fall into the wrong hands. His business competitors, his mother-in-law, or whoever. I doubt whether people would risk that sort of…er, exposure." His derisive laugh was devoid of all humour. "Easier to pay up and shut up."

"That's what blackmailers depend on." I took a long swallow of beer. "They seldom stop at one hit either."

"I think this one will. He's not stupid. He knows it's not our own money he's taking but that it belongs to our businesses. I don't have a partner to justify it to but I'm pretty sure some of the others he's tapped do. Christ knows how they've managed to pass it off as a good investment. As it was, I had to go against our solicitor's advice and sign the contract when he picked all sorts of holes in it and advised me not to."

"I take it the contract doesn't allow for a very beneficial return on your investment."

He shot me a look. "It's what you might call open to interpretation. I certainly don't expect to see my money again." This time his laugh was a little more genuine. "The most expensive blow job I ever got, that's for sure."

"Well, thanks for telling me. I know it wasn't easy

to admit that you've been played. But I enjoyed our hypothetical chat."

"Actually, it was a relief to talk about it."

"Confession is good for the soul, so the navel-gazers would have us believe."

"Yeah." He drained his glass and stood up. "I haven't asked you why you want to know all this and I'm not going to. Just get the bastard and bring him down, Charlie. I assume that's your intention." I nodded. "Well, good for you but for God's sake watch your back. This guy doesn't play by the rules."

I snorted. "Tell me something I don't know."

I WENT BACK to the boat, collected Gil and went off for a long walk. I spent an hour trying to convince myself there had to be another way forward other than the one that had lodged itself in my brain. When we returned I was no nearer to finding it. Having attended to Gil's culinary needs, I threw a sandwich together and retreated to the wheelhouse, still trying to figure out why Garnet needed money so badly that he was prepared to resort to blackmailing some of Brighton's leading businessmen.

His dog-racing scam had failed and he'd been short of cash. Well, short by his standards. I suspected that he'd still had more than enough to satisfy the average person's needs. But there was nothing average about Garnet. His blackmailing activities must have involved Miller, at least inasmuch as he would have drawn up the contracts for his marks to sign. He might not have known how Garnet was blackmailing them, but he would have known that no sane businessman would sign such one-sided contracts without coercion. Perhaps some of the entries in his latest notebook pertained to those dealings.

I opened a can of beer and leaned back with my feet up on my desk, pondering. Whatever he was doing, I was willing to bet that Garnet was doing it from his health club in Hove. It now appeared to be the hub of his operation and, unlike his nightclubs, was situated outside the city away from prying eyes. Still, there was only one way to be sure. I'd have to do what I'd spent the evening trying to talk myself out of doing and go there again myself. He'd invited me to try the place out anytime I liked. I didn't like, not one little bit, but I had no choice. It was either that or wait for Slater to find a way to fit me up for Miller's murder. With Slater on my mind I called Jimmy's mobile to see what progress he'd made with the mysterious D.H.

"Waste of fucking time, mate," he told me. "The guy was released from the slammer a month or so before Miller was topped. Miller defended him on attempted murder. Almost ripped the head off his wife's lover, he did. He was found guilty and started shouting about Miller not putting up the right witnesses. Told anyone who'd listen that he'd be made to pay."

"He sounds likely. Good for you, mate."

"Good for fuck all. He was back inside when Miller got done. Violated his parole."

"Ah. Don't suppose he contracted the job out?"

"I'm looking into it but I don't think so."

"Sorry about that."

"Yeah, so am I. Katrina Simpson is looking like a dead end too."

I could hear the frustration in his voice. He desperately wanted to get one over Slater. I wanted that too and not just because it would enhance Jimmy's career.

"Any other bright ideas?" he asked.

"I assume you're tracing Miller's final activities," I said, thinking of his dinner with Garnet.

"Well, Slater isn't exactly making it a priority."

I didn't need him to tell me what, or who, was top of her list. "I gather Miller liked to eat at the Rainbow," I told him.

"Gotcha! Thanks, mate."

"Keep in touch," I said before breaking the connection.

I phoned Garnet's club the following morning, before I could change my mind. The receptionist recognised my name—Mr. Garnet had told her to expect my call, apparently. She said it would be fine for me to use any of the club's facilities that day and would I like her to book me in for a massage? I said that I would.

It occurred to me as I rode the bike towards Hove, my gym gear stored in the top box, that I ought to have left word with someone about where I was going. Just in case. But who could I have told? Cleo didn't need to know about my suspicions. I didn't want to put her in harm's way. And Kara would probably have insisted upon coming with me. I hadn't forgotten the shit she dropped me in when she impulsively followed her sister into the lion's den. That wasn't what I was doing now. I was merely accepting an offer of a free workout and massage. Who wouldn't? Besides, Garnet still thought I was considering his offer. I wasn't in any danger.

Upon arrival an attractive employee was standing by to give me a guided tour of all the bits I hadn't seen during the party. Once again the swings above the pool were in use but this time their occupants wouldn't exactly stop traffic. An overweight middle-aged woman and two gangly teenagers. I was shown the gym stocked with state-of-the-art equipment, a swimming pool intended for serious use, and a long line of closed doors behind which a bewildering array of treatments apparently took place. What the fuck was a seaweed wrap, anyway?

My lovely guide pointed out a dining room where I'd be able to get anything I wanted to eat at lunchtime. I was tempted to ask if I could get a burger and fries but stopped myself. With the tour exhausted, Lydia handed me over to an attendant at the door to the men's room. He provided me with a locker for my valuables and a towelling robe to wear whilst in the club.

I used the gym but found no one in there worth talking to. Even so, I enjoyed the exercise and was ready to cool off afterwards by doing a few laps. I had the pool virtually to myself. The only other people in it were intent upon swimming hard too.

By the time I'd showered, I was starving. I had an hour to wait before my massage so I donned the stupid robe and headed for the food. Health drinks, salads, all sorts of stuff that Kara would approve of. I refrained from asking for a beer and took my meagre lunch to a corner table where I could watch the comings and goings.

It was almost all women using the place. I drew some curious glances but they barely stemmed their chatter about the treatments they'd just had, were about to have or were considering. I wondered if Garnet was on the premises. Even if he wasn't, I was willing to bet that he knew I was here. I'd half expected him to appear but so far there was no sign of him.

I demolished my food and wandered to the massage room, hoping one of the young ladies from the other night would be taking care of me. Instead I got a male masseur who barely spoke a word but did a professional job of easing out some of my knotted joints. The massage rooms were at the back of the club, close to a door marked private. It wasn't the door that led to Garnet's office—that was down another corridor. Nor did it lead to the staffrooms. I knew because I'd watched some of the employees coming and going through another door beyond the dining room.

What was so private that the door required a hefty great lock? I hadn't noticed locks on any of the other doors. Before I could figure out its significance the guy pummelling my back with the sides of his hands finally called it a day.

"All done," he said, throwing a towel over my buttocks. "Relax for a while. I'll be back shortly."

"Don't leave it too long or I'll be sound asleep."

"That's the general idea."

A minute or so after the door closed behind him I was about to leap from the table but stopped myself just in time. I was probably on candid camera. I opened one eye and glanced up at the alarm sensor blinking away in the top right-hand corner of the room. Well, that was what it looked like but I was pretty sure it served another purpose too. I lay where I was, facedown, and didn't move. But I listened. The walls were thin—plywood partitioning was my guess—and I could distinctly hear voices coming from the room behind the locked door. Frustratingly I couldn't quite make out what was being said. There was a lot of grunting and shuffling noises, as though something heavy was being moved.

The room I was in was a windowless cubicle so I couldn't look outside and get my bearings. All I could do was commit the layout of the place to memory as best I could. Garnet had coerced his partners into financing whatever he was up to. Presumably it was a room like this one where their sordid antics were recorded. Perhaps this very room. If Garnet knew I was here, he was probably keeping an eye on me. He trusted me about as much as I trusted him.

The door opened and my friendly masseur returned. I pretended to be asleep and let him touch my shoulder before I stirred. But when I opened my eyes I looked directly into the face of one of the girls I'd seen on those swings the other night.

"What happened to Boris?" I asked.

"Boris?"

"The guy who gave me a rubdown."

"I give better rubdowns."

*I'll just bet you do.*

She swiped the towel off my arse and I was completely naked. She didn't seem to mind but I did. Garnet had sent her, obviously. But why? He knew I wasn't married but perhaps he thought he could embarrass me by showing the pictures to Kara. Whatever, I needed to play along, purely for professional reasons and see if I could get the woman to…er, open up for me. She put some cream on her hands and started rubbing my shoulders.

"Relax," she said.

*Oh lady, that would be too easy for you.* "I am re-laxed," I said.

"Hmm, I don't think so."

"Didn't I see you here at the party the other night? You were on one of those swings."

"Yes, I was here. I saw you too." Her hands were working their way towards my waist. In spite of my best efforts to remain immune, I reacted to her touch. That was not good. "Are you going to be a member here?"

"Perhaps. How long have you worked here?"

"About a year."

"Where are you from? You don't sound English."

"I'm from Estonia." She leaned over me and her long hair brushed against my bare arse. Christ, she was kill-ing me! "But it is better here."

"How did you get the job?"

We played this game of cat and mouse for quite a while, asking each other questions, neither of us an-swering truthfully.

"Does that feel good?"

"Mmm, sure."

"Turn over. I must do your front."

*I don't think so.* I leapt off the table and grabbed the towel, draping round my hips to preserve my modesty. God knows why. She'd already seen all there was to see. "Sorry, love, can't stop any longer. I have to be somewhere."

"Oh, but you can't go!" She looked surprised and a little frightened by my determination. I guess she wasn't used to rejection. "You haven't had the full treat-ment yet."

I skedaddled, blurting out a halfhearted apology as I headed for the men's room. An hour later I was back at the boat, not a lot wiser. Far from being relaxed after the massage, the girl's expert ministrations had left me feeling wound up and frustrated. I briefly considered paying a visit to my exclusive girlfriend but dismissed the idea. She'd want to know why I was in such a state so soon after she'd left me. She'd get the truth out of me and probably insist upon helping me get to the bottom of Garnet's little scheme. A cold shower seemed like the more sensible option.

The following morning I logged on to the Land Registry. Since 1990 it's been possible for anyone to look at the title deeds of any property in the country. I stumped up a modest fee and was soon examining all the data in respect of Garnet's health club, including a very useful floor plan. As I already knew, the car park at the front was flanked by his own private country park. The flashy entrance area with relaxation salons on either side of it fronted the building. Directly behind that was the famous atrium which occupied the entire width of the building. Beyond was the gym and swimming pool, both windowless structures backing on to the staff car park. The building had spurs going off on either side, with windowless treatment rooms, offices that did boast a bit of daylight but with windows that looked onto the park. There were staff restrooms, kitchens, stores and whatever else it took to run a club of that magnitude.

What stood out was the fact that the staff car park wasn't overlooked by a single window from any of the public rooms. In fact, as I looked closer, I could see that only one small room had the luxury of a window facing in that direction. How weird was that? The entrance to that car park was from a narrow side road through solid gates that only opened if you had a zapper or pressed a button and spoke to a guard. The walls surrounding it were high, and there were an astonishing number of security lights for such a low-key area. The building came right to the edge of the corner plot on one side, providing no access to the area that interested me. On the opposite side there was a path, about the width of a car, presumably a service access.

And my only way in.

I had a good memory for layouts, and after studying the plans I was pretty sure the room with the locked door backed on to the car park as well. And it had an external door that let straight on to it. Very convenient for moving things you didn't want other people to see. Things that had to be kept under lock and key. It was either stolen goods or, more likely, drugs. That would explain why Garnet had needed a large amount of ready cash and resorted to blackmail to obtain it. He'd bought his way into the drugs market, using his base here on the south coast as a distribution centre. His nightclubs supplied a ready market for his merchandise but it would be almost impossible to trace the supply chain back to him unless a warrant was obtained to search his premises.

The Drug Squad had no reason to go after him. Drugs were sold in clubs all the time, everyone knew that. Garnet was now a pillar of the local community, high-profile in charitable causes and a close *friend* of the assistant chief constable. He was untouchable. It made perfect sense and I wondered why it hadn't occurred to me before now. The gear probably came in on the cargo ships that docked in Dover or Ramsgate. Busy ports where merchandise wasn't always properly documented and where customs officials could be paid to look the other way. Odds on the stuff came through Afghanistan's infamous Golden Crescent, via Pakistan. The drugs were most likely transferred here on one of Garnet's supply trucks, hidden amongst all the oils, lotions and cosmetics needed to keep his adoring lady clientele looking eternally youthful. Simple and hard to detect, like the best scams usually are.

Of course, I could be miles off base. I'd never get Slater, or anyone else, to come take a look-see unless I had something more than my own half-baked suspicions to go on. Which meant I'd have to go back and have a closer look for myself. I was counting on them moving stuff in and out after the club shut for the night. There'd be too many comings and goings, too many pairs of curious eyes, to make it safe during the day. For starters, any staff members who smoked probably nipped out to that car park to get their regular nicotine fixes.

Not knowing what sort of drugs he was shifting, it was hard for me to be sure but I was guessing that no cutting took place there. Garnet wouldn't want to have anything on the premises that couldn't be hidden at a moment's notice. This was just distribution headquarters, and that distributing would be done under the cover of darkness.

I sighed. It was going to be a long night.

I CALLED KARA, just to hear the sound of her voice, only to remember that she was going to something at the children's school that evening. I left a message on her voice mail instead, promising that I'd see her soon, hoping I wasn't making promises I wouldn't live to fulfil. I gave Gil his evening run and dropped him off with my fellow live-aboards on the adjoining pontoon. They often minded him when I was going places where he wouldn't be welcome.

Before heading for the club, I went in the opposite direction and called on an acquaintance who owed me a favour. I'd phoned him earlier in the day and he knew what I needed. I took the stuff he gave me and listened carefully to his rundown on how to work it.

"Are you sure it will function?" I asked.

"Have a little faith, Mr. Hunter," he said adopting a wounded expression. "I'm a professional. I have a reputation to protect."

"Yeah, I know. It's just that it looks so insignificant."

He chuckled. "That's the whole point."

"Right."

I gave him a few bob for his trouble and trudged down the street towards the parked bike. I had a bad feeling about this whole escapade. But suicidal missions based on nothing more substantial than a hunch had never stopped me in the past. Why change the habits of a lifetime?

I pointed the bike towards Hove and parked it in a pub car park about half a mile short of my destination. As soon as it was completely dark, I set off on foot and reached the club without anyone slowing their cars to ask me what the fuck I thought I was doing. I took that as a good sign. I mean, no one wearing biking gear walked by choice down the side of a country road after dark, did they? It would be just my luck to be intercepted by Garnet. Or have a public-spirited citizen insist on offering me a lift.

Fortunately that didn't happen. There were still lights on in the reception area of the club but only a few cars parked out front. It was gone ten o'clock and I couldn't help wondering what sort of person worked out at that time of night. Not that I really cared. I was more concerned with getting round the back without being detected.

I moved across the car park, not even trying to hide, mainly because there *was* no cover. If I looked like a man on a mission perhaps I wouldn't be challenged. I could see a security guard sitting behind a desk in the foyer, reading a paper. He hadn't once glanced up. I used his preoccupation with page three to get to the side of the building with the walkway.

Unfortunately there was also an eight-foot wall with glass embedded in the top to discourage opportunistic intruders. The plans forgot to mention that little detail. I studied it for a moment, wondering how best to tackle it. The height wasn't a problem but the glass most definitely would be. Fortunately I'd stuffed my biking gauntlets into my pockets rather than leaving them with the bike. I pulled them on. Hopefully they were thick enough to keep my hands from getting cut but I was already resigned to ruining a perfectly good, very expensive pair of gloves.

A swift examination of the area confirmed what I'd already feared, prompting a string of muttered oaths. It was scrupulously tidy and there was nothing lying about in front of the wall to help me. No bins, boxes, broken chairs, absolutely nothing I could stand on to

make my life easier. I interrupted my swearing to take
a deep breath, replaying the layout of the club in my
head. There had to be an easier way.

But short of strolling in through the front door there
absolutely wasn't. I was going to have to do this the hard
way, and I was going to have to do it now. That security guard might actually remember what he got paid
for and patrol the perimeter occasionally. If he did, he'd
have to be blind not to see me in such an exposed place.

Sighing, I placed my gloved hands on the glass frag-
ments on top of the wall and moved them about until
I had a firm grip. Before I could change my mind, I
hoisted myself to the top of the wall, using my feet
against the vertical surface to gain momentum and
ease some of the weight off my hands. But as soon as
I made the final push with my arms, I felt the gloves
rip. A sharp pain shot through one palm but I didn't let
it slow me down. I placed my feet, encased in strong
biking boots, on the embedded glass. Then I bent my
knees to absorb the shock and dropped to the other side,
rolling as soon as I hit the ground. I landed harder than
I'd anticipated and swore under my breath as I jolted
my shoulder.

I couldn't control my sideways momentum and went
with the roll, hoping I wouldn't crash into anything that
made a noise. Fortunately that didn't happen. I came
to a stop against the wall, sat up with my back against
it and caught my breath. Then I pulled off my gauntlets and assessed the damage. A nasty cut on my left
palm but otherwise I appeared to be more or less intact.
I wrapped a handkerchief round the injury and tied it

tight, rotated my shoulder and winced. It hurt like hell but wasn't dislocated. I'd live.

I turned my attention to the room that interested me. The blinds were closed but there was light coming from the gap at the bottom where they didn't quite meet the windowsill. Bent double to avoid presenting a shadow on those blinds or from triggering any automatic security lights, I walked like a crab until I was beneath the window. I waited there for several minutes, giving my heartbeat time to slow and wiped away the sweat running into my eyes with the back of my hand.

I couldn't afford to linger. The area was in darkness, but if a car came in through the locked gates I'd be trapped like a rabbit in its headlights. Still, since I was here… Slowly, I pulled myself up until I could see over the window ledge and peered through the gap. Inside the room was a long table. Glover and another guy I didn't recognise were making up parcels. It didn't take a brainiac to figure out what was in them.

I was trying to decide what to do next when I heard the gates opening. Using the sound as cover, I dived behind a line of wheelie bins seconds before a combination of car and security lights illuminated the entire area. I was pretty sure I'd made it in the nick of time but it had been a close-run thing. The 4x4 that drove in flashed its lights, the door opened, several boxes were loaded into the wheel recess in the boot, and the car drove off again. It took less than a minute, not one word was spoken, and I didn't get a proper look at the two men in the car.

But at least my suspicions had been more or less confirmed. Did I wait to see if another car arrived and sneak out the open gates to save myself the grief of climbing that wall again? Or did I hang about to see what else happened? I crawled back to the window and took another peek. They appeared to be packing it in for the night so I might as well do the same.

I was about to move when I sensed a presence behind me. I half turned, but before I could see who was there, something came down on the back on my head. Lights danced behind my eyes and an excruciating pain exploded inside my brain. The last thing I remembered was crumpling to the floor like a deflated balloon.

# Chapter Sixteen

"CHARLIE, YOU DISAPPOINT ME."

A voice brought me back to consciousness.

It needn't have bothered. It felt as though someone was pounding at my head with a claw hammer from the inside. I ached everywhere, felt physically sick and would much prefer to remain in oblivion. My eyes were reluctant to open, as if they knew what was coming and would just as soon not witness it. The room spun as I forced my eyelids upwards.

Peter Garnet's face swam in and out of focus, and for a few blissful minutes I couldn't remember where the hell I was. Garnet was sitting in a canvas chair, shaking his head as though I were a recalcitrant pupil who'd failed an easy test. I probably had. I ran a hand through my hair, wincing as I touched a lump the size of a duck egg at the back of my skull. My fingers came away sticky with blood. I also had a blood-soaked handkerchief tied round my hand.

Slowly it came back to me. I'd tried to spy on Garnet's drug operation and hadn't got past first base. Either I'd tripped an alarm somewhere or they'd been expecting me. I was on the floor and tried to sit up. A large booted foot pushed me down again with considerable force. I didn't have the strength to argue with it. Instead I needed to get my mind in gear and decide how to talk my way out of this hole. Not that I was too optimistic about my chances.

"Nothing to say for yourself, Charlie?"

Nothing he'd want to hear.

"What were you doing, breaking in?"

"Just checking out the employee benefits."

Glover's massive fist descended so fast that I was never going to get out of its path. All I could do was turn my face away. Even so, he hit me so hard that pyrotechnics exploded inside my skull. Again. I felt my lip split and the tangy taste of blood trickling inside my mouth. My left eye felt as though it had come out of its socket, and a ringing sound echoed in my ears.

"Don't get smart, Charlie. It's really not in your best interests."

"No health insurance perks then?"

This time Glover kicked me in the ribs, hard enough to crack them. *Shit, it hurt!* I groaned aloud and gave up on the tough guy act. Instead I curled into a ball and hugged my torso to nurture the pain.

Out of the periphery of my vision I saw Glover smiling. He'd got a reaction out of me and that obviously made his day. I remained huddled up, taking more time than I needed to recover, assessing my chances. I wasn't tied up but then we all knew I wasn't going anywhere. The security in this place could teach Fort Knox a thing or two. I was in one of the treatment rooms, probably the same one I'd been in for the massage. I saw the sensor still winking away in the corner. Glover most likely had a whole collection of his finest moments kicking the crap out of Garnet's enemies recorded for posterity, thanks to that little techno gadget. Each to their own.

It was hard to string together more than a few coherent thoughts. Given my situation, that probably wasn't such a bad thing. But I *did* have one ace up my sleeve. I had something Garnet wanted. Something I could bargain with. Miller's notebook. I didn't know if he knew and if so how he'd found out.

Bloody hell! I cautiously shook my head, deciding that I must be concussed. Of course he knew. Paul would have told him. Except, why would Paul have given it to me in the first place if he knew his boss wanted it? Still, information was power and right now it was the only ace I held.

"Sit up, Charlie."

It wasn't the sort of request it would be sensible to decline. I slowly pulled myself to my feet, using the wall behind me to help me stand. Even so, it wasn't an elegant manoeuvre. I was still wearing my jacket, which was just as well since it had deflected Glover's boot, just a little. Enough to avoid serious damage anyway, but I wasn't about to tell him that. Why spoil his day? I'd had a quick feel of my pockets whilst I'd been on the floor. I was pretty sure my wallet was still where it belonged, and most of my other possessions too. One of the few things missing was my phone. Big surprise.

Garnet pointed to the treatment table and I sat on its edge. It was either that or fall down because my legs didn't seem too keen to take my weight.

"So," Garnet said mildly. "Are you ready to tell me what you were really doing snooping about my property?"

*Hell, no.* "You asked me to work for you. Effectively to spy on one of my mates. I didn't buy your reasons for

that and wanted to find out what was really going on."
I would have shrugged but couldn't raise sufficient energy. "I don't like being played."

He shook his head. "You can take the man out of
the police but…"

"What can I say?" I spread my hands. "I'm suspicious by nature."

"And there was I thinking that we'd started to trust
each other."

"Trust is a two-way street, Peter. If you don't trust
me enough to tell me why you really want me to work
for you, we ain't gonna make comfortable bedfellows."

He hadn't yet raised the subject of the notebook. Perhaps he didn't know I had it after all. Time to drop a few
hints. I took a moment to choose my words carefully,
knowing that they might well keep me alive.

"Tell me, is your operation anything to do with
D.C.?" I asked, taking at random some initials I'd seen
in the notebook that I thought pertained to one of Garnet's offshore accounts.

He tried to disguise his reaction but I watched carefully and saw a gleam of satisfaction lighten his eyes.
"Ah, so you've got it. I thought as much."

"Sorry?"

"You've got something I need."

"And what would that be?" Like I didn't know.

"Something that belonged to my solicitor."

I cautiously shook my head, unwilling to set the claw
hammer off again by doing so too decisively. "I'm still
not with you."

"Oh, I think you are. And there was I, willing to play

nice." He let out a martyred sigh. "That's what comes of having a conscience."

I quirked a brow. It hurt. Everything hurt. "And you'd know that because…"

This time Glover did land another blow but I was ready for it and fended it off with my forearm. "Nice try, big boy," I said, feeling my lip crack open again when I shot him a taunting smile.

Glover growled but did as he was told when Garnet indicated the opposite wall. He leaned against it, massive arms folded over his chest, glowering at me like he couldn't wait to be let loose. I had a nasty feeling that his wait would be a short one.

"You obviously employ tame dogs, Peter," I said, deciding to rattle his cage a little. Unless I came up with some amazing delaying tactics I wasn't going to get out of this with all my limbs intact, anyway. To say nothing of my head. "Unfortunately I don't fall into that category. I have this innate sense of curiosity, you see, and—"

"Where is it?" Garnet thumped his fist against the wall. Good. I was obviously getting to him.

"Where's what?"

He sighed. "All right, we'll play it your way. The notebook you took from my solicitor's office."

"I'm still not with you."

"I'm very busy this evening." He consulted his watch. He'd done so several times during our little chat. He seemed on edge but there was no reason I could think of for *him* to be anxious. I was the one in deep shit. I wondered if he was expecting someone. If so, that person obviously mattered to him and that interested me. Garnet wasn't the subservient type. "I don't have time for this," he said.

"Then don't let me delay you." I pushed myself off the treatment table. "I'll get out of your hair and be on my way."

"You like to play the funny man, don't you, Charlie, but I'm not laughing."

"Well." I shot him an apologetic look. "Can't please 'em all."

"This is your last chance. I'm not going to ask nicely again."

"I can honestly say that I've never taken anything from your solicitor's office, other than the benefit of his advice."

"What were you doing at his building on the day he was killed, if you weren't killing him?"

"And why would I kill him, other than over his extortionate hourly rate?"

"Answer the question. We don't have all night."

"Actually, I wasn't there to see Miller. We'd concluded our business when I called on him a few days before that." I paused for effect. "I was there to see Paul."

"Paul?"

"Yes, you remember him. He's one of the lapdogs on your payroll."

"But you don't get on with him."

I managed a cautious shrug. "No, but he's still my stepbrother. We had family business to discuss. He wasn't home and that's why I was in and out of the building so quickly."

"All right, let's assume I believe you. Who do you think killed Miller?" His casually posed question took me aback. He was floundering in the dark, had even fewer theories about the crime than I did. With all his contacts, that surprised me. "I'm sure you have some ideas."

"Well, actually, Peter, don't take offence but since we're enjoying a frank exchange of views, I rather thought it might be you."

"Me!" He threw back his head and laughed. "Why would I want to kill Miller?"

"You've got me there."

"He was useful and it's damned inconvenient not having him around."

"It's impossible to get good help nowadays."

"So, just as a matter of interest, why did you go and see Miller on the day you did?"

He probably knew anyway but I'm a contrary bastard at the best of times and decided to tell him my version of the truth. I didn't want to mention my cover story and involve Spelling's widow.

"I wanted to know why one of your shell companies was paying Mike Kendall's wife's medical bills," I said offhandedly. "He said he couldn't help me because he didn't know what I was talking about." I paused, trying to look casually disinterested. "Obviously he was being economical with the truth, but he was in the legal profession, so what else could I have expected?"

"What?" Garnet's eyebrows shot skywards in a genuine show of surprise. "Why did you want to know that?"

"Because I don't think Kendall killed his best mate."

"But you still put him inside for the crime."

"Not me. It wasn't my case."

"Semantics." He paused, rubbing his chin as though

trying to decide if I was being truthful. "So why the interest now?"

"Idle curiosity."

He knew I was lying but didn't press me. "And the notebook? How did you come by that?"

"I still don't know which notebook you're referring to."

He expelled a long breath. "It's such a shame about that pretty face of yours."

There was a subtle change in the atmosphere and I knew I had to do something fast, before he let Glover off his leash.

"Do you know," I said, gently—very gently—smacking the heel of my hand against my still-thrumming forehead, "perhaps I do know something about a book. It was given to me for safekeeping."

"I knew you'd see reason." Garnet ushered Glover back to his place holding up the wall. I was glad about that, not being too sure how solid the partitioning actually was. "Where is it?"

"Is it the one that mentions a meeting between Miller and D.S. to sign some contract or other?"

"Very possibly."

"Ah, well, I listened to the advice of the person who mailed it to me and put it somewhere safe. In the event that I don't check in then obviously its contents will find their way to the police."

He laughed aloud. "Do you take me for a complete idiot?"

I figured that was probably a rhetorical question and didn't respond.

"I don't doubt that you have the book. Who gave it to you, by the way?"

"No idea. Like I said, it arrived in the post."

"Well, it doesn't matter. I know you're here off your own bat and no one's going to ride to your rescue. If your ex-colleagues were involved, I'd know about it."

That ploy about help being at hand always worked in the movies. Next time I saw Steven Spielberg I'd be sure and have it out with him.

"For the last time, where is it?"

I said nothing. Every time I opened my smart mouth I just seemed to make matters worse.

"You realise it makes no difference to me whether I get the book back or not. I just don't want it to fall into the wrong hands."

"I'm told that Miller kept notebooks detailing all his meetings. What about all the others?"

"Oh, don't worry about those. We already have them. Yours is the last one. We can search your boat and if that doesn't bring it to light we'll systematically work our way through the homes of all your loved ones. Now, Glover, what do you think?" That goon was capable of thought? Well, you learned something new every day. "Shall we start with Charlie's ex-wife and son or should we target the lovely Kara?"

I felt myself tense as the seriousness of my situation struck home. Anger coursed through me, helping to clear my fuzzy head. I thought I held the trump card but this guy had always been one step ahead of me. He knew Miller had wanted out, that much was evident from his entry in the notebook, but he obviously didn't know that Paul was his significant other. Not that I really cared. It was Emily, Harry, Kara and her kids who occupied my thoughts. I'd give the book up without a second thought but I knew the moment I did I'd be dead. And if they were going to kill me anyway, I might as well make life difficult for them.

"What did happen to Spelling, as a matter of interest?" I asked. I was counting on his overinflated ego to prompt a response. He paused, as though considering whether or not to tell me, but when he opened his mouth again I knew that pride would win out over caution.

"He was a bit like you. Stubborn. And worse, he was stealing from me." He sighed over-dramatically. "I told you before, I can't abide disloyalty. He had to be warned."

"Bit of an extreme warning, wasn't it?"

"He wasn't supposed to die. How could he repay me when he was dead? But Glover here sometimes gets a little overexcited." He offered me his shark's smile. "You'd do well to remember that. When he gets upset even I can't control him."

"And you let Mike Kendall go down for the crime?"

"Glover was more important to me. Anyway, I looked after Kendall's family."

"Until you stopped paying his wife's bills."

"That was an unfortunate oversight."

I thought of Cleo and all she'd suffered as a result of his unfortunate oversight and felt fit to explode with anger. But it was important not to let it show.

"Accidents happen," I said.

"Indeed they do. And unless you tell me where that book is, I regret to say that you'll soon become another statistic."

"You'd kill an ex-copper?"

"Oh no, not personally." He nodded towards Glover, who was smiling in anticipation. He cracked the knuckles on each hand, as though I ought to be scared. I was but he didn't need to know that. "In fact I rather like you, Charlie, I'd be sorry to see you leave us. But business is business. I'm sure you understand."

"Help me out here, Pete," I said. "What's in this for me? You said just now that you can't abide disloyalty. Now, you think I've been disloyal even though I don't work for you, which leaves me with a bit of a dilemma. Why would I make life easier for you by giving up that book? You don't actually *know* that it won't be released if I kick the bucket."

"It's a risk I'm prepared to take. Oh, I know you're tough. I've been impressed by your display of machismo, if that makes you feel any better. I've seen bigger men than you peeing their pants when they've been in your situation, begging me to give them another chance." He examined his fingernails intently. "I don't know about you but I can't abide seeing grown men beg."

"I'm with you there. It so lacks dignity."

"You really should have accepted my offer of employment, you know."

"I'm not good at taking orders. And I ask too many awkward questions. Can't help it." I managed a cautious shrug. "It's just the way I am."

"Such a shame." He watched me with an air of detached amusement but wasn't as relaxed as he appeared. Unless I missed my guess, he was anxious about something. "Anyway, where was I?"

"Search me."

"Oh, we already did. We took your phone for safe-keeping. And your little torch and a rather vicious-looking Swiss Army knife." *Shit.* "So much knife crime about nowadays. One must be a responsible citizen and keep knives off the streets."

"You ought to run the local Neighbourhood Watch. I'm sure you could give them a few useful tips."

"You're a funny man, Charlie." He stretched and stifled a yawn. "As I was saying, there's more than one way to crack a nut. No pun intended, of course." Footsteps sounded in the corridor. Disappointingly, it didn't sound as though it was the cavalry riding to the rescue. "And, unless I'm greatly mistaken, that alternative method is about to join us."

The door opened and Andrea Garnet stepped in. She was closely followed by someone else. Another woman.

"Charlie!" Kara cried, running straight over to me. "Are you all right?"

# Chapter Seventeen

MY HEART SANK. What the hell had she been thinking, coming here? I glanced at Garnet, no longer attempting to keep the seething anger out of my expression.

"Why?" I asked him, knowing what he'd say but still feeling the need to ask.

"Insurance," he responded succinctly. "I had a feeling you'd be the strong, macho type, not so easy to intimidate. But now…"

He merely shrugged, further explanation unnecessary. We both knew what he'd do if I continued to hold out against him.

"I didn't take you for the type to hide behind a woman," I said scathingly.

"You're mistaking me for someone who has a conscience."

"No danger of that."

"Darling," Andrea said. "Your other visitors are here. Best not keep them waiting."

"Right. If you'll excuse me for a short time." He stood, motioning to Glover to follow him. "I'll leave you two to your fond reconciliation and we'll resume this later." He paused, hand on the doorknob. "Do talk some sense into him, Kara. It will be so much more pleasant for everyone concerned. And I do mean everyone," he said, his eyes lingering on her, "if he sees reason."

"What is it that you want?" she asked.

"Oh, Charlie knows."

The moment the door closed behind them, Kara threw her arms round my neck. Every bone in my body protested at the light pressure as her torso collided with mine.

"Careful!"

"Oh, sorry. What have they done to you? Where does it hurt?"

*Everywhere.* "How long have you got?"

"Charlie, this isn't funny!"

"Do you see me laughing?" I turned my back on the blinking light in the corner of the room and spoke in not much more than a whisper. "What the hell possessed you to come?"

"I got a call."

"Shush." I turned her so that she too was facing away from the camera. "They're recording us and probably listening too. Keep your voice low."

"I got a call," she said again, more quietly. "I thought it was you. It came from your number."

"They took my phone."

"It was that Andrea woman. She said you were over here using the gym, that you'd pulled a muscle and couldn't ride your bike home. You were getting medical treatment from their in-house physio and had asked her to phone me to come and get you."

"And you fell for that?" I threw her a disbelieving look, blaming her for putting herself in danger when I knew it was my fault. "Did you really think I'd be working out at this time of night?"

"Well, how did I know you were over here playing

James Bond?" she asked, not unreasonably. "You didn't bother to enlighten me and you *do* tend to do odd things at strange times."

"Yeah, okay, point made." I stumbled into full view of the camera. "We need to give them what they want, Kara," I said in a loud voice.

"What!" Then she caught on. "Oh yes, it doesn't look as though we have much choice. I don't want them to hurt you any more." She lowered her voice and turned away from the camera again. "So, what do we really do now?"

Good question. "We try to get out of here. Garnet admitted that Glover killed Spelling, more or less on his orders." I spoke normally again. "I don't feel so good," I said, collapsing against the side of the treatment table.

"Let me help you." She went to the sink in the corner of the room, wet some paper towels and attacked my bloody face with them. "You're going to have a right shiner tomorrow," she said, playing to the camera.

*If I live that long.* "You should see the other guy. Ouch!" I'd taken too deep a breath and my ribs protested.

"Sorry."

She unfastened the handkerchief from my hand. "Can you walk to the sink?"

"I'll try."

She supported my arm and I made a big deal out of shuffling across the room, my movements clumsy and stiff. When we reached the sink she washed off the blood. I let her fuss over me whilst I waited for inspiration to strike but it appeared to be taking a vacation.

"This probably needs a stitch," she said. "The cut's quite deep."

"Tell that to Garnet. He's a compassionate man. I'm sure he'll let us pop out to the local A&E."

"Why do you always crack jokes when you're in trouble?"

"Defence mechanism," I said, winking at her. "And we're not finished yet," I added with more confidence than I felt. No point in us both stressing.

"Take your shirt off. I want to see what they've done to your chest."

I shook my head. "No you don't. Trust me," I hissed. She looked set to argue but something in my expression made her snap her mouth closed. "Not now."

"Oh all right, if you're sure. But at least lie down again." She dropped her voice. "How are we going to get out of here?"

Another good question. "I'm more comfortable standing," I said, avoiding giving her a straight answer. "Garnet wants the book that Paul gave me," I added in an undertone. "He doesn't want it to surface later and embarrass him. Personally, I think he's being a bit paranoid." I cautiously lifted my shoulders to emphasise my scepticism. Even that small gesture sent pain waves ricocheting through my rib cage. "Unless it falls into the hands of someone who knows what it was, what harm would it do? I mean, we *did* know but still couldn't figure it all out."

"He's a control freak. Hates to think there might be something out there to incriminate him, however obscure."

I made a loud complaint about my ribs, not entirely

for the benefit of the eavesdroppers. "The assistant chief constable," I said slowly.

"What do you mean?"

"Instead of getting him to put up money, he bought the man himself." I expelled a long breath. "What an idiot. I thought Bennett had more sense. If that book falls into police hands and the A.C.C. gets to hear about it, then this house of cards really will come crashing down. Perhaps Garnet's not being quite so paranoid after all."

"I repeat my earlier question that you so skilfully dodged," she said. "How the hell are we going to get out of here?" She glanced round the windowless box. "It seems hopeless."

"These partitions are pretty flimsy."

"But even if we had something to break the wall down with, which we don't, we're being watched. We'd never get away."

"Which leaves the door. If we could pick that lock, we'd have a fighting chance."

"Wouldn't they see us?"

"No, the camera points straight at the massage table. There are lots of blind spots in the room but if we disappear out of view for too long someone will come running."

"Are you any good at picking locks, Charlie?"

"Afraid not. It's not something they teach at police college."

"The English are so good at *not* equipping their officers for the real world."

"That's what I tried to tell them."

"They always make it look so easy in films. A credit card slid into the right place and Bob's your uncle."

"I assume Andrea took your bag from you."

"Yes, just as I came through the door. I was so shocked to see you in such a state that I didn't give it a thought."

"It was too much to hope that they'd let you keep your phone."

"Bugger it! I've been a bit of an idiot, haven't I?"

I smiled because...well because Kara could make me smile, even under such dire circumstances. It cracked open my lip again and I felt the warm trickle of blood dripping down my chin.

"Charlie, you're—"

"Leave it," I said, grabbing a plastic drinking cup and allowing the blood to drip into it. I also opened up my cut hand as far as it would go, tearing the wound open.

"Fuck it!" I said between clenched teeth, clasping my wrist as I waited for the stinging pain to subside.

"What are you doing?"

"I have an idea. Keep up the concerned chatter, stay out of range of the camera and search this room."

"What am I looking for?"

"Anything that could be used as a weapon. And bandages."

"Bandages?"

"I'll explain in a moment."

But there was little that would help us. This was a massage room, not a doctor's surgery.

"There's this." Kara held up a jar of what looked like massage oil.

"Now's not the time," I said, waggling my brows at her.

"So tell me all about this brilliant plan of yours," she said, rolling her eyes at me.

"Shush, I'm listening."

The voices coming from the locked room continued to drone on. One of them was Garnet's and his tone was respectful. Whoever had come to see him, Garnet was definitely in awe of him. That had been apparent when his wife told him his visitors had arrived. He'd been anxious to see them, to reassure them about something by the sounds of things. And all the time he was talking to those people he wasn't watching us. I doubted if anyone else was continually doing so either. He wouldn't want his visitors to know he had problems. Garnet's type never did.

That meant there was an outside chance that my crazy plan might work, but we couldn't afford to wait. As soon as Garnet's visitors left he'd be straight back in here and this time he'd be all out of patience.

I made sure we were well out of range of the camera and told her what I planned.

"We'll only get one shot at it though," I said after she'd heard me out in stunned silence, "so we need to make it convincing."

"But you're hurt. Are you sure you can do it?"

I wasn't sure about anything but now didn't seem like the right time to mention it. "It looks worse than it feels," I lied. "Shame I'm wearing black though. It would be more dramatic if I had blood all over a white shirt."

"You're doing it again," she said in a peevish voice. "Making jokes. This isn't funny."

I could see that she was seriously afraid. Sensible girl, she had good reason to be. "Come on," I said, trying to sound upbeat and confident. "It's now or never."

"Go on then. You're the star."

"I just want you to know that I've enjoyed our exclusive relationship." I allowed myself a moment's seriousness. "I'm glad I found you, Kara Webb." I held her against me for a second and immediately released her again. It was that or never let her go.

"I'm glad you found me too," she said, tears in her eyes. "Now, get on with it! We *are* getting out of this, and when we do I shall beat you to a pulp myself for getting us into it in the first place."

"Now there's something to look forward to."

"Come on, Charlie! Quit stalling."

"Right, here goes." I took as deep a breath as my protesting ribs would permit and let it out in a long screech. "Christ!" I said loudly, clutching my stomach and doubling over right in view of the camera. "That hurts."

"Charlie, what is it?" Kara rushed to my side looking suitably concerned. "Oh my god, you've got blood pouring out of your mouth." Well, *pouring* was stretching it but I'd done the best I could with the raw material available. I didn't fancy inflicting further punishment on myself to obtain a fresh supply, especially since our captors might well do the honours before this night was out. "Where does it hurt?"

"My gut," I said, staggering towards the bed.

"You missed your vocation," Kara whispered as she pretended to help me up. "You should have trod the boards."

"Arghhh!" I crumpled to the floor, still clutching my stomach, well out of range of the camera.

Kara hovered over me, close enough to the magic eye for her Oscar-winning performance to take centre stage. "Charlie? Charlie, talk to me."

I blew her a kiss.

"Help!" she yelled. "We need help in here."

"Okay," I said, crawling farther towards the door. "Get ready. Stay behind me and be ready to run like hell."

I took the jar of massage oil and spread a liberal amount over the floor immediately in front of the door. The voices next door had stalled when Kara screamed but it seemed like an age before anyone came to investigate. It was now a matter of how many people actually showed up. If it was more than one we were stuffed, but I reckoned that Garnet wouldn't want his visitor to see what was going on in here so wouldn't leave him alone. He thought I was out of it, and how many men did it take to subdue one hysterical female?

"What's taking them so long?" Kara whispered.

"I reckon the camera monitoring point isn't next door so they would have heard your shout but nothing else. Whoever's watching us will have to tell Garnet because I'm betting no one's allowed in here without his say-so. Just be patient," I said as much to myself as to her.

Eventually one set of footsteps sounded in the corridor. I breathed a sigh of relief and flashed a brief grin at Kara. The steps were too light to belong to Glover, which was an added bonus. We exchanged a speaking look as the key turned in the lock. Now that the time had come for action I was feeling deathly calm. I slumped on the floor again, eyes closed. I opened one—well, that was all I could open since Glover had half closed the other one for me. It hurt like a bitch. It was Mallet's head that poked round the door. He saw me out for the count and Kara flapping over me, yelling at him to do something.

Clearly satisfied that we weren't faking it, he stepped into the room, let out a surprised yelp and went arse over tit on the oily floor. He did that windmill thing with his arms, attempting to retain his balance but it was never going to happen. With a stifled oath he hit the floor hard. Kara and I were on our feet in seconds, staying well out of range of the camera as Kara kept up loud demands that Mallet do something to help me.

"Your boss won't be best pleased if he dies," she said. "He's got something he wants."

Mallet groaned and tried to scrabble to his feet. The fall hadn't knocked him out, that would have been too much to ask for. I had nothing to tie him up with and no way to keep him quiet for long enough to give us a fighting chance.

"Give me that empty oil jar," I said to Kara. "And a towel."

"What are you going to do with it?"

I grimaced. "What has to be done."

I wrapped the jar in the towel to lessen the possibility of it smashing against his skull and leaving him with glass embedded in it. I then gave Mallet a whack across the back of the head. Hard enough to knock him out, much as Glover had done to me earlier, but not hard enough to do any permanent damage. Like I gave a shit.

I searched the unconscious man's pockets and came up with the key to the room. And, pay dirt, his mobile phone.

"Come on!"

I reached out a hand to Kara. We carefully skirted the oily patch of floor and I opened the door, looking both ways to ensure the corridor was empty.

"We've got two minutes, maximum," I told her as I locked the door from the outside, and we headed towards the exit.

"Why don't you call reinforcement now?" she asked.

"No, we just need to get out of here. If we can get outside, that'll be the time."

"Just hit 999." She reached for the phone. "I'll do it."

"And tell them what?"

"That we've been attacked and…oh yes." Her face fell. "Garnet will get to us before the cavalry arrives and claim that we broke in."

"Exactly!"

We moved fast, still walking, but even that was enough to make my world spin. I didn't tell Kara I was suffering. She needed to think I was in control, not fighting concussion and struggling to remain upright. We'd almost made it to the reception area. Kara was smiling with triumph but something told me we weren't out of the woods yet. This was too easy.

My worst fears were realised when we turned the final corner and ran smack bang into a brick wall. A brick wall with tree-trunk legs planted apart and massive arms folded across a solid chest. Glover.

"Going somewhere?" he asked, grinning.

# Chapter Eighteen

I STILL HAD Mallet's phone in my hand and passed it to Kara, hoping she'd have the sense to put it somewhere other than her pocket. When she slid it down the front of her jeans I mentally applauded. Hopefully Mallet wasn't expecting a call. It would give her a hell of a shock if it started to ring inside her knickers, but I hadn't risked switching it off, just in case it needed a code to fire it up again. I turned my attention back to Glover, who was salivating like a hungry Rottweiler. He obviously thought this was going to be pretty one-sided. He was probably right.

He never should have gloated. It gave me just enough time to take stock of the situation. Even so, he still managed to land a massive punch in my solar plexus that knocked me sideways. I managed to get an awkward one back, down low. There was little strength behind it but my aim was good and I caught him right in the balls. He howled but recovered far too quickly. He was coming for me again, a murderous expression on his ugly face. Kara was hopping about, tugging at my arm, trying to get me out of his path. But that wouldn't help. Even if we reached the door we couldn't outrun him unless we first disabled him. This thing had to be settled, here and now.

I remained doubled over, causing Glover's grin to

widen. The cocky bastard thought it was all over, just as he was supposed to. There was an elaborate flower arrangement on a side table in a heavy crystal vase. Ideal for my purposes. As I straightened up, I knocked the flowers to the floor and grabbed the vase.

Before I could do anything more, his massive fist caught me squarely in the gut. Again. I folded in half, feeling such intense pain that I thought I might pass out. I'd never known anything like it but forced myself to ignore the nausea and concentrate on surviving. Kara screamed and I could see her in the periphery of my one-eyed vision casting wildly about for something to use as a weapon. I could have told her she was wasting her time.

Glover could easily have finished me off then and there, but I guess he didn't want to explain to the boss how an injured man and slip of a girl had managed to escape. Rational thought clearly didn't come naturally to him and he had to mull it over at his own pace. I used his momentary distraction to straighten up, smash the vase against the table to break it in half and thrust the jagged edge towards his face. He dodged it but not quickly enough. He screamed as blood gushed from his cheek and raised a hand as though trying to hold the jagged flesh in place.

"Move!" I yelled to Kara, dodging round the quickly recovering Glover.

The newspaper-reading security guard had finally reacted to the ruckus and sauntered over to investigate. Just before he reached us we pushed open the fire escape and rushed into the welcome night air.

"You're a dead man, Hunter," Glover growled, his heavy footsteps following us into the night.

But now we had the advantage. We were lighter and, in spite of my injuries, quicker on our feet. And we were running for our lives. That tended to make a person focus.

"Head to the left, away from the car park lights," I said to Kara, taking her hand and dragging her towards the meditation park.

The area didn't offer nearly enough cover but if we could get there ahead of Glover, I figured we'd buy ourselves a few precious minutes' respite. We almost tripped over something—probably a tree root. Yet again my battered body screamed in protest at the jolt it took but I ignored it, running on adrenaline and good old-fashioned fear as we plunged into the blessed darkness. We fell behind a sturdy tree trunk, both of us breathing heavily. I was having trouble focusing. Sweat and blood mingled on my face and I could feel my heart racing at twice its normal rate.

"The phone," I said as soon as I could find enough breath to speak.

She unzipped her jeans and rooted about, presumably inside her knickers. "Want a hand?" I asked.

"What *does* it take to get your mind off sex?" But her grouch lacked teeth and I could hear the jubilation in her voice. She thought we were home and clear.

I wished I could share her optimism as I took a moment to think about our situation. It all came down to whether or not they realised Mallet's phone was missing. If they didn't, we still had a chance. They knew we couldn't get to Kara's car. I could see it parked directly under a light, right outside the front door to the club. Besides, the keys were in her bag and I'd never have time to hot-wire it before they closed in on us. We couldn't use Mallet's phone to call a cab either. They'd be watching for any vehicles in the vicinity once they knew we'd escaped. If we were stupid enough to call the police, by the time they arrived at the club—always supposing they were willing to raid it on such flimsy evidence—they'd be no sign of illegal drugs. And even if we did somehow manage to slip this net, Garnet knew where we both lived and would assume he'd be able to pick us up again at any time of his choosing.

He just hadn't taken into account that I had a few tricks of my own up my sleeve. Kara had located the phone and handed it to me.

"Hmm, nice and warm," I said.

"Charlie, stop mucking about and get us out of here."

There was a full signal. Something was going right for us at last. I dialled a number that I'd looked up and memorised earlier, praying that he'd be at home. Bennett answered the phone himself.

"It's Charlie Hunter," I said to the assistant chief constable. "If you take a squad to Garnet's club immediately, you'll find drugs—a lot of drugs." I told him the precise location of the room in question. He didn't ask me any questions or once interrupt. "No lights or sirens," I said. "Oh, and be quick. We're in trouble." I told him where to find us.

"On our way."

Bennett broke the connection and I pocketed Mallet's phone.

"Will he come?" Kara asked.

"Oh yeah, he'll come."

"Is that why you called him and not Slater?"

"I wouldn't give Slater the time of day. Besides, she doesn't have the authority to get something like this off the ground. Garnet will have more than one informer inside the station, and Slater wouldn't mount the raid without doing all the necessary paperwork. By the time she got here, Garnet would know all about it and it would be too late." To say nothing of the fact that we'd have been caught by then but I decided not to dwell on that depressing likelihood.

"Will they still be looking for us?" she asked, snuggling against my side.

"Probably only Glover and the guard at the moment. It seems like ages but it's only been a few minutes since we ran from that building. Garnet will still be with his visitor, and Glover will hope to catch us before he has to admit we overcame him."

"You did, Charlie. I didn't do anything."

"Shush."

We heard two sets of footsteps coming towards us. Torchlight narrowly missed our hiding place as the men blundered through the trees. They'd missed us only because they weren't searching methodically, but they'd soon be back. What the hell were we supposed to do now? I glanced upwards. The tree we were sheltering behind was an old oak, with lots of low branches. It had to be hundreds of years old and was probably one of the reasons why Garnet hadn't been able to build on this part of his land.

"Any good at climbing trees?" I asked her.

She was on her feet in a flash and disappeared into

the leafy canopy. My ribs were giving me merry hell, and my ascent wasn't nearly so nimble. Even so, I made it seconds before Glover came stumbling directly below us. He cast his torch round the area but didn't once think to shine it upwards. I sent up a message of thanks for the cerebrally challenged as he moved on, shouting at the guard to do another sweep, cursing and swearing fit to bust a gut.

We didn't speak. In my case it took all my concentration to quell the pain in every part of my body and not lose my balance. Kara's rapid breathing told me that she was scared, worried about the children perhaps, if we didn't get out of this.

After what seemed like an eternity, several cars came down the adjacent road. I only hoped Bennett had the foresight to send several more round the back to block the exit from the staff car park. I had to assume that he had. Another long delay and then noise and lots of shouting.

"We can get down now," I said to Kara.

We were both stiff. I went first and helped her down, in spite of the fact that I could have done with some help myself. Hand in hand we emerged from the trees and waited at the periphery of the brightly lit car park. Police wearing Kevlar vests were everywhere. Even I was impressed by the A.C.C.'s ability to pull together so many men at such short notice.

The doors to the reception area burst open. There was lots of shouting and more people than I'd realised on the premises. They ran in all directions, obviously not prepared to go down quietly. The police took off after them. Several men were led out in handcuffs. Mallet was one of them. I obviously hadn't hit him hard enough. Andrea Garnet was struggling but easily restrained by two policemen.

Bennett was standing to one side, watching Garnet being handcuffed and read his rights, a smile of satisfaction on his face. We instinctively moved closer to watch the show. A big mistake, as it transpired. The blow came from behind, straight into my kidneys, sending me sprawling to the floor. Glover was screaming like a banshee, a torrent of abuse all aimed at me.

He was out of control, just as he'd probably been when he bludgeoned Spelling to death. Not a reassuring notion. Damn, I thought he'd be too concerned about saving his own skin to come after us, otherwise I'd have stayed up that damned tree. I rolled out of range of his boot and picked up a heavy branch, ready to use it as a weapon. But my grip was weak and Glover took it away from me with ease.

Now he had the weapon. It hardly seemed fair because he didn't need any help. I was in too much pain to move and there was absolutely nothing I could do to defend myself. I looked up into Glover's deranged eyes, prepared to accept the inevitable. He moved in for the kill, grinning like a maniac. There could be no question that he enjoyed his work. Then images of Harry flooded my mind, lending me superhuman strength. I grabbed his ankle and pulled as hard as I could, holding on with all my might. I guess I got lucky. I caught him off balance, one leg off the ground as he made to kick me. He tumbled over, cursing and swearing loud enough to wake the dead.

What I hadn't reckoned on was his taking Kara with

him. She was standing too close and he reacted with astonishing speed for a big man, grabbing her waist as he fell so she landed on top of him with a startled cry. Great, now he had a hostage! I could give him a taste of his own medicine and use my boot on his head, but anything I did to him, he'd retaliate by hurting Kara.

Where the fuck was Bennett? Surely he'd heard us yelling for his help. But he obviously hadn't. There was so much else else going down right now. What to do? Kara was making frantic eyes at me, trying to tell me something. She kept indicating his head. I'd be more than happy to kick it, but…then I caught on. She'd taken something out of her pocket and needed me to distract Glover. I nodded, moved my foot backwards and prayed.

Kara moved with the speed of lightning. As my foot made crunching connection with Glover's skull, she squirted the contents of the can she was holding straight into his eyes. He screamed, temporarily blinded, and instinctively moved his hands to his face. Kara took my hand and scrambled free. By the time Glover recovered, three policemen were holding him down and handcuffing him.

"Are you all right?" I asked her.

"Fine, what about you?"

I'd fallen to the ground again, totally spent now the action was over. Every square inch of me was in pain.

"I've had better days." I tried to sit up. It wasn't easy because the earth kept moving. "Thanks, by the way."

"My pleasure."

"What did you get him with?"

She grinned. "Hair spray. I found a handbag-sized

can in that desk drawer and put it in my pocket, just in case."

I sent up another message of thanks, this time in honour of vain masseuses. "Good thinking," I said, shaking my head in an attempt to clear my vision.

The A.C.C. joined us.

"Glad you could make it," I said caustically.

"Sorry, we had a bit of bother back there but we've got them all now."

"Good."

"How are you feeling, Charlie?" he asked.

"He needs medical attention," Kara answered for me.

"The paramedics are on their way."

"You got Garnet, that's all that counts."

"And the drugs," Bennett said with a grim smile of satisfaction. "He claims to know nothing about them but he doesn't have a leg to stand on."

I grunted, aware that he could afford the best brief. Equally aware how easily such people could cast doubt on even the most cast-iron evidence.

"Who was with him?" I asked. "He had some important visitor."

Bennett sighed. "There wasn't anyone else. He must have left minutes before we got here."

Damn. "Never mind, it was Garnet we wanted."

"You have no idea." He paused, casting a pensive look my way. "Although perhaps you do."

"Don't try to stand up, Charlie," Kara commanded. "Wait there for the paramedics."

"Thank you," Bennett said to me, bending to shake my hand. "Obviously, as soon as you feel up to it we need to talk."

"Of course."

"Here comes the ambulance now."

I was fussed over and generally assessed, right there on the edge of the car park.

"You'll need to spend the night in hospital," one of the paramedics said.

"Where's Gil?" Kara asked.

"With Mike. What about the kids?"

"Lily's watching them." She chewed her lip.

"Get the A.C.C. to arrange a lift home for you. I'll be fine."

"No way. Give me that phone."

She made a call, closed the phone and grinned. "Right, come on then, let's get you to the hospital. Lily's happy to stay with the kids all night so I'm staying with you." She held up a hand when I made to protest. "No arguments," she said, clutching my hand as I insisted upon walking to the ambulance. "I've always wanted to ride in one of these," she said to the paramedic. "Can we put the flashing lights on?"

I HAD CRACKED ribs, lots of bruising and several stitches in my hand. The X-rays showed no internal damage but I did have a concussion. Considering the beating I'd taken, I reckoned I got away lightly. I didn't want to stay the night in hospital but by the time they'd finished mucking me about, half the night had gone anyway. Plus the pain medication made me sleepy. Even if it hadn't, I couldn't have fought Kara when she was in such an intransigent mood. She sat beside my bed the whole time like a lively guardian angel, refusing to let me move a muscle.

She helped me to eat my breakfast the next morning

by consuming half of it herself and reliving the activities of the night before.

"So even if they do charge Garnet with drug possession and distribution, his brief could still get him off." She glowered. "It's infuriating."

I agreed with her. With Kara in that frame of mind it was the only sensible move.

"And you're no better off than you were when you went in there," she grumbled. "Worse really, because you now know Garnet was responsible for Spelling's murder but can't prove it."

The doctor interrupted her tirade. He took a look at me, chuckled at my blackening eye, told me I was no longer concussed and could go home.

"Just don't get into any more brawls for a while," he advised. "At least not until those ribs have healed. Keep them strapped as tight as you can stand."

We got out of there sharpish and took a cab back to the boat.

"What about the children?"

"Lily will take them to school along with her two," she said. "That's what neighbours are for. I've done the same for her once or twice."

"Okay. And Gil will have to stay with Mike for a while. We'll stop by and tell him on our way."

"On our way where?"

"After a shower and change of clothes, we need to stop off at the bungalow and collect the book and then we're off to see the A.C.C. He said he'd send a car to your place."

"So I should think." She sniffed. "It's the least he can do."

WE WERE SHOWN straight into Bennett's office. He offered up coffee, which we accepted, and asked me how I was.

"I'll live," I said.

"There's no permanent damage," Kara told him. "Apparently he has a hard head."

Bennett chuckled. So did Kara. I didn't get the joke myself.

"Garnet's lawyered up and isn't saying a word," he told us, sobering.

"Well, there's a surprise."

"But he won't slip out of this one."

"And you're not frightened—"

Bennett looked me squarely in the eye. "I take it you know what he was doing."

"I pretty much guessed."

"I was an idiot for going anywhere near the man. I knew he was nothing more than a thug in a Savile Row suit." He pummelled his forehead with a closed fist. "There's no fool like an old fool."

"Well, if it's any consolation, he fooled a lot of people."

"Not much, no. I hated what I'd become because of him."

"Had you actually given him anything you shouldn't have?"

"No, but I knew the day would come when I had to make that decision," he said with refreshing candour. "And I decided a couple of days ago that I just couldn't do it. I came clean to my wife about what happened." He let out a mirthless chuckle. "After all that agonising about her reaction she didn't turn a hair. She just said she thought that sort of thing happened all the time at those places and knew I wasn't to blame. She was more worried about how it might affect my career."

She was right to be so but he didn't need me to tell him that. "So, now's the time he'll try and call in that favour. Make you have evidence magically disappear, stuff like that."

"He can try but it won't happen."

And I could tell from the light of determination in his eye that it wouldn't.

"How did you get involved with him, Charlie?"

I told him about Cleo. He listened without once interrupting, appearing to remember the case.

"And Garnet admitted to Charlie that his goon killed Spelling," Kara said. "But we've got no way of proving it."

"If we could, that would certainly seal Garnet's fate."

"Oh, I think I can help you there."

Two heads swivelled to look at me. "What do you mean?" Bennett asked.

I extracted a thick pen from the inside pocket of my jacket and waved it under Bennett's nose. "Fortunately Garnet's minions don't know how to do a proper search."

"What is it?" Kara asked.

"Unless I'm much mistaken," Bennett answered, "it's a digital pen recorder."

"Right."

Kara's face lit up. "And it recorded everything Garnet said to you about Spelling's murder."

"Sound and pictures. I let my jacket fall open, made sure the camera was pointing towards him and let him hang himself." I flashed a brief smile. "He ain't the only one to make good use of spyware."

"Where did you get it?" Bennett asked.

"Off the record?" I asked. He nodded. "Someone we put away for hacking into his MP's email."

"Why would he want to do that?" Kara mused.

"The guy had pissed him off and he wanted to make a point. Deliberately left a trail that led straight back to him so he could have his day in court. Someone here wanted to pin other unsolved crimes of that nature on the guy and I made sure that didn't happen."

Bennett slowly nodded. We both knew I was talking about Slater.

"Anyway, the guy's owed me a favour ever since."

Kara grinned. "How do we view what's on there?"

I unscrewed the pen and showed her the memory stick inside. "It even works as a proper pen," I told her, demonstrating. "Once we've attached the stick to a computer we use this little disc to read everything on it."

I held my breath, worried now that it might not work and that I'd suffered in vain. Fortunately that didn't prove to be the case. The picture was a bit grainy and jumped whenever Glover walloped me, but the sound was spot-on. The three of us watched it in stunned silence. When it came to an end Bennett was the first to speak.

"What made him think you had that book?" he asked.

"I don't think he knew for sure but I'd been to see Miller and could have lifted it then."

"So could anyone else who'd been in his office."

"True, but when he caught me breaking into his club he knew I'd never work for him and wouldn't have let me walk out of there alive. So when he suggested I had the book I denied it in a way that implied just the opposite. That's what kept me alive."

"You really are tired of living, aren't you," Kara said, looking really angry. "What an idiotic thing to do."

"Hey, we survived, didn't we?"

"More by luck than your good judgment."

She had me there. I produced the book that had caused so much trouble from my inside pocket and slapped it down in front of Bennett. "It's all yours now," I told him.

"Okay," he said flipping through the pages. "I know you won't tell me where you got it from and it's probably better if I don't know. But perhaps you can tell me what's in it to cause Garnet so much stress."

"It's written in a sort of shorthand. Just initials and cryptic notes about his meetings with his various clients. Kara and I could make educated guesses about some of it but didn't find anything especially incriminating. My guess is that Garnet laundered his drug money through his nightclubs and there's something in there about the offshore accounts where he's got it tucked away."

"Could well be," Bennett agreed. "I'll get our experts to give it the treatment. I'm sure we'll find whatever he's trying to hide."

"Garnet's brief will try and get any information you glean thrown out on the grounds that the book was illegally obtained," I warned Bennett.

"He's welcome to try," Bennett said, clearly spoiling for a fight. It was revenge time and he planned to enjoy every minute of it. "But before he even gets to hear about it, I think we'll show it to Glover and see if he wants to do a deal."

"Good thinking," I said, flashing a wary grin and immediately regretting it. Even smiling hurt.

A detective came to get us. It was time for us to make our formal statements.

Bennett stood and warmly shook my hand. "Thank you, Charlie," he said. "I'm in your debt. Any time you need anything, anything at all, my door will always be open to you."

"Thanks, I appreciate it."

We walked through the squad room and received a round of applause. The only person not to join in was a scowling Jillian Slater.

"Don't forget she still thinks you're a murderer," Kara said sweetly.

As if I could.

# Chapter Nineteen

WE COLLECTED KARA'S car from the police garage, Gil from my neighbours and went back to the bungalow. The downside of living on a boat was not having a bath. And right then what I really needed was a long soak to get some of the kinks out of my battered body. With Kara offering to scrub my back it inevitably turned into something a lot more interesting, which was how I discovered that when the spirit was willing, weakness of the flesh didn't mean a damned thing.

Later she dropped me back at the boat and dashed off to collect the kids from school. I promised to see her again soon but had other things to clear up first. Cleo was on my conscience. I'd been avoiding face-to-face meetings with her, unsure what to say about the intimate side of our relationship, even less sure what her expectations were. Anyway, we arranged to get together. She was horrified by the state of me, especially when she realised I'd acquired my injuries whilst trying to help her dad. When she heard that he'd most likely soon be released, she couldn't contain her joy.

"I don't know how to thank you, Charlie," she said, tears shining in her eyes.

"Glad to be of help."

"But you shouldn't have put yourself at risk."

"Well, it turned out okay, and your dad will probably

get compensation for wrongful imprisonment. He'll be able to return your savings and have a bit left to get his life back together."

"That's all I've ever wanted." She smiled at me and touched the back of my uninjured hand. "Like I told you at the beginning, murder's not his style."

"There'll be a lot of publicity. The press will be all over you for comments," I warned her. "I'd rather not be dragged into it."

"But you deserve the glory."

"No, I don't." I'd let Jillian Slater put an innocent man away without doing much to try and stop her. I didn't deserve anything. "If you want to thank me, just keep my name out of it."

"Fair enough. If you're sure."

"I'm certain."

"And I'll be able to pay you."

"I don't want your money, Cleo. Keep it."

"No, really I—"

"I won't take it and there's an end to it."

There was an awkward pause. I still hadn't figured out if she thought the end of the investigation meant the end of our personal relationship. Either way, she didn't deserve to be left hanging in the breeze.

"Cleo," I said awkwardly. "About us, I—"

"It's all right, Charlie," she said, smiling. "I never thought there'd be a happy ever after."

"Ah, so you were using me then?"

"Just taking solace where I could find it. I don't need complications in my life right now." Well, that told me. "I need to be there for Dad."

"He's lucky to have you," I said, meaning it.

She stood up, leaned over me and dropped a kiss on the uninjured side of my face.

"Goodbye, Charlie," she said. "And thank you."

I watched her as she walked away. So did half the other men in the pub. Her seat had barely been vacated before Jimmy Taylor sauntered in and plonked his arse on it.

"I'm surprised the conquering hero has time to spare for us humble foot soldiers," he said, shaking my hand. "Congratulations, mate, you're the talk of the nick. Slater's shitting bricks."

"Good."

"How do you feel?"

"Like I've been run over by a truck."

"Yeah, well, that truck is singing like a canary. Garnet stupidly didn't bother to get Glover a top-notch brief, thinking he'd keep stum. He would have done too, if you hadn't recorded everything Garnet said."

"So Slater's now doubly keen to get me for murder."

"I reckon."

I watched him make healthy inroads into a pint of bitter. "I might just be able to help you there."

"Okay," he quipped, "I'll take your confession."

I offered him a wry smile, produced a photograph of Miller's former lover from my jacket pocket and placed it on the table between us. My other theories about Miller's killer had come to nothing so perhaps it was time for Jimmy to look at this guy.

"Who's that?" Jimmy asked.

I told him.

"Hang on, Miller wasn't gay, was he?"

"He hadn't come out but he and this guy were an item

for quite a while. Miller threw him over for someone else and he didn't take the rejection well."

"So you like *him* for doing Miller now? A man scorned, and all that?"

I let his sarcasm wash over me. After all, I'd given him two dead ends to chase. Three if you count Garnet, who was actually innocent of this particular crime. "I think he's worth looking at."

"But he wasn't there that day."

"He didn't go through the lobby, no." I explained about the garage.

"But how can we prove that?"

"Check his alibi. And check the CCTV on the corner of the street. If he came that way then he'll be on it, but if he came from the other direction…"

"It's a fifty-fifty shot then." Jimmy wasn't exactly champing at the bit.

"Check it out on your own. If it is him, I want you to have the collar, not Slater."

He grinned. "You and me both, mate."

I lingered a bit in the pub after Jimmy left, taking my time to finish my drink. The doctor had warned me not to take alcohol with the painkillers he'd given me and just one pint was making me feel a bit woozy. For the first time in living memory I didn't finish a beer and made my slow way back to the boat.

Two days later I rode the Harley all the way to Torquay. Kara thought I was mad but, perhaps sensing that I needed to do this, took Gil for me so I could make the trip. Hal's team were doing a final practise against another couple of teams off the Devon coast. I needed to talk to him about his problems. I also needed to see Paul and was curious to see the boats in action. Hal offered to send a car for me but I needed to prove something to myself by doing it the hard way. Em still told anyone who'd listen that stubbornness was one of my most unbecoming traits.

I arrived to a carnival atmosphere. The seawall was lined with spectators, probably tempted out by the fine weather. There were fast-food stalls, ice cream vans and vendors wandering about selling tacky souvenirs. Six boats were competing, all painted in garish colours, advertising their sponsors' wares. Support boats swarmed round the fleet like flies, as did launches carrying local press and VIP spectators. I noticed television cameras too. Scantily clad girls working for the sponsors were getting a lot of attention from the male spectators.

Hal waved when he saw me and ushered me into his launch. "Glad you could make it, Charlie," he said, doing a double take when he saw my array of bruises but making no comment on them. He was clearly preoccupied, probably worried that something would happen to snarl up the practise.

"Which two are your boats?" I asked as the launch stopped just clear of the start of the course.

"The two painted in my corporate colours. Green and blue flashes."

"Got them."

"French and Mason are in number one. Paul's driving number two with Alan as throttleman."

"I thought you only ran one boat."

"I have, up until now, but the rumours about the team and my ability to finance it are growing in strength."

I chuckled. "So you're countering them by running a second boat. Very astute."

"Not necessarily. Depends if Paul's learned enough to make it worth my while. He's been bugging me about it for long enough. This is his chance."

"Who decides which boat gets the best starting position?" I asked. "Obviously the one on the inside is best placed."

"At races it's decided on practise results. Today we drew lots."

"And your two are right in the middle of the pack."

"Yeah, it could be worse."

The roar of engines being revved, the smell of diesel oil, asphyxiating exhaust fumes and an overload of testosterone made for a heady atmosphere. Men in the flotilla of launches surrounding ours shouted advice and instructions into microphones and I was soon caught up in the excitement. Someone in another launch sounded a Klaxon.

"The one-minute warning," Hal said.

The rev of engines increased.

"Here we go," Hal muttered to himself.

With an additional roar and plume of exhaust smoke, six boats pelted towards the first buoy, so close together that I couldn't believe there wouldn't be a collision. I recalled Mason telling me that the seas were never calm and I could see what he meant. The wake from other boats smashed against the flimsy hulls as no quarter appeared to be asked for or given.

Hal had binoculars pinned to his eyes. I picked up a spare pair and focused them on Paul's boat, astonished to find that I was willing him on. He was tucked into third position, riding the rough waves with total concentration and not attempting to cut up the boat in front. At least not yet. He must have learned something from his chequered career. All the boats took the first buoy without mishap and thundered towards the next.

"Eighty knots down that straight," Hal said to no one in particular.

"Makes Formula 1 look like a wimp's game," I remarked, impressed.

No one in the launch responded and I returned my attention to the race. I didn't know whose boat was in the lead but French was second, Paul still in third. Then the boat in fourth recklessly pulled level with Mason and I heard a sharp intake of breath on Hal's part.

"What's that idiot doing?" he growled.

They were going to touch. There was no way they could avoid it unless French ceded his position because the guy on the inside wasn't giving way. I could see Mason shaking his fist and shouting at the other driver. French had no choice but to turn to starboard but Paul was already legitimately hogging that position. This was where he could take the lead and prove himself at the expense of the man he must badly want to beat. To my utter astonishment he throttled back and gave French room. French regained second place and took the next buoy.

Paul's consideration had cost him third place but I suspected that it had also earned him Hal's respect. He already had mine.

They were on the third leg now and something odd happened. The leading boat suddenly slowed. The three boats behind it left it standing, which was when Paul made his move. With a daring manoeuvre that left every one of us in the launch gasping at his audacity, he increased his speed and cut inside the boat in front of him as they both swerved towards the next buoy.

"That was impressive," I said.

Hal turned towards me, actually smiling. "Yes," he said. "It was."

The boats were now on the final lap, French just ahead of Paul as they fought one another for the lead.

"What happened to the leader back there?" I asked Hal.

He shrugged, glasses still glued to his eyes. "Could be anything. I'm just glad it wasn't us for once."

French and Paul had left the others behind. It was a two-horse race to the final turn. This was where Paul was bound to do something stupid. I found myself willing him not to take chances. Needless to say, he did. He switched course, came up on French's starboard bow, cutting inside him and the final buoy, leaving French with no choice but to give way.

"Is that legal?" I asked.

"Oh yes," Hal said, grinning. "And very risky. The boy's learning."

It was a bit of an anticlimax when we got back to shore. Hal was taken up with organisational matters and it was some time before we could sit down with a beer.

"Thanks for coming down, Charlie. Hope you enjoyed it."

"I hate to say this but I have new respect for my stepbrother."

Hal quirked a brow. "You and me both."

"And nothing went wrong for you today."

"No, but that leading boat had a clogged fuel line."

"I don't know how that happened but I think I know who's responsible for your problems."

"Come on then," he said, when I didn't immediately say more. "Don't keep me in suspense."

And so I told him, explaining Angie's connection to Katrina Simpson and Simpson's relationship to Garnet.

"God, why didn't I make that connection myself? I followed the trial in the press and knew someone had testified for Katrina." Hal shook his head. "When Angie came to work for me, I just didn't connect the name."

"Why should you have? It was some time later and I assume you didn't interview her yourself."

"No, no I didn't, but even so."

I told him that we'd seen Angie entertaining one of his maintenance crew on his boat the Sunday before. I'd sat out more than my share of deafening silences in my time but this one was in a class of its own. I stayed quiet as well, leaving him to digest all I'd said.

"You have no idea how bad I felt about Katrina Simpson going to prison," he finally said. "I had sleepless nights about it, wondering if I should have testified, to help her."

"You didn't have firm evidence. If you'd gone into court and explained that conversation you'd overheard, you can bet your life that the prosecution would have come up with a dozen other explanations, all more plausible than an affair."

"Yes, that's what I thought at the time." He paused. "But a few months after Katrina went to jail I happened to see Max in a restaurant with a young lady."

"Ahh."

"Exactly. I left immediately. No way did I want to confront him, but I knew then that Katrina had probably told the truth about the affair."

"But she still opened those accounts for Max, even if she didn't steal the money. She must have known they weren't kosher, so she's not entirely innocent."

"Even so, I should have spoken up for her."

"You did the right thing with the information you had at the time."

"Then how come I feel so shitty about the whole fiasco?"

"Life's like that sometimes." I took a swallow of my beer. "What will you do about the two saboteurs? Will you involve the police?"

I wasn't surprised when he said no.

"I'll get rid of them, of course, and make sure they know why. Angie was clever choosing someone comparatively junior in the maintenance crew to help do her dirty work. Suspicion didn't once fall on him. And he's immature enough to be flattered by a pretty girl's attentions."

"There you have it then."

"You don't think Garnet was trying to wear the team down so he could take it over?"

"I did wonder about that in the beginning but I'm pretty sure he wasn't. He had his hands full with all his other gigs. He's just a megalomaniac who sees a slight against someone close to him as personal."

Hal sighed. "I won't see Angie in trouble with the law. She was only trying to exact revenge for a friend, however misguidedly. Besides, if I'd spoken up for Katrina, she might not have been found guilty."

"Well, you don't need to worry about Peter Garnet anymore. My former colleagues will be detaining him for the foreseeable future."

He didn't ask why and I didn't elaborate.

"I'm glad it wasn't Paul, Charlie. I know you suspected him."

"I'm glad too," I said, meaning it. What it would have done to Dad and Brenda didn't bear thinking about and my relationship with my father, such as it was, wouldn't have survived the fallout. Besides, now that Paul had revealed a little of his soft underbelly, I was having a hard time keeping up the vendetta. We would never be mates but we didn't need to be at each other's throats all the time either.

"I'll make it up to Katrina Simpson," Hal said, signalling the barmaid for refills.

"How?"

"When she gets out I don't suppose people will be queuing up to employ her."

"But you'll offer her a job."

"If she'll give me the time of day."

"Why don't you write to her inside?" I suggested. "Tell it from your point of view and make the job offer in your letter. Give her time to get used to the idea."

"That's a brilliant idea, Charlie. I'll do just that." He reached into his pocket and handed me an envelope. I could tell that it was stuffed with cash. A lot of cash. "This is for you."

"I don't want your money. What are friends for?"

"Don't be an idiot. You've saved me a fortune and you've earned it. Besides, in case you've forgotten, you're out of work."

I grinned. "Well, there is that. Thanks, Hal."

My phone rang and I excused myself to answer it. It was a jubilant Jimmy.

"Miller's ex has coughed to the whole thing," he told me. "Broke down in tears and said if he couldn't have Miller then no one would."

I rolled my eyes. "Is it sound?"

"Oh yes. He tried to pretend he wasn't there but we got him on CCTV, just like you said we might. As soon as we told him that, he gave us chapter and verse. I think he was glad to be caught actually."

"Congratulations, mate. That's quite a feather in your cap."

"Thanks to you. I won't forget that."

"Well, you stuck your neck out for me."

"Yeah, but even so I—"

"How's Slater taking it?"

Jimmy's raucous laughter echoed down the line. "She tried to take over when she realised what was going down but I basically told her it was my collar and to fuck off."

"Good for you."

"Then she wanted to know who tipped me the wink about Miller being gay. I said it was a snout."

"Just as long as you kept my name out of it."

"Course I did. That would only make her more determined than ever to involve you. Slater looked like she was sucking on a lemon when we charged the bloke."

"She always looks like that. How could you tell the difference?"

"Yeah well, the word is that she's being moved sideways."

"Brighton's gain will be another patch's loss." I heard a burst of laughter in the background and loud music that sounded as though it was coming from a juke-box. The guys were letting off steam. "Are you in the boozer?"

"Course we are. We're celebrating. That's why I'm ringing. You ought to be here."

"No, I'm still off the sauce." Well, that wasn't strictly true but I wouldn't have crashed Jimmy's party and stolen his thunder even if I had been in Brighton. "It doesn't mix with the painkillers."

"Sorry to hear that."

"Don't be. It won't be for much longer. Well done again, mate. Enjoy the moment. I'll let you get back to your beer."

Paul joined us as soon as I hung up.

"Well done," I said. "That was quite a show."

"Yes, good work," added Hal. "That's the first time you've beaten French."

Paul grinned. "He's not a happy camper but he can't complain, not when I gave way to him."

"Hmm, I can imagine." Hal drained his glass and stood up. "Excuse me, I have things to do so I'll leave you two to catch up."

"Did they get him?" Paul asked as soon as Hal left us.

"Yes, it was Miles and he was charged this afternoon."

Paul let out a long sigh. "Good. But will Jason's dirty linen have to be washed in public? He would have hated that."

"Depends upon whether he pleads guilty. He's confessed so he really doesn't have a lot of choice, and the evidence is stacked against him. Now that they have his prints they're bound to be found, if not in the flat then certainly in the garage. But he might lawyer up and renege on his confession."

"Can he do that?"

I shrugged. "It happens."

"Won't he get a lighter sentence if he pleads guilty?"

"That's the way the system works. It saves the hard-pressed taxpayer from the cost of a trial. But his brief might claim mitigating circumstance. He could try and persuade the judge that he was emotionally unbalanced at the time and didn't know what he was doing."

"Will that fly?"

I wobbled one hand. "Depends on the shrinks. And on the judge."

Paul ran a hand through his hair and sighed. "Thanks, Charlie. It helps to know what happened and why. I just wish I didn't feel I was to blame."

"You?" I looked at him askance. "You weren't even there."

"No, but I made a big play for Miller even though I knew he was in a relationship."

"It takes two to tango, mate. And your name won't come up, if that's what's worrying you. Not if Fisher didn't know about your relationship with Miller. I didn't tell anyone."

"No, he didn't know for sure. He might have suspected, that's all."

"That's all right then. If your name stays out of it, no one will know where I got Miller's last notebook from."

"Well, that's good," Paul said. "And one good turn deserves another. About your mother…"

Two nights later Kara and I were curled up in the salon, listening to mellow jazz, talking, doing quite a lot of kissing. Drinking wine. Feeling content. The kids were with her mother and she was spending the night on board. She'd be doing a lot more of that in future if I had any say in the matter. Where our relationship would go beyond that was anyone's guess. She certainly wasn't putting pressure on me to commit.

"You look like you've gone five rounds with a heavy-weight," she said, reaching up to gently stroke my bruised face. "Can you see out of that eye yet?"

"I can see all the bits of you that interest me."

"Those bits not including my face, presumably."

I chuckled. "You seem to forget that I'm still trau-matised."

"We were lucky, weren't we?" she said. "To come out of it all unscathed, I mean."

It was the first time our escapade had been men-tioned since my return from Devon. I'd been waiting for her to bring it up.

"Hey, I'm not unscathed. I have serious injuries that need careful nurturing."

"Don't push it, Hunter."

"The sympathy round these parts is totally under-whelming."

"You're quite the hero of the hour, Charlie. None of this would have been possible if it weren't for you but you're letting everyone else have the glory."

"That's me, modest to the bone. But at least Garnet won't be around for a good long time. The entry in the notebook that had him so steamed up wasn't about his lunch with Miller but the location of some of his ill-gotten gains. Whether or not the powers that be will ever get their hands on them is another matter."

"Why not?" Kara asked. "If they can prove they were obtained illegally."

"The proof will be almost impossible to find. Besides, some of these offshore locations interpret international banking law rather laxly and will drag their feet. But at least the accounts have been frozen whilst their contents are disputed so Garnet won't have access to them either."

"Is Andrea Garnet being charged?"

"Oh yeah. They can't pin any of the drug trafficking on her but at the very least they can get her for luring you into a kidnapping situation."

"Will she go to jail?"

"Probably not. If it's a first offence she'll get probation and community service. But she *will* be poor, what with most her husband's assets being seized."

Kara laughed. "That will kill someone like her."

"Exactly."

"What about Mike Kendall?"

"Well, the wheels are turning quickly and he's likely to be out on licence as early as next week, pending a full pardon."

"That's good," Kara said. "Cleo will be pleased."

I chuckled. "She is."

"What's so funny?"

"Well, she rang me to tell me the news and was highly incensed because her sister wants to play happy families again."

"The bitch!"

"Right. She wouldn't even help Kara with their mother's medical expenses but now she wants to be on the courthouse steps when her father's released, basking in the media attention."

"What did Cleo say about that?"

"She basically told her to fuck off."

"Good for her."

"My sentiments exactly."

"But where will he go?" Kara asked. "Has he got anywhere to live?"

"Well, that's the other thing Cleo told me. It seems that Jeff Spelling's widow visited him regularly in jail. She never thought he'd done the killing, you see. She was most emphatic about that when I went to see her, but I didn't realise she and Mike Kendall were quite as friendly as they actually are. Anyway, she's offered to take him into her place."

"How sweet."

"Well, stranger things have been known to happen, and the guy deserves a break."

"There's something else on your mind, Charlie," Kara said after we'd lapsed into a long silence. "Come on, out with it."

"It's something Paul told me," I said reluctantly. "I don't quite know what to do about it."

"Are you still letting him get to you? I thought you'd patched things up."

"About my mother. He doesn't know who ordered her to be killed or even if she was the intended target. But he's pretty sure Marianne was plotting something. He was at a party at their house once, not long before Mum died. Marianne took a phone call during the middle of it. Paul said she seemed agitated. He's always been a nosy sod, wanted to know what she was up to and watched her through a gap in the door. She talked for a long time, Mum's name was mentioned and so was a large sum of money."

"She paid an assassin?" Kara's hand tightened on mine.

"There were no large unexplained amounts of money missing from her account but she could have paid it in small instalments to avoid suspicion, I suppose. I'll have to take another look now that I know what I'm looking for."

"Did Paul know who she was talking to?"

"No."

She looked discouraged. "Oh, well then—"

"But he pressed last number redial when Marianne left the room." The air left my lungs in an extravagant whoosh as I relived Paul's revelation. "She was talking to Graham Sullivan, a very mediocre saxophonist who was always hanging round my mother. His presence wasn't welcome and, as Paul suggested, we have first-hand experience of what men scorned are capable of."

"You have a lead at last but it will be impossible to find Sullivan after so much time." She smiled her sympathy. "No wonder you're so frustrated."

I chuckled mirthlessly. "That's what I said to Paul but he told me to have more faith. He'd made it his business to keep tabs on Sullivan over the years."

Kara jerked upright. "So he knows where he is."

"Oh yes. He bought a house in France just after Mum died and paid cash for it."

I fell silent, recalling how Paul had stood up and shook my hand firmly. "Now we're even," he'd said. "And friends, I hope."

"Yeah, friends," I'd said, too numb to disagree.

Kara was quiet for a long time but I could see that she was dying to say something.

"Go on then," I said. "Get it over with. Tell me to give it up and get a life."

"Actually, Charlie," she said, reaching up to kiss the side of my face, "I was going to ask when we're planning to go to France."

\* \* \* \* \*